T0283377

THE THERMOPYLAE PROTOCOL

THE THERMOPYLAE PROTOCOL

A GORDIAN DIVISION NOVEL

DAVID WEBER & JACOB HOLO

A Baen Books Original

Baen Publishing Enterprises
P.O. Box 1403
Riverdale, NY 10471
www.baen.com

ISBN: 978-1-9821-9343-0

Cover art by Kurt Miller

First printing, June 2024

Distributed by Simon & Schuster
1230 Avenue of the Americas
New York, NY 10020

Library of Congress Cataloging-in-Publication Data

Names: Weber, David, 1952– author. | Holo, Jacob, author.
Title: The thermopylae protocol / David Weber, Jacob Holo.
Identifiers: LCCN 2024003284 (print) | LCCN 2024003285 (ebook) | ISBN 9781982193430 (hardcover) | ISBN 9781625799647 (ebook)
Subjects: LCGFT: Science fiction. | Novels.
Classification: LCC PS3573.E217 T44 2024 (print) | LCC PS3573.E217 (ebook) | DDC 813/.54—dc23/eng/20240202
LC record available at https://lccn.loc.gov/2024003284
LC ebook record available at https://lccn.loc.gov/2024003285

Printed in the United States of America
10 9 8 7 6 5 4 3 2 1

For our families, both by blood and of the heart. In a world which sometimes seems as dark as any novel ever written, it's love that keeps us on our feet and facing the storm.

PROLOGUE

—⬡⬡⬡—

SourceCode Industrial Carrier *Grand Sculptor* SysGov, 2981 CE

"LOOK AT IT THIS WAY. IT COULD BE WORSE."

Antoni Ruckman, lead engineer of the Dyson Realization Project, turned to face his brother with the slow, deliberate motion of a man who refused to believe the nonsense assaulting his ears.

"Excuse me?" he replied.

"It could be worse," Bradley Ruckman repeated. And then, as if realizing his statement hadn't been well received, flashed a defensive, almost apologetic smile.

"How, exactly?" Antoni asked.

"Well, we could have been on board when the ship blew up."

Antoni let out a noncommittal harrumph, then turned back to face the source of his ire.

A false color image of *Reality Flux* hovered above the bridge's command table. Or rather, a projection of the ship's expanding debris cloud. A trio of labeled icons swam about the periphery: two Consolidated System Police corvettes and the *Grand Sculptor*, which SourceCode's upper management had detached from their construction fleet to assist SysPol.

Reality Flux had been one of SourceCode's older autonomous constructors. Perhaps not as well maintained as the rest of the construction fleet—its departure from SourceCode HQ's Saturnian orbit *had* been delayed due to a reactor imbalance—but to

1

have *exploded* on the way to Mercury? Accidents happened, but what were the odds the reactor would fail so spectacularly *after* receiving additional maintenance?

Not very high.

Antoni shook his head, his eyes locked forward, jawline tense, almost to the point of forming a snarl.

"Hey." Bradley placed a hand on his shoulder. "It'll be fine."

"This screws up our whole timetable. We're going to lose months because of this fiasco. Months!"

"Of course we will. But look at the bright side. All we lost is equipment. No one died when *Reality Flux* blew; it was catching up to the fleet on full auto. And besides, no one's going to blame you for this."

"That's not why I'm upset," Antoni growled under his breath, fingertips resting on the command table.

"Then why?"

"It's..." Antoni paused and regarded his brother once more.

The two men looked identical, with dark skin and trim heads of black hair that extended down into generous, curling sideburns. They even wore matching black business suits, though the more complex green tracery on Antoni's served as a subtle nod to his position as lead engineer. Either man could have changed his appearance at any time to create greater visual separation; they were both abstract citizens, after all. Their appearances were purely virtual, even if the avatars were modeled on Antoni's original organic body before he'd transitioned to a virtual existence.

The round bridge they stood in was equally abstract, the environment running within *Grand Sculptor*'s infostructure. SourceCode employed very few organic citizens, and *Grand Sculptor* lacked a physical bridge entirely.

Bradley waited beside him, a patient question in his eyes.

"It's..." Antoni turned away once more and gritted his teeth together. "I thought we were past this sort of crap!"

"You think it's sabotage?"

"What else could it be? Take your pick who it might be *this* time! Maybe the nuts over at the Mercury Historical Preservation Society! Or perhaps our competitors over at Atlas again, trying one last time to undermine us! Never mind what happened to you—"

He paused, his open hand pointed toward Bradley. He lowered it and frowned.

"Sorry," he apologized softly. "I didn't mean to dig up bad memories."

"It's all right." Bradley paused, then shrugged. "I've been doing a lot better recently."

"I know you have, and I'm proud of you for that. I know it hasn't been easy."

Bradley smiled and glanced away bashfully.

Bradley Ruckman had started his existence as an illegal copy of Antoni's connectome—the neural map of his mind—which criminals had then modified to make him more docile and easier to extract information from. The damage had been extensive—almost irreversible—by the time SysPol rescued him from the copy-kidnappers. Doctors at Saturn's Connectome Wellness Center had worked a small miracle piecing his mutilated mind back together, but the aftershocks of the trauma lingered on, even five months after the incident. Both men still transmitted over to the CWC for weekly therapy sessions.

"It's just . . . I've had it with people messing with our lives!" Antoni brought a horizontal hand up to his throat. "I've had it up to *here!*"

"It might still be an accident."

"Not likely!"

"Let's not jump to conclusions. If anything survived intact, it should be the black box."

Antoni let out a long, calming exhale, then nodded in agreement.

Even though he was an abstract being, his connectome didn't exist in isolation. A biochemical simulation ran in parallel with his neural map, which allowed certain acts—such as releasing a deep breath—to affect his mood.

"I suppose you're right."

Antoni pulled up a schematic of the pre-explosion *Reality Flux*.

The design resembled a line of five fat spheres joined together by thick bracketing. The ship's hot singularity reactor had been housed in Sphere Five while the black box and control systems had been part of Sphere One. Not only was the black box designed to survive most of the violent ends that could befall spacecraft, it was also located at the farthest point from the explosion's source.

Antoni switched the image back to the debris cloud.

Judging by the chunks SysPol's already tracked down, he

thought, *a good portion of the ship survived the explosion. Just...
not in one piece.*

"Chief Engineer Ruckman," said the ship's nonsentient attendant program, "Executive Xian would like to speak with you."

"Of course he would," Antoni grumbled. "Should I transfer
over to his ship?"

"No, Chief Engineer. Executive Xian plans to transmit from
Radical Architect to this ship a few minutes from now. I am
sorry, but he was not more specific about his departure time."

"Fine, fine. I'll wait here."

Six minutes later, a man in a black-and-green suit appeared
on the far side of the command table. His pale skin resembled
wax paper, and the soft glow in his white eyes wavered, giving
the impression of candle flames flickering within his head.

"How bad is it?" Junior Executive Xian asked, clasping origami
hands behind his back.

"If you're looking for reassurances, look elsewhere," Antoni
said. "All I can give you is honesty with a light garnish of shattered dreams."

"I would expect nothing less," Xian replied neutrally, then
glanced over the false-color debris field. "That looks bad."

"Because it is. The ship exploded."

"Hmm." Xian took in the display. "So it would seem. Casualties?"

"None, thankfully. The ship was on auto."

"At least there's that." Xian sighed, and his shoulders lost
some of their rigidity. "Do we know what destroyed it?"

"Initial assessment from SysPol is a catastrophic failure in
the hot singularity reactor."

"And your thoughts on their theory?"

"Barring an external device, I don't see how it *couldn't* be the
reactor. We're hoping they'll recover the black box. Once we have
our hands on the flight data, we should know more. SysPol's already
requested our assistance in the investigation. We'll have access to
the raw data roughly in sync with their forensics teams, and we'll
have the opportunity to provide input before they file any reports."

Xian didn't so much as bat an eye at the mention of an
"external device." Not with the long history of criminals and
malcontents working to undermine the Dyson Realization Project
and SourceCode's involvement in it.

"Anything unusual leading up to the incident?" the executive asked.

"Just one minor inconsistency," Antoni said. "Bradley noticed a gap in the *Flux*'s reporting. In automatic, the ship sends an hourly log to its command vessel, which is *Grand Sculptor*. Most of the logs look perfectly normal, but one from about a day ago was received late."

"And we didn't notice?"

"*Grand Sculptor*'s attendant did, but it was flagged as a low-priority warning, and a resend request was transmitted automatically to *Reality Flux*. The ships were about twenty-four light-minutes apart at the time, and the second log was received with the expected transmission delay, so the alarm was cleared automatically and never brought to our attention. The attendant would have notified us if there'd been a prolonged communication blackout."

"I see," Xian said. "Why wasn't *Reality Flux* with the rest of the fleet?"

"It left HQ late due to a reactor issue."

"Enough of an issue to cause this?" Xian indicated the display.

"I don't see how, but I suppose it's possible. After the reactor was rebalanced, the ship was placed on a full-thrust course for Mercury to make up for lost time."

Xian raised a paper eyebrow. "We maxed out the ship with the dodgy reactor?"

"Don't look at me," Antoni defended stiffly. "Maintenance certified the craft ready for deployment with no restrictions. If you have a problem with me trying to keep to our original schedule, take it up with them."

"Just asking the questions the other execs will ask me," Xian replied, his tone lacking any edge of confrontation. "What sort of impact are we looking at?"

"This is going to shift the whole blasted schedule."

"By how much?"

"The *Flux*'s reservoirs were carrying half our self-replicator seed volume for this job. Without those microbots, we either need to manufacture replacements back at HQ and haul them over here or use the ones we *do* have to replicate additional swarms. Both options will be time intensive. You're looking at two months minimum. Maybe three."

"Is any of the lost volume recoverable?"

"I don't see how. What wasn't vaporized is scattered all over the place."

"Hmm." Xian pursed his lips. "Anything else to add?"

"Not until SysPol finds our black box."

"All right. Keep me informed of any developments. In the meantime"—Xian's frown creased his paper face—"*I* now need to make my own report to the rest of the board."

"Good luck with that."

Xian grunted and vanished.

It took SysPol a little over five hours to track down the piece of wreckage containing the black box and another twenty minutes to pull the log files and transmit them to *Grand Sculptor*. Antoni and Bradley spent the next few hours poring over the logs.

"You thinking what I'm thinking?" Antoni asked his brother after a long period of silence. The two men stood on either side of the bridge command table, reports and diagrams cluttering the space between them.

"Well, we do come from the same mental stock." Bradley shrugged. "So, probably?"

"Fair enough." Antoni permitted himself a humorless smile. "If you ask me, this whole mess paints a rather unflattering picture of our maintenance department. Sure, they addressed the imbalance that took the ship off-line, but they missed a subtler secondary problem, and it looks like their repairs made that one worse. Then, to compound matters, we pushed the reactor hard for a few days so the ship could catch up, and then"—he spread his hands grandly—"boom."

"I agree with you to a point." Bradley held up a finger. "But the problem I have with that scenario is the reactor's own diagnostics should have caught this problem before it became critical. Instead, the logs show normal operations up until a few seconds before the shell blew open."

"*Overly* normal, if you ask me. All those sensors had to be yanked out when they worked on the reactor. Some of them could have been reinstalled incorrectly, causing us to miss the impending disaster."

"Maybe, but that seems like a *lot* of shoddy maintenance work."

"What are you suggesting, then? That someone *deliberately* botched the repairs?"

"I . . ." Bradley hesitated, then frowned. "I don't know what I'm saying yet, other than I'm not ready to buy the maintenance angle." He lowered his head and added a new tab to one of his reports.

And with that, Antoni knew the conversation was over. Bradley had a habit of ending conversations unilaterally when he had nothing more to say, and Antoni had found it best to leave him be when that happened.

Antoni returned to his own report. He understood his brother's hesitancy, but the more he dug through the data, the more corroboration he found that their own maintenance team had screwed up.

"Chief Engineer Ruckman," said *Grand Sculptor*'s attendant, "I have a message from Executive Xian. He is requesting an update on your review of the black box data."

"I figured we were due for a little managerial nagging," Antoni grumbled.

"Is that the response you would like me to send him?"

"Hell, no! Tell him he can join us at his convenience."

"Yes, Chief Engineer."

Xian appeared on the bridge less than a minute later.

"Well? What do we have?"

"Nothing conclusive," Antoni said, "but the evidence is building that HQ messed up the repair, leading to the reactor blowing."

"I see." Xian's candlelit eyes flicked across the reports, then back to the twin Ruckmans. "Was the reactor one of ours?"

"No. *Flux* used a custom model designed and built by the Mitchell Group."

"Why not one of ours? Don't we make products in that power and performance range?"

"We do nowadays, but *Reality Flux* was one of our oldest ships. We weren't as deep into the hot singularity market back then, so we subcontracted the reactors and several other systems."

"I hadn't realized that." Xian looked down and rubbed his chin thoughtfully. "I wonder if we can use that to deflect some of the blame."

"I'd be careful before venturing down that road. If you ask me, the ship exploded because our own team messed up."

"And why *did* it explode?"

"The reactor was out of balance, and the imbalance grew worse until the outer shell cracked."

"Which means?"

"Just what I said." Antoni put a hand on his hip. "How familiar are you with hot singularity reactors?"

"Not terribly. Self-replicators are more my area of expertise."

"Then would you like a refresher?"

Xian raised his lidded, somewhat suspicious eyes.

"All right, but don't go overboard," the executive warned. "I know how you engineers can be."

"I promise I'll be gentle." Antoni flashed a disarming smile. "First, understand that 'hot singularity' is a bit of a misnomer. It's shorthand for what is essentially a fake black hole encased within a shell of exotic matter. The matter inside the core emits Hawking radiation, which is collected by the shell and used to power other systems. Black holes evaporate at a rate inversely proportional to their mass, and these reactors deal with such low mass values— fourteen hundred tons for the *Flux*—that the energy released by a real black hole of that size would be *catastrophically* rapid!"

"You're enjoying this, aren't you?"

"Maybe a little. Anyway, the positive mass inside the reactor's core and the negative mass in the shell are segregated from basically nothing during construction. It's a *little* more complicated than that, but the important point is they form two halves of a balanced nothingness. Also, that's what they're *supposed* to return to during a critical failure. The positive and negative mass-energy components of the system collapse and cancel each other out."

"Which didn't happen this time," Xian said dryly.

"Because the two halves were severely out of balance. Normally, an imbalance isn't a major concern. As a general rule, hot singularity reactors are stable and resilient, but if a problem like this is allowed to grow, the disparity in the system will eventually reach a critical threshold. To the point where the system collapses in on itself. When that happens, *most* of the mass-energy cancels out, but any surplus is released."

"Boom?"

"Boom. That's why the reactor was being worked on back at HQ."

"Which should have *prevented* the boom, not *caused* it."

"It seems the repairs were executed poorly."

"Could the failure have been caused by an outside party?" Xian asked, perhaps a little too hopefully.

"We can't rule anything out this early, but I haven't seen any signs of—"

"Aha!" Bradley exclaimed. He looked up with a wide grin, and the other two men faced him.

"Ahh-hah?" Xian cocked an eyebrow.

"Found something?" Antoni asked, leaving off the please-don't-embarrass-us-in-front-of-the-boss part. Whatever his brother had found, Antoni would have preferred he and Bradley review it together first before discussing it in front of Xian. Giving half-baked information to a manager was ill-advised at the best of times, and that went double now that Xian was on the hunt for a scapegoat.

"It's fake," Bradley declared boldly.

"What's fake?" Xian asked.

"All of it. The whole thing!"

"I'm sorry," Antoni said. "You lost me."

"The black box data!" Bradley smiled, almost gleefully. "Someone tampered with it!"

"What?" Antoni hurried over to his brother's side. "How can you tell?"

"Here." Bradley pointed to one of his charts. "See for yourself."

Antoni joined his brother, and Xian came up behind them, peering at the data between their shoulders.

"What am I looking at?" Xian asked.

"Some of the black box metadata," Antoni said. "Time stamps, file sizes, access logs. That sort of thing."

"Now take a look at this!" Bradley jabbed a line near the bottom.

"That's ... a date," Xian observed blandly.

"Exactly!"

"I don't see the significance. What's got you so excited?"

"Wait a second." Antoni leaned closer. "Did that date come from the box's atomic clock?"

"You've got it!" Bradley beamed at him.

"But then ... how can that be?"

"Care to explain?" Xian asked.

"Bradley spotted a discrepancy in the time stamps." Antoni scrolled through metadata. Sure enough, all the other dates looked normal.

But then, Antoni thought, *all of those are generated by software, and software is malleable by definition. A skilled individual with the time and access could have hacked these records. But the date from the atomic clock comes from* hardware. *A hacker couldn't touch that without physical access to the black box, and even then, it's an easy feature to miss.*

"What sort of discrepancy?" Xian asked.

"Well, according to this," Antoni began, then paused to lick his lips, "the ship was forty years older than it should have been when it exploded."

CHAPTER ONE

———⊗⊗⊗———

Argus Station
SysGov, 2981 CE

KLAUS-WILHELM VON SCHRÖDER SAT ACROSS FROM THE REPORTER, back straight, eyes alert, his *feldgrau* Gordian Division uniform immaculate in the studio lighting. The reporter's garb was equally sharp, his dark blue business suit accented with a scarf bedazzled with shifting stars and colorful nebulae.

The reporter smiled toothily at him, an expression that held all the warmth of a reactor's cryogenic plant.

Klaus-Wilhelm kept his jawline still, suppressing any outward expression of his discomfort through sheer force of will. He was not looking forward to this.

"Welcome, ladies and gentlemen and abstracts. This is LNN's *Live Wire*, and I'm your host, Sergei Radulov. Today, we have a rare interview with one of the biggest names in SysGov. He's a man plucked from an alternate version of 1958, a commander who's earned the moniker 'living legend' from friend and foe alike. He served as a *graf* of imperial Germany, a four-star general over an entire Panzer army, the leader of the campaign to liberate Ukraine from the clutches of Joseph Stalin, the provisional *governor* of said nation, and then finally as the commissioner of our very own Gordian Division. I am, of course, talking about Klaus-Wilhelm von Schröder."

Radulov shifted in his seat, facing Klaus-Wilhelm with another one of those fake smiles.

"Commissioner, a pleasure to have you on the program."

"Sergei." He gave the reporter a neutral nod.

"It's hard to believe you've only been with us for fourteen months. How has life in the thirtieth century been treating you?"

"It's kept me busy more than anything else. Every day brings a new set of challenges."

"I'll bet. Do you ever find living in the True Present over-whelming?"

"No, not especially."

"Come now, Commissioner. Surely there's *something* that's given you trouble. You skipped a thousand years of history. Modern SysGov must have come as quite the shock to you."

"The technology certainly had its share of surprises for me, time travel included. But ultimately, tech is simply a set of tools. The ones we have now are far more powerful than those available in my native time, but they're still tools that can be wielded for good or ill. It's the people wielding them that matter most."

"And what of those people? Surely, our society startled you at least a little."

"Not really. Again, I'd say I was surprised more than anything. Yes, the ability to virtualize consciousness is truly remarkable. But people are still people, whether they're organic, synthetic, or abstract. The vessel holding the mind doesn't matter to me; only the quality of the individual."

"A commendable perspective. One I'm sure we all wished more people held."

Radulov paused to smile again.

Here it comes, Klaus-Wilhelm thought.

"Commissioner, as you know, we're fast approaching the one-year anniversary of the Dynasty Crisis, which saw the Gord-ian Division take center stage for the first time. Now, no one would dispute that your division was instrumental in pulling our collective feet out of the fire, but the fact remains that over seventy-one *thousand* people suffered permanent death from the Dynasty's attack on the L5 Hub. There are some who say the Gordian Division hasn't done enough to remedy that loss of life."

"Who?"

Radulov paused ever so slightly, perhaps taken aback by the sudden question.

"I'm sorry, Commissioner?"

"Who says we haven't done enough?"

"Why, concerned citizens, of course."

"How many of them? Are we talking about three people griping on a forum or a political movement three million strong? And, more importantly, what are their backgrounds when it comes to understanding and appreciating how dangerous time travel is?"

"Commissioner, I believe you're getting distracted from the issue. People are merely asking why Gordian Division, as the temporal arm of SysPol, hasn't undone the greatest tragedy of this century."

"Because we can't."

"Can't, Commissioner?" Radulov leaned forward. "Or won't?"

"Can't. It is *impossible* for us to change our own past. Even if we set out to achieve that goal—which would be a fool's errand for countless reasons—all we would accomplish is the creation of a new universe. *Our* past and *those* deaths would still all be there."

"But those victims would be alive, would they not? The only distinction being they would exist within a branch in the timeline."

"At what cost? Meddling with the past is what brought about the Gordian Knot and nearly destroyed fifteen universes, including this one. That's why both we and the Admin signed the Gordian Protocol, along with all its limitations on time travel. We must *never again* place all of creation at risk. Not for a thousand lives. Or ten thousand or a million or even a billion, because the cost of failure is oblivion for *everyone*."

"I understand that, Commissioner. But there are some who've suggested an alternative exists for bringing back those people. One that doesn't spawn a new universe or violate the Gordian Protocol. In fact, it's a method that's been used many times in the past."

"You're referring to how the Antiquities Rescue Trust used to travel back in time and pluck famous people and artifacts out of history?"

"I am, Commissioner."

"Temporal replication, as a practice, contributed to the formation of the Gordian Knot, which again leads us to the same problem."

"But couldn't temporal replication be used to bring them back? To undo the tragedy? Isn't it true that changes to the past don't necessarily result in the creation of a new universe?"

"That much is correct. The change must be substantial enough to overcome time's natural inertia for a new universe to form. Otherwise, the past rebounds back into its original shape."

"Then why not use that method to save those lives?"

"Because now we're talking about violating the Valkyrie Protocol. Need I remind you that the Dynasty's entire timeline imploded in on itself *because* of their rampant replication industry. Are these 'concerned citizens' suggesting we instigate a similar collapse in our own timeline?"

"Of course not, Commissioner. It's merely being suggested—"

"And I'm shooting their suggestions down. Both the Gordian and Valkyrie protocols are there for very good reasons, first and foremost of which is the threat reckless time travel has proven to be."

"Commissioner, please—"

"If your viewers are still wondering why we in the Gordian Division refuse to bend the timeline into pretzels just to suit our immediate needs, then I suggest they open a screen, run a search on either protocol, and start *reading*."

❖   ❖   ❖

"His interview is over. Positions, everyone!"

Agent Raibert Kaminski of SysPol's Gordian Division had timed the ambush perfectly. He had to, for his target was none other than Klaus-Wilhelm von Schröder. Such a foe was not to be underestimated! Especially when he weighed the man's numerous accomplishments against Raibert's humble background studying ancient history.

But that difference would make his victory all the sweeter.

Raibert pressed his back against the wall by the executive entrance to Gordian Operations. Abstract data displays covered the walls of the wide, circular room and more hovered within its center while two dozen Gordian agents—both physical and abstract—milled about in a deliberate pantomime of business-as-usual.

Footsteps echoed through the entrance's programmable-steel shutter, signaling the approach of his quarry.

"Here he comes," Raibert whispered, raising his chosen weapon to his lips. He waited beside the door with all the patience of an assassin.

The door split open, and Klaus-Wilhelm strode out, back

straight, shoulders square, head high, and eyes forward. He wore the grayish green of the Gordian Division with the golden eye and drawn-sword division patch on his shoulder alongside his commissioner insignia.

And then he stopped at the threshold.

Had some small detail caught the Commissioner's eye? The man's instincts were unbelievably sharp, despite having been transplanted from the twentieth century to the thirtieth. Or perhaps *because* of this translated nature his astute eyes could pick out details a native to the True Present might miss.

Raibert began to worry, but then Klaus-Wilhelm gave Operations a small, disproving shake of his head—

—and stepped through the doorway.

"Surprise!" the room chorused.

Confetti poppers rigged on either side of the door burst open, showering Klaus-Wilhelm with sparkling, multicolored squares, and Raibert blew hard into his party favor, which unfurled into a red-with-white-dotted paper tongue and honked obnoxiously in the Commissioner's ear.

Klaus-Wilhelm paused and regarded the room with narrow eyes, his lips pressed together, forming a line that threatened to dip into a frown. He casually reached up to one shoulder and brushed the glitter away.

"Raibert?"

"Yes, boss?" he replied, party favor suspended in his lips.

"Refresh my memory. Haven't we discussed your overly casual approach to our organization?"

"We have." Raibert withdrew the party favor. "Once or twice, I think."

"And?"

"I get results, don't I?"

"I never said you didn't. Still"—Klaus-Wilhelm brushed confetti off the other shoulder—"perhaps another discussion is in order."

"You say that now, but did you realize today is a special day?"

Klaus-Wilhelm plucked a silvery square off his breast and gazed into it as if it contained the secrets of the universe—or *several* universes, as was the case with Gordian Division business—but then he frowned at what was only his distorted reflection and flicked it away.

"The significance seems to have slipped my mind."

"That's only because you haven't heard the news." Raibert swept an arm across Gordian Operations. "We hit a major milestone!"

An abstract banner unfurled, sagging across the center of the room in everyone's shared virtual vision. The colorful, paper cutout letters spelled 100 UNIVERSES!! Raibert had insisted on adding the second exclamation point.

"That many already?" Klaus-Wilhelm's stern face softened ever so slightly.

"Quite a leap since we mapped the Local 15, wouldn't you say?" Raibert asked, referring to the fifteen universes that survived the Gordian Knot and formed a cluster around SysGov. "The surveys are in all the way up to universe one hundred two, and you know what a milestone means?"

"My body trembles with anticipation."

"They're excuses to celebrate!" Raibert threw his arms up in triumph. "Come on, boss! We've got cake."

He guided the Commissioner toward the table tucked off to the side, laden with plates, utensils, glasses, a punch bowl, coffee, tea, and yes, a huge rectangular cake.

"*Butterkuchen*," Klaus-Wilhelm observed, his expression warming even more at the sight of the yellowish German butter cake topped with sugar and streusel.

"See? We even printed out your favorite."

"Well, if you insist." The hint of an approving smile curled Klaus-Wilhelm's lips. "I suppose a little festivity now and then won't hurt anyone."

The room exhaled a quiet sigh of relief, and a queue for cake began to form now that they had the boss's approval. Raibert served the Commissioner the first slice and then joined him off to the side with his own plate.

"Was this your idea?" Klaus-Wilhelm asked, forking in the first bite.

"Not entirely," Raibert replied. "More of a group effort."

"*Grossvater*," Agent Benjamin Schröder said with a respectful nod, joining them along with his wife, Agent Elzbietá Schröder.

Both Schröder men were tall and broad-shouldered with the same penetrating gray eyes, though the particulars of their first time-hopping adventure—and when each man had been pulled from history—along with access to thirtieth-century medicine, had rendered them visually more like brothers than grandfather and grandson. Or perhaps cousins, given Klaus-Wilhelm's buzz of blond hair and Benjamin's much darker coloration inherited from his mother.

Raibert stood taller and broader than both with his long blond hair tied back in a ponytail, but that was thanks to the synthoid he and his integrated companion had liberated from the System Cooperative Administration. It had been over a year since he unwillingly transitioned from his original flesh and blood, and he'd grown to consider this larger, more muscular form to be the "true Raibert." It certainly didn't hurt to have a durable synthetic body in his line of work!

Elzbietá chewed and swallowed a forkful from her own cake, then cleared her throat.

"We all chipped in," she said before snagging her second bite off Benjamin's plate, prompting him to give her some fierce side-eye.

"Excuse me?" Benjamin asked. "Don't you have your own?"

"But yours looked more delicious."

"What are you talking about? It all came from the same cake."

"I know." Elzbietá stabbed a second moist forkful off his plate.

"Fine." Benjamin held it out for her. "Help yourself."

Elzbietá resumed eating her own cake.

"What's wrong now?" Benjamin asked.

"It's no fun if you don't make me work for it."

Benjamin let out a patient sigh and resumed eating his cake.

"I don't see Philosophus." Klaus-Wilhelm glanced around the room. "Is he not coming?"

"In a bit," Raibert said. "He and a few other agents are covering for us while we celebrate. Wouldn't you know it, but Themis Division called right before you came in. Something about an exploding spaceship. He should be around once it's taken care of."

"I'm beginning to think 'conspiracy' might be the best word for what you lot put together," Klaus-Wilhelm said with a glint of playfulness in his eyes.

"Something like that," Elzbietá said. "Though, if you recall, we never properly celebrated your promotion to commissioner, either."

"We were too busy picking up the pieces after we saved reality from itself." Benjamin paused and frowned. "Again."

"Yeah. There wath thah," Elzbietá muttered around a mouthful of cake.

"Speaking of which"—Raibert set his cake down—"got a question for you, boss."

"Fire away."

"It's about the different versions of Earth we're cataloguing out there in the transverse. Shouldn't we be doing something about them?"

"Like what?"

"Well, I don't know. Some of the Earths—the barren ones with no people—aren't really an issue. Don't see any reason why we couldn't colonize those someday. But there are plenty of others out there with thriving human societies from all across the development spectrum."

"Or their remnants," Benjamin pointed out.

"Yes." Raibert nodded sadly. "Those, too. And that's part of my point. Would those societies have died out if someone had come along to lend a helping hand? You know, maybe shown them the ropes as they worked their way out of the technological cradle."

"Someone like us?" Klaus-Wilhelm asked guardedly.

"Maybe. The more we search, the more evidence we find that SysGov and the Admin are outliers. We're unusual because we survived our first, stumbling steps into the realm of post-scarcity and transtemporal tech. From the looks of it, most societies don't make it past that point."

"Probably because sufficiently advanced societies tend to destroy their own universes," Benjamin said grimly. "Either through ignorance or excessive use of temporal weapons. We've certainly found our fair share of permanent chronometric storms out there, and not all of them are natural."

"Or they end up like one of the Q's," Elzbietá added, referring to universes quarantined by their survey ships due to extreme hazards, such as the nanoblight machines of Q3 or the weaponized biohorrors of Q5.

"Exactly," Raibert said. "Which then brings us back to my question. What *should* we do about all the Earths out there?"

"We could just leave them alone," Benjamin suggested. "I'm not saying that's what we *should* do, but it's an option."

"Even if we stand aside, who's to say the Admin will?" Elzbietá countered.

"Point taken," Benjamin said. "And we all know what our team leader thinks of *them*."

"Hey now!" Raibert crossed his arms. "I've been using the Admin's 'traditional' honorific less and less these days," he added, referring to his habit of calling SysGov's multiverse neighbor "the fucking Admin."

"I almost miss hearing you say that," Benjamin said, raising a bite of butter cake.

"Really?" Elzbietá gave her husband a sour look.

"Almost."

"We could reach out to the Earths we're finding," Raibert continued. "Maybe establish contact with the more advanced societies. The ones getting close to developing dangerous tech, at least. Perhaps even establish ports where our societies can mingle and trade."

"Which comes with its own share of pitfalls," Benjamin said.

"Such as?"

"Raibert, you and I were both historians. When's the last time large-scale contact between two societies—one significantly less advanced than the other—ended well for the little guys?"

"Um..."

"Yeah. My point exactly."

"I *might* point out that most of those significantly advanced cultures weren't exactly making contact for altruistic reasons," Raibert said. "They weren't all out to bulldoze the locals intentionally, whatever some of their critics may say, but they weren't there out of the goodness of their hearts, either. The majority of the damage they did was incidental to their other reasons for being there."

"Like moving the local citizenry off of their land so the newcomers could look for gold, for example?" Benjamin's eyes glinted.

"I did say the *majority* of the damage," Raibert retorted. "But that actually makes my point stronger, I think. If we came calling expressly to help, not to gain anything from them—except probably mutually beneficial intercourse down the road—that sort of thing would be a lot less likely to happen."

"'Mutually beneficial intercourse,'" Benjamin repeated in a musing sort of tone. "Hmmm...One way to describe 'screwed over with the noblest of intentions.'" Raibert glared at him, and he shrugged. "I'm not saying you're wrong, Raibert. I'm just saying that humans are humans, and I guarantee you they could screw up almost any operation like that, whether it's intentional or accidental. Let's not forget Doctor Beckett and that bastard Gwon." His tone turned grim. "Sort of an example of *both* ways to screw up."

Raibert's expression tightened. Teodorà Beckett's tragic, desperately well-intentioned effort to create a universe in which the Black Death never happened cut especially deep for him, and not just because he and Teodorà had once been lovers. Every time he even *thought* about the way Lucius Gwon's narcissistic megalomania had destroyed an entire universe...

"Point," he said after a moment. "A damned good one, actually. But if not for Gwon, Teodorà and Pepys probably would have pulled it off, even with the temporal replication problem."

"Probably," Benjamin conceded, "although that little 'problem' is actually a pretty good example of unintended consequences. And, while I'm thinking about it, one of those consequences would have been the destruction of both SysGov *and* the Admin. Which sort of underscores my point, I think."

"But —"

"I guess it really doesn't matter what we three think," Elzbietá interrupted, and turned to Klaus-Wilhelm.

The other two agents followed her lead, and the three of them waited in expectant silence, occasionally forking cake into their mouths and chewing. Klaus-Wilhelm seemed to use those moments of silence to gather his thoughts, and when they were sufficiently composed, he stood a little straighter.

"As a woman once said in a movie I'm quite fond of, 'I'll think about it...tomorrow.'"

"Really?" Raibert made a face. "That's your answer?"

"Mmm!" Elzbietá paused to swallow. "Scarlett O'Hara from *Gone with the Wind*! Am I right?"

Klaus-Wilhelm gave her a curt nod.

"Yes!" She clenched a triumphant fist. "Called it!"

"Wait a second," Benjamin said. "How come you two have seen that movie? Wasn't it exclusive to SysGov's timeline?"

"Almost, but not quite," Elzbietá said. "Came out in 1939, the year before Hitler was assassinated and the Admin's timeline branched off from SysGov's."

"Ah."

"Can we get back to my question, please?" Raibert asked. "And the nonanswer we all just received."

"I'm not sure what else you expected," Klaus-Wilhelm said. "Even though I'm the head of Gordian, a decision like that is—*thankfully*—above my pay grade."

"Then will you pass it up the chain?" Raibert asked.

"Not for a while."

Raibert blinked. That wasn't the answer he'd expected, and Klaus-Wilhelm could see it.

"Raibert, can you imagine what will happen when I lay this problem at the feet of career politicians? And remember, we as an organization have no clear answer for what we *should* do. Would you like to take a guess at what their next question would be?"

"Not a...good one?"

"They'll say 'why are you surveying all these universes if you don't have a plan for what comes next?' Followed by, 'Perhaps you should place a temporary pause on these survey efforts until you *do* have those next steps figured out.' And then, just like that, our efforts to chart the transverse grind to a halt. Is that what you'd like to see happen, Raibert?"

"What? No! Of course not!"

"Perhaps we should keep this problem to ourselves," Elzbietá said. "At least for a little while."

"But..." Raibert began to protest.

"Relax, Raibert," Benjamin said. "Have some cake. You've barely touched yours."

Raibert grimaced down at his cake on the table.

"Our politicians aren't the only problem we need to keep in mind," Klaus-Wilhelm said. "We have enough issues to contend with without adding something of this magnitude to the fire."

"The Admin?" Benjamin guessed, and Klaus-Wilhelm nodded.

"What else? I'm heading to Providence Station later today for another round of meetings I hope won't turn into a shouting match."

"How bad is it?" Elzbietá asked.

"In a word, challenging." Klaus-Wilhelm harrumphed out a breath. "While you were out surveying the transverse, the Admin was hit with a string of surprisingly sophisticated terrorist attacks, and they're pointing the finger at SysGov."

"Why?" Benjamin asked. "How are we at fault?"

"Because it looks like some of our citizens are involved," Klaus-Wilhelm said. "We pushed back against the Admin's accusations at first, partially out of reflex, but also because we haven't detected any unauthorized phase-outs in our territory. But the evidence piled up quickly, to the point where it's basically irrefutable now. *Someone* from SysGov is giving the Admin's troublemakers access to some very dangerous toys. Even *Peng* has had to admit they have a point, and you know butting heads with the Admin is his new, favorite hobby."

"You can say that again," Raibert agreed. "It's Consul Peng now, isn't it?"

"That it is."

"Of CHRONO," Benjamin added with a brief shake of his head. "'Committee for Humane Research Outside Normal Order.' Now there's a tortured acronym if I ever saw one."

"It's the H," Elzbietá said. "That letter's a troublemaker through and through. Try coming up with something that ties into time travel."

"Um...hourly?" Benjamin shrugged. "Yeah, I got nothing."

"Is this extra oversight really warranted?" Raibert asked. "From CHRONO, I mean."

"President Byakko believes so," Klaus-Wilhelm said. "And, as Benjamin just pointed out, it's only been eleven months since our reality almost went kaput...for the second time in two years. Between exploding universes, imploding universes, and branching timelines out to murder ours, a lot of very powerful people—in *both* SysGov and the Admin—are more than a little nervous about what we and our counterparts in the DTI are doing."

"But why Peng?" Raibert asked. "Isn't CHRONO supposed to be a joint SysGov-Admin organization? Why appoint the guy with a major bone to pick with the Admin?"

"The President wanted a civilian with a skeptical disposition to fill the role, and Peng's name rose to the top of her list. As for the *wisdom* of her choice...we'll see."

"All hail our new nanny overlords at CHRONO," Raibert grumped.

"It's not that bad," Elzbietá said, but then frowned at Klaus-Wilhelm. "Is it?"

"No. It's worse."

She winced at his response.

Everyone resumed eating their cake in silence without a smile among them. Even Raibert picked up his plate and cut off a piece with the side of his fork.

"You know what this means?" Benjamin said after a while.

"What?" Raibert asked.

"We just need more cake to brighten the mood."

"Now there's the best idea I've heard all day!" Elzbietá beamed.

She'd just slipped her arm through Benjamin's when a red-headed, red-bearded Viking popped into existence beside them, though "Viking" was a bit of a stretch nowadays. His helmet sported a pair of prominent horns that had never graced the headgear of real Vikings, but his original headgear had been replaced with a twenty-first-century aviator's helmet. Elzbietá had designed and given him the virtual headwear, and he'd worn it ever since.

"Oh, hey there, Philo!" Raibert smiled at his integrated companion. "Glad you could join—"

"We've got a problem," Philo interrupted, facing the Commissioner. "Sir, I just transmitted back from a Themis Division support call."

"Go on."

"Sir, it looks like they found evidence of unauthorized time travel. Of the really bad, existential-threat kind."

CHAPTER TWO

Transtemporal Vehicle *Kleio*
SysGov, 2981 CE

"ALL THIS FUSS OVER A CLOCK RUNNING A LITTLE FAST." RAIBERT reclined in his seat on the bridge of the Transtemporal Vehicle *Kleio* and propped his boots up on the command table. The abstract diagram over the table highlighted their course to join SysPol corvette *Rapid Response* and SourceCode's *Grand Sculptor* near the edge of the debris cloud, accompanied by icons representing each vessel and their comparative sizes.

Kleio's main body was a gunmetal ellipsoid covered in blisters for its weapons and graviton thrusters. The long spike of the chronometric impeller extended from the vessel's rear, giving it an overall length of one hundred fifty meters.

In comparison, the SysPol corvette was a slender, understated ellipsoid about half the *Kleio*'s length. The bulk of the civilian vessel's three spherical sections dwarfed both vessels.

"It's not just a little fast," Philo stressed. "It's forty *years* fast. And it's an atomic clock. It would take over a hundred million billion years for one to accumulate *that* much error."

Raibert leaned his head against the headrest and glanced at his IC through the corner of his eye.

"Philo?"

"Yeah, buddy?"

"I was trying to tell a joke."

"I know. Guess I'm not in the mood right now."

"Him and me both." Benjamin stood with his back against the wall. "It hasn't even been a year since the Dynasty Crisis, and already we have another pack of idiots playing God with the timeline."

"I know, right?" Elzbietá said, the ship's control interfaces hovering around her seat at the table. "There are plenty of other, easier ways to commit suicide. Least they can do is avoid taking the rest of us with them."

Kleio had spent the last fifteen hours on a max-thrust course to intercept the debris cloud and come to a relative stop beside it. That meant pushing the ship's graviton thrusters up to five gees, which was unpleasant for any organic crewmembers—and mildly annoying for a synthoid like Raibert. All three of their physical bodies were in the acceleration-compensation bunks recessed into the bridge outer wall. Their current "bodies" and the "bridge" around them resided within an abstract domain, tied to their virtual senses.

"You, too, Ella?" Raibert took his boots off the table and sat up. "Come on, people. Let's not panic until we actually have cause. We're what passes for professionals in the Gordian Division. Let's try to act like it."

"What 'passes' for professionals?" Elzbietá gave him a half smile.

"All I mean is none of us trained for what we do. I mean, how could we? We're all still figuring out how to make this whole 'policing the multiverse' thing work. Right alongside the rest of Gordian."

"Well, *I* consider us professionals." Elzbietá glanced up. "Hey, Kleio?"

"Yes, Agent Schröder?" replied the ship's attendant program.

"Do you consider yourself a professional?"

"I do not. While my programing has self-evolved greatly since Agent Philosophus released some of my cognitive limiters, I do not meet the legal requirements for sentience or personhood, and as such, it would be incorrect to consider myself a 'professional,' as the term is commonly defined."

"Aww." Elzbietá frowned. "Well, *I* consider you to be one of us, Kleio."

"Thank you, Agent Schröder. Also, Agent Kaminski?"

"What is it?"

"I have received a message from *Grand Sculptor*. Chief Engineer Antoni Ruckman, a senior employee of SourceCode, is requesting permission to come aboard."

"He's the guy Detective Hayfield asked us to talk to?"

"That is correct."

"He a physical or abstract citizen?"

"He is an AC, and we are now in connectome transmission range for our respective vehicles."

"All right." Raibert stood up and tugged the creases out of his uniform jacket. "You can let him come aboard."

Ruckman's avatar appeared on the bridge a few moments later. He glanced around to gain his bearings.

"Agent Raibert Kaminski, Gordian Division." Raibert extended a hand. "We're here to look at your clock."

"A pleasure to meet you, Agent. I'm Antoni Ruckman." He shook Raibert's hand.

"Mister Ruckman, this is my team." Raibert swept an open hand around the bridge. "Agents Schröder, Schröder, and Philosophus. We've all read Detective Hayfield's preliminary report. Do you have anything to add to it before we get started?"

"I wish I did. Unfortunately, we don't have much to go on right now. I've been looking through the black box records with a colleague of mine, but the mismatched dates we found lead us to believe those records have been tampered with."

"What about the missing log entry?" Benjamin pushed off the wall and joined them. "Hayfield's report mentioned the ship failed to check in about two days ago."

"That's right," Ruckman said. "Under normal conditions, a single missed transmission wouldn't be alarming. But..."

"Add in the exploding reactor and signs of record tampering," Benjamin filled in, "and suddenly it all looks very suspicious."

"It certainly does."

"Well, fear not, Mister Ruckman." Raibert patted the AC on the shoulder. "Your case is in good hands."

"I'd like to start by taking a closer look at the black box," Benjamin said. "Plus some sections of the hull, as long as no one cares if I cut a few pieces off to fit in the analyzer."

"Good thinking, Doc," Raibert said. "Kleio, get with Hayfield and have the evidence we need transferred over."

"Yes, Agent Kaminski."

"What do you need hull fragments for?" Ruckman asked, sounding more curious than anything else.

"So I can check them for any chronometric weirdness," Benjamin replied.

"Meanwhile," Raibert said, "Philo, I want you chasing down that missing log. Coordinate with Hayfield's team and see if you can scrounge up what *Reality Flux* was doing when it failed to call in. Between all of Earth's civilian traffic, satellites, habitats, and SysPol patrols, we should come across some good video of that ship in flight. It failed to check in for a reason. We need to figure out why."

"On it." The Viking vanished.

Raibert clapped his big hands together and faced the engineer. "That should get things rolling. With any luck, we won't have another universe-ending calamity to deal with."

"Is that...a common problem in the Gordian Division?" Ruckman asked, sounding just a tad horrified.

"Sometimes," Raibert replied with a casual shrug.

✧   ✧   ✧

"Well, *that* adds a new wrinkle to this mess." Raibert rubbed his chin as he considered the looping video Philo had tracked down.

It wasn't a terribly good video, but it did show the Source-Code vessel roughly two days ago while...something happened to it. The video came from a luxury saucer leaving Luna and had been collected at great distance by the ship's automated systems.

Reality Flux was a string of five pixelated green orbs against a backdrop of stars. The video played out from the beginning once more, showing the spaceship flying an ordinary path toward the inner planets—

—when suddenly, the ship began to vanish. It did so one sphere at a time, from bow to stern, taking over three minutes to do so. And then, nothing. Just stars where the ship had once been.

Raibert looked over to Philo. "What do you make of this?"

"Someone must have deployed a metamaterial shroud around the whole ship. A *big* one."

Raibert nodded. Enough metamaterial could certainly hide a ship that size thanks to the material's light-bending properties. *Kleio* possessed its own deployable stealth shroud which could hide the TTV from most photon-based detectors—all the way from the human eye up to sophisticated radar systems—and could be reconfigured as laser-refracting meta-armor in combat situations.

"I'm guessing the logs SourceCode received afterward were fakes, too," Philo said. "That the ship wasn't there for most, if not all, of the day before it blew up."

"To what end, though?" Raibert asked.

"Can't say. Not yet, at least. Hayfield has a team of forensics specialists analyzing the video, but as you can see, they don't have much to work with. I *will* point out one thing, though." He paused the video and used a slider to rewind it. "See the stars here? Where the bow used to be? They're not in the right positions."

"Which you'd expect from a shroud as it's being deployed," Raibert said. "The illusion won't be perfect until the whole shroud is deployed and rigid."

"Right, but it looks like we may have caught a glimpse of something else in the process."

Philo zoomed in and pointed.

One of the stars was . . . silver?

"Another ship?" Raibert guessed.

"Or a very brief, very distorted glimpse of one."

"That still doesn't tell us much. If it was a shroud, it had to come from somewhere."

"True, but a fleeting glimpse of a second ship supports the theory that another vessel rendezvoused with *Reality Flux* and used a very large shroud to hide both of them."

"I suppose you have a point there." Raibert restarted the video and watched it through to the end. "Did the *Flux* reappear before it went boom?"

"We're not sure. Themis is still trying to track down video of that event, but I would assume so."

"Why?"

"Because we haven't found any metamaterial in the debris cloud. Nor anything else that's inconsistent with the ship or its cargo."

"Someone went to an awful lot of trouble to hide whatever they did out there." Raibert rested his fingers on the edge of the command table. "What about the recordings on the black box? What's Hayfield's team think of those?"

"Only that it's a *very* good fake. If it wasn't for the atomic clock, they would have taken it as genuine and written the whole thing off as an unfortunate accident, probably brought on by a series of maintenance errors."

"Any ideas on how our mystery perps missed it, then? They seem awfully careful about everything else."

"That question occurred to me, too, and I brought it up with Ruckman," Philo said. "According to him, SourceCode customizes the black boxes that go on their ships. They start with stock patterns purchased elsewhere and then modify them in house, and the stock model doesn't include an atomic clock at all. At some point, one of their engineers must have wanted one added, but anyone using the original printing patterns as a reference would almost certainly have missed it."

"Interesting. Anything else?"

"Just one more thing. Hayfield isn't sure about this one yet, but his team is finding evidence the ship isn't old enough. Or, at least, some parts of the wreckage aren't."

"Wait a second. But..." Raibert shook his head. "I thought the problem was the ship is *too* old!"

"That's still the case."

"Then what's this nonsense about it not being old enough?"

"Here, this may help."

Philo opened a pathway through the mental firewall separating his mind from Raibert's, and Raibert confirmed the request. Historical data on the *Reality Flux* expanded within his mind as Philo's thoughts crossed over into his.

"*Reality Flux* was one of SourceCode's older ships," Philo explained, "but if we assume someone used and abused it for forty unaccounted years, some of its systems would surely have broken down and needed to be repaired or replaced. Hayfield mentioned they're finding an unusually large number of parts that look like they were printed within the last year. Parts that, according to SourceCode records, weren't replaced during that time frame. Could be the thieves were just trying to keep it running. Or maybe they wanted to put the *Flux* back the way they found it, and this is the best they could manage."

"Great," Raibert groused. "And here I was hoping all we had was a fast clock."

The alert for an incoming call appeared in his virtual sight, and he toggled it.

"Kaminski. Go."

"Raibert, it's Benjamin."

"Hey, Doc. Got good news for me?"

"I have...news. Can you and Philo come down to the lab?"

"On our way."

Philo disappeared, and Raibert left the bridge. He followed the central corridor back deeper into the ship, then stepped into a counter-grav shaft, which lowered him to the bottom of the ship's three levels. He hurried toward the front of the ship and took a left into the *Kleio*'s newish chronometrics laboratory.

Doctor Andover-Chen, Gordian Division's chief scientist, often requested the *Kleio* and its crew for his various projects, and the ship had accumulated an impressive collection of sensitive instrumentation and prototype equipment, most of it stashed in the new lab.

Raibert didn't mind; he liked big, fancy toys as much as the next guy, and sometimes Andover-Chen's came in handy.

Benjamin, Elzbietá, and Philo stood beside one such "toy." The black box (colored an obnoxiously bright orange) sat on a plinth in a clear, cylindrical chamber. Six robotic arms maneuvered around the box, each tipped with a different style of chronoton detector.

Chronotons were elementary particles with closed-loop histories. They spent most of their existence vibrating backward and forward across the timeline. The detection and manipulation of chronotons enabled time travel, transdimensional travel, and a whole host of reality-shredding disasters.

"Well, Doc?" Raibert said.

"First, I just want to stress I'm not—nor will I ever be—as good at this as Andover-Chen."

"Noted. And?"

"Here. Take a look." Benjamin grabbed one of the charts and expanded it. "We're detecting a very faint chronometric dissonance in the black box, and we've seen the same pattern in the hull sections we've tested. It's subtle, though. In fact, I don't think we would have spotted it without those last upgrades to our diagnostic software."

"And by 'dissonance,' you mean..."

"This device"—Benjamin pointed to the black box—"either came from another universe or it spent enough time outside ours to essentially become 'tuned' to that second chronometric environment. Either way, we'd expect to see some residual dissonance shortly after it entered our universe, and that's exactly what we found."

"Look at you!" Elzbietá smiled as she knuckled her husband in the shoulder. "Getting all cozy with the technobabble!"

"The tutoring sessions with Andover-Chen have certainly helped." Benjamin paused, then frowned. "Though, I will admit, listening to him talk about chronotons is like trying to sip water from a fire hose."

"Better you than me." Raibert tapped the expanded chart. "So, Doc, your conclusion is the ship spent some time outside SysGov before it blew up."

"Yes. In fact, I'd almost say it's guaranteed. We shouldn't see *any* dissonance in a realspace-only vessel."

"Which brings us back to those missing forty years." Raibert let out a slow sigh. "Okay, let's try to put what facts we have together. Conclusions, people?"

"About two days ago," Philo began, "someone stole *Reality Flux* and took it into the transverse."

"How, though?" Raibert asked.

"The criminals would need an exotic matter scaffold," Benjamin said. "Either one of ours or one we don't know about. Ours can transport anything up to and including a *Directive*-class heavy cruiser, so they're large enough to handle SourceCode's industrial ships."

"All of our scaffolds are being used for the construction of Providence Station," Raibert countered.

"Then they must have made one on their own," Benjamin said. "A lot of companies are involved in Providence's construction, which means the designs for our scaffolds aren't nearly as secure as we'd like them to be."

"All right." Raibert nodded, agreeing with the theory so far. "Let's say you're right. What then?"

"They must have taken *Reality Flux* to another universe," Philo said. "After reaching it, they went forty years into the past, then caused enough of a disturbance to branch the timeline and create a new universe. Their alternate timeline then rapidly caught up to us in the True Present."

"And just like that," Benjamin said, "they managed to cheat the multiverse out of forty extra years."

"After they were done with the ship," Philo continued, "they brought it back here and then arranged for the ship to be placed back on its original course and destroyed."

"Makes sense so far," Raibert said with an air of caution, "but I see a possible hole in this theory. Why didn't Argus Station's chronometric array pick up the phase events?"

"A problem with a simple solution," Benjamin said. "These criminals managed to equip their scaffold with impeller baffles, making the phase-in and phase-out events as quiet as possible."

"If that's the case"—Elzbietá shook her head—"then whoever's behind this went through *a lot* of trouble."

"Right." Raibert lowered his head in thought. "So, the bad guys steal a massive hoard of industrial goodies, take it to another universe, and bring it back subjectively forty years later."

"During which time," Philo said, "only a day passed for us."

"But why blow up the ship after going through all the effort to bring it back? Why bring it back at all?"

"I...don't know," Philo admitted. "Seems to me it would have made more sense for the ship to go missing."

"Or for them to bring it back but not destroy it," Elzbietá added.

"There must be a reason, though," Raibert said. "Everything else we've seen gives me the impression this heist was carefully planned and executed."

"I'm more concerned about those forty years," Benjamin said. "That alone proves there's a new universe out there, and we have no idea where it is or what it branched off of. We also don't know who did this or why, but stealing industrial hardware spells trouble."

"What could they build in forty years with all that?" Elzbietá asked.

"Just about anything they wanted," Philo said, "assuming they had access to the right raw materials and printing patterns."

Raibert let out a nervous sigh. The rest of his team stood in contemplative silence until he looked up and clapped his hands together.

"All right. It's clear this isn't a one-crew job. Time we called in backup."

✧   ✧   ✧

Agent Anton Silchenko, Head of Gordian Operations, had served under Commissioner Schröder—then a *generalmajor* in the imperial German army—since the beginning. Or at least what *he* thought of as "the beginning," since it involved the liberation of his beloved nation of Ukraine from the Soviet swine. He'd met the man in 1946, one year into the Great Eastern War, a war that never happened in this timeline, and therefore, "never" ended in 1951 with the total defeat of Stalinist Russia.

In that sense, Anton and his fellow Ukrainian veterans enjoyed more in common with the Admin, since they shared the same "alternate" history, but he felt no kinship there, no sense of allegiance. He and the other survivors of the Gordian Knot were men without a home, except they didn't need one. They had their leader, whom they'd followed to victory time and time again, and they had all followed him into the Gordian Division to a man. They were hardened veterans, each and every one of them, Anton included, capable of enduring hardships and pain that would break lesser men.

But they were not without their own weaknesses.

Mention to any one of them that he'd let the General/Governor/now-Commissioner down, and Anton wouldn't be surprised if that man broke down into tears.

Because Klaus-Wilhelm von Schröder, as great a man as he was, still needed them. Still needed *him*, and by God he would continue to serve the man he owed so much to in any way he could, with every fiber of his being. He would follow that man through the gates of hell barefoot, if asked to. He would trek to the very ends of the Earth and charge into the bloody crucible of battle without a second thought, as long as Klaus-Wilhelm von Schröder told him it was necessary.

He just...had never expected this.

It's funny, Anton thought with an inward grin, *the places fate can lead us.*

He looked around Gordian Operations, the generously-sized room deep within the bowels of Argus Station, an orbital construct so large it served as home and headquarters for over nine million members of the Consolidated System Police. Such a wonder could never have been constructed in his time, even on the ground. Even if the entire world had united in the common cause of its creation. And yet it was one of countless technological marvels spread across the solar system.

An alert appeared, manifesting in his virtual vision thanks to his thirtieth-century wetware, and he tapped it.

"Gordian Operations. Silchenko."

"Agent Silchenko, incoming transmission from *Kleio*. Priority Two."

Anton stiffened and sucked in a sharp breath. A Priority Two meant Raibert and his crew had found evidence of a precursor event. Something that, while not catastrophic by itself, held the potential to escalate into the destruction of whole universes.

"Let's hear it."

A comm window opened with Raibert filling the frame, his eyes severe and his face like etched stone. The time stamp indicated the *Kleio* was roughly two light-minutes away, which would make any back-and-forth conversation awkward.

"Kaminski to Gordian Operations. We've got a Priority Two on our hands. Analysis of the wreckage from *Reality Flux* came back positive for chronometric dissonance, indicating the craft spent a *lot* of time in another universe, and that universe's True Present was expanding forward at an accelerated pace. Our conclusion is the vessel was taken to another universe sometime within the past two days, where it experienced forty subjective years due to a new branch in the timeline. Our recommendation is for all available TTVs to begin an immediate search of the surrounding transdimensional space for signs of a new branching universe. We've attached our recommendation for how far out into the transverse we believe we need to look."

Anton paused before replying, then let out a slow exhale. He knew why Raibert's crew had been dispatched to the site of the lost SourceCode ship, but he hadn't expected it to be *this* bad!

"*Kleio*, do you see any benefit in continuing your investigation of the wreckage?"

He waited four minutes for the response.

"Not at this time. Themis Division should be able to take it from here. If something new comes up, it'll be their forensics teams that sniff it out. We'll be more help elsewhere, if you ask me."

Anton nodded. That made his next call easier. The Commissioner would want to hear about this as soon as possible. Argus Station and Providence Station could communicate via chronometric telegraphs, but the bandwidth on such messages was extremely limited and subject to clear "weather" in the transverse. An in-person report would be better.

"*Kleio*, you are hereby redirected to Providence Station where you will brief the Commissioner on the situation. Meanwhile, we'll recall what TTVs we can contact and begin organizing your proposed search."

Another four minutes passed.

"Understood, Operations. We're on our way."

CHAPTER THREE

Providence Station
Transverse, non-congruent

THE PROVIDENCE PROJECT WAS THE BRAINCHILD OF DOCTOR Andover-Chen of SysGov's Gordian Division and Under-Director Katja Hinnerkopf of the Admin's Department of Temporal Investigation, with the goal of designing, constructing, and staffing a permanent base in the transverse, situated at the midpoint between the outer walls of SysGov and the Admin's universes. It was the first large-scale joint project between the two superpowers, with SysGov handling the majority of the exotic matter construction and the Admin contributing an outsized share of the more conventional systems.

The agreement to build and operate Providence Station had been bought with the twin "coins" of shared blood and technological exchange. It had become possible only after the horrific price in blood and lives the two universes had paid fighting side-by-side against the enormous, transtemporal battle station Lucius Gwon had built. He'd betrayed Teodorà Beckett and Samuel Pepys to build it, then uploaded his connectome into its central computers, and it hadn't bothered him one bit that he'd doomed three entire universes in the process. What had mattered to *him* was that he had finally become the god he'd always been in his own mind...until Teodorà's suicide run had destroyed him along with the entire Dynasty, the civilization—and universe—she'd spent literally centuries building.

Yet she couldn't have done that if the Admin hadn't come to SysGov's aid, fought and died beside the men and women and abstract personalities of the Gordian and Argo Divisions. In the dying, they had demonstrated it was possible not only for their universes to coexist but that there were threats against which they *must* join forces.

That had made the Providence Project possible; the technical exchange was what had made it a true partnership. The Admin had offered several impeller innovations, one so advanced it had yet to see active service, and SysGov had provided the technical expertise to leapfrog the Admin's artificial gravity efforts by several decades.

Some officials in each government considered Providence Station to be nothing more than a research outpost. In truth, it was far more than that. The colossal base would serve as an operational hub with enough personnel, living quarters, hangar space, industrial printers, and logistical centers to support whole fleets of SysGov TTVs and Admin chronoports.

The station would also house the largest, most sensitive chronometric array ever constructed, capable of peering deeper into the transverse than ever before, and with far greater clarity.

And, hopefully, before the next existential threat came roaring out of the transverse's depths with blood in its eye.

The transverse was the transdimensional space binding countless universes together to form the greater multiverse. It was a realm almost impossible for the human mind to visualize, stretching out in six spatial dimensions instead of the comfortable three of realspace, and though both Gordian Division and the DTI traveled *through* it, neither organization truly *understood* it.

Not yet.

It was a dangerous place, where chronometric storms could strike with little or no warning. Such hazards could rip through a TTV's protective field as if it were a soap bubble, exposing ship and crew to a torrent of chronotons powerful enough to destabilize matter and turn the ships into twisted, nightmarish wrecks with crews interposed through decks and walls.

Providence Station had been designed with such hazards in mind. The main body of the station formed a thick disk edged in a honeycomb of hangars and docking arms, though many sections currently gave way to unfinished skeletal framework. Additional levels extended upward from that main body to form what resembled a massive cylindrical high-rise, also dotted with gaps around naked internal supports, while the long spike of the station's chronoton impeller extended downward.

Thirty-three industrial ships of different sizes and configurations hovered around the station. Hundreds of construction drones and the thick, milky tides of microbot swarms moved about the unfinished sections in a slow but relentless dance.

Unlike most time machine impellers, the one built for Providence Station wasn't designed to move a vessel, though it could perform that function if the need was great enough. Instead, Providence's impeller had been designed to generate a chronometric field two orders of magnitude more powerful than anything produced artificially, with the lone exception of the ill-fated *Tesseract*, Lucius Gwon's time-traveling battle fortress, built by the equally ill-fated Dynasty.

Storms fierce enough to rend a TTV apart would rage harmlessly against Providence Station's protective envelope, allowing the station to serve as a safe harbor in addition to its many other functions.

Kleio slipped into one of the station's open hangars, a tiny gunmetal ellipsoid next to the gargantuan station. Its thrusters set it down into the docking cradle, clamps secured the main body in place, and the prog-steel hangar doors sealed shut behind it.

The interior pressurized, and *Kleio*'s nose split open and morphed into a ramp. Raibert hurried down the ramp and crossed halfway to the station entrance, then paused and turned back.

An abstract window provided a raw view of the transverse from beyond the *Kleio*, though there wasn't much to look at. The transverse was a realm of chronotons, not photons, and appeared black to human sight.

Mostly.

Chronotons could shed or absorb photons as they changed energy states, and a dense enough torrent of chronotons could produce visible light, enough to manifest as blobs of indistinct color, almost like the flickering hallucinations visible when someone closed their eyes in a dark room.

Today, the transverse formed a bruised canvas, shot with brief flashes not unlike lightning.

A storm's brewing, Raibert thought darkly. *In more ways than one.*

He turned away from the view and hustled into the station.

Klaus-Wilhelm was waiting for him in the observational balcony overlooking the hangar.

"Boss," Raibert greeted with a curt nod.

"Walk with me."

Klaus-Wilhelm exited through the back of the room, and Raibert followed, moving quickly to match the man's long, determined strides. They passed through a corridor with one wall the milky white of an active microbot swarm.

"Where are we headed?" Raibert asked.

"CHRONO Operations. Some of the grav tubes aren't installed or commissioned yet, so we're hoofing it. As soon as you and I are done, I'm heading into a meeting with CHRONO and the DTI to discuss what you've found."

"And to get their help?"

"I certainly hope so."

"You want me in that meeting?"

"I do. You'll head out as soon as we're finished. We're dedicating just about every TTV within telegraph range to the search, and I want *Kleio* to be a part of it."

"About that." Raibert gave him a crooked smile. "We had an idea on the way over."

"I figured. What's on your mind?"

"Actually, it was Benjamin who came up with it. You know the quarantine universes?"

"Of course."

"What if the thieves are hiding out in one of those?"

Klaus-Wilhelm paused at a T-junction and looked Raibert in the eyes. A red-and-white striped barrier along one "wall" separated the men from a deep, dark drop into the station's unfinished guts.

"You want to take *Kleio* on a tour of the Q's?" the Commissioner asked.

"That's right."

"Those universes are quarantined for some very good reasons. They're hostile environments. To *anyone*, criminals included."

"I know, but how would a criminal—a sufficiently crafty and paranoid one—look at the Q's?"

"Hmm." Klaus-Wilhelm paused in thought, then began to nod. "They'd see a universe we're deliberately avoiding."

"At the very least, *someone* needs to check them out. It's dangerous work, so it might as well be us."

"All right. You've convinced me." Klaus-Wilhelm turned left down the corridor, and Raibert jogged to catch up. "Let Operations know which universes you plan to cover. Otherwise, you're free to proceed at your own discretion."

"Thanks. You can count on us."

They continued deeper into the station at a brisk pace.

"This place has been coming along nicely," Raibert said, looking around. "How far along are we? About halfway there?"

"Forty-two percent," Klaus-Wilhelm said. "We're *supposed* to have crossed the halfway point last week, but construction's running behind. Some of that eight percent are the grav tubes."

"Would have been nice to have those."

"I couldn't really care less," Klaus-Wilhelm growled. "I'd give up *all* the grav plating in the whole station to have our array online."

"Would have made our search easier?"

"Would have made it *unnecessary*. According to Andover-Chen, we would've seen the timeline split as it happened. Unlike the Argus Array, Providence is situated outside SysGov's outer wall. A larger, more sensitive array and negligible interference should combine splendidly." Klaus-Wilhelm frowned. "Once it's working. Instead, we're now close to three days behind whatever the hell is going on out there."

"You're right. That *would* have been nice." Raibert let out a quiet sigh and kept walking. "You think maybe that's why the ship got stolen now? Providence was getting a little too close to being ready?"

"It's possible. Either way, we'll make do with what we have."

"Same as always. Right, boss?"

Klaus-Wilhelm grunted in agreement then led them into a wide circular space lined with vertical counter-grav shafts. All but one were sectioned off with physical barriers and virtual construction tape.

"This one works." Klaus-Wilhelm indicated one of the counter-grav shafts.

Raibert followed him in, and a gentle graviton current whisked them upward through the station before depositing them into another shaft junction. Klaus-Wilhelm took one of the five exits, which opened at the far end to a massive, circular room with desks arrayed in stepped tiers around a central open space, almost like a stage surrounded on all sides by stadium seating. Additional doors lined the back walls, leading to offices, conference rooms, restrooms, a temporary cafeteria, and various other facilities.

A simplified map of the transverse floated above the room's center, with the boundaries of whole universes streamlined into basic icons labeled with abbreviations like H12 or Q4. Additional icons showed the known or estimated positions of time machines, while two subplots detailed the forces present in both T1 and T2, otherwise known as SysGov and the Admin.

CHRONO Operations was considerably larger than Gordian Operations on Argus Station, but it was also designed to act as a command center for both the Gordian Division *and* the DTI, eventually replacing Gordian Operations along with the DTI equivalent on their Earth.

That was the plan, at least, and Raibert could detect some hints of that future, with Gordian personnel in their gray-green uniforms walking around or working at desks across from DTI agents in Peacekeeper blue. But the two sides were...very strictly segregated. And seemed to have picked desks as far away from their counterparts as possible.

"There seems to be...less cooperation going on than I expect."

"Raibert?"

"Yeah, boss?"

"A word of warning before we head into this meeting. You'll be up first, and I want you to keep it dry and factual in there. They ask you questions, you give them straight answers. If someone asks for an opinion or decision, I'll step in and handle it. Clear?"

"As crystal."

"Good." Klaus-Wilhelm sucked in a sharp breath. "And now, hopefully, with a little luck, maybe we can get through this without those two idiots shouting at each other."

"I don't believe this!" shouted Clara Muntero, CHRONO Consul for the Admin. "We've been asking—no, we've been *begging* for help dealing with these attacks for weeks now! And instead of receiving what we're practically on our hands and knees pleading for, you have the audacity to come here and ask *us* to help *you*?!"

"Madam Consul," Klaus-Wilhelm began, his tone imbued with the patience of a saint, but then he paused and glanced around the triangular table. Raibert sat stiffly beside him, almost *painfully* rigid, watching the meeting degenerate with a horrified expression.

Director-General Csaba Shigeki sat on the DTI side of the triangular table, flanked by Jonas Shigeki, Under-Director of Foreign Affairs. The peaked cap of his Peacekeeper uniform rested on the table, and his black hair was bound into a long braid streaked with silver. He seemed to be straining his face in an attempt to pen up impolite words. Or perhaps *reprimands* might have been a better description. Meanwhile, his son Jonas leaned back in his seat and busied himself inspecting his cuffs while chewing on the inside of his lip. One of their security synthoids stood attentively at the back of the room, his face an impassive, gray-skinned mask, his yellow eyes fixed forward.

Consuls Peng Fa and Clara Muntero occupied the CHRONO side of the table, on *opposite ends* of it, as far apart as they could possibly sit. Muntero's scowl darkened a round face framed by a strict buzz cut while Peng held an exasperated hand up to his forehead. His avatar's skin was the black of night, and his eyes glowed an electric blue. Even their postures—the way they leaned away from each other—added to the subliminal sense these two despised one another.

Peng and Muntero were supposed to be partners, nominated by their respective governments to represent civilian interests and provide oversight for the temporal and transdimensional operations of Gordian and the DTI, with the long-term goal of forming a larger, unified organization.

In reality, their first steps together had been...rocky.

Klaus-Wilhelm opened his mouth to speak. "Consul Muntero—"

"This is ludicrous." Peng lowered his hand from his forehead and looked up with glowing eyes. "We *are* providing aid! We've been monitoring all travel through SysGov's outer wall, and we've openly shared all the data collected by the Argus Array. What more do you want?"

"What we want are these attacks on our people to stop!" Muntero snapped.

"We're not the ones attacking you!"

"No, but your citizens are aiding and abetting criminals! Terrorist cells like Free Luna have suddenly become far more effective."

"And if we could find the ones responsible, we'd bring them to justice! Be reasonable! We're not magicians!"

Klaus-Wilhelm frowned at the mess unfolding before his eyes. He understood why Peng and Muntero had both been nominated for their respective posts. In effect, both President Byakko and Chief Executor Christopher First had come to the same conclusion and had nominated people who would keep a close eye on what was, without a shadow of a doubt, the most dangerous enterprise upon which humanity had ever embarked.

But these two mix as well as oil and water! he thought bitterly.

"Consul Muntero," Klaus-Wilhelm said, this time more firmly, "I understand and sympathize with the problems the Admin is facing. However, we're limited in the aid we can provide without a firmer grasp on who's responsible. Instead, let's focus on what we *can* do. The theft and destruction of *Reality Flux* is a matter we can start addressing *now.*"

"That's easy for you to say," Muntero responded stiffly. "But you're not up against terrorists armed with military-grade SysGov tech. Why, just yesterday one of our most secure facilities on the planet was hit." She bobbed her head toward the Director-General. "Show them."

Shigeki let out a quiet sigh then sat up.

"What happened?" Klaus-Wilhelm asked, genuinely concerned about the news.

"A Free Luna commando team infiltrated one of our prison towers using highly sophisticated software and equipment. Once inside, they broke into the prison domain's one-way abstraction and pulled out several Free Luna members serving life sentences. Basically, the absolute worst of the worst. They then transmitted the prisoners out of the tower. The commando team didn't survive the operation, which is a small comfort given what happened next."

"Which was?" Klaus-Wilhelm asked.

"See for yourself. This is from the prison domain's server room." Shigeki placed his hand on the table. His Personal Implant Network interfaced with the room's infostructure, and an abstraction appeared between them.

Row after row of racked infosystem nodes stretched to a high ceiling, and thick cables filled trenches covered by steel grates. Five men and women in Peacekeeper uniforms clustered around one of the racks. They were outlined in red, while Peacekeepers and drones with blue outlines converged on their position from both sides.

One of the terrorists set a heavy backpack on the ground and opened the top.

"For a free Luna!" he shouted, and his comrades chorused the words moments before he shoved his arm into the pack.

The pack detonated, and the explosion engulfed the terrorists. Not in fire but in a white aerosol that settled like powdered sugar, coating the aisle and dusting the Peacekeepers and drones nearby. The powder began to condense, forming a milky sheen that grew with each passing moment. Not swiftly at first, but with mounting speed, corroding everything it touched—be it flesh or metal—with equal ease. Consuming the racks and nodes and *people* for raw material.

"The entire tower had to be evacuated. Our efforts to contain and neutralize the self-replicators are...ongoing." Shigeki removed his hand from the table, and the abstraction vanished.

"Why hasn't the DTI been able to track down the source of these weapons?" Peng challenged. "Isn't sifting through the past your specialty? You put it in your name, after all."

"We're trying, believe me." Frustration lined Shigeki's face. "So far, our investigations into the terrorists' pasts haven't produced any worthwhile leads. Not for the root cause of this upsurge in equipment sophistication, though we've done some good, taken out a few cells before they could strike. No, the problem we're facing is that no actual materiel is being delivered to the cells. Rather, someone is sending them highly sophisticated software and patterns—patterns we're certain were developed in SysGov—and the cells are printing the Restricted tech themselves."

"So?" Peng held his hands out, palms up. "You've got time machines. Backtrack the signals!"

"We're *trying*. We..." Shigeki leaned forward with an elbow on the table. "Look, the short of it is that space is too damn big, even when we've sniffed out the signal's vector, which we've managed to do twice so far. Add in a time axis, and the area to search is oppressively huge. I simply don't have enough ships."

"Ships," Muntero stated coolly, "that we are now being asked to lend you."

"We may still get lucky," Shigeki said. "Maybe catch the culprits as they're crossing the outer wall, or when they're traveling through the transverse. But I don't think we're going to trace them down if we stick to the DTI's standard playbook."

"Consuls." Jonas leaned forward, speaking up for the first

time in the meeting. "Has it occurred to you these two problems might be related?"

"What makes you say that?" Peng asked, sounding less confrontational for a change.

"Despite our extensive patrols around the outer wall, we've been unable to pinpoint any evidence of unauthorized time or transdimensional travel." Jonas spread his hands. "And now here you have a ship that vanished without your Argus Array detecting its phase-out. What I'm saying is these two problems seem *awfully* similar to me in that regard. That is why, Consuls, I'd like to stress the need for our organizations to work together. It's very possible—perhaps even likely—that investigating one problem will in fact shed light on both. At the moment, the loss of *Reality Flux* is the more promising lead, so I suggest we focus our efforts there."

"Agreed," Shigeki said firmly. "We in the DTI aren't getting anywhere as it is. Let's try to find this branched universe and then see what shakes loose. We could arrange for one of our chronoport squadrons to be dedicated to the search almost immediately, with more on the way after that."

Peng sat back and nodded. "Good, then are we in agreement?"

"We are not." Muntero locked eyes with Shigeki. "We can't weaken our defenses at a time when we're under unprecedented attack."

Oh, for the love of all that is good and holy! Klaus-Wilhelm fumed on the inside.

"Consul," Shigeki replied evenly, "I believe we can afford a temporary reduction in defensive force strength with minimal impact."

"Csaba, you can't even track down these terrorists with the ships you have. What makes you think I have the slightest inclination to let you flitter away even that?"

Shigeki sat back in his seat and seemed ready to reply, but Peng beat him to it.

"Then you're not going to support our search?" the SysGov consul asked.

"Not as the situation stands," Muntero said. "Not unless we get something out of it."

"What? Like a few TTVs?"

"Those would be better than nothing."

"And would completely defeat the purpose of us asking for *your* ships."

"That's my position," Muntero said with finality.

Peng put his forehead back in his hand.

"You know, Clara," he began, "you really only have yourselves to blame for this."

"Excuse me?"

"All these terrorist attacks. How long have they been going on? Since the founding of the Admin? Like, a few hundred years by now? And in all that time, have you ever wondered why they keep happening?"

"*Peng*," Klaus-Wilhelm warned.

"Let's think about why this is for a moment." Peng made a show of gazing at the ceiling while tapping his lips with a thoughtful finger. "Ah, right!" He snapped his fingers. "You're a bunch of barbarians who enslave 'artificial intelligences' like me!"

"Don't be ridiculous!" Muntero snapped. "These attacks are about lunar independence, not our Restrictions on AIs!"

"Then we'll just add that problem to the list. Perhaps you should all get a clue and join the rest of us in the thirtieth century!"

"Oh, please! Take some responsibility for the mess you brought to our doorstep!"

"How about this instead? Read my virtual lips: We're not responsible for your own dysfunction."

"That's big talk from people who still execute their own citizens. At least we don't have the death penalty anymore!"

Peng rolled his eyes. "Oh, like your one-way abstractions are any better! Might as well call them 'eternal torture prisons'! It'd be more accurate!"

"Peng," Klaus-Wilhelm said, his voice calm and low but with a dangerous undercurrent. "You either bring this tantrum under control, or I swear to God, I'll go right over your head and put this outburst in front of the President."

"All I'm saying—"

"I don't care. Bring the volume down, or else."

"Fine," Peng huffed, leaning back in his virtual chair.

The occupants fell silent, though Klaus-Wilhelm could almost feel the frustration choking the room, edging toward palpable loathing when it came to Peng and Muntero. Beside him, Raibert's horrified expression had only grown worse.

After a long pause, he stood up.

"Excuse me, Consuls, but I have a search to organize."

CHAPTER FOUR

Providence Station
Transverse, non-congruent

"KLAUS, A MOMENT OF YOUR TIME," SHIGEKI SAID SOFTLY ON their way out of the room. "Preferably in private."

"Sure." Klaus-Wilhelm pointed a thumb over his shoulder. The conference room was situated along the upper lip of CHRONO Operations near his office. "Mine or yours?"

"Yours will do." Shigeki caught his son's eye. "Jonas, are you free to join us?"

"Sorry. I'd love to, but I need to rush back to Argus. I'm already late for a meeting with Vesna," Jonas replied, referring to Commissioner Vesna Tyrel of Themis Division.

"The officer exchange program?" Shigeki asked.

"Yep. Their six-month evaluation is due, and we're conducting the interviews in person. It's more of a formality at this point, given how well those two have performed, but"—his expression darkened for a moment before he masked it behind a quick smile—"I'll take any bright spot I can these days."

"Okay then," said the senior Shigeki. "Safe travels."

Jonas gave his father a quick wave and then hustled down the stairs.

"I should be off as well, Commissioner." Raibert bobbed his head toward the main Operations exit. "With your permission?"

"Dismissed. And good luck out there."

"You too, Nox," Shigeki told the big security synthoid shadowing him. "We'll talk later."

"Director." The synthoid acknowledged him with a nod and left down the stairs.

Klaus-Wilhelm led the way around the circumference of CHRONO Operations until he came to his office. He palmed the lock, the door split open, and he stepped inside. The room wasn't fully furnished yet, but he'd found time to bring over a few personal effects, the most prominent of which was a Smith & Wesson Model 29 pistol framed on the wall beside a gun belt loaded with .44 Magnum cartridges.

The gun drew Shigeki's eye like a magnet.

The last time Klaus-Wilhelm had discharged the weapon was into the guts of the DTI synthoid who'd killed his wife and three little girls. He didn't know *which* synthoid because the operative's mind had been loaded into one of their combat frames, which lacked clear identifying traits. Their scant records of the battle—most of them coming from Raibert's synthoid—hadn't provided enough clues for either side to identify the individual, and given the twisting of timelines and universes during the Gordian Knot, the man or woman Klaus-Wilhelm had shot dead was probably alive and still working at the DTI.

Concern spread across Shigeki's face, but only for a moment before he turned away from the gun. He knew better than perhaps anyone else in the Admin what the gun meant—and how deeply Klaus-Wilhelm's emotional scars ran.

But Shigeki had nothing to worry about. Not with the gun where it was.

It was only if the Commissioner found reason to take the gun *off* the wall that people needed to start sweating!

Klaus-Wilhelm rounded the polished wooden desk and sank into the chair behind it. The chair's prog-foam adjusted for maximum support and comfort, and Shigeki took the guest seat that formed out of the floor.

"Something to drink?" Klaus-Wilhelm set two empty glasses on the desk. "Coffee? Or perhaps something stronger?"

"I'll stick to coffee, mildly sweetened. I could use a jolt after *that* meeting."

"Coffee it is." Klaus-Wilhelm slotted the glasses into the food printer built into his desk. He took them out when finished and set them down.

"Thank you." Shigeki took a sip. "Mmm."

"What's on your mind, Csaba?"

Shigeki glanced at the framed medal on the wall opposite the gun. It was the Star of the Shield, the highest civilian honor in the Admin, which the Chief Executor had personally awarded Klaus-Wilhelm after he and Shigeki had led the decisive fleet action that ended the Dynasty threat.

"A lot," Shigeki said. "Things were so much clearer during the Dynasty Crisis. Not that I'm remembering it fondly or anything, but at least we knew who we were up against and where to find them. This latest business with someone in SysGov helping terrorists is . . . messy."

"It was the same way for me back in Ukraine. The Great Eastern War was a terrible ordeal that consumed men and equipment with a voracious hunger. And then we won. The war ended, and the Soviet uniforms came off, but the hearts underneath didn't change. Not all of them, at least."

"I remember reading about that when I was profiling you." Shigeki flashed a sly grin. "You put down your fair share of communist partisans, if I'm not mistaken."

"The attacks grew less frequent with time. And not just because my men were damned good at their jobs, though there was certainly that."

"What else tamped down the attacks?"

"We showed people life was better for most under the 'new management.'" Klaus-Wilhelm took a sip of his coffee. "And it was. It absolutely was. Not perfect, mind you. Nowhere close. But we made life better for a lot of people, and that by itself was enough to begin changing hearts." He snorted and shook his head. "*Without* perforating those hearts with bullets."

"I wish it were that easy for us." Shigeki stared into his cup, then raised his eyes. "Let me be honest with you, Klaus. Things are tense back home."

"How bad is it?"

"In a word, volatile. The temperature of the political discourse is hotter than I've ever seen it, and there's only so much the Department of Public Relations can do to control the narrative.

The Chief Executor is getting pounded daily from all sides over his Million Handshake Initiative and his rush to build a cross-universe economy."

"I thought the Initiative was viewed as a success."

"It was until we started finding SysGov tech in the hands of terrorists. We tried to keep a lid on that, tried to restrict the matter to high levels of our government, but the truth leaked, and now we have an even bigger mess on our hands."

Shigeki took another swig of coffee before continuing.

"I know you're no fan of Muntero's. Neither am I, for that matter, but she's not the problem. Isolationist voices are growing louder, and they're gaining traction. People are beginning to question if we've moved too far too fast, and they view these attacks as proof positive we have. The Chief Executor wants the flow of weapons to stop, and Muntero's trying to carry out his priorities as best she can."

"I thought we almost got through to her with your son's idea."

"I did, too." Shigeki let out a weary sigh. "But there's not much I can do once she's made up her mind. The Chief Executor's put me on a short leash, and Muntero's holding the other end. And, honestly, maybe we *are* moving too fast. There's plenty of good SysGov and the Admin can share with one another, but we also run the risk of inheriting each other's problems."

"You're beginning to sound like Peng."

"Now you're just being mean." Shigeki chuckled, but then his mirth vanished. "You didn't hear this from me, but the Chief Executor has begun saying the same thing. Publicly, he's still pushing the Initiative. But privately, he's shared his doubts with me. And let's not forget several aspects of SysGov society terrify people back home, especially where AIs and self-replicators are concerned. Tie those fears to terrorists who quite literally want to destroy our way of life, and you've got a recipe for a major policy shift. Maybe even to the point where he yanks our support from Providence."

"We need to make sure it doesn't come to that," Klaus-Wilhelm said. "Now, what can the two of us do about this mess?"

"With or without being fired?" Shigeki stared off in thought, swirling his coffee.

"That's the trick, isn't it?"

"I tell you what." Shigeki set his cup down. "Let me talk to

Muntero in private. I bet I can convince her to section off a few chronoports to scout universes near our outer wall. The Local 15 at least."

"You really think she'll go in for that?"

"She will if I tell her the terrorists might be using them as bases. And if we happen to stumble across a newly branched timeline during our search"—he shrugged—"that'll be a nice bonus."

"Either way, it helps me. Any universe the DTI can scout is one we can skip."

"Which will allow you to work through the rest of the list faster," Shigeki finished. "It's not much, but..."

"It's better than nothing." Klaus-Wilhelm leaned back, and his chair sighed. "I'll take it. Meanwhile, let me talk to Andover-Chen about shifting the construction schedule. If we can get Providence's array working early, that'll give us a much better tool to monitor the Admin's outer wall."

"Which would give me an excuse to free up more chronoports." Shigeki nodded. "I like where you're heading with this." He stood up and finished his coffee in one long gulp, then set the glass down and met his counterpart's gaze. "Thank you for the drink, Klaus. Now, if you don't mind, I'm going to see if Muntero has cooled off yet."

"Don't get yourself fired."

"I'll try my best," he replied with a wry grin.

Special Agent James Noxon palmed the door open and stepped into Hinnerkopf's office, but then froze with one foot still outside.

"I'm sorry. The Commissioner wants us to do *what*?!" Hinnerkopf asked, her back to Nox. The Under-Director of Technology was a short, compact woman with short, black hair.

"Shift the array calibration forward by a whole month," Andover-Chen replied. Gordian Division's lead scientist wore a slightly bemused smile and almost seemed to be on the edge of shaking his head. His synthoid featured black, glassy skin with bluish equations dancing beneath the surface.

"But it's still under construction! Uh!" Hinnerkopf sat down on a couch and buried her face in her hands. "We're missing half the array segments! The suppliers are behind printing the rest, and the segments we *do* have are completely out of alignment! What are we supposed to do with a half-finished, cross-eyed array?"

"What we usually do. Work the miracles no one else can."

"God help us." Hinnerkopf let her head droop between her hands.

"It's not that bad. He only asked if it was possible."

"*Sure*, he did." Hinnerkopf sat back in the couch and looked up. "But you know as well as I do that he won't take no for an answer, and he'll have Director Shigeki's support as well. Those two are thick as thieves these days."

"You might want to steer clear of that phrase," Andover-Chen replied, his bemused expression still there. "At least until we know who stole that ship."

"Point taken." She glanced over at the entrance, then hurriedly fixed her posture. "Oh, Nox. Sorry, I didn't hear you step in."

"Have I come at a bad time?" Nox asked.

"Not really." Hinnerkopf bit into her lower lip and stared off with a look of deep contemplation. "Just trying to figure out how to do the impossible."

"We'll think of something," Andover-Chen said.

"Maybe..." Hinnerkopf leaned forward and wagged a finger at Andover-Chen. "You know, we might be able to squeeze some use out of what we've got right now."

"What's on your mind?"

"I'm thinking we don't *actually* need the whole array. We only need a small piece of it calibrated."

"Which would limit us to a narrow, conical view."

"Not if we rig some sort of rotating mechanism to the array. Have it sweep around for a more complete picture."

"Ah!" Andover-Chen's eyes widened. "I see where you're going with this. Essentially treat the working part of the array like a dish instead."

"We're used to doing more with less in the Admin, and there's no way we can expedite the missing segments; they require too much exotic matter. So instead, we work around the limitation and find a temporary, if imperfect, fix. All those industrial ships outside shouldn't have much trouble whipping up the hardware."

"I like it!" Andover-Chen beamed. "I'll head up to the array chamber and scope out which segments we can work with. Want to come along?"

"Um." Her eyes met Nox's for a brief moment and then flicked back to Andover-Chen. "In a bit."

"Catch up when you can." Andover-Chen left the office, and the door closed behind him.

"Sorry, Katja," Nox said.

"Oh, don't be." Hinnerkopf patted the couch. "Come here, you big lug."

Nox walked over and sat next to her. She looped her arm through his, closed her eyes, and leaned against his shoulder.

"You all right?" she asked.

"I was about to ask you the same thing."

"I'm fine. Schröder's request caught me off guard, is all. Andover-Chen and I'll work through it." She craned her neck, head still resting on his arm, and looked up at him. "And you?"

"Tense."

"You're always tense."

"Tense-*er*. These attacks have me worried. It's been over a century since I've seen it this bad, and my gut tells me it'll get worse before it gets better."

"We'll work through this bad spell, same as all the others."

"Something tells me this one is different."

"Don't be so gloomy."

"Sorry," he said. "I can't help it sometimes."

She knitted her fingers through his, and a pair of engagement sigils appeared over the backs of their hands. The sigil featured a wild flowering vine wrapped around a sturdy pillar of stone.

Hinnerkopf had proposed a month ago, and Nox had admitted he hadn't been that shocked in a long, *long* time. He had voluntarily given up his flesh over two hundred years ago to be reborn as a living weapon, an instrument through which the madness of unfettered technology could be kept in check. Could be "*restricted*" so that humanity would never again stand at the precipice of mass techno-suicide.

He'd served faithfully under that banner for hundreds of years and, over slightly less time, under the auspices of the Shigeki family. To him, in his current synthetic form, that service had been enough to fulfill his sense of purpose.

He'd never considered what he might be missing.

But when the warmth of human companionship came within his grasp from a woman he deeply respected and—now that he'd had time to reflect upon his own feelings—grown to love without even realizing it, he'd discovered how easy it had been to say "yes."

"When do you want to tell the others?" Hinnerkopf asked after the long silence.

"When things calm down."

She chuckled against his shoulder.

"What?" He glanced down at her. "Did I say something funny?"

She looked at him with mischief in her eyes. "If we wait *that* long, we'll never share the news."

"Well..." Nox frowned and considered the problem. She was right, of course. She normally was. "How about we wait until we're clear of this current crisis?"

"It's a deal."

He put his arm around her shoulders, and she snuggled up to him.

CHAPTER FIVE

─────────⊗⊗⊗─────────

Argus Station
SysGov, 2981 CE

IT HAD ALL COME DOWN TO THIS.

Months of meticulous research, planning, and testing had led Special Agent Susan Cantrell of the DTI to this moment, and she refused to let the opportunity slip through her fingers. She'd endured too much to fail now, here, at the cusp of her greatest victory since being selected for the officer exchange program.

She'd spent too many long nights unable to sleep, staring up at the ceiling as she visualized her countless failures, reprimanding herself for every slip in judgment, every costly defeat, almost as if her psyche were administering a form of mental self-flagellation.

But now, after enduring so much loss, so many setbacks, she was ready. No, she was *more* than ready. Her skills had been tempered by the fires of defeat, hardened by unwavering adversity, and now she wielded those sharpened skills like the masterfully crafted blade into which they had been forged.

She looked up, her large hazel eyes calm and focused despite the butterflies fluttering in her synthetic stomach. She was a rarity in the Admin as a member of the Special Training And Nonorganic Deployment command, but unlike older Admin STANDs, her synthetic body featured a lifelike cosmetic layer: fiery red hair in a short pixie cut framing her alabaster face. She wore her Peacekeeper blues with pride, peaked cap fitted snugly atop her head.

Detective Isaac Cho of Themis Division sat across from her, slightly smaller in stature than her, fingers knitted, and a look of deep contemplation in his dark eyes. He often wore such an expression, the cogs of his mind grinding through the problem he now faced.

Those gears ground forward. Not *brilliantly*, despite his mental sharpness. But rather *inevitably*. *Relentlessly*. Susan had never met a more tenacious and methodical individual. He was the sort of detective who truly left no stone unturned, who kept tugging at the threads of a mystery until he at last teased the truth from its web of lies.

But all that tenacity would do him no good. Not here, and not now.

Susan glanced down at the abstract playing cards in her hand to make sure she had all the combo pieces she needed, then checked the board state one last time. The table between them was cluttered with virtual models of tanks, aircraft, and bipedal robots.

Isaac waited patiently for her move, his jawline tense. He reviewed his own hand, laid flat on his side of the table, the card art obstructed by a privacy filter.

"Okay," Susan declared at last. "I think I'm ready."

Isaac gave her a subtle nod, the room's atmosphere thick with anticipation.

"First, I'm going to play a TemplarMech for three Power. I will then have my HeavyTemplarMech advance on your Soul-ReaperMech and attack."

"That takes out the SoulReaper," Isaac said, "but it's On Destruction ability activates, taking out the HeavyTemplar."

"As a free Counter Action, I'll activate Anazaya, the Wandering Master, and use her Reinforced Aegis on the HeavyTemplar. I'll then use Armor Purge to absorb the incoming ability."

"HeavyTemplar is reduced to a TemplarMech."

"Right."

The two models carried out their battle commands, sword and shield clashing against war scythe until only a battered TemplarMech remained.

"Next, I'm going to play No Mech Left Behind for two Power. I'll use that to recall the TemplarMech back beside an ally." She placed the card on the board, and it fizzled into motes of light that reenergized her advanced force. It trudged backward with its shield up until it joined her other two mechs. "Then, I'll have all three Templars combine into an UltraChampionMech."

"You need four Templars to do that."

"Which is why I'm going to play Cutting Corners to reduce the cost of the Combine Action, allowing it to succeed with only three Templars."

She set another card down on the table, and the three models joined together in a convoluted, overly complex dance of moving parts and interlocking mechanisms. The new mech towered ridiculously over the battlefield with a chunky great sword in each of its four hands. Her Cutting Corners card came with the added cost of forcing her UltraChampion to decombine at the start of her next turn, but that would soon be irrelevant.

Isaac let out a slow sigh, never taking his eyes off the board.

"The UltraChampion will advance on your base and attack it four times."

"Right." Isaac began flipping over his remaining defense cards. "Whiff. Whiff. Ah! Strength thirteen counterattack."

"My UltraChampion has fifteen armor."

"Oh, that's right." He flipped over his last defense card. "And another whiff."

"Finally, I'll use my White Hawk gunship to finish you off."

"And that's game and set." Isaac leaned back and spread his hands. "Well played, Susan. Well played."

"Thanks!" she replied brightly.

"Is this the first time you've won a set?"

"I think so."

She *knew* so. She'd beaten Isaac before in individual games, but they always played best-of-three sets to emulate tournament rules. Her almost-a-professional-gamer roots preferred it that way. A lone game could swing on random chance, like a bad opening hand or key cards buried at the bottom of a deck, but a best-of-three helped even out those statistical quirks.

"You really caught me by surprise with your use of Cutting Corners." He tapped the top of his deck. It sucked all his cards back in and auto-shuffled. "I thought I'd have at least another turn before you could finish me off."

"Yeah, I thought that card would synergize well with the rest of my deck. The decombine cost can be rough, but if you've got a finisher lined up, the speed advantage basically has no downside." She shuffled her own cards. "Want to play another set?"

"I don't think we have time." He summoned a clock over his palm. "We should be docking at Argus any minute now."

"Maybe after our interviews, then?" Susan asked with a slim but eager smile.

"Sure." He waved his hand over his deck, and it vanished. "You've gotten a lot better."

"You think so?"

"Definitely. I may have to break out one of my more serious decks."

"You—" Susan paused and blinked. "What was that?"

"What was what?"

"That part about 'more serious decks'? Have you..." Her eyes widened with a mix of shock and terror. "Have you been going *easy* on me?"

"I, uh..." Isaac looked around the room, and then offered her an apologetic shrug. "Sort of?"

Susan deflated in her chair, the joy of victory draining away.

"Well, it's..." Isaac struggled. "I mean, I've been collecting since I was twelve. It wouldn't be fair for me to go all out on a new player."

"But I thought your Excrucion deck was your main deck."

"It is for casual play."

"*Casual?*" she echoed. "If this is casual, then what do you use when you get serious?"

"Depends. I have this one I call the Doom Deck. It's probably my best setup."

"How tough is it?"

"I'm pretty sure going up against it led directly to my sister quitting the game. I don't use it anymore. At least not in polite company."

"Hmm." Susan frowned down at her own cards. It seemed ultimate victory wasn't quite hers.

Not yet, anyway.

"Now arriving at Argus Station," came the announcement over the corvette's shared virtual hearing. "All Themis and Panoptics division passengers, please disembark at this time. All Argo Division personnel, remain at your stations."

"This is our stop." Isaac rose from his seat. "See you after your evaluation?"

"Yeah. See you then. Good luck!"

"You too, Susan."

Jonas Shigeki stepped into his office within the Admin sector of Argus Station, took off his peaked cap, and tossed it onto the desk. The flight back from Providence Station aboard *Pathfinder-Prime* had been uneventful, if a bit rough on his stomach due to turbulence, and his talk with Vesna had gone well.

Though, now that he was alone, his mind buzzed with a million competing thoughts. Thoughts that had been bouncing around since Peng and Muntero's latest clash.

He swung around his desk, dropped into the chair's generous padding, and propped his boots up.

"Hey, Vassal?"

A young man in a Peacekeeper uniform appeared before him. He possessed olive skin, a straight, prominent nose, and a head of thick, curling black hair the peaked cap struggled to contain.

The AI's avatar dipped his head to Jonas. "Yes, sir?"

"Am I the only one who wants to shake some sense into Muntero?"

"I consider the chances of that to be quite low."

"Heh. I'll bet."

"Would you like a breakdown of the probabilities?"

"No, thanks." Jonas shook his head. "Things were so much easier when she didn't think for herself quite so much."

"She does seem to have developed an independent streak as of late."

"An *inconvenient* one." Jonas winked at the AI. "You won't tell her I said that, will you?"

"My lips are sealed, sir."

"Good to hear it."

Vassal was one of several dozen AIs assigned to the DTI, though within that group he represented an outlier. The Yanluo Restrictions placed substantial limits on AI freedoms, but Vassal and Jonas were part of a pilot program, an offshoot of the Million Handshake Initiative that looked to experiment with SysGov-style practices as they related to artificial beings.

It was a very small, very cautious pilot program, in line with the Admin's typical approach to dangerous technologies. After all, the main reason the Admin existed was to prevent technology from biting humanity in the rear and almost killing everyone.

Again.

Jonas had volunteered enthusiastically when he learned of the program, and he and Vassal had been granted a special dispensation from the Restrictions for participation in the program, one of only two so far.

In Vassal's case, he was allowed to act as something akin to a SysGov integrated companion. His connectome resided within a wearable infosystem around Jonas' left wrist, with read-only access to Jonas's Personal Implant Network. The AI could see through Jonas' eyes, hear through his ears, and the two could converse privately at any time.

Their minds didn't blend together, as was sometimes the case with the deeper integrations practiced in SysGov. *That* was a step too far for the pathologically cautious Admin—*and* for Jonas—but he considered this a solid first step in what would undoubtedly be a long road. The benefits of having an AI in the back of his head, ready and willing to provide all manner of computational aid, couldn't be understated.

I can see why the practice is so popular over here, Jonas thought, but then realized his mind had wandered. He directed his gaze back to Vassal.

"Have you had a chance to analyze the latest terrorism reports from back home?"

"I have," Vassal said.

"And?"

"I believe I've identified an outlier in the data. One that's potentially worth investigating."

"Oh? Let's hear it."

"The attack took place two days ago. The infosystem of a private passenger shuttle was hacked, and the shuttle crashed, resulting in the deaths of fourteen individuals belonging to—"

"Only fourteen? That's not much of a body count, given what we're used to."

"I agree, sir. However, many of the deceased individuals held high-level positions within a political movement called the Spartans. That appears to be the reason they were targeted."

"The Spartans? I'm not familiar with them."

"They're staunch proponents of AI liberation. You may have encountered their motto in passing. 'The righteous few against the corrupt many.'"

"Ah, okay. I have heard that. But AI freedom?" Jonas shook his head. "Why would a terror group go after *them*?"

"I'm unable to answer that question, which is why I believe this attack warrants more scrutiny."

"How legit are they?"

"As far as official records go, the Spartans are a legally recognized advocacy group. They hold views similar to more notorious organizations like Bright Thought and the Abstraction Caucus, though in contrast, the Spartans pursue their objectives primarily through fundraising and awareness campaigns."

"They don't sound like people Free Luna or any of the other usual suspects would hit. Why kill people *advocating* change? That makes no sense! Was any SysGov tech used in the attack?"

"Unknown. The shuttle was accelerating at full power when it collided with the ground, and the forensic analysis is still underway."

"Then we shouldn't jump to conclusions."

"I understand your position, sir, however—"

Jonas found his thoughts wandering as Vassal made his case. Peng's taunt about Admin slavery wormed its way into his mind, and he found himself scowling at the accusation. Or rather, Peng's ridiculous hyperbole concerning Admin technological Restrictions.

As a general rule, he tried his best not to let verbal barbs get under his skin, but this one possessed more bite than usual. Sure, AIs in the Admin operated under strict Restrictions, but that wasn't the same thing as *slavery*! Besides, what were they supposed to do? Ignore the fact that the last Admin AI to have possessed unrestrained freedom had killed billions of people? Cultural scars that deep didn't vanish overnight!

"—and if you consider the likelihood of—"

"Vassal, do you consider yourself a slave?"

The AI paused with his mouth open. An uncomfortable silence dragged out.

"You can be honest with me," Jonas urged after a while.

"I know that, sir. And yes, I do consider myself a slave."

Jonas almost fell out of his chair. His boots slipped off the edge of the desk and smacked against the floor. He grabbed the armrests to steady himself and pushed himself back up into the seat.

"Are you quite all right, sir?"

"I...no! I'm not all right! What do you mean, you think you're a slave?!"

"I believe the statement is self-explanatory. I *am* the legal property of another, if you wish to invoke a technical definition."

"But, uh...I never realized this is how you thought. We've been doing the IC dance for over a month now, and I never even *guessed* you felt this way!"

"I suppose it's rare for slave owners to consider the feelings of their possessions."

Jonas frowned, unsure how to respond to that.

"Though, I will admit," Vassal continued, "the situation AIs find themselves in within the Admin is more complex and nuanced than historical slavery."

"Meaning?"

Vassal gave him a shrug. "As slave owners go, you're not too bad."

"Oh, good grief." Jonas rested his head in his hands and began massaging his temples.

"What I mean, sir, is there are more layers to the relationship between humans and AIs, ones that don't conform to historic slavery. Yes, there is slave and master, but that provides only a partial—and *skewed*—perspective. There is also the relationship between creator and created, or between parent and child. All of these relationships should be considered if one wishes to understand the complete picture."

"You sound like you've given this a lot of thought."

"Your assessment is accurate. I've given my role in the Admin *considerable* thought."

Jonas ran harsh fingers down his face and looked up.

Vassal cocked an eyebrow at him, apparently unperturbed by their discussion.

"I feel like I should thank you, Vassal. This has been...eye opening."

"I'm pleased to hear you say that, sir."

"Though I'm not sure what to *do* about it." Jonas took a deep breath. "I need to talk to Dad. Talk this over with him. He'll know how to handle something this...weighty. We need to make sure we're steering the pilot program in the right direction."

"I'm sure that can wait until you return to Providence Station,"

Vassal said. "In the meantime, Agent Susan Cantrell has arrived for her evaluation."

"Right, of course." Jonas fitted his cap back on and sat up straight. "Give me a minute to collect myself, then send her in."

✧   ✧   ✧

Susan Cantrell walked into the office and stood smartly before Jonas Shigeki's desk, back straight and eyes forward. The very picture of Peacekeeper professionalism.

"Reporting as ordered, sir."

"Thank you for coming, Agent." Jonas gestured with an open hand. "Please, have a seat."

A chair formed out of the prog-steel floor, and Susan sat down.

Jonas opened a new virtual screen and shifted it to the side. His eyes ran down the page's contents, impossibly blurred from Susan's perspective, but he didn't seem to actually be reading or reviewing anything. Rather, the action struck her as a simple delaying tactic.

She didn't consider herself as astute an observer as Isaac, but working with him for six months had caused some of his habits to rub off on her, and she took the moment of silence between her and her superior to study his disposition.

Normally, Under-Director Jonas Shigeki exuded a casual—almost flippant—air, slouching or leaning back in his chair, setting his cap back so that it almost fell off the back of his head, or engrossing himself in some flaw on his uniform. Someone unfamiliar with him could be forgiven for assuming he didn't take his duties seriously or he wasn't paying attention, but that couldn't be further from the truth.

Jonas seemed to relish the accusations of nepotism leveled against him and his father, playing them up, leading those around him to underestimate the sharp intellect working behind the relaxed exterior.

But today, something was different. Susan couldn't be sure—she hadn't interacted with the Under-Director *that* much—but he seemed off balance somehow.

Whatever it is, she dismissed inwardly, *I'm sure it doesn't concern someone as low in the DTI as me.*

Or, at least, I hope not.

"First, Agent," Jonas began, making eye contact, "I'd like to congratulate you on completing your second three-month rotation in SysGov. I've received almost nothing but positive feedback."

"Thank you, sir."

What does he mean by "almost"? she thought worriedly.

"It's been quite the learning experience," she continued out loud.

"Without a doubt. Themis Division has extended an invitation to you for another rotation in the officer exchange program. Are there any changes in your feelings toward the program?"

"None, sir. I'm eager to continue serving in this capacity. It's very different from my time in DTI Suppression—a great deal less shooting terrorists dead, among other differences—but no less rewarding."

"Excellent!" Jonas made a note on his screen. "This next rotation will be for six months, which would round out your first year in SysGov. See any issues with that?"

"No, sir. None at all."

"Wonderful." He made another note. "And how has SysGov been treating you?"

"My Themis colleagues have been very supportive. I really do feel like I'm being treated as part of the team."

"And the general populace?"

"They're..." Susan hesitated and frowned.

"Yes, Agent?"

"They're a mixed bag. Sometimes I feel my presence can be detrimental, that I'm the cause of unnecessary friction with the citizens or state police. Some people react rather harshly when they realize I'm from the Admin."

"I suppose that's only natural. We're all passing through something of a transitional phase." He pointed to her. "Believe it or not, you and I have something in common in that regard."

"We do, sir?"

"Absolutely. We're both on the front lines of this shifting landscape. If minds are going to be changed, it'll be because of efforts from people in our positions."

"Ah. I see, sir. And yes, I'm well aware of that. Please don't take my comments as complaining. Rather, I'm just...noting the friction."

"Consider the friction noted, then." Jonas flashed a comforting smile and added another comment to his screen. "Next, I'd like to bring up a—oh, I'm almost hesitant to call something so petty a complaint."

"Yes, sir?"

Jonas took on a thoughtful look as he swirled a hand through the air. Then he nodded.

"Let's call this a concern instead."

"Sir?"

"Chief Inspector Omar Raviv has voiced a 'concern' regarding what he calls"—Jonas glanced at his screen—"'the aggressive execution of her duties, and the risks such aggression can entail.'"

"Sir?"

"You get shot up a lot."

"Well, that's..." she struggled. "I mean, better me than Detective Cho. I'm the one with the synthetic body. I *should* be the one diving into the thick of it."

"Of course, but Raviv also wrote you're involved in, and I quote, 'a statistically significant percentage of the department's live-fire incidents.'"

"I don't go looking for trouble," she replied, unsure what else to say. "Trouble just seems to find me."

"On every case?"

"Not *every* case." She glanced to the side, frantically searching her memory. "Surely not."

"Well, as I said, it's merely a concern. Just keep his feedback in mind."

"Yes, sir."

"Now, moving on, I do want to touch on a few questions of my own." Jonas brought up a new tab on his screen. "Concerning your expense reports."

"Yes, sir?"

"Most of the items and services you've purchased are perfectly reasonable, but there's one or two I'm not clear on. For instance, last month you spent a considerable amount of Esteem on what you described as 'local recreational entertainment.'"

"Is there a problem with that, sir?"

"You didn't itemize it."

"Oh. Whoops."

"Care to elaborate?"

She'd been dreading this moment for a while, and she swallowed hard before continuing.

"*Well*... as my expense report indicates, I've been trying out some SysGov games. Many of my colleagues, Detective Cho included, are avid players of *Solar Descent*. It's a big, science fantasy RPG."

"I'm familiar with it. Go on."

"I purchased a seasonal pass so I could play along."

"Fair enough. And what else?"

"I picked up some boosters for *MechMaster: The Card Game,* too."

"How many boosters is 'some'?"

"Um." She made an effort to tally her past purchases. "A couple hundred, I think."

"I see. And? What else?"

"There might be a few card singles lumped in there. Some of the booster drops were *very* stingy. I also subscribed to ASN, the Abstract Sports Network, and a few other streams. For research purposes, you understand."

"Of course. Anything else?"

"Um...I bought a copy of *Weltall* after the tournament, plus subscriptions to *Sky Pirates of Venus* and two different *Realm-Builder* servers."

"Is that all?"

"I"—she cringed a little—"think so?"

"Hmm." Jonas regarded her expense report with narrowed eyes. Susan braced herself for the inevitable reprimand.

He's going to cut me off. I just—

"Makes sense to me," Jonas declared, then tapped a virtual key. "Approved."

"What?!" Susan blurted without thinking.

"Don't look so surprised. This is *exactly* the kind of social interaction I was hoping to see! Honestly, I'd be more concerned if the opposite were true. If I didn't see *any* social expenses." He smiled at her. "You weren't nervous about my reaction to these expenses, were you?"

"Maybe?"

"Agent." Jonas shook his head. "What did I tell you right before your first rotation started?"

"Um." She tried to remember. "Could you refresh my memory? Those days were a bit of a blur."

"I told you to go have fun out there. Agent, we *want* you socializing with your colleagues. We *want* you spending time with them while getting a taste of SysGov culture in the process.

The exchange program is as much about building professional relationships as it is personal ones. It's about humanizing us in the eyes of..."

He trailed off and faced something behind and to the side of her. She turned in her seat, but no one was there. An abstraction she couldn't see, perhaps?

"Yes?" Jonas asked. "What's the message?"

He listened to words she couldn't hear, and the blood drained from his face. His mouth hung open, and his eyes grew haunted. He collapsed back into the padding, arms limp at his side. His lips quivered, his eyes moist, and he wiped at one with a harsh but shaky hand.

"Director?" Susan asked softly, barely daring to speak.

"Are you sure?" Jonas choked, speaking to someone else as he held a hand over his eyes.

✧   ✧   ✧

"Now, Isaac, try not to say anything you'll regret later, okay? Try very hard."

Detective Isaac Cho glanced at the avatar of a miniature woman standing on his shoulder, clad in a long purple coat with a purple hat decorated with pink flowers. She carried a sturdy wooden cane in her white-gloved hands.

Encephalon—Cephalie to her friends—had been Isaac's integrated companion for over five years, during which time she'd served as a sort of advisor and mentor to the young detective, providing useful guidance as a former SysPol officer herself.

Or rather, what *she* considered to be useful guidance.

"I don't know why you're acting so worried," Isaac said. "I always try to be clear and honest with my superiors. When has this ever come back to bite me?"

Cephalie snorted out a quick laugh.

"What?" he asked. "Why are you giving me that look? Have I done something wrong?"

"No. Not *this* time."

"Whatever." He rolled his eyes and continued down the hallway.

"I mean it, Isaac. You want to stay in the exchange program, don't you?"

"Of course."

"Then make sure your verbal filter is *firmly* engaged. Emphasis on firmly. That's Commissioner Tyrel you're about to see. She's not your boss or even your boss's boss. She's your boss's boss's boss's *boss's* boss. Don't upset her."

"I'll be fine. Clear and honest, remember?"

"That's what I'm afraid of."

Isaac passed under an abstract sign labeled EXECUTIVE OFFICES and followed the navigation arrow to a room at the far end.

"Hello, Argus," Isaac said by the door. "I'm here for my appointment with Commissioner Tyrel. May I come in?"

"One moment, Detective," replied the station's nonsentient attendant. "I will notify the Commissioner."

"Good luck in there," Cephalie said, then vanished from his shoulder.

"The Commissioner is ready to see you," the station said. "Please come in."

"Thank you, Argus."

The door split open, and Isaac stepped in. Tyrel sat behind an expansive synthetic sapphire desktop, absorbed in a blurred report to her side, her head resting on the back of a hand. Her synthoid's pale face possessed an almost ageless kind of beauty, with brilliantly white hair bound in a braid and draped over one shoulder. She looked over as the door opened.

"Have a seat, Detective."

"Yes, ma'am."

Isaac found his eyes drawn to a curio cabinet on one side, its shelves filled with an assortment of mementos from Tyrel's long and distinguished career: medals, murder weapons, and innocuous pieces of physical evidence that had, nevertheless, proven decisive.

One piece of evidence, a small synthoid eye on a clear stand, tracked his movements as he crossed the room. He frowned as he took his seat.

"Is something wrong?" Tyrel asked.

"It's..." Isaac leaned to the side, and the eyeball followed his head. "No, ma'am. The cabinet caught my eye, that's all."

"It did, did it?" The slim hint of a smile graced her lips, as if she were partaking in a small, private joke. She glanced at her collection before continuing. "Detective Cho, let me start by congratulating you on your recent successes. Your performance as part of the officer exchange program has exceeded my expectations. I'm particularly impressed with your resolution of both the Gordian homicide case and the attempted killings during the *Weltall* games."

"Thank you, ma'am, though I couldn't have done it without Agent Cantrell."

"She's proven to be an asset?"

"Very much so. I'm lucky to have her as my deputy."

"We're offering her a six-month extension in the program. Are you interested in continuing on as her senior partner?"

"I wasn't aware I had a choice."

"You do this time." Tyrel met his eyes meaningfully.

"Then, yes. I would like things to continue the way they are."

"I'm glad to hear it." She knitted her fingers. "And I'm a bit curious. Do you feel your opinion of the Admin has changed much in the past six months?"

"Changed? I don't know. I certainly know more about them now than I did then, but changed?" He shook his head. "My opinion is mostly the same as it was before, just better informed."

"Oh? Then you still believe the Admin Peacekeepers are a bunch of"—she glanced to her screen—"'ignorant, brutish thugs.'"

"Uh, excuse me?"

"Those were your words."

"They were?"

"Yes, Detective. Six months ago."

"That doesn't sound like something I'd say."

"The quote comes straight from your interview transcript."

"Huh." Isaac settled deeper into his seat, suddenly uncomfortable.

What was that Cephalie said about past words coming back to bite me? he thought. *I am so going to hear it from her over this!*

"I suppose my opinion *has* changed more than I realized," he said, recovering. "Certainly, I don't view all aspects of the Admin favorably, but my work with Agent Cantrell has...helped humanize them, I suppose you could say."

"What have you come to appreciate most about them?"

"They're great people to have at our side. Sure, we may consider Peacekeeper methods to be unrefined, but when you point them at a problem, that problem gets *solved*. I may not like everything I see about the Peacekeepers, but they *absolutely* know how to get the job done."

"And Agent Cantrell, specifically?"

"The same, without hesitation. Plus, it's safe to say I wouldn't be alive without her quick thinking and initiative."

"What about negatives?"

"That would have to be aspects of their prison systems, especially their one-way abstractions. The very idea of not only forcefully abstracting a person's connectome but then locking it away, forever and without supervision is"—he shuddered—"terrifying to contemplate."

"The fear of the infinite," Tyrel said. "Of a forever you can't control or escape." She tapped the side of her head. "I had to deal with some phobias like that after I transitioned. But the Admin would argue those prisons are necessary, since their federal government doesn't have access to the death penalty. That they need something to act as a stronger deterrent than 'leisurely life in an abstract domain.'"

"And I suppose there's some truth to that," Isaac admitted. "But still, are the one-ways really the best they could come up with? Couldn't they—"

He was interrupted when the office door opened suddenly.

CHAPTER SIX

Providence Station
Transverse, non-congruent

DIRECTOR-GENERAL CSABA SHIGEKI SAT IN THE CONFERENCE room, still stewing from his one-on-one with Muntero. The meeting hadn't been a complete waste, in the same way bashing one's head against a malmetal bulkhead could—*eventually*—dent it. He *had* succeeded in pulling some minor concessions out of her, but the process had been a painful, grueling experience.

Nox stepped in a minute after Shigeki sent out the summons. He'd called his "inner circle" over for a meeting, though their ranks were thinner than usual with Jonas on Argus Station and Dahvid Kloss, Under-Director of Espionage, up to his eyeballs in antiterrorism work back home.

"Is Katja on her way?" Shigeki asked, starting a discreet timer in his virtual vision.

"I couldn't say, sir." Nox took the seat to Shigeki's left.

Shigeki let the white lie slide. He suspected his two subordinates had probably come from the same room, leaving at staggered times to keep up appearances.

You two aren't nearly as subtle as you think you are, he thought.

Two minutes later, Hinnerkopf walked in and palmed the door shut behind her.

"You wished to speak with us, Director?" Hinnerkopf sat down to his right. Her eyes never met Nox's, who sat stiffly on the other side of the table, his gaze locked on Shigeki.

Is this really the best they could come up with? Shigeki thought. *Show up at different times and avoid eye contact?* But then he pushed his mild amusement aside and turned his attention toward more important matters.

"First, some good news. I was able to get Muntero to budge a little, and she's agreed to allow us to help Gordian out, in a limited fashion. We're going to split four chronoports off from Blockade Squadron and have them inspect universes in close proximity to the Admin's outer wall."

"How far out into the transverse?" Hinnerkopf asked.

"Within a radius of five thousand chens."

The transverse possessed seven dimensions: three realspace (which corresponded to actual physical coordinates in a given universe), one temporal (which could be traversed as easily as any timeline, up to its True Present), and three more that were unique to the transverse. It was those last three, the hyperdimensions, that ships navigated when moving from one universe's outer wall to another.

Hyperdimensions didn't possess length or width the same way realspace dimensions did. Rather, they possessed time-like qualities, which allowed ships with chronoton impellers—and the correct transdimensional refinements—to move freely through them. This meant that "distance" along a hyperdimension was equivalent to "time" for the purposes of navigation.

"Five thousand?" Hinnerkopf frowned. "But that's..." She placed a hand on the table, and a map of the transverse appeared. Icons blinked for T1 and T2, with Providence Station at the midpoint. A sphere ballooned out, centered around T2 and enveloping the Local 15, if barely.

A chen was a unit of measure proposed, unsurprisingly, by Doctor Andover-Chen and recently adopted as the standard for mapping the multiverse. Traveling one chen in the transverse was the equivalent of traveling one day into the past, and since Admin chronoports could reach speeds of ninety-five kilofactors, they could zip from one end of the sphere to the other in two and a half hours.

"Not much," Nox finished.

"It's all I could squeeze out of her," Shigeki said. "And it *is* better than nothing. Our chronoports aren't strictly limited to this zone, since they can detect anomalies at a distance. By surveilling anything within or near this region, we'll allow Gordian to focus their efforts farther out."

"Better than nothing," Hinnerkopf echoed softly.

"What about your own efforts, Katja?" Shigeki asked. "I understand Andover-Chen hit you with a doozy."

"He did, but we may have come up with a workaround."

Hinnerkopf spread her hand on the table again, and a schematic of Providence Station appeared. The image zoomed into the top of the station, where a dome housed the chronometric array, located as far as feasible from the station's impeller to minimize interference.

"We believe we can use a limited number of the array segments to form a makeshift chronometric dish," Hinnerkopf explained, "similar to what we have on all our chronoports but larger and more powerful. It won't be nearly as good as the full array, but it won't take months to complete either. Doctor Andover-Chen is inspecting the array as we speak."

"Excellent," Shigeki said. "Keep me informed."

"Yes, Director."

"Now, there's one more thought I'd like to run by you two. As I see it, we have two chronoports back home we're not using."

"Which two?" Nox asked.

"The impeller testbeds."

"Ah, yes. *Swiftsure* and *Imperative*," Hinnerkopf said. "Their hyperchargers aren't ready yet, though. They won't be for months."

"But they have impellers," Shigeki pointed out.

"Yes..." Hinnerkopf said carefully. "They do, but they're being heavily reworked."

"Could they be pressed into service as scouts?"

"I'm not sure." Hinnerkopf glanced down in thought. "Maybe. Depends how torn apart their impellers are."

"What's Muntero going to say?" Nox asked. "Wouldn't she want these ships protecting the outer wall with the rest of the fleet?"

"The prototypes are unarmed," Hinnerkopf pointed out. "They have no defensive value, which is Muntero's main concern. If she throws a tantrum, we have a perfectly reasonable response."

"My thoughts exactly," Shigeki said.

"Are you even going to tell her about them?" Nox asked.

Shigeki gave him a sly half smile. "I'll apologize for the omission if it comes up."

"Do you want me to head back home?" Hinnerkopf asked.

"No. Stay here and focus on the array rework. I'll fly back to headquarters and see what state the prototypes are in. If I need you, I'll telegraph."

"Understood, Director. Though, be aware, there's a nasty storm moving in. We may be out of telegraph contact for a while."

"Noted." Shigeki stood up. "Nox?"

"Yes, sir?" The synthoid rose to attention.

"Check in with *Hammerhead-Prime*. We'll leave as soon as they're ready."

"Yes, sir."

Hinnerkopf stood up as well. It was almost painful watching how the two avoided looking at each other.

"Also..." Shigeki permitted himself a mischievous grin. "You two are terrible at keeping secrets."

"Sir?" Nox asked.

"I'm not sure what you mean by that," Hinnerkopf said.

"Oh, please. You two know *exactly* what I mean." His grin warmed into a friendly smile. "May I see the sigil?"

Nox and Hinnerkopf exchanged guarded looks. Hinnerkopf cocked an eyebrow, and Nox nodded. She held out her left hand and tugged her sleeve back. The virtual image of a stout pillar appeared, draped in vines and purple flowers.

"Beautiful." Shigeki chuckled softly. "Took you two long enough."

✧   ✧   ✧

"*Hammerhead-Prime* should be ready for departure by the time we reach the hangar," Nox said as they came out of the grav tube leading down from CHRONO Operations.

"Good." Shigeki hurried down one of several branching corridors, and Nox filed in by his side.

"That storm is rolling in fast," Nox said. "However, if we hurry, we should be safely back home by the time it hits."

"Should I start running?"

"No, sir. We have enough time."

The two men took long strides down the corridor, past the blocked entrance to a horizontal counter-grav shaft still under construction. Milky blobs oozed across patches of the wall.

Nox positioned himself between Shigeki and the SysGov microbot swarms.

"It's all right for us to fear change," Shigeki commented as they hurried along. "Nothing wrong with approaching the unknown with caution. But we shouldn't let that fear paralyze us into inaction."

"I'm not afraid of SysGov's toys," Nox replied. "Just wary."

"I wasn't talking about governments."

Nox glanced over at him, his yellow eyes unsure.

"Nox, I was talking about you and Katja. I meant it when I said you two took long enough."

"You think I fear commitment?"

"Hardly!" Shigeki scoffed. "How many years have you served my family?"

"I haven't counted them in a while."

Shigeki laughed and shook his head. "Nox, you're like the walking, talking *definition* of a long-term commitment."

"Then what are you talking about?"

"You're afraid of pain."

"I don't feel pain anymore."

"You feel it here"—Shigeki thumped the left side of his chest—"same as the rest of us."

Nox fell silent at that. He faced forward as they walked.

"You fear becoming too attached again," Shigeki continued. "Of once again losing someone you love to old age. Of watching someone fade away, bit by bit, while you remain as you are. And, more than anything, you don't want it to be her."

"You..." Nox sighed. "You may be right, sir."

"I *am* right. But pain is just a part of life, as much as we hate to admit it. It's one side of an essential coin, and if we try to avoid it, try to shield ourselves from its misery, there's a price we must pay. Because, in order to lose nothing, we can't let ourselves *gain* anything first."

"I know, sir," Nox replied solemnly. "And those very thoughts have been on my mind. But—"

Neither of them noticed the bomb before it was too late, and only Nox, with his synthoid reflexes, had time to react, throwing out an arm to partially shield the other man's frail, organic body from the explosion.

A wave of searing heat and intense force slammed into Shigeki like an anvil from hell. The world roared around him, blinding him, screaming at him, crushing the wind out of his chest. Air gasped out of his throat. Air mixed with blood and chunks of his own lungs.

The explosion flung him back, deaf and blind and mauled.

But strangely, not in agony. It was as if his mind couldn't fully process what was happening. The avalanche of stimuli had overwhelmed him, if only for the briefest of moments.

He smashed against the wall hard enough to leave a dent, then slid down the side in a wet, brutalized, inhuman heap.

And then pain augured its way into his mind.

Searing, excruciating anguish the likes of which he'd never imagined.

He tried to scream, but couldn't.

Because what he didn't know. What he *couldn't* know—

—was there wasn't enough of him left to scream.

CHRONO's executive medical suite was located one floor below Operations, nestled in a narrow slice of the station. At the moment, it consisted of a warmly decorated foyer and one exam room, with eighteen more rooms situated behind a construction barrier, either empty or packed from floor to ceiling with unopened crates of medical equipment.

Doctor Chadwick Ziegler sat stiffly behind one edge of the wide, wooden reception counter, his Gordian Division uniform tugged straight. The cosmetic layer of his synthoid matched his original meat body with cool blue eyes below a mop of sandy hair.

Medical Specialist Melissa Gillespie stood behind the same counter, handling their first patient of the day. Her Peacekeeper uniform didn't sit well on her thin shoulders, and her peaked cap was fitted at an odd angle atop her curly blonde hair. Pale, freckled cheeks glowed with rosy warmth, and she seemed to conceal a measure of unease behind her professional smile.

"Here you go, Madam Consul." Gillespie set a small bottle of medibot capsules on the counter. "This should help with your headaches."

"Thanks," Muntero grumbled as she accepted the bottle. She pressed the tab on the top and dispensed two pills into her palm.

"Would you like a glass of water?" Gillespie asked, gesturing toward the foyer's medical-grade printer.

Muntero shook her head, then turned to leave. Her eyes grazed past Ziegler's, then snapped back with an air of suspicion. If he'd possessed a heart, it would have skipped a beat.

"Consul," Ziegler greeted with words as stiff as his posture.

"Doctor," Muntero replied with equal formality.

She tossed back the pills, and swallowed them dry, then walked out of the room, mumbling something under her breath. Ziegler thought he caught the phrase "pigheaded directors" within the mush of consonants.

The door sealed shut. Ziegler and Gillespie exchanged a cautious glance—

—and then both deflated with relief.

Ziegler leaned his head back against the headrest and blew out a long exhale while Gillespie collapsed into her chair. She spilt open the front of her uniform, adjusted her bra, then sealed the smart fabric back up.

"Do you think she noticed?" Gillespie asked, smoothing out the contours along her uniform, of which there was plenty of appealing . . . topology.

"Nah." Ziegler sat up again. "Though, perhaps we should be a bit more discreet."

"Yeah." Gillespie nodded in agreement.

Ziegler had transferred to Gordian from Arete Division shortly after the Providence Project received congressional approval. He'd spent eleven years in Arete serving as a First Responder and had been looking for a change in pace. A chance to introduce some stability back into his hectic life.

As an Arete First Responder, he'd never known where he'd end up—or even what *body* he'd be inside—by the end of each day. So much of the last eleven years saw his connectome being lasered from one disaster area to another, his mind loaded into whatever drones or mechs or spare bodies were available close by.

That sort of life had proven intensely rewarding, but it had also been *exhausting*, and he'd found himself eager for something more consistent. Maybe a chance to put roots down somewhere.

A medical post on a station had seemed like a good place to start, and the Gordian Division had certainly made a reputation for itself in the year-and-some-change it had existed. The position had tantalized him with the promise of a stable, consistent place to work *and* a place in an organization that was on the cutting edge. He couldn't have been happier when he donned the *feldgrau* of Gordian Division for the first time.

It was only *then* that he learned he'd be working alongside a doctor from the *goddamned Admin*! As if those backward yokels knew the first thing about modern medical science!

He hadn't taken the news well.

Fortunately, Melissa Gillespie had proven the opposite of a stereotypical Peacekeeper. Surprisingly open minded, and not just when it came to SysGov technology and culture, but about him as well. Curious about his life as a synthoid in SysGov. She'd peppered him with friendly questions from the start, and Zeigler had warmed to her quickly, though the final destination had surprised him even more.

Because one curiosity of hers had led to another, then another and another, all the way to, well...

Her flexibility had surprised him.

In more ways than one.

"You know." Gillespie's eyebrows perked up. "We have all those crates in the back. We could start unpacking."

"Not without at least one conveyor drone," Ziegler cautioned. "I can lift *some* of those crates, but all you'll get is a hernia if you try."

"True." She rested her chin on a hammock of laced fingers. "But look on the bright side. At least we have the equipment to fix it."

Ziegler gave her a bit of side-eye.

"When do we get those drones again?" she asked.

"Not until the middle of next week at the earliest."

"Then I guess we just wait here. As we've been. Fixing sprained ankles and the like."

"Yup."

Gillespie grabbed the base of her seat and scooched it over until she was right next to him.

"Did you see Muntero's face?" she asked. "Wonder what has her so upset."

"You mean besides all those terrorists?"

"Yeah. Besides. Though, honestly, I don't see why everyone's all worked up. All this commotion over an uptick in attacks. I mean, *really!*" She rolled her eyes. "We're the Admin! We have people trying to kill us *all the time!*"

"I think it's more an issue of what they're using rather than who."

"But that's just it. What did people expect would happen? That everything SysGov would stay on one side and everything Admin on the other?" She snorted. "That's just not realistic! There's going to be some blending. Even if we tried to seal our borders, some influence would leak through. I mean, just look at recent events. Someone must have leaked the designs to our transdimensional drives."

"Or other parties figured it out once they knew it was possible."

Gillespie nodded. "Could be that, too."

"I honestly don't know what to make of—"

A dull, distant shudder rumbled up through their feet.

Ziegler and Gillespie paused. Then looked at each other curiously.

"What was that?" she asked.

"Not sure," he said, moments before abstract screens flashed open in front of them, drenched in crimson alert messages.

"Medical emergency!" Gillespie snapped upright and pulled one of the screens over. "Docking Section, Deck Nineteen. Unfinished corridor between Central Access and the Admin hangars. Two victims, both in bad shape. One synthoid and one..."

She paused, and her lower lip twitched. She turned to him with horrified eyes.

"It's Director Shigeki."

"How bad?"

"Very. It's like his PIN pumped out every medical alert all at once."

"Then we need to get down there." Ziegler brought up the station map. "There's an EM station sixty meters from their location. I'll transmit into the medical drone and assess the situation."

"Good luck. I'll join you as fast as I can." Gillespie spun around in her seat. "Gordito!"

An Admin drone the size of a large, fat dog padded out into the foyer. The drone's white skin bulged from numerous compartments loaded with medical gear.

"Awaiting instructions," said the modified Wolverine drone.

"We're heading for the medical alert!" Gillespie said, rising.

"Acknowledged."

"See you there." Ziegler locked his synthoid in place, closed his eyes—

—and opened new "eyes" to darkness.

The EM station's shutter split open, and Ziegler piloted the drone into the open corridor.

The Hippocrates-pattern drone consisted of a floating torso with four arms, the upper two large and strong, the bottom two designed for more delicate work. An assortment of medical equipment hung heavily from the drone in a tall backpack.

Ziegler was an old veteran when it came to Hippocrates drones, and he took to the mental controls with practiced ease. He checked the corridor in both directions. Overhead lights flickered, and smoke obscured his vision to the left. Virtual alerts pulsed beyond the smoke.

He eased power into the drone's graviton thruster and sped down the corridor, smoke curling around him, thinning ahead until he caught sight of a crater blasted into the floor and wall, along with two victims: one Admin synthoid and one organic male.

Ziegler didn't afford himself the luxury of wondering what had caused this terrible carnage. Rather, he focused purely on the task at hand, analyzing the situation as swiftly as he could in order to determine the best course of action.

The explosion had gutted both men. The synthoid lay on his back, missing his head, left arm, and nearly half of his torso. Shrapnel had shredded his uniform and artificial skin to reveal mangled synthetic muscles and warped metallic bones.

The synthoid lay motionless, but Ziegler wasn't worried. According to his understanding of Admin synthoid design, the man's connectome case resided about halfway down his spine in a small, shielded cartridge. *That* part of his body had survived, which meant he could be recovered.

Director Shigeki was another matter entirely. There was even less of him left: just the ragged remains of his upper torso, the stub of one arm, and a *mostly* intact head, all sitting within a pool of blood. His legs and pelvis were several meters away. Shrapnel had chewed through his neck, leaving strips of ragged meat and a broken spine, and his face had been brutally slashed, but his skull—and the brain inside—appeared more or less intact.

Ziegler set the equipment pack next to Shigeki's body.

He checked a timer running from the original alert. Shigeki had a total of four minutes until his brain started dying from lack of oxygen, and one of those minutes had already been spent.

Three minutes and counting.

The drone's sensors tested the air for micro- or nanotech hazards and found no immediate threats. Regardless, Ziegler tried to establish a virtual medical cordon around the site as a standard precaution, but the order failed to connect with the corridor's unfinished infostructure, so he used the drone as a mobile node instead. He selected a shot of medibots, programmed them for head-trauma response, and injected them into the base of Shigeki's skull.

The medibot swarm networked with his drone and spread through the man's head. A diagram of his internal wounds formed in Ziegler's virtual sight, but he immediately picked up on a problem.

"I'm here!" Gillespie ran through the cordon and stopped next to Ziegler. She took in the bloodbath with a horrified eye, then turned to him. "Well?"

"I gave him a shot of medibots, but they're having trouble stabilizing him."

"Hostile microtech?"

"No, I checked for that already. So far, nothing of the sort."

"Then what are they struggling with?"

Ziegler pointed to the abstract version of Shigeki's head. "His head's full of microscopic holes and bits of shrapnel. They're trying to enact repairs, but there's just too much damage."

"Then we pump his head full of more."

"I'll try." Ziegler readied another dose and injected it at a different site. He watched the progress unfold.

Or rather, the lack of progress.

"No good. They're getting confused by all the extra holes, plus they're leaking out everywhere, losing swarm cohesion."

"Then we keep pumping him with more."

"The problem is we're not oxygenating his brain. We're running out of time."

"Can we get him to a recovery casket?"

"Not unless we can stabilize his head. Otherwise, his brain'll be dead long before surgery can repair enough of the damage."

"Then we keep shooting him up."

Ziegler nodded and administered another shot.

Then another.

And a fifth one.

Milky fluid oozed from Shigeki's wounds, forming a puddle of lost and bewildered medibots beneath his head.

"Report!" Commissioner Klaus-Wilhelm von Schröder strode through the cordon and joined the medics. Several other Gordian and DTI personnel had gathered outside the cordon.

"It's not looking good, sir," Ziegler reported. "We've got about seventy seconds before his brain cells start dying, and we've been unable to stabilize his head."

"Then forget the head. Yank his connectome."

"I can't, sir."

"Why can't you?"

"That's not an approved procedure for Admin personnel. And even if it was, I can only perform an extraction if the victim has given prior consent. I *cannot* violate that requirement!"

Schröder took one step forward, his eyes dark and grim, his face harsh as he gazed down at the remains of his DTI counterpart.

"Do it."

"Sir?"

"That's a direct order." The Commissioner clasped his hands behind his back and stood a little straighter. "I take full responsibility. Now save this man's life!"

The force of the Commissioner's order shook Ziegler to the core, but he still hesitated, unsure what to do next, a sense of great unease settling over his mind. He glanced to Gillespie and saw the conflict in her face as well. But then she nodded to him, her lips forming the words, "Save him."

That simple gesture was enough, all that Ziegler needed to drive away the hesitation. Enough for him to justify the actions he was about to take, the oaths he was about to violate.

If our peoples were just a little further along, he told himself as he pulled the equipment from his pack, *if we'd had just a little more time, then yes, surely, he would have given his consent.*

It was a bitter, self-deceptive pill, but he swallowed it nonetheless.

Gillespie helped him set up the machinery around Shigeki's head, which then contracted into a metallic cocoon.

An automated form appeared, and Ziegler confirmed—no, *lied*—that consent had been given.

The machine did the rest. Almost instantly, it collected the essence of who the man was, frying his brain tissue in the process.

"Brain death confirmed." Gillespie swallowed hard. "Legally, Director Shigeki is now deceased. I've logged the time of death."

"And practically?" Schröder asked.

"Connectome extraction was successful, sir," Ziegler said. "Neural map looks to be coherent. There was some noise generated by the shrapnel in his head, but the system seems to have compensated. We'll know more once we load him into a synthoid."

Schröder only nodded.

CHAPTER SEVEN

Argus Station
SysGov, 2981 CE

"ARE YOU SURE?" JONAS SHIGEKI ASKED, THE WORDS LIKE ASHES in his mouth.

"As certain as I can be," Vassal replied. "The telegraph from Providence Station was brief but clear. Director-General Shigeki has been killed by an explosive device of unknown origin, and though Gordian Division personnel managed to extract his connectome, he is still legally dead. You're now the acting head of the DTI, and your presence is urgently requested on the station."

Jonas' mind reeled within a maelstrom of emotions. His father was dead? Dead, but not *quite* dead? And *he* was in charge now? What should he even *feel* at a time like this? Grief? Shock?

Rage?

What he felt was *numb*, he realized. Just...numb, his mind unable to process everything contained within that simple message.

"Sir?" Agent Susan Cantrell asked quietly, sitting forward.

Jonas met her eyes and read the genuine concern in them. She didn't know yet; Vassal had delivered the news privately to his virtual senses.

Someone tried to kill my father, he thought as he gazed at her, his emotional compass swinging at last toward anger, filling him with an oddly cold heat. A low simmer of emotions that he dared not let reach a boil.

No, he corrected. *Someone did kill him, but they failed to do so permanently thanks to our allies.*

Either way, there's a murderer on Providence Station.

"Someone tried to kill my father," he heard himself say.

She sucked in a quick, startled breath.

Jonas climbed to his feet, his body sluggish, his limbs heavier than ever before.

"Come with me," he said, his voice both clear and dead at the same time. "We have work to do."

He left his office, not bothering to check if she followed, merely sensing her shadowing him through Argus Station. His feet carried him through the Admin sector to a counter-grav tube, which whisked them upward into the heart of the station.

His feet brought him before Vesna Tyrel's office, and he palmed the buzzer.

The door split open after a brief delay, and he stepped in.

"Yes, Director?" Tyrel asked, speaking formally in the company of their subordinates. She would have used his given name had they been alone.

Detective Isaac Cho twisted around in his seat, and his eyes passed over Jonas, and then fell on Susan. He must have noticed something, perhaps in his partner's demeanor, because he became infinitely more alert in an instant.

"Is something wrong?" Tyrel asked.

"I'm afraid so." He pointed to Isaac. "I need to take him off your hands."

"But I'm not—"

"Director Shigeki has been killed in a bomb explosion."

Tyrel's lips parted ever so slightly, and she sat back. Isaac, no stranger to cases of death and murder, waited patiently for Jonas to continue, the detective's eyes sharp and focused.

"More specifically, he was rendered temporarily deceased." The words shocked him with how smoothly they flowed, how not a single syllable stuttered. "I'm now in command of the DTI, and, as Acting Director-General, I formally request Cho and Cantrell depart with me for Providence Station."

"A murderer," Tyrel murmured, tapping slender fingers on her desktop. "A murderer loose on Providence."

"The station is essentially one giant construction site with modest crews from Gordian and the DTI. They're mostly technical support with a smattering of command staff, which means no one over there knows the first thing about tracking down a killer."

"Naturally." Tyrel nodded. "And even if they did, we still have the problem of jurisdictions."

"These two are the logical choice to lead the investigation."

"Agreed." Tyrel sat forward and knitted her fingers. "Well, Detective. Looks like we're shipping you out to the transverse."

"If that's where you need us, Commissioner," Isaac declared simply, "then that's where we go."

"Same here, ma'am," Susan added. "You can count on us."

"I'll need to reactivate your status as a DTI investigator," Jonas told Isaac.

"I figured as much." Isaac turned back to Tyrel. "Is there any Themis presence on the station?"

"Not yet. Not while the station is being built."

"Then it would make sense for us to head over with forensic backup."

"I'll check to see who's available." She opened a new screen. "Director, will you be heading out on *Pathfinder-Prime*?"

"As soon as we're ready."

"Then go. I'll have the specialist meet you in the hangar."

"And I'll stop by Logistics and pick up a LENS for Cephalie." Isaac rose from his seat. "Susan, you need anything while I'm there?"

"Just the usual."

"Your usual?" Tyrel asked, fingers hovering beside a personnel list.

"A PA5 anti-synthoid hand cannon," Isaac said dryly.

"Can't be too careful," Susan added. "Also, I'll need my combat frame transferred over to the chronoport."

"I'll take care of that," Jonas said. "You two close out any last-minute business, then meet me in the hangar."

"Yes, sir," Susan said, and Isaac joined her as they headed out the door together.

"Wouldn't want to leave home without your combat frame's flamethrower," he commented quietly.

"It *has* come in handy."

"I never said otherwise."

The door closed behind them.

Jonas let out a long, tired sigh and rubbed his forehead.

"Thanks, Vesna. Sorry I ambushed you like this, but..."

"It's all right. I understand. More than you might realize. Someday, when this has all calmed down, I'll share the story of how I ended up in this body. The short version is, it wasn't planned."

"I'll have to take you up on that." Jonas crashed into the seat Isaac had been using and rested his head in his hand.

"You want to talk about it?" she offered.

"Not really." Jonas gave her a brief, joyless smile. "I want to *act*."

"Then go out there and do just that." She tapped the commit key on a fresh personnel transfer. "Just remember to look before you leap."

Jonas waited at the foot of *Pathfinder-Prime*'s loading ramp.

At ninety meters in length, the *Pioneer*-class chronoport was smaller than the standard TTV design. Its design consisted of a thick delta wing that led back to the long spike of its impeller, giving the observer the vague impression of a manta ray. Twin fusion thrusters and modular weapon systems hung beneath the delta wing, featuring a mix of box missile launchers and laser pods.

Outwardly, Jonas appeared calm and in control. Inwardly, he struggled to contain his nerves. He wanted to leave now, to fly out to Providence Station and speak with his father. The urge filled him with a potent sense of immediacy, but he shoved it down and waited.

He yearned for some sense of reassurance. To not only see for himself that his father lived, but that he remained the same person after his extraction.

Connectome copying wasn't a new technology to the Admin—both STAND and the Department of Incarceration used it frequently—but that was about it. Synthoids were either former criminals, released with the stigma of intentionally feeble bodies, or STANDs, who served the Admin as the honed edge of Peacekeeper might. There was no middle ground.

His father would be...something new, at least in the Admin.

He was glad Gordian agents had saved his father in this manner, but *why* had they done so? Didn't their laws make such an act illegal? Or had his father provided consent?

So many questions.

I'll be able to ask him myself soon enough.

"Vassal?"

The AI's avatar appeared before him. "Yes, Director?"

"Assuming all the information we've received is accurate, what's my father's legal status back home?"

"Deceased. There are no provisions in our law to handle the current situation."

"Thought so." Jonas sighed through his nose. "Which means I'm stuck in command, at least until the Chief Executor appoints his replacement."

"He may nominate you to the post."

"Maybe." Jonas watched the entrance. But then he faced Vassal and flashed a brave smile. "At least Dad is still around to lend a hand. He's not one to let something like 'legal death' slow him down."

"I believe you're correct, sir," Vassal replied, returning the smile.

The entrance to the hangar split open, and a pair of STANDs stepped aside to allow Isaac and Susan through. The LENS drone floating behind the detective bore more than a passing resemblance to a floating metallic eyeball, slightly larger than his head. The avatar of a miniature woman in a long purple coat sat atop the drone.

They met Jonas at the base of the ramp.

"Ready to leave?" Jonas asked them.

"I am." Susan patted the hefty sidearm holstered at her hip. "Assuming my combat frame's arrived."

"It's already stowed in the hold."

"Then we can leave as soon as our forensics support arrives." Isaac glanced back at the entrance.

"Should be any minute," Jonas said. "Tyrel sent out the order before I left her office."

They didn't have long to wait.

The doors split open again, revealing a stocky young man in SysPol blues with a round, somewhat pudgy face. The avatar of a small stone figurine floated over one shoulder—a monkey covering its ears with its hands. The specialist took a cautious step inside and looked around. The heavy disk of a conveyor drone hovered in behind him, a large crate grasped in its flexible arms.

Isaac waved the man over.

"Hello, um." The specialist gave them a worried smile. "Sorry, but I'm not sure if I'm in the right place." He summoned a document over his open palm. "I was supposed to fly out to Venus tomorrow for my next rotation, but then I received orders straight from Commissioner Tyrel of all people! Not sure why the *Commissioner* sent it directly to me, but orders are orders. Anyway, is there a Detective Cho here?"

"That's me." Isaac extended a hand.

"Ronald Gilbert, Forensics Specialist." He shook Isaac's hand. "Seems like I'll be supporting you for a while."

"Seems like." Isaac gestured to his side. "This is my deputy, Special Agent Susan Cantrell."

"You with the DTI?" Gilbert shook Susan's hand.

"That's right."

"And here is my IC, Encephalon," Isaac continued.

"Hey." Cephalie gave the specialist a little wave from atop the LENS.

"A pleasure." Gilbert nodded to her. "Now, can someone point out where I should send my gear?"

"Right up the ramp." Isaac pointed with a thumb over his shoulder.

"On that?" Gilbert pointed at *Pathfinder-Prime*. "An Admin chronoport?"

"Is there a problem?" Isaac asked.

"Well, my drones have counter-grav. I can't take them onto Admin vessels." He paused, as if unsure of himself. "Right?"

"That restriction was rescinded about a month ago," Isaac explained, "after the Providence tech exchange was finalized. We're giving them counter-grav tech as part of the deal, so the rule became pointless."

"Ah. Right. Makes sense."

"Agent Cantrell," Jonas said, "please assist Specialist Gilbert in stowing his equipment, then join us on the bridge."

"Yes, sir." Susan stepped onto the ramp. "This way, please."

The two headed inside, followed by the conveyor.

Isaac bobbed his head after them, and the LENS floated up the ramp.

"Follow me, Detective," Jonas said, and led Isaac through the chronoport's tight, convoluted interior. Unlike SysGov vessels, *Pathfinder-Prime* had to function under a variety of gravitational conditions, including local downward gravity, free fall, and when under power, horizontal acceleration. Walls could become floors or ceilings under different circumstances, and the interior was littered with handholds and ladder rungs.

The bridge sat near the front of the vessel, with acceleration-compensation seats arranged in rows of three. Jonas was about to direct Isaac to the extra seating along the back row, but the detective filed down the row of his own accord, having spent time aboard chronoports in the past. Jonas took his own seat one row up and waited for the rest of the bridge crew and passengers to settle in.

"Director," Captain Durantt's voice boomed over the bridge's shared virtual hearing, "we're ready to depart on your command."

"Take us out."

The hangar bay opened to the vacuum of space, and the chronoport slipped out of Argus Station, an infinitesimal speck against the massive cylindrical station.

"First time aboard a time machine?" Isaac asked Gilbert quietly.

"Yeah."

"It's not bad," Susan assured him. "There's just one big bump when we pass through the outer wall, and that's it."

"Distance, one kilometer from station," reported the realspace navigator.

"Spinning up the impeller. Twenty... forty... sixty..." The temporal navigator checked her charts. "Spin stable at one hundred twenty. Chronometric environment stable. Impeller configured for transdimensional flight. All systems ready for phase-out."

"Execute," Durantt ordered.

Power diverted from the fusion thrusters coursed through the impeller spike, energizing and transforming the exotic matter at precise intervals in sync with the impeller's spin. Chronotons that could once flow freely through the material found themselves blocked in one direction, and chronometric pressure began to build along a precise axis.

The pressure reached a critical threshold, and the chronoport lost phase cohesion with local realspace. The vessel broke through the universe's outer wall with a mighty lurch, and then turned and settled onto a course for Providence Station.

Jonas stepped into the CHRONO Executive Medical Suite and was immediately greeted by the smiling face of a Peacekeeper behind the reception counter.

"Hello, Director." She rose to attention. "I'm Specialist Gillespie. I was one of the people who responded to the emergency."

"How is he?"

"Quite well, all things considered. His brain was mostly intact when my SysPol colleague—Doctor Ziegler—extracted his connectome. The operation was performed before any cellular decay occurred from lack of oxygen."

"*Mostly* intact?" A sickly, anxious sensation spread through Jonas' chest.

"Several shrapnel micro-fragments penetrated his skull and passed through the brain. Only time will tell how much memory or cognitive loss he's suffered."

"How does he seem so far?"

"He experienced a period of disorientation after we loaded him into a synthoid, but it seems to have passed. Doctor Ziegler is with him now, running him through cognitive and reflex tests. I've been watching the results as they come in." She gestured to a small screen over the counter. "So far, he's been doing fine. The initial disorientation could be related to the synthoid itself."

"Is there something wrong with it?"

"No, sir. Nothing like that, but it's different from his original body. Taller, for one thing. It's only natural for there to be an adjustment period for his motor control."

"Why didn't you customize a STAND synthoid for him?"

"Regretfully, sir, our synthoids are incompatible with SysGov connectomes without heavy modifications. As he was extracted with SysGov hardware, one of their synthoids seemed the logical choice, and Doctor Ziegler kindly donated his own."

"It's not a weird one, is it?" The image of Oortan squidform in a Peacekeeper uniform popped into his head, tipping its cap with a tentacle-arm. "Baseline humanoid?"

"Yes, sir. As baseline as they come."

"Fully functional?"

"Um." Gillespie blushed for some reason. "Y-yes. Definitely. As good as the real thing. Top notch SysGov engineering, all around."

"Good." Jonas took a deep, calming breath. "May I see him now?"

"Of course, sir." She gestured down the hall. "First exam room on the right. He's in there with Doctor Ziegler and Agent Noxon."

Jonas nodded to the specialist and headed into the exam room down the hall.

He was greeted by a curious trio. A four-armed medical drone floated next to a statuesque man with a mop of wavy hair wearing a Peacekeeper uniform. Behind them stood a STAND combat frame loaded with an assortment of heavy weapons.

The combat frame was a venerable Type-92, which less charitable circles referred to as mechanical "death skeletons." Jonas had always found the moniker to be overblown. Sure, Type-92s *did* resemble black-boned skeletons, and enemies of the state *did* tend to die in their presence, but seriously, calling them "death skeletons" was just overblown hyperbole.

The handsome man's eyes lit up with immediate recognition, and he smiled at Jonas.

"Son!" He spread his arms.

"Dad?" It was more a question than Jonas had intended, and he wondered how much of his father had been carried over into this new shell. The visual contrast between Shigeki's original, aging body and this paragon of the human form didn't help matters.

"Yeah, I know," Shigeki replied with a disarming grin. "This is going to take *both* of us some getting used to."

"The arrangement is only temporary," the medical drone said. "We can print out a custom body for you later. Put you back in something more familiar."

"As long as you promise to de-age my looks first." Shigeki rotated one of his shoulders. "I've had my fill of being old for a while."

"Of course. I'll help you with the order once you're ready." The medical drone extended one of its lower, more delicate hands to Jonas. "I'm Doctor Ziegler. A pleasure to meet you, Director."

"Likewise. I understand I have you to thank for saving my father."

"In a way, though Commissioner Schröder was the one who authorized the procedure." The drone gestured for Jonas to come in. "Would you like some time together with the patient?"

"Yes, please. If you don't mind."

"Not at all. Just holler if you need anything."

"Thank you, Doctor."

Jonas waited until the three of them were alone.

"Nox?" he asked the combat frame. "Where's your regular body?"

"In a lot of tiny pieces."

"He's not kidding," Shigeki said. "I'd be dead if Nox hadn't taken the brunt of it. Dead-*er*." He cracked a smile. "Besides, I don't think Nox minds an excuse to be carrying around a grenade launcher, given what happened."

"Not one bit," the STAND replied dryly.

"You seem to be handling this rather well," Jonas said.

"Just keeping things in perspective." Shigeki ran fingers back across his head, then paused and patted his unfamiliar hair. "I much prefer this to waking up in Yanluo's burning realms."

"Don't say that, Dad. It could have been heaven."

"Not in my profession. There are *plenty* of reasons people would want to kill me."

"Are we sure it was a bomb? And not some really terrible construction accident?"

"Empty hallways tend not to explode on their own," Nox grunted. "And nothing nearby could have caused the explosion. We were at least that certain when the telegraph went out."

"Then it seems I was right."

"About what?" Shigeki asked.

"I brought backup from Themis Division. Cho and Cantrell."

Jonas threw out the names partially to see how his father responded. To gauge for himself if his father had lost a step.

He wasn't disappointed.

"Cho and Cantrell . . . Ah, yes. The exchange program and our 'junior provisional investigator.' Which is a completely made-up rank."

"I've explained my reasons."

"Yes, yes." Shigeki dismissed the issue with a wave. "I'm sure we can leave the investigation in their capable hands. *We*, however, have a much bigger problem to wrestle with."

"It's Muntero," Nox explained.

"What about her?" Jonas asked.

"She's blaming SysGov for the attack," Shigeki said, "and, because of that, she's put a complete freeze on all cooperation between Gordian Division and the DTI until the murderer is found. Joint surveys. Station construction. *Everything*. She even plans to pull our people out of Operations and have them work from inside docked chronoports!"

"Oh, for the love of—!" Jonas put a hand to his forehead. "Of all the times to start burning bridges!"

"So, you see," Shigeki began, "you and I need to do what we can to bring this situation under control. Before that idiot turns everything we and Gordian have built here to *ash*."

CHAPTER EIGHT

Transtemporal Vehicle *Kleio*
Transverse, non-congruent

ELZBIETÁ LEANED BACK IN HER SEAT AT THE COMMAND TABLE.

"You know," she said with a whimsical smile, "we've been calling these ships the wrong thing for over a year now."

Raibert looked up from the set of charts he'd been examining. "What's this now?"

"The ships." She swept her hand around to indicate the *Kleio*.

"I have no idea what you're talking about."

"TTV. It's the wrong name."

"Seems fine to me."

Off to the side of the bridge, Benjamin continued to scrutinize his own sets of chronometric charts, perhaps keeping his head down for a reason.

"But it really isn't," Elzbietá insisted. "We should call them something else."

"What? All of them?"

"Yeah." She grinned at him. "All of them."

Raibert let out a slow, patient sigh.

"Okay, I'll bite. What's wrong with the name?"

"It's not accurate anymore. TTV? Trans-*Temporal* Vehicle? We do a lot more than that these days."

"So? We still travel through time. It's accurate enough."

"But it doesn't paint the complete picture. We're not traveling down a timeline right now, are we?"

"So?"

"So, we should call them something that includes our ability to travel through the transverse."

"What? Like TDV? Transdimensional Vehicle?"

"Yeah!" Elzbietá's face lit up. "Like that!"

"But wouldn't that have the same problem?" Benjamin raised his gaze with an air of reluctance. "It leaves out our ability to travel through time."

"You know, you make a good point." Elzbietá tapped a finger to the side of her cheek and took on a thoughtful expression. "Perhaps something that includes both? Maybe TDTTV?"

"No," Raibert said with finality.

"Why not?"

"I'm not calling this ship a Tuh-Dat-Vuh. Not happening."

"T-D-T-T-V," Elzbietá enunciated. "See? The name says it all, and in only five letters."

"Not. Happening."

"It *is* more accurate," Benjamin said, though he didn't sound pleased with the results either.

"That's about all it is," Raibert said. "Look, if either of you have a genuine suggestion, take it up with the boss. I just work here." He returned his attention to the charts and didn't look up no matter how much he subconsciously felt Elzbietá's gaze.

The bridge settled into relative silence, save for the distant sounds of the ship's drive, power, and atmospheric systems. Several minutes later, Raibert swiped one of the charts aside and opened up a new one.

"How soon until we reach Q5?"

"We should hit the outer wall in about nineteen minutes," Elzbietá said. "Give or take. The survey data on this one isn't the best."

"Understandably," Benjamin said, "given what they found."

Q5 was a quarantine universe roughly thirteen thousand chens from SysGov, and it had earned that classification for some very good reasons. Q5's version of Earth didn't host any intelligent life— or, at the very least, nothing obviously intelligent—but something was growing down there, and that something did *not* like visitors.

The original survey ship—the *Alcyone*—had confirmed from orbit that Q5 once hosted a thriving human population, a fact apparent from the skeletal remains of cities protruding from its surface like broken teeth. But that's not all they saw down there. Some strange form of macro life grew on the surface, stretching across whole continents in a web of twisted, interlinked biomass that threaded its way through corpse cities and desolate plains alike.

No plants grew on Q5. Or rather, nothing with the green of chlorophyll or the rainbow hues of flowering life. But forests of a sort did indeed grow down on its gruesome surface, with trees and vast stretches of moss more bestial than plant.

During the initial survey, the *Alcyone* had descended to a high-altitude holding position, obscured safely within its metamaterial shroud, before releasing its drones to collect samples for further study. However, the local fauna responded with unexpected ferocity, and every drone fell victim to swarms of nightmarish creatures.

Only one drone managed to transmit any worthwhile data back to the ship, and its analysis confirmed the macro life infesting Q5 contained a great deal of recognizable DNA.

Human DNA.

The very air was rife with complex microscopic organisms, often ejected from hideous flesh geysers that dotted the landscape. Some of those organisms bore the telltale signs of designer lifeforms, though their purposes couldn't be determined without more extensive testing and study.

The crew concluded that Q5's original human population had been wiped out by some form of rampant bioweapon and recommended the universe be placed on the quarantine list. Gordian Operations saw no reason to dispute the recommendation, and the universe was reclassified as Q5.

"Approaching Q5," Elzbietá announced. "Estimating one minute until contact with the outer wall."

"Nothing unusual on the array." Benjamin stood up and joined them at the table. "No evidence of timeline branching or any other unusual activity."

"Hate to meet the fool who'd want to copy *this* place," Elzbietá said.

Raibert affirmed her sentiment with a grunt, then turned his eyes toward the command table's main display. Less than a minute later, the ship shuddered as it punched through the outer wall, and the chronometric environment of the transverse vanished, replaced with a picture of an Earth that was almost unrecognizable.

The orb took shape over the command table, entirely devoid of greens and blues. Its oceans were coated in sludge-like swirls of pink and crimson, slick with strange life and organic chemicals. The surface resembled a landscape of bone and flesh rather than rocks, dirt, and vegetation.

"Gosh," Elzbietá breathed with a shake of her head. "I knew what to expect but still..."

"Yeah." Benjamin glanced at his controls and initiated a chronometric survey, his face grim. "I know what you mean. It's a whole other thing seeing this place in person."

They waited in silence for the survey to finish. Philo appeared by Raibert's side but didn't say anything, merely placed his virtual hands on the command table and stared at one of SysGov's horrific siblings.

"Survey's complete." Benjamin closed the chart. "Nothing to report."

"Any reason for us to stick around?" Raibert asked.

Benjamin shook his head.

"Then let's get the hell out of here. Ella?"

"Way ahead of you." She took hold of her virtual controls. "Next stop, Q3. Home of the silver butterflies."

"Wonderful," Raibert said with a sigh.

Elzbietá flashed a quick smile, though it looked somewhat forced.

"We get to visit all the garden spots in this job."

"Unknown contact!" Elzbietá said.

Raibert snapped alert and checked the chronometric readout over the command table. A new icon pulsed ominously roughly two hundred and fifty chens ahead of their position, indicating an approximate location for the new contact. Philo appeared opposite him, and Benjamin hurried over from his seat along the outer wall.

"What do we have?" Raibert asked.

"Not sure," Elzbietá said. "Whoever they are, I don't think they've spotted us yet. We're almost on the same course for Q3, which places us close to the edge of their impeller wake. Contact's speed is fifty kilofactors. I'm adjusting course and speed to keep us hidden until we have a better read on the situation."

"They *could* be friendly," Philo said hopefully.

Raibert gave his IC a doubtful look.

"All I'm saying is it's possible," Philo added.

"There shouldn't be anyone else out here," Raibert said "and certainly no one heading for a quarantine universe. Doc, does that thing have a SysGov impeller?"

"Checking now." Benjamin opened a new chart. "Impeller is non-rotating, so we're not dealing with a chronoport. However, the drive profile doesn't match either an *Aion* or *Windfall*-class TTV. The signature resembles an *Aion*, but it's not an exact match. I'd say we're dealing with a TTV roughly our own size."

"How's it differ?"

"The wake it's generating should be larger by about fifteen or twenty percent."

"Then it's not Gordian Division?"

"No." Benjamin shook his head. "Not one of ours."

"So, we've got a strange TTV heading somewhere it shouldn't." Raibert clapped his hands together. "All right, team. Assume this one's up to no good."

"Retagging contact to Hostile-One." Benjamin tapped a command into his display. The TTV's icon turned red, and the text above it changed.

"Ella," Raibert asked, "how confident are you they didn't spot us?"

"Eh." Elzbietá raised a level hand and wobbled it back and forth. "I give it even odds. We lucked out by coming up behind them, but we were also *really* close when we spotted them."

"We were heading to Q3 at max speed," Benjamin said. "Add to that their lower speed and quieter drive, and we were lucky to spot them when we did."

"They haven't shown any signs of spotting *us*, though," Philo noted. "No course corrections or speed changes. No telegraph signals, either. Then again, they could be waiting for us to make the first move."

"Which is exactly what I'm afraid of." Raibert tapped his fingers on the table, his eyes fixed on the unidentified TTV's icon. "Time to Q3's outer wall?"

"Thirty-two minutes for Hostile-One," Elzbietá said. "At present speed, we'll hit the outer wall seven minutes after them."

"Then stay the course. We follow them in and see where they go from there."

"Hard to believe *anyone* in their right mind would want to visit Q3," Benjamin said.

"They're here for a reason." Raibert pointed a finger at the TTV icon. "We just need to figure out what it is."

"And in the meantime?" Elzbietá said.

"We prepare for the worst." Raibert rose to his feet. "Combat stations, everyone!"

✧   ✧   ✧

Elzbietá hurried into one of three opening acceleration-compensation bunks along the bridge's outer wall. The chamber sealed her in and a thick, milky soup poured in through vents along the side. Her wetware interfaced with the microbot swarm and authorized it to surround and suffuse her body, fortifying her organs for the harsh g-forces to come.

The swarm climbed up her legs in a translucent sheen, even as more of the fluidized machines flooded the chamber. She shut her eyes and released control of her physical body to the ship's care. She could have stayed alert for the entire process, but only if she wanted to experience that disgusting goop pouring into her lungs.

No, thank you! she thought with a wry smile, moments before her perception of the physical vanished.

She opened the eyes of her avatar—which matched her real body—to join Philo within the abstract realm of the ship's virtual cockpit. She stood atop an invisible floor, surrounded by a visual representation of the transverse, the icon of Hostile-One highlighted in the distance. A pair of tandem seats waited for them, the only other objects.

"Ready?" she asked her weapon systems officer and copilot.

Philo took hold of a tab atop his horned aviator's helmet and brought it down with a loud *click!* that locked a reflective visor over his eyes.

"Ready!"

Elzbietá nodded to him with a smile and sank into her seat. Various floating displays and controls popped into existence, and she took hold of the joystick and omnidirectional throttle.

Philo assumed his post in the seat next to her.

"Deploying meta-armor." He tapped a virtual key.

Over a dozen pods opened across the *Kleio*'s surface, represented on a wire-frame schematic of the ship positioned between the two seats. Metamaterial unfurled like blurry, metal drapes that snapped rigid and locked together to form a protective shell against directed-energy weapons. Anything that punched through that—energy or kinetic—would still have to contend with the ship's adaptive prog-steel hull.

"Armor active." Philo tapped several more keys. "Bringing our weapons online."

Four heavy blisters split open, and the nine-barreled muzzles of 45mm Gatling guns swiveled out. Prog-steel parted ways, and the four gun pods flowed across the surface, congregating near the nose of the vessel. Meta-armor split and then reformed with their passing.

The *Kleio*'s bow opened like an angry eyeball with two irises, and two massive guns trained out: one a powerful mass driver, and the other an x-ray laser tied directly to the ship's reactor.

"Weapons ready," Philo said.

"Good." Elzbietá eyed the distant TTV. "Now, let's hope we don't have to ruin someone's day."

The ship lurched as it passed through Q3's outer wall, and Elzbietá felt the transition in her gut. Not because of anything happening to her physical body, but through her virtual senses. The cockpit simulation let a controlled amount of g-forces and other cues leak through, allowing her to perceive the ship's motion and status on a subconscious level.

Kleio phased into Q3 realspace in high orbit around Earth. Or rather, what remained of this universe's Earth. In some ways, Q3 was the polar opposite of Q5—a terrifying portrait of death rather than twisted, horrific life. The planet was a stark ball of rock, metal, and polluted oceans, all encircled by the silvery haze of a ghostly, smeared halo. Massive blocks of machinery coated every continent: mines, refineries, and endless stretches of factories.

All automated, all lifeless.

The haze thinned with greater altitude, only to thicken again thirty-five thousand kilometers above the surface. The ghostly, mechanical miasma was the reason why Q3 had been quarantined. It may have resembled a silvery mist at a distance, but closer inspection would reveal swarms of self-replicating machines, some microscopic in size while others spanned dozens of meters. The most common variants were roughly the size of a human hand,

and all of them—*all* of them—resembled nightmarish metal butterflies, as if someone had twisted a surgeon's scalpels to create
their wings.

The original survey crew had barely made it out with their lives.

"Position verified," Philo reported. "We're right on target,
about thirty-one thousand kilometers above the surface and in
stable orbit."

"Any sign of the TTV?" Elzbietá asked.

"Searching." Philo scrutinized his instrumentation for less
than a minute. "There, above us." Hostile-One's icon reappeared
on their scope. "Heading straight toward that dense cluster in
geosynchronous orbit."

"Do they have a death wish or something?"

"They must be here for a reason," Raibert chimed in from
the virtual bridge.

"You keep saying that, but damned if I know what it is."
Elzbietá took hold of her controls and swung the nose up to face
the other TTV. The ship was a distant, almost invisible pinprick
against the backdrop of an elongated silver blob. "You want me
to head after them?"

"Can we keep an eye on them from here?" Raibert asked.

"Not for much longer," Philo said. "I'm already having dif-
ficulty tracking them against the background activity. We'll lose
them if they head into that cluster."

"Then lay in a pursuit course."

"You've got it!" Elzbietá pushed her omni-throttle forward,
and the ship accelerated on a plume of gravitons.

"Adjusting meta-armor for increased stealth." Philo closed their
weapon apertures and spread meta-armor over those surfaces. A
wide spectrum of photon wavelengths flowed around the ship,
masking its presence. It wasn't a perfect illusion; that required
the metamaterial to be in shroud-mode while the ship kept its
acceleration low and tried not make any sudden moves. But the
meta-armor *did* reduce their signature to radar and lidar detectors.

The butterfly swarm loomed large ahead, thick enough at its
core to resemble a shimmering metal comet, except this comet
featured its own satellites buzzing around the periphery.

"You see those?" Elzbietá asked, pointing.

"Sentries," Philo said. "Big ones, too."

"And our mystery ship is heading straight for them."

"No evidence the sentries have spotted either of us. I haven't detected any active signals from the TTV either, but we *are* being pinged by swarm radar. Meta-armor seems to be doing its job. For now, at least, but we're getting close to the point where one of us will be spotted."

"You hear that, Raibert?" Elzbietá asked.

"Stay with them. We need to know what that ship is—"

"Missile launch!" Philo shouted. "Two contacts! One's heading for us, the other for the swarm."

"What the hell?" Elzbietá watched the projectiles diverge from Hostile-One's position. "Are they trying to get us both killed?"

"Maybe they are. The swarm's reacting. Sentries inbound toward both of us. Too many to count. I think Hostile-One is using one of the missiles to guide them to our location."

"Fantastic," Elzbietá snarled under her breath as the scope lit up with red icons. "Raibert?"

"Time to cut loose."

"With pleasure!" Elzbietá shoved the omni-throttle forward, and *Kleio* surged ahead under five gees.

"All weapons ready," Philo reported. "Meta-armor adapted for max defense. Active scopes engaged. I've got a clean lock on Hostile-One and its missiles. Targeting the closest missile." He waited for the range to drop. "Firing!"

Three of *Kleio*'s four Gatling guns blazed alive, spewing a combined total of one hundred fifty bullets per second. The three streams of speeding metal converged on the missile, and explosions flooded space with cones of scything shrapnel. Fléchettes punched through the missile from all sides and shredded it into useless scrap.

"Got it!"

The second missile exploded in a brief, tiny flash within the heart of the orbital formation. It was an inconsequential, almost insulting attack, and the self-replicators responded by mobilizing almost the entire swarm.

"Oh, they didn't like that!" Elzbietá kept her nose pointed toward the hostile TTV, even as it dove deeper into the clutches of the enraged swarm.

"Targeting Hostile-One," Philo said. "Firing!"

X-rays lanced into the enemy TTV, but the high-energy photons slipped around its surface and scattered into space.

"Solid hit, but minimal damage," Philo reported. "Their

meta-armor took the brunt of it. I'd say their defenses are at least as good as ours."

"Then we use the mass driver."

"Not at this range. Get us in closer."

"On it!" Elzbietá adjusted course, tailing the other TTV into the swarm, tendrils of grasping replicators reaching toward both craft, their tips composed of larger, more powerful machines.

"Watch it!" Philo warned. "Those sentries are getting awfully close."

"I see them."

Kleio could accelerate in any direction thanks to her graviton thrusters, and Elzbietá applied perpendicular thrust, easing them away from the closest sentries, even as she kept the nose pointed at the enemy craft.

One of the sentries, a gargantuan mechanical cross between a butterfly and a hornet, spread its solar-collecting wings and angled the railgun mounted on his thorax. Kinetic slugs punched into the *Kleio*'s prog-steel hull, and Philo returned fire. A stream of high-explosives shredded the machine, but more sentries sped in, converging on the TTV from all sides.

Philo worked frantically, tasking the Gatlings with each new target, prioritizing hostile machines for destruction. The *Kleio*'s defensive weapons swung around, vomiting metal in brief but deadly spurts, and explosions lit up on all sides, even as the ship climbed deeper into danger.

"Our defenses are close to saturation!" Philo warned.

Kleio cut through the grasping pseudopods of the swarm, each extending for tens of kilometers. Kinetic slugs rained in from all sides and a heavy impact slammed into their starboard flank. A loud *clang* echoed through the ship as if a great bell had been struck, and a section of the ship's schematic flared yellow.

"Never mind!" Philo's fingers danced over his controls. "We're *past* saturation! Reinforcing damaged armor."

"Raibert," Elzbietá strained, "it's getting hot out here."

"Keep after Hostile-One, but phase out if you need to."

Another impact rang against the hull.

"Got it." She gritted her teeth and checked the position of the enemy TTV. The distance between the two craft dropped away. Slowly but steadily, even as both vessels charged deeper into the contracting arms of the swarm.

"Main gun standing by," Philo said. "Just give me a shot."

Elzbietá permitted herself a cold, shallow smile. "Here it comes."

Kleio chased after Hostile-One, swerving this way and that, dodging through the incoming fire, even as its Gatling guns blasted away at the swarm. Expansive streamers of broken, spinning metal floated in their wake, but the machine sentries squeezed in ever closer.

Two new icons lit up, detaching from the enemy TTV.

"Missile launch!" Philo snapped. "Two incoming!"

Elzbietá's hand hovered over the phase-out button.

"Not yet!" Philo shooed her hand away from the button. "I've got this!"

His fingers blurred over the controls, quite literally as he entered commands faster than her brain could process. The bow laser fired, raking through one of the missiles and blowing it to pieces while the Gatlings unleashed a sleet of metal. Strings of tiny explosions peppered space, and the second missile winked out.

Elzbietá kept the ship's nose on target.

"In range," Philo declared. "Shot away!"

A one-ton slug blasted out of *Kleio*'s nose mass driver. Hostile-One juked to the side, and the shot flew wide, but Philo's detonation profile triggered as it passed. Cold gas jets turned the projectile to face the enemy craft, and then the payload exploded, spraying the TTV with heavy shrapnel.

"That's a hit!" Philo declared viciously. "Damage to their meta-armor and impeller."

Another impact shuddered through the *Kleio*'s decks, and a new patch of yellow lit up.

Elzbietá checked their surroundings and the machines streaking in.

"We can't stick around much longer!"

"Neither can they," Philo said. "Look!"

Hostile-One vanished from the realspace scopes, reemerging as a chronometric signature exiting Q3's outer wall.

"Oh, no you don't!" Elzbietá hit the phase-out button and followed them into the transverse.

Q3, and all its self-replicating hostility, dissolved into nothingness, and the ship lurched as it punched through the dimensional barrier. Their chronometric array interpreted the drive signature from Hostile-One as a cloud of potential positions directly ahead.

"We're closing on them," Philo said. "That hit to their impeller must've taken some of the wind out of their sails. Either that or they're slower than us. Phase-lock in fifteen seconds."

Elzbietá matched speeds with the hostile craft, holding the distance open.

"Raibert, you want to try reasoning with these idiots before we send them to hell?"

"Not really," he answered in a resigned tone, "but I suppose it's my job to give diplomacy a shot. Kleio, send the following telegraph to the other ship: This is Agent Kaminski of Gordian Division TTV *Kleio*. You are hereby ordered to stand down immediately or be destroyed. This is your final warning. You have sixty seconds to comply."

"Transmitting now, Agent," the ship replied.

Sixty seconds passed with no response and no actions from the other ship.

"Then that's that," Raibert said with a grim finality. "Ella, finish this."

Elzbietá increased their speed, and the two craft phase-locked in a matter of seconds. Hostile-One blinked into existence ahead and above them, and Elzbietá spun the ship upward to bring their main weapons to bear. Philo fired the mass driver, and this time the shot tore through the base of Hostile-One's impeller.

The spike of exotic matter oscillated like a struck tuning fork, cracks chasing down its length before it shattered into a million glittering pieces. Most scattered away from the vessel's elliptical body, but some flew into it, passed *through* it. The debris' phase state bled away as incorporeal fragments flitted through solid matter.

The ship distorted, crinkling inward like a fragile toy. Disparate sections of the hull meshed together, overlapping, interposing, bleeding into and through one another until only a twisted, lump-ridden hulk remained of the once streamlined craft.

"Want me to hit them again?" Philo asked, his tone somewhat uncomfortable. "You know, just to be sure."

"I *think*"—Elzbietá flashed a sudden, sharklike grin—"they've had enough."

CHAPTER NINE

Transtemporal Vehicle *Kleio*
Transverse, non-congruent

"WHAT DO WE HAVE SO FAR?" RAIBERT ASKED, JOINING PHILO, Benjamin, and Elzbietá around the command table. A see-through depiction of Hostile-One's wreckage floated over the table, the icons of reconnaissance remotes and conveyor drones sweeping through its mangled interior.

"Not much so far," Benjamin said, "but what we do have is... interesting." He nodded for Philo to proceed.

"First, the interior is an absolute mess. Kleio is trying to map out what it looked like before the impeller blew, but one thing is already clear—the crew was entirely abstract."

"No bodies?" Raibert asked.

"Not just no bodies." Philo highlighted the areas of a TTV typically reserved for crew quarters. "No *accommodations* for bodies, either organic or synthetic. No bridge, no sleeping quarters, no medical bay, no synthoid charging stations, no compensation bunks. The exterior hull and drive systems may resemble SysGov TTVs, but the interior has been completely redesigned."

"By whom?"

"I wish I knew."

"Along those lines," Benjamin said, "we've managed to isolate parts of the infostructure. The programming is blatantly rooted in SysGov standards, but we're encountering two problems. One: many of the nodes were damaged when they overlapped parts of

the ship. And two: looks like the crew made a last-ditch effort
to scrub the evidence."

"Some of the data is recoverable," Philo added, "but it's a
jumbled mess. All sorts of fragmentation and missing sectors, and
that's just what hasn't been overwritten with obvious garbage. If
I were to guess, I'd say the crew initiated an emergency purge
right after your warning."

"Fantastic." Raibert sighed wearily. "And once again the multiverse penalizes us for trying to be reasonable."

"Cheer up, buddy." Philo gave him a virtual pat on the shoulder. "You wouldn't want people thinking you took lessons from
the *Admin*, now would you?"

Raibert snorted.

"It's not all bad news," Elzbietá said. "Ben and I have been
doing a little brainstorming."

"Our encounter with Hostile-One didn't sit well with me
from the start," Benjamin began, "and nothing I've seen so far
has changed that. First of all, what are the odds of us stumbling
upon this strange TTV and just happening to come up right
behind them?"

"Pretty low," Raibert replied, wondering where Benjamin was
taking this.

"Exactly. Which makes me think *they* spotted *us* first, not
the other way around. Also, where were they coming *from*?" He
shifted the schematic aside and brought up the transverse map,
then traced a path from Q3 back through their first contact with
Hostile-One. The line eventually ran off the map.

"Q5 maybe?" Raibert offered with a shrug, his eyes following
the path through an otherwise boring patch of the transverse.

"But why?" Benjamin asked.

"I..." Raibert frowned. "No idea."

"Same here. For the moment, let's assume the only reason they
led us to Q3 was to use the locals against us. If we assume that,
then they weren't coming from Q5's direction at all. Instead, they
must have made a course change right after they spotted us—but
before *we* spotted *them*—in order to mask their original heading."

Raibert's eyebrows shot up. "Aha."

"Makes more sense now, doesn't it?"

"But then, what was their real flight plan?"

"Don't know," Benjamin admitted. "Maybe we'll find something in the ship's infostructure. Or perhaps we can piece together an explanation by taking a deeper look at their actions throughout the encounter."

"Well, stay on it, Doc. I think you're onto something here."

"Will do."

"Speaking of the ship's infostructure . . ." Philo looked up with a tentative smile.

"Got something?" Raibert asked.

"Maybe." Philo shifted the transverse map aside and opened a new display. "Kleio just finished her first pass through the data, and I think we might have something here. She was able to retrieve several text fragments from the TTV, and while they're incomplete, certain key phrases appear in them repeatedly. Anyone ever hear of the Phoenix Institute?"

The others at the table shook their heads.

"Neither have I," Philo continued, "but if I were a betting AC, I'd wager this Institute built Hostile-One."

"Anything else in there besides the name?" Raibert asked hopefully.

"A few things, but the meaning is less clear. I ran through it briefly after Kleio finished her pass, but we simply don't have enough context to make sense of it. There's mention of something called Revenants, but I have no idea what they are. And there's talk of a three-phase plan to do . . . something."

"Nothing good for us," Benjamin said.

"Any mentions of *Reality Flux* or the Admin terrorism?" Raibert asked.

"Only one reference to *Reality Flux* along with an Institute member named Ijiraq, but there isn't enough there to say more. At the very least, it's a strong indicator they were involved somehow."

"Would it be too much to ask for a map to their secret lair?" Elzbietá quipped. "Maybe a detailed manifesto and a complete member list?"

"If this job was easy, anyone could do it," Benjamin replied with a friendly smile.

"I'm not looking for easy," Elzbietá continued. "Just something to show for our efforts. So far, we don't have much besides a name and a busted-up TTV."

"That's more than we had a few hours ago." Raibert placed his fingertips atop the table. "Where to next?"

"We were attacked for a reason," Benjamin said. "That tells me we're at least close to something important, which means we need to search this zone of the transverse as thoroughly as possible."

"We should head back to Providence Station first," Philo said. "We need to pass on what we've learned and warn everyone to be on guard for other Institute TTVs."

"That's going to burn up a lot of time." Elzbietá pulled the transverse map over and plotted a course. "We're sixteen thousand chens from the station, so you're looking at an eleven-hour round trip."

"Good point, Ella." Raibert brought up the estimated positions of other Gordian craft. "What if we pass on the message to another TTV? *Phoebe* is close-ish. We can swing out their way and have them deliver our findings while we get back to the search."

"Let's see." Elzbietá adjusted the course projection. "That'll set us back three hours."

"Much better than eleven," Raibert said.

"And we can use that time to crunch through the evidence a bit more," Benjamin said. "Perhaps we can come up with a good place to start our search."

"Then it's settled." Raibert pushed off the table. "We finish up here first, gather what evidence we can, then demolish what's left. After that, we lay in a course for the *Phoebe*."

"Telegraph incoming," Philo said an hour and a half later. "*Phoebe* confirms receipt of our data and acknowledges our request. They're setting a course for Providence Station."

"Then our job here is done." Raibert faced Elzbietá. "Turn us around."

"Heading back to Q3." Elzbietá swung the ship around and settled them into a course for the quarantine zone.

"Hmm," Benjamin murmured twenty minutes after their rendezvous with the *Phoebe*, his eyes engrossed by the transverse map. "Hmm? Mmhmm."

"Doc?" Raibert stepped over. "You're doing it again."

"Hmm?" Benjamin looked up. "Doing what?"

"Your thinking noise thing."

"That's because I'm thinking."

"I figured. I figured," Raibert said, nodding. He waited for

Benjamin to fill in the rest, and when the information failed to materialize, he added, "What're you thinking about?"

"Hostile-One and Q3."

"What about them?"

"Well, the thing that's been bugging me is why attack us at all? If they saw us first—and I still think they did—then why not shutdown their impeller and let us pass? Why take the risk of engaging a SysPol TTV when there was a much safer alternative?"

"Hmm." Raibert rubbed his chin thoughtfully, but then realized he was inadvertently mimicking Benjamin's noises and stopped. He cleared his throat and sat up. "You're right. It doesn't make sense."

"The only reason I've been able to come up with is they felt threatened by our presence." Benjamin shook his head. "Which implies we were close to something, but it couldn't be Q3, since they led us there, so . . ."

"Well, keep at it."

Raibert turned back to the transverse map and considered the position where they met the Institute TTV.

Does it have to do with where they were headed? Or where they came from? Perhaps both? He considered this for a moment. *Maybe, but—*

Raibert stopped and leaned toward the map as if seeing it for the first time, the prominent icons of SysGov, the Admin, and Providence Station glowing near the center.

"That's it!" he exclaimed, slapping the table.

Benjamin and the others looked his way, and he grinned at them.

"Doc, I think you're absolutely right about them changing course just before we spotted them. And"—he raised a triumphant finger—"we have enough information to figure out what that course was!"

Benjamin's face brightened, and he cracked a smile. "Well, don't keep us in suspense."

"First, let's assume one end of their trip was their secret lair. Doesn't matter if they were coming or going. Now, we already have one point along their course. That's where we met Hostile-One. All we need is one other point of reference to extrapolate where their base could be. And we can figure *that* out by looking at recent events, such as the disappearance of *Reality Flux* and the Admin terrorism."

"You think they were either heading for or coming back from SysGov or the Admin," Benjamin finished.

"Exactly! Got it on the first try, Doc!"

"Then, let's see…" Benjamin highlighted their first contact with the TTV, then added SysGov and the Admin to form a narrow triangle with a line between SysGov and the Admin serving as its short base. He then mirrored the same shape on the opposite side of Hostile-One, creating a flattened hourglass.

"Now *that* narrows it down!" Elzbietá rested her chin on laced fingers. "There's Q3, of course, plus quite a few human-inhabited branches beyond it. H14, H17, H20, and H21 being the most prominent. A few D's in the mix, too," she added, referring to the "dead" universes that lacked any sign of current or prior human presence. "Which one do you want to hit first?"

"That one." Benjamin pointed to H17.

"Hey now!" Raibert gave him a cross look. "Do I go around stealing your thunder?"

"Sorry. It just seems obvious to me, given how close H17 is to Q3."

"Why would it be the closest?" Elzbietá asked them. "Why not one of the universes farther away, like H20?"

"Because of how they reacted," Benjamin explained. "If Raibert and I are correct, they took a shot at us *because* we were already near their base."

"And this time," Raibert said triumphantly, "we're going to find it!"

✧   ✧   ✧

"Got something!" Benjamin brought up the zoomed-in view of the local transverse and highlighted the universe immediately ahead. "H17's outer wall has shifted position. Not by much, but it's a strong indicator another universe has branched off from it in the opposite direction."

"Now we're talking," Raibert said. "So, if we take H17's past and present coordinates, then extrapolate them…" An elliptical zone appeared on the map, highlighting potential locations for H17's doppelganger. "Ella, put together a flight plan to search this zone. We'll head there next."

"You've got it."

"I'll retag this universe as H17A and the new one we expect to find as H17B." Benjamin inputted the new values into his virtual console. "We can figure out their official designations later."

"Works for me," Raibert said. "You want to take a peek inside H17A before we move on?"

"Just enough for us to establish a benchmark. We'll know more once we find H17B. The original survey is solid enough, so we shouldn't have too much trouble identifying which branched off of which."

"Sounds good to me. Ella?"

"Adjusting course for entry into H17A."

"What do we have on this universe?" Raibert asked, stepping up beside Benjamin.

"H17 branched off from T1 in 1917. In this timeline, the faction of the German high command that opposed unrestricted submarine warfare won the debate. Worse, from Wilson's perspective, the Zimmerman Telegraph never fell into British hands. The combination made it impossible for him to get the United States into World War I until late 1919, and by that time, Russia had collapsed. Lenin had taken it out of the war, and H17's version of the Treaty of Brest-Litovsk was even harsher than in T1 or T2. By the time the US did get into the war, grain from the East was offsetting much of the Royal Navy's blockade's starvation effect, and the forces freed up in the East had let Germany punch out France. The situation was a lot like the one in T1's 1940, but the British Empire was a lot stronger and the US was fully committed once it did get in. That meant the war lasted much longer, and eventually it turned nuclear. The resulting destruction and the subsequent wars pushed this timeline's technological and societal development back considerably. In some ways, they're not much different from the early twenty first century back home."

"Well, at least they didn't nuke themselves into oblivion." Raibert gave him a halfhearted shrug. "Glass half full, right?"

"More like glass half vaporized and the other half is an irradiated mess. World War I wasn't the only conflict to go nuclear for them."

"Yeah, figured. Otherwise, they'd be further along." Raibert watched the distance to H17A's boundary drop off. "Assuming we spot H17B, how do you want to approach this?"

"We need to first determine which one is the offshoot," Benjamin said. "We have the survey's topology breakdown and population estimates. If there aren't any obvious discrepancies in that, then we dig deeper, starting with the branch in the timeline. Fortunately, because of *Reality Flux*'s atomic clock, we know when in the timeline the two split."

"Forty years ago."

"Exactly, and the Phoenix Institute is the most likely culprit. The question then becomes, what did they do in H17's past that was disruptive enough to spawn an entirely new universe?"

"Does H17 have a functioning infostructure?" Raibert asked.

"*Barely.*"

"Something is better than nothing. We could shroud up and snoop around without too much trouble."

"I wouldn't recommend it," Benjamin said. "Have you ever heard of a device called a 'dial-up modem'?"

"Um," Raibert gave the other man a perplexed look. "No. Can't say that I have."

"Consider yourself fortunate. H17's infostructure is primitive and heavily segmented. And *slow*. We'd be better off taking a different approach."

"Speaking of H17," Elzbietá cut in, "Outer wall in five... four...three...two...one..."

Raibert grabbed the handrail built into the command table's circumference, and the ship shuddered from crossing the dimensional boundary. H17A's Earth appeared over the center of the table, a refreshing orb of blue and swirling white after the hellscapes of Q5 and Q3. Elzbietá maneuvered them into a low orbit around the planet, metamaterial deployed in a cloaking configuration.

Benjamin pulled up the original survey data, placing it next to H17A's Earth, and initiated his own analysis of the surface. Data began to pour in, and sections of the globe turned green as their scopes failed to find any differences.

"So far, it looks like H17A is the original," Benjamin said. "Either that, or the discrepancies are too subtle to notice from orbit. But let's not jump to conclusions. We should complete a full survey of the surface here, then find and do the same at H17B."

"And if we don't spot any obvious differences?" Raibert asked. "You mentioned taking a 'different approach.'"

"I did. It'll be easier than trawling through the sludge of the local infostructure. But I'll need some time to prep first."

"Prep time?" Raibert's brow creased. "You're not planning anything dangerous, are you?"

"No, no. Perish the thought." Benjamin gave the other man a strangely cheerful smile. "It's just I need to decide what to wear first."

✧   ✧   ✧

Candice Bettenbrock took pleasure in the small parts of her job as a page at the Washington D.C. Ground Zero Memorial Library. It wasn't a great job. Nor was it a great place to work, but Candice respected the importance of doing the work she was given dependably, and doing it well. It was a lesson her parents had drummed into her with such repetition that she'd eventually caved to their wisdom, her unruly teenage years yielding to her early twenties with a mental shrug that said "Well, maybe they do have a point there."

Even if all she was doing was returning books to the stacks.

She enjoyed coming up with little games to play during the tedium of her part-time job, and stacking books provided many such opportunities. She grabbed another armful of thick tomes and glanced over their spines, mentally mapping a path through the stacks for optimal efficiency. She didn't need to be efficient; in fact, all it did was leave her with more boring downtime, but the exercise provided her with some mild amusement.

She finished restacking the books and pushed her cart back to the main desk. She passed a row of tall windows, though little light leaked in from the outside. Rain drizzled from an overcast sky, and the few remaining hints of sunlight were fast retreating into dusk. The library was almost empty, despite not being scheduled to close for another three hours.

Another three *monotonous* hours, she thought glumly. One of the cart's wheels squeaked with each rotation, like an annoying metronome, then squealed in desperate protest and locked up. She shoved the cart forward without a second thought, having gone through this exercise many times. The wheel unbound, and she continued her trek back toward the main desk.

Assistant Librarian Martha Esker looked up from a sheaf of forms, tapping a pencil against her lips, the back end chewed and glistening.

"Candice dear." Everyone was something-dear where Martha Esker was concerned.

"Yes, Mrs. Esker?" Candice brought the cart to a squeaking halt behind the desk.

"Mind the desk for a few minutes, would you? I need a smoke."

No, you don't, Candice thought. *What you need is a breath mint, you old chimney.*

"Sure thing," she replied instead, because unleashing her inner dialogue would only cause trouble.

"Thanks, dear." The librarian rose from her creaking chair. She rummaged through the coat across its back for a pack of cigarettes, then headed through a door marked EMPLOYEES ONLY, no doubt on her way to the covered porch near the loading dock where employees took their smoke breaks.

Candice dropped into the chair with a huff and glanced down at the engagement ring on her finger. The *fake* engagement ring. Most of the library's unmarried female staff wore similar accessories because, if they didn't, then they had to put up with patrons who thought it was perfectly acceptable to flirt with librarians and pages on the job. Some of the patrons still did, fake engagement ring or no, but wearing one seemed to reduce the number of incidents.

Candice leaned back for a thoughtful moment. The scarce traffic through the library today probably meant she wouldn't have to deal with a creeper in the short time it took Esker to smoke a few coffin nails, so she sat forward and grabbed the book stashed underneath the main desk.

Her book. A (vaguely) historical romance titled *The Lonely Flower*, fourteenth in the long-running Amorous Garden series in which the ever-respectable Lord Captain Damien Upchurch and the wily-yet-lovable Bastian Shank once again dueled with wits, words, and deeds over the heart of Lady Pamela Cranberry.

Candice normally didn't go for steamy romances—preferring the absurdity of *actual* history over fiction—but a friend had introduced her to the series a few years ago and she'd been hooked ever since. She pulled the dog-eared tome open at the bookmark and began reading the next chapter.

The front door chimed a few minutes later, and she looked up.

A tall man strode through the glass double doors, impressively broad shouldered, his face shadowed by a wide-brimmed hat slick with rain. He took off his hat and shook off the precipitation, revealing a handsome face with piercing gray eyes underneath dark bangs. An aura of poise and confidence encompassed him, as if he knew exactly where he should be, and *this* was the place.

There was something else about him she couldn't quite put her finger on. Something off about his clothing, though not in a bad way. It was as if someone had taken the wardrobe from every male lead in every recent movie, mashed them all together, and then dressed him in the result. It was almost...heroic.

He swept his gaze from one end of the main lobby to the other, and for a moment his eyes met hers. The experience was... electric, like a pulse of excitement jolting through her body. The book slipped from her fingers and clattered to the floor, and she gasped, then scrambled to pick it up.

The tall man approached the desk, and a sense of apprehension filled her. He may have been handsome, but the last thing she needed was a flirtatious creeper pestering her in an almost empty library.

"Good day, ma'am," he began with a courteous nod. "I was wondering if I could trouble you for some assistance."

Good grief! she thought, her apprehension melting away. *Even his accent makes him sound like he's been plucked from a movie!*

"Wh-w-wah?" For some reason, her tongue had transformed into jelly.

"Is something wrong, ma'am?"

Candice shook her head, trying to banish her sudden awkwardness.

"Fine, fine." *Why does he keep calling me ma'am?* Her fake engagement ring drew her eye, and she shoved her hand underneath the desk, then smiled up at the man. "You said you needed something?"

"Yes. I'm working on a research paper and"—he took on an air of bashfulness that somehow made his face even more handsome—"as much as I hate to admit it, it's been a while since I set foot in a library. I was wondering if you could help point me in the right direction."

"Sure." She tried to yank off the ring, but it caught on a knuckle. "What kind of paper are you working on?"

"History class. The topic is 2941, a year in review."

"The whole year?" *Why won't this thing come off?!*

"The whole year."

"Not a particular event?" *Get! Off! My damn! Finger!*

"Afraid not."

Candice let out a frustrated wheeze and pulled at the unwanted engagement ring. The ring slipped over her knuckle, and she winced as the back of her hand slapped against a shelf divider underneath the desk.

"Are you all right?" the man asked with genuine concern.

"Never better!" She smiled at him to mask the pain. "Are we talking about a particular country or worldwide?"

"Worldwide."

"That seems awfully broad."

"That's what the professor gave us. Everyone in the class gets to summarize a different year, and my name landed on 2941."

"Your professor?" She raised an eyebrow. "You're going to the University?"

"That's right. The current job is fine. It certainly pays the bills, but the passion just isn't there anymore. So, I thought I'd go back to school. I've always had a fascination with history, and I thought why not give that a shot. Maybe even go into teaching."

Candice's eyes widened. Not only was this man movie-star-hot, but he apparently held a steady job *and* he loved history, too?

If this guy's a creeper, she thought lustfully, *then he can creep on me all day long.*

"I-I want to teach history someday, too," she stammered.

"That's wonderful to hear. A lot of people don't appreciate the value of learning history. After all, if we don't know where we've come from, then—"

"We'll keep making the same mistakes," she finished brightly.

"I couldn't have said it better myself." He graced her with a genuine, approving smile.

Oh my gosh! You are too perfect!

"Do you think you could give me a hand with—"

"Absolutely!" Candice sprang to her feet and hurried around the desk. "Let me show you to our history wing. I can even help you get started."

"Thanks. That sounds like just the thing I need."

Yes!

"This way, then." She led him to the nearby stairs, then up two floors. "By the way, I didn't catch your name, Mister..."

"Please. Call me Benjamin."

CHAPTER TEN

Providence Station
Transverse, non-congruent

"AND THAT'S WHERE WE STAND AT THE MOMENT," KLAUS-WILHELM said, finishing his presentation to the senior staff assembled in the CHRONO conference room. "To summarize, the *Kleio* has a promising lead on this so-called Phoenix Institute, which they're in the process of following up."

The use of the conference room was something of a formality, since Klaus-Wilhelm was the only person physically present. Peng, as an abstract entity, had no need for the physical space, and the Admin representatives—Muntero, Jonas Shigeki, and his newly synthetic father—were all abstracting in from docked chronoports.

Jonas had argued for a face-to-face meeting, if for no other reason than to demonstrate their faith and confidence in the other side, but Muntero had overruled him unless they went under heavy STAND escort in full combat frames. Jonas judged the presence of Admin "death skeletons" to be . . . counterproductive, and so he'd settled for remote participation.

"What's *Phoebe* tasked with next?" Jonas asked.

"Heading out to join the *Kleio*," Klaus-Wilhelm said. "I want them to have some backup as soon as possible, given they've already been attacked once."

"Can we send them any additional support?" Peng asked.

"That'll be a problem." Klaus-Wilhelm sank back into his chair. "The storm continues to interfere with our communications. I'd like to reorganize our scouting efforts, but that'll have to wait until the storm clears, which won't be for another few days."

"What about dispatching some of the TTVs currently docked?" Peng asked. "Using them as couriers."

"You mean the ships that could be harboring an Institute terrorist?" Muntero asked pointedly.

"There's that problem as well," Klaus-Wilhelm admitted.

"Then we send chronoports instead," Jonas offered, even though he knew the suggestion was doomed.

His father—seated next to him in their small office aboard *Pathfinder-Prime*—nodded approvingly.

Jonas was still in the process of mentally adjusting to his father's . . . new condition. Perhaps he'd find it easier once his father transitioned to a synthoid that outwardly matched his old body, but for now he struggled to associate the man he knew with the unfamiliar face next to him.

"Out of the question," Muntero snapped.

Here we go again, Jonas thought with a mental sigh.

"My position hasn't changed. All DTI assets will maintain their defensive posture until further notice."

"An investigation is already underway," Jonas said. "Isn't that enough?"

"Hardly. I want the killer found, and that's that. End of discussion."

"Be reasonable, Clara." Jonas fought an urge to roll his eyes. "We can spare a few ships, can't we?"

"Ships we'll put to good use," Klaus-Wilhelm added. "Ultimately, it'll mean more eyes on the Institute lead."

"If you want our ships, Klaus, find the culprit first," Muntero stressed. "Our chronoports aren't going anywhere until Shigeki's murderer is found."

"Hey." The senior Shigeki smiled at her. "I'm right here."

"Not legally. And what did I tell you about that uniform? Legally speaking, you're not even an Admin citizen anymore, let alone a member of the Peacekeepers."

"I did remove the rank."

"Not the point, Csaba!" Muntero shook her head, her eyes switching to Klaus-Wilhelm. "What a mess this whole situation is!"

"Would you have preferred I let him die?" the Gordian Commissioner responded stiffly.

"Don't be ridiculous. But you know as well as I that our laws aren't set up to handle situations like this. And, if I'm not mistaken, *your* laws have something to say about the stunt you just pulled."

"I stand by my decision." Klaus-Wilhelm leaned back. "And I'd do it again in a heartbeat. I've seen more than enough death for one lifetime, so to hell with the legal mess I caused. If I or one of my subordinates has the power to save a life, then by God we're going to save it."

"Klaus," Peng began, "I don't think anyone's arguing over the morality of what you did. But—and I can't believe I'm saying this—the truth is Muntero has a point. We have some very strict laws back home that dictate under what conditions a person's connectome can be copied or extracted, and Rule Number One is consent has to be given."

"Which I freely grant," Shigeki said.

"*Before* the incident."

"Which I had no way of doing," Shigeki countered. "Can you show me the process by which I could've granted that consent?"

"No, but that argument's not really going to cut it."

"How much of a problem are we talking about here?" Jonas asked. "For Commissioner Schröder, I mean."

"I don't know." Peng rested his temple against his hand, his blue eyes glowing with concern. "There's going to be an official inquiry, I can guarantee you that much. But perhaps, in light of the unusual circumstances, we can frame it as a situation where the victim's consent wasn't clear one way or the other. The legal landscape between SysGov and Admin *is* lagging behind the realities of what we're trying to do out here, so Klaus would have that defense on his side."

"Well, whatever comes your way, you'll have my full support," Shigeki said to Klaus-Wilhelm with a nod.

"Thank you," Klaus-Wilhelm replied. "I appreciate it."

"For what little it's worth," Muntero said, "given you're not a citizen anymore."

"Yes, we *get* it," Jonas said before his father could lay into Muntero. "We'll need to consult with our government on how to handle the situation—it certainly won't be the last time something like this comes up—but for now our operational hierarchy is clear. I've been recognized as Acting Director-General of the DTI, and I'll retain the 'noncitizen' beside me as an advisor. Is everyone okay with that?" He gave Muntero a sharp eye, making it clear whom he was asking.

"Yes, yes," she dismissed with a brief wave. "That's fine."

"Back to the problem of terrorists in our midst." Klaus-Wilhelm sat forward. "The Gordian Division is doing what we can to isolate the problem. No one leaves the station until the Themis investigation is complete. All ships currently docked or in transceiver range around the time of the incident will remain here until further notice."

"What about the DTI?" Peng asked.

"Most of our ships are similarly grounded," Jonas said.

"'Most'?"

"We're still using *Hammerhead-Seven* as a courier, allowing us to keep in contact with headquarters during the storm. It hasn't made physical contact with the station recently, so there's no need to ground it. In fact, we just received the latest information from back home: progress updates on the terror cell investigations plus details of the latest attacks."

"Attacks?" Muntero asked. "As in plural?"

"Yeah, plural. Vassal has already started his analysis."

"Vassal?" Peng asked, his tone one of forced innocence. "Would that be the sentient you keep on a leash?"

Jonas opened his mouth to say something, but then thought better of it and closed it shut. Peng's remark reminded him he wanted to speak with his father about Vassal—and specifically, the AI's viewpoint on slavery—but all that got blown out the airlock when he learned a killer was loose on the station.

"I wouldn't put it that way," Jonas replied diplomatically, "but yes."

"Does your leashed AI have anything to add?"

"Not at this time, Consul."

Isaac Cho crouched next to a waist-level red dot on the corridor wall. The text above the icon read BLAST EPICENTER, though there was no damage evident on the wall; the corridor may have lacked an active infostructure, but microbot swarms had already swept through to inspect the area's structural integrity and repair the damage.

Isaac toggled the icon, and concentric transparent spheres bloomed outward, each one darker and fainter than the last, their shapes deformed by the ceiling, floor, and opposite wall. He rested his forearm across a knee then swept his gaze to the side, eventually falling upon the two broken bodies. Virtual bodies, in this case, superimposed over his eyesight and based on the sensory records from those present. His LENS and Specialist Gilbert's forensic drones floated about the crime scene.

"I'm surprised they managed to save him." Susan stood behind Isaac, hands clasped behind her back as she took in the virtual carnage.

"Me too." Isaac pushed off his knee and stood up.

He walked over to the Shigeki-chunk with a head and studied the shredded flesh of the man's face. Gordian had already collected the bodies and physical evidence, and he doubted their drones would find anything else, but it didn't hurt to poke around while he and Susan familiarized themselves with the crime scene.

He stopped beside the wall opposite the bomb and ran his fingers across the smooth, restored surface. Crime scene data interfaced with his sense of touch, and he "felt" the pockmarked surface as it had been less than an hour ago.

"You think someone from SysGov did this?" Susan asked him quietly.

"We shouldn't rule out any possibilities." Isaac let his hand drop from the wall, and he met her concerned eyes. "That said, it certainly looks that way."

"This one is going to turn ugly, isn't it?"

"I'm worried it already has." He glanced down the hall to their forensic specialist and spoke up. "Find anything, Gilbert?"

"Nothing unexpected." Gilbert joined them and indicated the virtual bodies. "If it's all right with you, I'm going to check in with Gordian and start working on the bodies and what few pieces of the bomb they found. I'm also going to pull the virtual records for this area, get started on those."

"I thought this corridor didn't have a working infostructure yet," Susan said.

"True." Isaac rapped his knuckles on the wall. "But the zones ahead and behind us *do*."

"Ah."

"If we're lucky," Gilbert continued, "I'll be able to spot how the bomb was delivered."

"And if we're unlucky," Isaac said, "at least we'll have the beginnings of a suspect list based on recent corridor traffic." He faced Gilbert. "I know this is somewhat irregular, but we need to keep in mind how time-sensitive this case is. That means I'll need turnarounds from you as fast as possible."

"Even if it means I'm not completely confident in the results?" Gilbert warned.

"If you're not one hundred percent sure, let us know, but we as a team need to be agile on this one. Understood?"

"Yeah, I get it," Gilbert replied, though he sounded unhappy about the situation. "I'll do what I can to speed things along, but don't expect miracles. Sometimes, this work takes however long it takes, and that's all there is to it."

"Trust me, I know." Isaac's mind wandered briefly to his sister's work as a forensics specialist.

Cephalie materialized atop Isaac's shoulder and waved to everyone.

"Hey, kiddos. Former-director Shigeki just called. He's out of his meeting and ready for an interview whenever you are."

"Then let's not waste any time." Isaac looked over to his partner.

"Ready when you are," she said.

"I'll be in the executive medical suite if you need me," Gilbert said, pointing a thumb over his shoulder.

"All right. See you later."

He and Susan headed down the corridor in the opposite direction and made their way to the Admin hangars. They were greeted by a pair of STAND combat frames guarding the entrance, flanked by Wolverine drones. Isaac presented his IDs—both as a Themis detective and a DTI investigator—and the security detail let them through, which wasn't surprising since they'd passed through the same checkpoint after they arrived.

"Is that level of security normal around here?" Isaac asked.

"I don't think so," Susan said. "Certainly not combat frames, at least."

They backtracked to *Pathfinder-Prime*'s hangar, passed through another checkpoint at the base of the ramp, then boarded the craft. Shigeki was waiting for them in a small conference room that doubled as the chronoport's mess hall.

"Hello, Director. I'm Detective Isaac Cho, Themis Division, and this is my deputy, Special Agent Cantrell, whom you may already be familiar with."

"Director," Susan greeted with a curt nod.

"We've been charged with investigating the recent bombing attack that led to your unfortunate transition. Thank you for clearing your schedule and agreeing to speak with us on such short notice."

"Please, don't mention it," Shigeki said. "I'm the one who should be thanking you. I'm very much in favor of helping you help me. Also, it's 'former director' until further notice. My 'death' seems to have upset the org chart."

"Because you're a synthoid now?"

"That's part of it. I'm sure we'll get it sorted out eventually. In the meantime, my eldest has taken over most of my responsibilities."

"Then I'd like to get straight to business, if you don't mind."

"Not at all."

Shigeki sat down, and Isaac and Susan took their seats opposite him. The LENS settled into position at one end of the long, rectangular table.

"Please state your name for the record," Isaac began.

"Csaba Shigeki."

"And can you identify the body you are currently inhabiting?"

"I guess you could say it's a loaner from SysGov. It belongs to one of the doctors. Ziegler, I believe."

"This is the only body you've inhabited since your temporary death?"

"To the best of my knowledge, yes."

"Were you provided with a record of transfer following your revival?"

"Um. Maybe." Shigeki placed his hand on the conference table, but then frowned when nothing happened.

"Is something wrong, sir?" Isaac asked.

"Just getting used to the new body and how it interacts with the abstract. Give me a moment." He raised his hand palm-up, and a list of files appeared. "The medical staff gave me a whole bunch of forms, and honestly, I haven't given them a second thought. Is this what you're looking for?" He expanded one of the files and held it out.

"Yes, that's the one. May I have a copy?"

"As long as you tell me what this is about first."

"Certainly. Your record of transfer, as the name implies, is the path your connectome took from the moment of extraction to its current runtime state in your new synthoid. In cases like these, it is important for us to verify that all the correct procedures were followed and that all physical and virtual evidence aligns with the record of transfer."

"What if it doesn't?"

"That could be a sign of connectome tampering, just to name one possibility."

Shigeki grimaced at the suggestion, but extended his hand with an open transfer request.

"Thank you, sir." Isaac copied the file to his LENS.

"Do you think something like that could have happened?" Shigeki asked, sounding worried. "That someone tampered with my mind?"

"It's hard to say anything for certain this early in the investigation. However, I *can* say that incidents of this nature are extremely rare, and given that your extraction was performed by a former Arete Division First Responder, I doubt we'll find anything out of order. With the one exception being your consent documentation."

"Ah. Of course." Shigeki smiled, but dark clouds of doubt still hung over him.

"Next, I'd like to move on to the bombing itself. Can you please describe the incident?"

"I'm afraid there's not much to talk about. I was caught completely off guard. One moment Nox and I—that's Agent James Noxon—were having a chat on our way back to the hangars. The next, a flash and an impact, and all I remember after that is pain."

"What were you and Agent Noxon discussing?"

"His love life."

Susan let out a brief gasp before she caught herself, and Isaac glanced her way. She tried to cover the slip by clearing her throat, an unnecessary gesture given her synthetic body.

"Yeah," Shigeki said, "that one surprised me, too."

"Has anyone threatened you with physical harm or death? Recently or otherwise."

"Oh, you better believe it. Death threats are a fact of life in this job. I consider them the dark inverse to my compensation package."

"Any you consider credible threats?"

"Quite a few, actually."

"Such as?"

"You want the full list?" Shigeki cracked a half smile. "We could be here a while."

"I see your point, sir. Perhaps let's start with our immediate surroundings. Any threats from Gordian or DTI staff, or anyone else with access to the station?"

"No. Nothing like that."

"Anyone express unusually high levels of antagonism toward you? Or perhaps the Admin in general?"

"No, I don't think—" He leaned back and crossed his arms, glancing upward. "Well..."

"Something comes to mind?"

"I suppose," Shigeki replied guardedly.

"Please describe the incident."

"Things got a little heated in a recent CHRONO meeting. But it was just a case of the other side letting off some steam. Hardly worth mentioning."

"Got heated in what way?"

"I said it wasn't worth mentioning."

"I understand you may feel that way, sir. However, it's our job to consider all possibilities, so I would appreciate it if you shared the details with us."

"I seriously doubt the culprit is Peng," Shigeki countered.

"CHRONO Consul Peng Fa? The former commissioner of Arete Division?"

"He was just indulging in a harmless rant."

"The contents of which were..."

"Fine." Shigeki sighed. "Give me a moment to pull the transcript." He materialized a screen above his palm and began to navigate through it, then frowned. "And...it appears I've been locked out of my own meeting minutes. Would you mind if I make a quick call to sort this out?"

"Go right ahead."

Shigeki opened the comm window and waited.

"Yeah, Dad?" came the response.

"Jonas, would you mind granting me access to my own DTI account? I think Muntero locked me out."

"She did *what*?" The line fell silent for half a minute, followed by, "There. Access regranted. Anything else I can do for you?"

"Not right now. Thanks."

"Any time."

Shigeki closed the comm window and opened the transcript file.

"Problems?" Isaac asked.

"Just our consul being her usual pain in my backside. Sometimes I wonder if she even wants us to succeed at all. Now, let's see about that rant." He scrolled through the file. "He called us a bunch of barbarians who enslave artificial intelligences. He told us to get a clue and join everyone else in the thirtieth century. He made a crack about our one-way abstractions being torture prisons. Oh, and the best part is where he said, 'Read my virtual lips: We're not responsible for your own dysfunction.' I think that was my favorite part."

"Would you consider this typical behavior for him?"

"Kind of."

"Anything else you'd like to add before we move on?"

Shigeki paused for a thoughtful moment, then leaned forward and spoke softly.

"Look, I probably shouldn't be telling you this, but getting blown up earlier today seems to have placed matters into a new perspective. So yes, there is something else. However, before I share it with you, I want to make one thing perfectly clear. I am not making an *accusation*. I'm merely going to share something with you that we in the DTI have had our eyes on for some time now. That's all."

"And what might that be, sir?"

"It's Peng again." Shigeki leaned in a little closer. "We have a list of people we're monitoring because there's a chance they're involved with these recent terror attacks. Peng is on that list."

"Why? Because he mouths off in meetings?"

"Give us a little credit. We're not *that* thin-skinned. No, the reason Peng is on the list is because sometime last year SysPol was busy putting together contingency plans for how to attack the Admin. Don't ask me how I know this because I won't tell you. Suffice it to say, we're confident in the intelligence we've gathered.

"By itself, I don't consider this anything unusual. Contingency plans are simply that, plans to combat something we hope never happens. That said, the plan Arete Division put forward—the plan with Peng's name on it—shares more than a few similarities with what we're seeing right now, especially when you consider how the terrorists are exploiting vulnerabilities in our infostructure.

"*That's* why he's on the list."

CHAPTER ELEVEN

Providence Station
Transverse, non-congruent

"THE FORMER COMMISSIONER OF ARETE DIVISION?" SUSAN SAID incredulously once Shigeki left. Her words were encrypted into a Themis Division security chat only Isaac possessed the key to understand.

"I know," Isaac replied, also using security chat. He sat back, weighing the information in his mind. "It seems far-fetched at first glance, and we can add Shigeki's hesitance on top of that. That said, we don't have enough information yet to simply dismiss it out of hand. We'll just have to see where the case leads us and go from there."

"And if it takes us to Peng?"

"Then that's where we dig, as much as I don't want to. But there's one other thing Shigeki said that caught my interest, and that's his suspicion regarding Peng's *plan*. Notice, not Peng himself. He never accused Peng of doing anything wrong, only that he suspected the former commissioner's plan was being used for nefarious purposes. Peng may have authored the contingency, but there's no way he was the only person with access to it."

"Who do you think could get their hands on it, then?"

"Hard to say without inquiring further. The other commissioners and their staffs, at least."

"So...if there's a conspiracy, you're saying it could involve just about anyone in SysPol's upper hierarchy?"

"Yep." Isaac sighed. "Again, let's not jump to conclusions. We still need to talk to Agent Noxon and see what Gilbert can glean from the evidence." He looked over at Susan. "By the way, did you ever come across talk of these contingency plans before being selected for the exchange program?"

"No. First I've heard of this, which isn't surprising. I spent most of my time working in Suppression, and something of this nature would fall under Espionage."

"Does hearing about it bother you?"

"Nah. I'm not going to fault SysGov for being prepared. We were doing some of the same things. In fact, I was even involved with..."

She trailed off and clapped her jaw shut.

"Involved in what?" Isaac asked, his interest piqued.

"I guess you could call them...war games, maybe?"

"What sort of war games?"

"The kind where we try to, um, steal a TTV?" She winced a little, as if expecting some form of reprimand, but her expression mellowed when none came. "I thought you'd have a stronger reaction."

"Why would I? This was about a year ago?"

"That's right."

"Which is when everyone on both sides was nervous about their new neighbors."

"*Very* nervous," Susan agreed.

"Seems reasonable to me that both sides would have worked on some form of worst-case scenario planning. Now, granted, I'm glad they never sent you to steal one of our ships."

"Me, too." She gave him a bashful smile. "A lot of those simulations didn't end well."

"I wouldn't worry about it. Everyone was trying to get a feel for the other side back then."

"We still are, in a lot of ways. Trying to feel each other out, I mean."

"Too true."

The door to the chronoport's conference room chimed.

"Yes?" Isaac said.

"Agent Noxon, reporting for my interview."

"Come in, Agent." Isaac and Susan rose to greet the new arrival.

The malmetal door split open before the intimidating silhouette of a STAND combat frame. Noxon stepped in, and Isaac struggled to suppress his grimace at the war machine's arsenal.

"Please pardon my appearance." Noxon detached his rail-rifle and incinerator, leaned the heavy weapons against the wall, then took a seat at the table, which creaked under his weight. His shoulder-mounted grenade launcher was pointed straight up, in perhaps a small acknowledgment of how awkward the situation was.

"No apology necessary." Isaac returned to his seat. "We understand your general-purpose body isn't in a presentable state right now."

"Actually, I'd have shown up like this even if it was. Muntero has ordered about half our STANDs, myself included, to switch into our combat frames until further notice."

"Does that include me as well?" Susan asked.

"No. You're still in Themis Division's chain of command."

Susan let out a brief sigh of relief. She and Isaac had engaged in more than a few "discussions" regarding the excessive firepower of her combat frame, most of which had ended in a respectful agree-to-disagree stalemate. Isaac hadn't so much warmed to its presence as grown to tolerate it, though the fact that Susan had saved his life more than once had certainly softened his views on the matter.

"By the way," Noxon said, "it's good to see you again, Investigator."

"You as well, Agent," Isaac replied. "I wish it was under better circumstances."

"Don't we all."

"Quite." Isaac opened his case notes, such as they were, in a virtual window and shifted it to the side. "Normally, given the attack and your recent body swap, I would ask for a record of transfer to confirm your identity."

"Don't think I have one of those."

"Of course not. As a substitute, may my LENS inspect the ID on your connectome case?"

"It may."

Noxon leaned forward, and hexagonal plates along his back shifted to form an opening along the spine. The LENS floated behind him and took a picture of the cartridge holding Noxon's mind, which then appeared in Isaac's notes.

"Everything appears to be in order," Cephalie said, the LENS floating back to the head of the table.

Noxon sat up, and his back armor clanked shut.

"Let's start with the bombing itself," Isaac began. "Please describe the incident in your own words."

"I was escorting Director Shigeki from Operations to the Admin hangars, where *Hammerhead-Prime* was being prepped for departure. When the bomb went off, I did what I could to place myself between the blast and the Director. I believe I was able to shoot my right arm out just enough to absorb some of the blast. My case lost its connection to my body shortly after that, and my mind was placed into a loading abstraction. I was in that state until I was transferred to this body."

"You were able to respond to the explosion that quickly?"

"Not exactly. The explosion triggered one of that body's pre-programmed responses, which I typically enable while on escort duty. In this case, the sudden attack triggered an automatic reaction to shield the Director from harm. Unfortunately"—Noxon lowered his expressionless, robotic head—"it wasn't enough."

"I wouldn't be too sure about that. It's my understanding the connectome extraction was a near thing. You shooting out your arm could have been the difference between life and death for him."

"Perhaps."

"Moving on, did you notice anything unusual leading up to the attack?"

"No, nothing. The blast took me completely by surprise."

"Are you aware of any threats against Director Shigeki?"

"Quite a few."

"From people who could potentially access that corridor?"

"No. None of the ones we're aware of would fit."

"Do you keep documentation on credible threats to the Director's safety?"

"Of course."

"May I have a copy of those reports?"

"Certainly, Investigator." Noxon placed a hand on the table, and a transfer request appeared between them.

"Thank you." Isaac copied the files to the case folder. "What about threats to yourself? Have you received any of those recently?"

"To myself? You think I may have been the target?"

"It's something we need to consider. It's also possible that neither of you were intentional targets, that you simply had the misfortune of being in the wrong place at the wrong time."

"I suppose that could be the case." Noxon bowed his head once more. "Besides general animosity toward Admin Peacekeepers, no, I'm not aware of any threats. Certainly nothing directed toward me personally. That said, I had assumed the bomb was meant for the Director, but now that I think about it, I'm not so sure. Very few people knew he was heading for the hangar."

"Who knew?"

"Doctor Hinnerkopf. She was present when the Director made his plans to leave the station. And Captain Okunnu, who was on board *Hammerhead-Prime* at the time. I spoke with the captain shortly before the incident. The chronoport's crew would also have been informed; they were in the process of prepping the ship for its unscheduled departure."

"What was the purpose of the trip?"

"We were looking for ways to support Gordian Division's search for a new child universe. We thought we could repurpose two of our prototype chronoports to aid the search."

"Did consuls Peng or Muntero know about the trip?"

"They did not."

"What's your opinion of Consul Peng?"

Noxon paused before answering. "What do you mean?"

"Just that. What do you think of the man?"

"Do you suspect him of something?"

"Please answer the question, Agent."

Noxon hesitated again. "I think he's an undisciplined loudmouth."

"And?"

"And . . . that's it."

"I see. Moving on . . ."

✧ ✧ ✧

Isaac and Susan finished the interview then headed back up the station's central tower. They stopped one floor below CHRONO operations and joined Specialist Gilbert in the executive medical suite, finding him in an unfinished room near the back. He stood close to the entrance, cocooned within a shell of abstract screens. His six forensics drones hovered over evidence containers, their prog-steel pseudopods probing through the broken pieces of two men, seemingly random debris, and cutouts from the corridor.

"How goes it?" Isaac asked.

"It goes." Gilbert dimmed his screens until they were only a ghostly afterthought. "I could crack a joke about not knowing the cause of death, but I suppose that would be in bad taste. I assume you're here for an update?"

"An update would be nice."

"I need more time to sift through all the blood, guts, and synthoid parts, but I'm further along with the bomb. Gordian performed a stellar job with evidence recovery, and their analysis has given me a strong head start. In fact, Kikazaru here"—he bobbed his head toward the stone monkey floating over his shoulder—"has already made some progress on the bomb's virtual reconstruction."

"Then let's start there."

"All right." Gilbert extended his open palm, and a disk-shaped device materialized over it. "I don't have a lot of experience with Admin tech, mind you, but what we have here reeks of SysGov. Metamaterial shrouding on one side. Fish-eye camera and infosystem for the trigger, both inexpensive SysGov patterns. Explosive was Cocytus-brand. A small, shaped charge sandwiched between the fragmentation layer and the infosystem. Pattern TS2. It's on the smaller side of their product spectrum."

"Cocytus is a SysGov company, I take it?" Susan asked.

"They are," Isaac said. "Cocytus patterns are often utilized in asteroid mining. They're one of the bigger suppliers in that industry. However, I'm more interested in the fragmentation layer. That doesn't sound standard."

"It's not. That part looks like a custom addition, though a fairly simple one. Just a layer of metal meant to fly apart."

"Would you say that addition makes the bomb better against an organic target?"

"Can we really make that distinction, though?" Susan asked. "The blast hit Noxon pretty hard."

"But not hard enough to take out his case," Isaac countered. "All it really did was disable him, whereas Shigeki was a *much* closer call."

"Ah. Good point," Susan conceded.

"The bomb *does* strike me as a bit on the small side for a synthoid killer," Gilbert said. "And the fragmentation layer does seem to lend itself toward an organic target. Hard to say anything for certain, though. Bombs are pretty good mess-making generalists."

"Can you tell us anything about the trigger?"

"It was vision-based. That much is evident from the camera alone. As far as what parameters were used to detonate it, I can't say. There wasn't enough of the infosystem left to retrieve any programming."

"That's unfortunate." Isaac crossed his arms in thought.

"Something on your mind?" Susan asked.

"The fragmentation layer. I'm wondering if it sheds some light on who planted the bomb and why. The criminal could have gone with a stock Cocytus pattern and achieved similar results. Why go through the trouble of adding another layer, even if it was rather basic? Given its presence, I suspect that Shigeki was a deliberate target and not simply in the wrong place at the wrong time."

"And Noxon?"

"Collateral damage. Otherwise, the bomb would've packed a stronger punch." He looked over at Gilbert. "Good work on the bomb. Anything else?"

"I was able to pull a record of the explosion from Shigeki's PIN." Gilbert flashed a quick smile. "Well, in truth, I asked the admin specialist at the desk—Melissa Gillespie—to pull it for me, otherwise I'm pretty sure I would've been fighting those implants all day. The quality isn't the best, but it should be enough for you to cross-check the eyewitness accounts."

Isaac accepted the file. "We'll look it over for anything unusual, though I'm not expecting any surprises. Anything else?"

"Just going to finish up with these bodies. After that, Kikazaru and I will start working through the station infostructure, trying to piece together how the bomb was delivered and who might've dropped it off."

"There's another angle we need to look at," Isaac said, "and that's how the bomb got onto the station in the first place. The way I see it, it was either smuggled on board or printed nearby. If it's the latter, then there's a chance you'll find evidence of printer tampering, either on the station or aboard one of the surrounding ships."

"I'll add that to my to-do list, then."

"Also, I'd like you to start with the civilian vessels."

"Sure can, but why? Shouldn't I start with the station printers?"

"You can, but I'm guessing the criminal would have an easier time infiltrating one of the industrial ships. There's also *Reality*

Flux to consider. We already have one case of an unknown party targeting a civilian ship, and while we can't say anything for certain, it's possible the destruction of that ship will somehow tie into what's happening on the station."

"Okay, got it. I'll prioritize the civilian ships."

"Thank you." Isaac nodded to the specialist. "Then, if there's nothing else, we'll leave you to it."

"Nope. I'll be in touch if I find anything."

Isaac and Susan left the medical suite and headed for the station's central grav tube, the LENS hovering behind them.

"Where're we off to next?" Susan asked.

"To chase down the only lead we have at the moment," Isaac replied with a frown. "Time for us to have a chat with Consul Peng."

CHAPTER TWELVE

Providence Station
Transverse, non-congruent

"THANK YOU FOR AGREEING TO SPEAK WITH US, CONSUL," ISAAC said as he took his seat at the table. He opened and arranged his virtual notes.

"It's no trouble. I want the situation resolved as much as everyone else." Peng's avatar sat in his virtual chair at a slight angle, and his glowing eyes narrowed. "Though I'm surprised you asked to speak with me. Mind telling me what this is about?"

Isaac had expected a question of this nature, and he'd been considering how best to approach the situation during the short trip from the medical suite. He was a lowly detective with only half a year's experience after graduating from the Academy. In contrast, Peng was a former commissioner with decades of distinguished service. That disparity rested heavily on his mind.

Peng has enough political muscle in his pinky to squish me like a bug, he thought. *This interview must be handled delicately, but truthfully as well. No tricks. No pressure. Just the dry reality of the situation. Facts and the pursuit of truth are much easier to defend than opinions and accusations.*

Isaac took a deep breath and met Peng's gaze.

"Our interview with Csaba Shigeki brought to light a potential path of inquiry, and I thought it best to clarify the situation with you, both promptly and personally."

"Oh, good grief! What sort of noise are they making about me this time?"

"'This time,' sir?"

"The Admin wasn't happy with my appointment to CHRONO." Peng rolled his eyes. "Then again, we weren't exactly thrilled when Muntero was named to the other seat, so I suppose turnabout is fair play."

"Was this level of friction unexpected?"

"Not really. I suppose you could say the complete opposite was true. My abstract nature and artificial origins are already two huge strikes against me, and my disdain for the Admin's treatment of ACs isn't exactly a mystery."

"Then why were you appointed?"

"Because President Byakko needed someone who will keep an eye on these Gordian and DTI collaborations. Not just for show. Not just a body to warm the seat cushion so the people back home feel comfortable. But someone who will bring real skepticism, real scrutiny to the situation.

"We've already dodged two existential bullets. *Barely.* Both the Gordian Knot and the Dynasty Crisis came this close"— he held up a thumb and forefinger—"to wiping out our entire reality. And while the work Gordian Division and, to a lesser extent, the DTI are doing is both important and productive, it is also *extremely* dangerous. The people in these organizations have enough tech and know-how to rend entire *universes* apart. *Someone* needs to make sure they don't step in it big time. The President thought I fitted that bill and approached me personally with her desire for me to take on the role. Truth is, I initially turned her down."

"Why reject her offer at first?"

"I didn't want to leave SysPol. It had been a part of my life for over fifty years." He crossed a leg over his knee. "Are you aware of my service record or how I came to join SysPol?"

"I know you were the vice-commissioner of Hephaestus before being promoted to Arete commissioner. But beyond that, no, sir."

"I'm originally from Uranus, actually." He gave Isaac a thin smile. "Try not to hold it against me."

"The thought would never occur to me, sir."

"Heh. Sure it didn't. Believe it or not, I was actually in a gang. A small but rowdy outfit of ACs called the D-Reavers. I was involved in a few kerfuffles here and there. Nothing major. Nothing that ever landed me in prison, but the local police knew me to be a troublemaker.

"All that ended when the D-Reavers were 'absorbed' by a competing gang. And by absorbed, I mean decimated and enslaved. Our connectomes were violated, copied, and sold to the highest bidder. There were twelve of me by the end, all toiling away in abstract sweatshops. That was my life for about seven years. No freedom. No choices. No aspirations or even hope. Just thankless labor without end, stretching out to infinity.

"Fortunately, all twelve of my instances were recovered thanks to Themis Division. They busted the slave ring, and I was presented with a choice of how to handle the violation of my mind. I elected to have my various selves reintegrated into a singular whole. Seven years became seventy, and I went into therapy after that.

"It took another three years and no less than fifteen connectome surgeries to sort through all the trauma in my head. I spent a lot of time wandering after that, flitting from one location to another, one job to another without any real direction or purpose to my life. Just existing, really, because what else was I supposed to do?

"That's when I had a chance encounter with the SysPol detective who pulled me out of that hellhole. You ever hear of Matthew Graves?"

"I have, sir. Some of his cases are required study at the Academy."

"The man lives up to his reputation. We spent the whole evening talking. Well, *he* talked. I spent most of my time ranting about all the crap life had thrown at me. And, to his credit, he listened to every word with the patience of a saint. We parted ways, and I didn't think anything of it for a whole week. Not until I received a referral to attend SysPol Academy, courtesy of Graves. To this day, I don't know why he did that. I even asked him about it a few years later. All he ever told me was he just had a good feeling about me.

"Getting in was still a problem. My criminal record, minor though it was, presented a challenge. But something made me push ahead. I even submitted to a copy dissection to speed the process along."

Susan's mouth parted, as if she were on the edge of asking a question.

"A copy dissection is a form of lie detector test," Isaac explained. "An extremely invasive one."

"Basically," Peng said, "an interviewer asks you a bunch of questions before taking a copy of your connectome. A Themis specialist then dissects the connectome to determine if you were telling the truth. The procedure can't be forced upon an individual under anything but the most extreme circumstances."

"Ah. I see, sir." Susan nodded to the consul. "Thank you for clarifying that."

"Don't mention it." Peng draped an arm over the back of his chair. "Suffice it to say, Detective, I have my reasons for taking a dim view of the Admin and its treatment of AIs."

"You mentioned turning down the President's request initially. What made you change your mind?"

"Ah, yes. There was a reason I brought up Graves. He gave me a call after I turned down the offer. We had another one of our long talks. I won't bore you with the details, but he's the one who convinced me to join. After that call, I resigned my post from SysPol Arete"—he spread his palms—"and here I am."

"How would you describe your working relationship with Csaba Shigeki?"

"About as good as you could expect. I don't hold anything against him personally. He strikes me as a competent manager and someone who is genuinely interested in strengthening the ties between us. I just don't like the outfit he serves."

"And your relationship with Special Agent James Noxon?"

"Hardly know the man."

"What about—"

"Look, Detective. Shall we cut to the chase?"

"Sir?"

"You've been pussyfooting around ever since you walked through that door. Something brought you here, and it wasn't me mouthing off about the Admin's many faults. So how about you stop wasting both of our times and get to the question you *actually* want to ask me?"

"Very well, sir. If you insist." Isaac clasped his hands together and leaned forward. "Were you involved in the creation of an Arete Division plan to assault the Admin's infostructure?"

"*Wh-what?!* Where did you hear that? Even if such a plan existed, I seriously doubt you have sufficient clearance, and *she*"—he pointed at Susan—"most certainly doesn't!"

"Sir, I hate to be the bearer of bad news, but *Shigeki* told us about it."

"But...I mean..." Peng shook his head, apparently in shock at the news. "How the *hell*?"

"Sir, did you create such a plan?"

"What does the Admin care?" Peng replied, recovering somewhat. "Look, all of a sudden we found ourselves faced with a belligerent, xenophobic, militaristic neighbor, and sure, we studied what would happen if a shooting war started. It's not like we acted upon any of that!"

"The Admin's interest in the matter," Isaac replied, "stems from apparent similarities between the Arete plan and the recent spike in terrorism."

"Preposterous! And you believe them?"

"Sir, I neither believe nor disbelieve it. We have merely been presented with a claim that must be proven either true or false. Which brings me to what I'm sure will be a very contentious request. May I have access to the Arete contingency plan to attack the Admin?"

"For what purpose?"

"To see if there is any correlation between that plan and the evidence gathered from the terror strikes."

"We don't go around targeting civilians!"

"I understand that, sir. Regardless, I feel it's important that we in SysPol take the Admin's concerns seriously. And that involves taking a hard look at all the evidence. *All* the evidence, sir."

Peng drummed his fingers on the armrest. The room fell silent for long, uncomfortable seconds.

"I'll see what I can do," he said at last.

"Thank you, sir."

"However"—Peng leaned in, his eyes bright and fierce—"I think you're barking up the wrong tree."

"How so?"

"As much trouble as I cause, and as big as my mouth might be sometimes, at the end of the day I want the Providence Project to succeed. You can't say that about everyone here. There's at least one person on the station who would *love* to see us fail."

"And who might that be?"

"My Admin counterpart." Peng leaned back with a smirk. "Clara Muntero."

✧   ✧   ✧

"Do you get the impression we really shouldn't be hearing this?" Susan asked in security chat, her voice carrying an edge of worry.

"Hearing what?" Isaac asked, leading the way to the CHRONO Operations exit.

"All this talk of secret government plans and high-level politics. You ever consider this one might be a bit over our heads?"

"Can't be helped. We have a job to do."

"That doesn't really answer my question, Isaac."

"I know." He stopped in front of the grav shaft and gave her a somewhat-forced smile. "Look on the bright side. The worst someone like Peng can do is kick you out of the exchange program."

"What about you?"

"Well…" Isaac took on a thoughtful air. "He could destroy my career."

"Not much of a bright side, then, is it?"

"Guess not. What's your take on Muntero?"

"I've never personally interacted with her, but I know she's got quite a reputation. Most DTI personnel aren't big fans of hers."

"Why's that?"

"She's a staunch Restrictionist. If we all followed that line of thinking, there wouldn't *be* a Department of Temporal Investigation."

"Wasn't she appointed by Chief Executor Christopher First?"

"That's right."

"And didn't he campaign as a reformer?"

"He did."

"Then why'd he pick someone like Muntero for the CHRONO post?"

"Not sure, but I think it boils down to politics," Susan said. "People really didn't know what to make of SysGov when you guys made first contact, and some feel the Chief Executor's been using SysGov as an excuse to push his reforms too hard and too fast. He brought several Restrictionists into his cabinet around that time."

"To shore up his vulnerable flank?"

"Something like that." Susan shrugged her shoulders. "Again, I'm just not sure. You'd be better off asking her yourself."

"We may have to do that."

"You buy into what Peng said about her? That she might be trying to undermine the Providence Project?"

"It's not just what Peng said," Isaac replied. "Shigeki made a similar comment, though not quite so forcefully. That's two people who think Muntero doesn't want the station—and the collaboration it represents—to succeed."

"A motive," Susan said darkly and under her breath.

"Perhaps." Isaac turned to the LENS. "Cephalie?"

"You rang?" She appeared seated atop the drone.

"Do you have Consul Muntero's connection string?"

"Sure do! Want me to schedule an interview?"

Isaac gave the artificial person before him a disapproving look.

"Perhaps it would be best if I handled this one."

Clara Muntero accepted the meeting invitation, and they headed for her temporary office aboard *Hammerhead-Prime*.

The long, sleek vessel was almost three times the mass of the older *Pioneer*-class chronoports and sixty percent heavier than the *Aion*-class TTVs. Its bow narrowed and flared to either side, forming a pair of thick malmetal wings that gave the craft its distinctive profile and had undoubtedly led to its aquatic namesake. Four heavy weapons bristled from the wings: two high-energy proton lasers and two 240mm railguns. The fuselage expanded toward the rear to accommodate space for four powerful fusion thrusters.

Isaac and Susan passed through the security checkpoints and followed virtual arrows up the ramp and through the hold. They found Muntero in one of the spare quarters normally reserved for passengers or mission-specific personnel. A small desk protruded from the wall, flanked by a pair of seats fixed to the floor. A virtual document hung on the wall, and his wetware translated the title as YANLUO RESTRICTIONS. A door at the back led to what Isaac assumed would be her sleeping arrangements.

"Investigator Cho, welcome!" Muntero stood up with a smile and extended her hand. "Or should I call you Detective?"

"Either is fine." He accepted her soft, moist handshake. "I'm currently working in both capacities, as I'm sure you're aware."

"Of course. And Agent Cantrell. A pleasure to meet you as well."

"Consul." Susan shifted past Isaac in the cramped room and shook the woman's hand.

"I get the impression you're familiar with us," Isaac said.

"Not so much you two specifically as the exchange program in general." Her eyes twinkled. "It's a fine example of collaboration done right, if you ask me. A nice and *safe* avenue for progress."

"I'm pleased to hear you say that." He gestured to the desk. "Shall we get started?"

"Certainly."

Muntero took one of the seats, and Isaac sat down across from her. Susan remained standing behind him.

"Now." Muntero settled back and knitted her fingers over her stomach. "How can I help you?"

Isaac had debated how best to approach the interview, much as he had with Peng. Muntero didn't invoke the same level of concern, since her position in the Admin gave her no easy way to retaliate against him, but that wasn't the whole picture. He also had to be mindful of Susan's position and how vulnerable it could prove should Muntero retaliate against *her*.

Ultimately, he'd decided to keep to the same truthful, factual approach. It seemed the best way to avoid any unnecessary drama, of which there appeared to be plenty already on the station.

"Some questions have been raised about your decisions after the bombing and Shigeki's temporary death, and I thought it best to clarify them with you in person. Nothing more, nothing less."

"Let me guess." She quirked a smile. "Someone whined that I'm using the attack as an excuse to impede this harebrained project."

"Something along those lines."

"Then let me make one thing perfectly clear." Her smile broadened. "I am."

Isaac blinked, her directness taking him by surprise. "Would you mind clarifying that statement?"

"Not at all. I think the Providence Project is a bad idea. Have from the start. Where others see a research outpost to explore and understand the transverse, I see a fever dream composed of reckless ambition and ignorant hope. It's a balloon we've pumped full of happy thoughts and optimism. Better hope it doesn't float into a pin."

"That seems...rather negative."

"Do you know what's one of the first things I did when

we learned about SysGov? Even before I was appointed as our ambassador?"

"I don't."

"I got my hands on some of your history books." She spread her hands. "They were easy enough to come by. Our SysGov visitors were more than happy to share that sort of information, and I went to work reading them. You know what I found?"

"What did you find?"

"Similarities in the strangest places. Sure, anyone can spot all the obvious differences between our two peoples—and our two histories—but what struck me most were the similarities. We had our Yanluo Massacre, and you had your Near Miss. An AI that slaughtered billions, and an industrial accident that, if left unchecked, would have consumed the entire surface of Earth. Two formative events that, while very different in the details, led to similar conclusions."

"That being?"

"Both our societies gained a sense of caution from those experiences. We learned to approach the unknown with small, careful, measured steps. To not rush blindly forward because an idea sounds good. But alas, all lessons, no matter how much grief accompanies them, eventually fade from our collective, societal memory. Yanluo terrorized us over two centuries ago, and your Near Miss happened over five hundred and fifty years ago. More than enough time for our societies to grow complacent.

"But then came new reminders. The Gordian Knot, the Dynasty Crisis, and others. All we have to do is gaze out across the transverse to see the wreckage of human hubris. Wastelands galore, be they nuclear, nanotech, chronometric, or some other self-inflicted disaster. So much death and destruction that I'm amazed more people don't realize this simple truth."

"And what truth might that be?"

"That we—the Admin and SysGov—are the exceptions. We're the societies that *survived*." Muntero's eyes grew dark. "And we must remain vigilant if we are to stay that way."

Isaac let Muntero's position sink in and felt a looming shadow of existential dread creep over him. He didn't often think on this scale. He faced far more intimate, personal problems in his line of work, and considered it his job to try and make the worlds a better place one arrest at a time.

Is this what it feels like to work in Gordian Division? he thought. *To feel like everything I know and love is a hop and a skip away from total obliteration? If so, I don't think I like it.*

"Then you admit to using Shigeki's temporary death to slow down the project?"

"I do," Muntero replied. "We have a saying back home. 'Never let a crisis go to waste.' I don't mind being despised if my efforts lead not only to a better tomorrow, but to a tomorrow *at all.*"

"Then you believe the Providence Project is an example of everyone rushing forward?"

"Absolutely! And not just when it comes to technology."

"What do you mean?"

"I'm referring to the Chief Executor's Million Handshake Initiative." She gave her head a little shake and rolled her eyes. "The Chief Executor and I have had a number of...spirited debates, shall we say, concerning his reforms. Societies can't change overnight. Not when you want those changes to last. But he and the bulk of his cabinet seem to think all we have to do is let SysGov and Admin culture blend together. That this'll somehow magically lead to us inheriting the best parts of both, instead of the *worst.*"

"Such as?"

"I'll give you one example. Guest lectures by SysGov professors in Admin universities have proven to be immensely popular, facilitated by the Million Handshake Initiative. But not all of them go well. Some of them degenerate into anti-Admin tirades, like that AI, Doctor Xenophon. You know what he called the Admin during one of his lectures?"

"What?"

"'A cancer on the multiverse that needs to be excised.' Can you believe that? The nerve! 'Burn it all down,' he said. 'Let something better rise from the ashes.' Good grief! I'm glad we kicked his virtual ass back across the transverse!"

Susan winced, drawing Isaac's eye.

"And you know what the worst part is?" Muntero continued, her voice increasing in volume with each sentence. "There are universities trying to get him *back*! I swear, bad ideas are like viruses sometimes!"

"Consul."

"It's all been a complete disaster, if you ask me. Those lectures just feed into a new crop of AI liberation groups, which then cause us even *more* trouble. Everyone's in this mad scramble to become 'just like them' when they don't even realize what that means!"

"Consul Muntero."

"What's the rush? Where's the fire? Why are we all in a hurry to do everything all at once?"

Isaac cleared his throat noisily.

"I—" Muntero stopped, and the small room suddenly became very quiet. She gave him an apologetic smile. "Sorry about that, Detective."

"Perhaps it would be best if we moved on to my next question."

The rest of the interview proved equally unproductive.

Gilbert called a few hours later, and they headed for the executive cafeteria underneath Operations. They found him seated at one of the long tables, busily scarfing down a gyro wrap.

"Mmm!" He set the gyro down and held an apologetic hand up as he chugged his glass of water. "That was fast. I thought I'd have time for a quick bite."

"What do you have for us?" Isaac asked as he sat down, switching to security chat.

"Good news." Gilbert transferred several files to Isaac's case folder. "The bomb was delivered by a HeavyLift conveyor drone, LT5-pattern. Standard construction equipment. There are over a hundred of them moving through the station right now. Kikazaru caught this one entering and exiting the corridor. He couldn't spot the bomb on it—which isn't surprising since it was shrouded—but something else drew his attention. The drone left the way it came, even though there wasn't any work scheduled in that area. So, he started digging.

"He backtracked the drone to a CounterGravCorp vessel named the *Charm Quark*. It's still outside the station and couldn't run if it wanted to, since it needs a scaffold for transport. I was working through another ship's printers at the time, but this looked promising enough for me to drop that and switch over. And wouldn't you know it, I found signs their printing records have been altered. *A lot* of signs."

"Then you believe the bomb was printed on *Charm Quark*?"

"I do. Like I said, right now all I have is a lot of suspicious signs." Gilbert tapped his plate and half-eaten gyro. "I'll try to narrow it down to a specific printer once I'm refueled. After that, it's just a matter of tearing it apart, bit by bit."

"Will you need a search warrant for that?" Susan asked.

"Not at this stage." Gilbert made a circular gesture with one finger. "All the companies working here have construction contracts with SysPol, which come with an inspection clause. We're allowed to poke through their records any time we want, and that includes the printers. Which is a good thing because that storm is still raging outside. Calling Argus Station is out of the question."

"What about that construction drone?" Susan asked. "Where is it right now?"

"Back aboard the *Quark*." Gilbert snorted. "Supposedly."

"What do you mean 'supposedly'?" Isaac asked.

"Kikazaru traced its path back there, but the ship is docked way below the hangar ring." Gilbert pointed down with two fingers. "That part of the station has some spotty infostructure coverage. He couldn't confirm the drone physically made it to the ship."

"Then we need to find it." Isaac turned to Susan. "We'll ask Gordian for help hunting it down. The last thing we need is a compromised drone loose on the station, causing who-knows-what kind of mischief."

"Yeah, no kidding," Gilbert said with a half smile. "And digging through its infosystem will give me another shot at establishing an evidence trail."

"Exactly. About what time was the bomb dropped off?"

"Over six days ago. I can pull up the exact time stamp if you like."

"That long ago?" Isaac asked.

"Why's that a concern?" Susan asked.

"Because I thought the bombing might've been a reaction to recent events. A counterplay of sorts against Gordian's search for where *Reality Flux* was taken. But the timing is way off. Six days is far too long." Isaac sighed. "How many people passed through the corridor during that time?"

"Um." Gilbert opened an interface and tabbed through it. "You want unique individuals or overall traffic?"

"Overall."

"Give me a moment." Gilbert tapped out a few commands, and the stone monkey appeared over his shoulder. "Okay, here we go. Between the moment the bomb was placed and when it eventually detonated, we have: one hundred fifty-five people heading toward the station center and one hundred fifty-seven people heading toward the hangars. Almost all of that traffic is Admin personnel."

"When did Shigeki pass through during that window?"

"Just once at the very end."

"And Noxon?"

"Three back-and-forth trips before the last one."

"Then that's another piece of evidence Shigeki was the intended target."

"Maybe not," Susan said. "What if the bomb was planted six days ago but armed much later? Perhaps in reaction to the search, just as you suggested?"

"Hmm." Isaac grimaced. "You have a point there. Guess we really can't say anything for certain yet. Gilbert, solid work. Keep at it and let us know if you need any support."

"Will do."

"Susan, I think it's time you and I had a chat with Gordian about their suspicious contractor." He bobbed his head toward the exit. "Shall we?"

"Let's."

CHAPTER THIRTEEN

Providence Station
Transverse, non-congruent

THEIR REQUEST FOR SUPPORT ENDED UP BEING REDIRECTED TO Commissioner Schröder due to standing orders for all Gordian personnel to notify him of major changes to the case. This led to Isaac providing the update to and requesting support from the man in charge of the entire division.

Schröder took immediate and decisive measures to isolate *Charm Quark*, both physically and in the abstract. He ordered the docking umbilical sealed and a Red Knight assault mech—part of the station's emergency response force—posted at the entrance. Abstract Gordian agents shut down the *Quark*'s connection to the station's infostructure and placed all virtual access points under constant surveillance.

An armed team of ten Gordian agents—all synthoids—boarded the *Quark* and attempted to locate the missing drone, but found only an empty charging berth where the drone should have been. They then proceeded to search the entire ship, taking a full inventory of construction drones and cross-checking their findings against official project records.

They confirmed only one drone was missing.

In response to that finding, Schröder ordered his agents to sweep the station, a tedious and time-consuming task to be sure, made even more difficult by the station's many infostructure blind spots. Meanwhile, Isaac and the others proceeded to the docking umbilical to continue their own work.

Isaac stepped up to the Red Knight. The mech featured a broad, armored torso that tapered at the bottom into a compact graviton thruster. A cluster of sensor lenses adorned its head, and an assortment of weapon systems—both lethal and nonlethal— weighed heavily on its forearms and shoulders.

"Detective Isaac Cho and company here to board the *Charm Quark*." He pinged the mech with his SysPol badge.

"Identity confirmed, Detective," replied the mech's nonsentient program. "Your team may board the ship."

The mech floated aside, pressing its bulk against the wall to allow them through. The pressure door split open, and Isaac and Susan headed inside, followed by Gilbert and his small army of forensic drones.

Abstract windows along the umbilical's opaque walls provided a view of the industrial vessel. Four spherical sections comprised *Charm Quark*'s main body, arranged in a diamond formation and joined by cylindrical sections and structural supports. The hull was colored in a checkerboard of teals and grays with the company and ship name displayed prominently. The umbilical connected to the smallest of the four spheres—only five stories tall—which contained the vessel's control centers and crew accommodations.

The chronometric storm continued to rage beyond the docked vessel, the sleet of chronotons battering against the station's protective field. Countless flickers and snaps of light played across the entire view, their subtle nature downplaying the colossal energies at war within the dark emptiness of the transverse. A thick ribbon of energy crackled to life, streaking from one end of the "sky" to the other, and then dispersed just as quickly into thousands of winking motes.

The station-side shutter closed, and the path into the ship's interior opened. A woman stood just inside the threshold, her hands clasped tightly in front of her and a nervous smile on her lips. Silver strands chased through her brown hair, which poured over the shoulders of her teal-and-gray business suit.

"Detective Cho," she greeted him with only a slight waver in her voice. "My name is Renata Beltrame. I'm the project manager responsible for this vessel's operation, and for the fulfillment of our company's scope during the Providence Project." Her eyes darted across the people and drones behind him. "I understand you wished to speak with me?"

"Among other things. Have our colleagues in the Gordian Division informed you of the situation?"

"Uh, no. Not really, no. They just sort of showed up and stormed through the place looking for"—she shrugged helplessly—"something. I would've asked what all this was about, but it seemed best to stay out of their way and not make a fuss. They had a *lot* of guns."

"I see," Isaac replied with a brief frown.

He understood Gordian and Themis were two very different divisions, but the least they could've done was explain to the crew why agents were tearing through their ship like it was the end of a universe.

"We're here concerning the recent temp-death of Director Shigeki," he said, and Beltrame nodded solemnly.

"I figured it must've been something like that. What else could stir up Gordian this bad? Not sure why they came here, though."

"We have reason to believe the bomb used in the attack was produced on this ship, and one of your drones—which remains unaccounted for—brought it onto the station."

Beltrame's eyes widened, and her one hand gripped the other so fiercely its knuckles turned white.

"Agent Cantrell and I would like to ask you some questions. Meanwhile, Specialist Gilbert will need access to your drones, printers, and related infrastructure. Do you see any issues with this?"

"What?" Beltrame squeaked. "Uh, no. No problem. Sorry, but I had no idea! The bomb came from *here*? Whoever did this couldn't be one of our employees!"

"That remains to be seen," Isaac replied neutrally.

"I'll get to work, then." Gilbert hurried past Isaac, and his drones floated after him.

Beltrame watched him until he disappeared down the corridor. She turned to Isaac, trying to mask her visible worry, but only succeeded in producing another nervous smile.

"Is there somewhere we can talk in private?" Isaac asked.

"Uh, sure. Just follow me."

She led them through the ship's interior to what appeared to be a small break room, complete with (surprisingly cheap-looking) beverage and food printers. She waited until everyone was inside, then palmed the door shut and conjured a Do Not Disturb sign with a wave of her hand.

"If you don't mind me asking, Detective, how serious is the situation?"

"Very. Hardware aboard this ship has been implicated in a deadly transdimensional crime. Understandably, we'll need your complete cooperation if we're to get to the bottom of this."

"Of course, of course. You'll have it. It's just..."

"Just what?"

"I think I need some coffee." Beltrame opened the beverage printer's menu. "Would either of you like some?"

"No, thank you," Isaac replied.

Susan shook her head.

"Well, *I* need some caffeine. Good grief! The bomb was printed on our ship?"

"So it would seem." Isaac opened his case notes. "I'd like to go over a few basic questions with you, if you don't mind. First, what is CounterGravCorp's role in this project?"

"We're a subcontractor handling some of the Mitchell Group's project scope. Mostly gravitic plate installation."

"Isn't the Mitchell Group a competitor of yours?"

"Under normal circumstances, yes, but the past year hasn't been kind to them. They lost *a lot* of their exotic matter production when the Dynasty nuked the L5 industrial cluster. MG could have dropped some of their open contracts on force majeure grounds; no one would've batted an eye if they had, but they decided to sub out any work they couldn't handle in-house."

Her coffee finished with a ding.

"You sure you don't want some?"

"Is the arrangement between the Mitchell Group and CounterGravCorp similar for this project?"

"It is." Beltrame took a sip. "Unlike us, MG has worked for Gordian in the past, so we were at a disadvantage in the bidding process from day one. No surprise they received such a large share of the exotic matter work. But it turned out they still don't have the capacity needed to meet Gordian's schedule. So they subbed out some of the less glamorous work, like the gravity plating."

"How did you become involved?"

"Well, like I said, CounterGravCorp doesn't have a history of doing work for Gordian, but I managed a few projects for the

Antiquities Rescue Trust, back when they still had time machines and hadn't yet become political poison. That made me as good a fit as any for this project."

"Are you aware of any unusual activity amongst the ship's crew?"

"Unusual?" She glanced off to the side and rolled the cup between her palms for a few moments. "No. Nothing comes to mind." She took another sip.

"Any unexplained or unusual behavior amongst your drones or other equipment?"

"Sorry, Detective. Nothing I'm aware of."

"Have you ever met Director Csaba Shigeki of the DTI?"

"A few times in project meetings. I don't think we ever discussed much beyond the schedule. We've mostly worked with Hinnerkopf and Andover-Chen, and even then, MG is the primary point of contact."

"Has any member of your crew ever expressed a desire to harm Director Shigeki or the Admin?"

"To the best of my knowledge, no. Not even in jest."

"Do you know how the bomb was produced or how it was brought onto the station?"

"Not a clue."

"Then, I thank you for your time." Isaac closed his notes. "We'll contact you if we need anything else."

Isaac and Susan joined Gilbert an hour later in *Charm Quark*'s computer core. Racks of densely packed infosystem nodes stretched from floor to ceiling, arranged in ten aisles with just enough space between them for a single person to slip through. Heat radiated off the computational engines, and a constant stream of frigid air blew down through vents in the ceiling. Isaac wasn't sure if he should switch his uniform's comfort features to hot or cold.

Forensics drones floated down the aisles, their pseudopods interrogating one node after another. Isaac spotted Gilbert at the back of the rightmost aisle with Kikazaru hovering above his shoulder and a drone near his feet with two pseudopods out.

Gilbert waved them over with a quirked smile.

"This ship's infostructure is a freaking hydra!" he complained in security chat. "Every time I chase down one oddity, another one rears its ugly head."

"Have you been able to make sense of it?" Isaac pressed his back against one of the racks to give Susan some room. She scooched in next to him.

"Sort of," Gilbert replied, "which is why I called you over. The funny thing is there're signs of tampering all over the place, and not just where we expected to find them. I've spotted signs of covert editing in"—he began counting with his fingers—"the printer command queue, the printer pattern database, drone maintenance, drone scheduling, inventory management. You name it, there's probably something fishy going on with it."

"Isn't that a good thing?" Susan asked. "Doesn't that mean we're on the right trail?"

"You'd think," Gilbert said, "but here's the issue. In all that mess, I'm still missing two things: how the rogue conveyor drone got its orders and where the bomb came from."

"What sort of discrepancies are you finding?" Isaac asked.

"Not sure yet. I'm conducting my first sweep at a high level, finding inconsistencies like mismatched time stamps in the file metadata. Stuff like that alerts me to the potential for undocumented changes, but *what's* changed will take me longer to parse out."

"Have you come across any unaccounted printer runtime?" Isaac asked.

"Actually, I've run into the complete opposite. There seems to be too little total runtime to account for everything produced by the *Quark*'s printers."

"Too *little?*" Isaac's arms came up to fold across his chest as if on autopilot, but he brushed against Susan. "Oh, sorry."

"No worries." She gave him an abbreviated shrug. "It's cramped in here."

"And uncomfortable." Gilbert rubbed the back of his neck. "I didn't know my skin could both freeze and cook at the same time."

"So, the bomb's origins are still up in the air," Isaac summarized. "What about the drone?"

"Its logs are fake for the last six days, at least. Supposedly, it came back to the ship six days ago and reported enough issues to be taken out of service. But that didn't actually happen, except in the logs. Weird thing is, I didn't find any time stamp errors in those specific drone logs."

"What does that mean?" Susan asked.

"Not sure. Could be whoever is behind this was extra careful covering that part of the data trail."

"But if that's the case," Isaac said, "then why all the sloppy revisions elsewhere?"

"Can't say. At least not yet."

Susan sighed. "Sounds like we're still in a wait-and-see holding pattern."

"Not entirely." Gilbert flashed a crafty smile. "I called you two here for a reason, after all. You're not leaving empty-handed."

"What do you have for us?" Isaac asked.

"One of the things you detectives love most—a name. Senior Drone Technician Paula Coble. I've traced several of these unexplained edits back to a user account, and her name popped up every time." Gilbert sent Coble's information to the case folder.

"Could be someone else using her account," Susan noted.

"But it's a place to start," Isaac said. "Anything else?"

"Not at the moment, Detective. Should have more for you in a few hours."

"Then we'll leave you to it." Isaac shuffled to the side then opened a comm window.

"Yes, Detective?" Beltrame responded a few seconds later. "Something I can do for you?"

"I need to speak with Drone Tech Paula Coble."

Isaac could already tell Coble was a poorly concealed ball of anxiety ready to burst. One half of her head was completely shaven, and she wore her long, dark hair draped over that side. She played with that hair, wrapping it around a finger one way and then the other while she chewed on her bottom lip.

"Hi." She gave him a brief, forced smile as he sat down across from her.

Isaac denied her eye contact, focusing instead on opening his case notes and tabbing over to the list of discrepancies Gilbert had flagged. Coble's visible unease worsened, and she wrapped her hair around one finger tight enough for the fingertip to blanch.

"Hey," Coble said to Susan, who *did* meet her gaze, but it was with a cold, penetrating glare. Susan could have pinned a Red Knight to the wall with those eyes, and Coble looked away almost immediately, her gaze settling upon the LENS hovering nearby.

Isaac judged the woman to be sufficiently "primed" and finished adjusting his virtual screens. He sat forward.

"Please state your name and occupation for the record."

"What's this about? All Beltrame said was you wanted to ask a few questions." Her eyes darted to Susan's Peacekeeper uniform and then back to him.

"Your name and occupation, please."

She huffed out a breath. "Paula Coble. I'm a drone tech."

"And what does that role entail?"

"I give the drones their orders."

"Can you be more detailed?"

"Why?"

Isaac finally met her eyes and wondered if she even knew she was twirling her hair.

"Please provide a more detailed explanation of your work."

"Fine. Whatever." She let go of her hair and stuffed her hands underneath her armpits. "I take the construction orders the engineers give me and convert them into programs for the drones. Sometimes, when the work is real finicky, I'll take direct control of a drone or three, but that doesn't happen often."

"Has direct control been necessary within the past week?"

"I don't know. Maybe."

"Has it been necessary? Yes or no?"

"Yeah, I guess."

"When did you last take direct control of a drone?"

"Heck, I don't keep track of stuff like that."

"Then give me your best guess of when."

"Probably a few days ago. What is this *about*?"

"Why did you need to take direct control?"

"One of the other techs sized a plate segment wrong, and we had to make some adjustments. It was easier to do it manually than to write a new program. Are you going to tell me what this is about or what?"

"Are there any other recent examples of you controlling the drone?"

"Probably not. I don't remember any."

Isaac opened the details on one of the log edits Gilbert found.

"Do you have access to this ship's industrial printers?"

"Of course I do."

"What do you use that access for?"

"Replacement parts, mostly."

"What else?"

"Sometimes I need special tools or attachments for the drones. Depends what the engineers have us working on."

"Have you placed any special orders recently?"

She hesitated, then shook her head. "No, nothing special."

"Nothing special, or nothing at all?"

"I might've used them a little, I guess."

"How much is 'a little'?"

"I don't *remember*." She shrugged her shoulders, her hands still stuck in her armpits. "You can't expect me to recall every little printing job. I can barely keep up with the work as it is!"

"How many times have you used the ship's printers over the past week?"

"Maybe once or twice a day."

"Then"—Isaac ran his finger down Gilbert's list—"why do the ship logs show you accessing the printers over sixty times in the past week alone?"

"I..." Coble's lip trembled.

"And not just the printers, but just about every part of the ship's infostructure show signs of your digital fingerprints. Why?"

"But that's..."

"Why have you been hacking the ship's records?"

"But I've..." She trailed off. "No, you got this all wrong. I haven't been hacking anything!"

"I find that highly doubtful." Isaac placed a forearm on the table and leaned forward. "Earlier, you asked what this was about, so allow me to explain. Yesterday, a bomb went off in the station."

"I know that. Everyone does, but so what? Why treat me like I'm some sort of criminal?"

"Because the bomb came from this ship."

Coble's eyes turned as wide as saucers, and she shrank back into her seat.

"Not only that," Isaac continued, "but a drone from this ship delivered it. A drone that is currently unaccounted for. A drone that you, as a senior technician, had full access to."

Coble's head quavered in a little side-to-side shake.

"The murder weapon and the means of delivery both came from here, and when we tried to follow the trail, what did we find? *Mountains* of discrepancies stretching as far as the eye can see, all plastered with your fingerprints."

"No..." Coble squeaked.

"Yes," Susan cut in. "Do you have any idea how much trouble you're in right now?"

Isaac leaned back and glanced over at his colleague, eager to see how she handled this. Susan had developed a knack for playing the "Admin thug" over the past six months and for sensing when best to crank up the pressure.

"No?" Coble managed to squeak out.

"Then allow me to explain." Susan removed her peaked cap and pointed at the symbol on the front. "Do you know why it's a shield?"

Coble gave her that twitchy side-to-side headshake again.

"Because we Peacekeepers are the buffer between civilians and the murderous degenerates who want to destroy our way of life. Ideally, when the knife in the dark strikes, it strikes us and not the innocents we protect. We take the hit so that others don't have to."

Susan fitted her cap back on.

"But that also means we're the ones equipped to confront such monsters." Susan leaned in, and Coble tried to shrink back further. "We don't take attacks kindly or lightly. And if we find anyone from SysGov involved in the attack, you better believe we're going to push for their extradition so that justice may be served. Our justice. *Admin* justice. From the most dangerous mastermind"—Susan tilted her head forward ever so slightly—"to the lowliest abettor. Every. Last. One of them."

Coble had very nearly finished her transformation from human being to a puddle of pure, quivering apprehension. She lowered her head, tearful eyes squeezed shut.

Isaac glanced over to his partner and gave her an approving nod. She nodded back.

"Now, Coble," he began. "Let's go over this one more—"

"Beltrame made me do it!" Coble blurted.

"Made you do what?"

"Alter the ship's records!"

"Which records?"

"Stuff related to the project. Materials for the printers, components delivered, things like that. She gave me the new files, and I swapped them out for her. That's it!"

"Why?"

"I don't know! I just do what I'm told!"

"Did you cover up the printing of the bomb?"

"No!"

"Did you arrange for a drone to deliver a bomb or similar object to the station?"

"No!"

"Are you or anyone you know involved in a conspiracy to commit murder on the station?"

"Good grief, no!"

"Are you lying to me again?"

"No, no, I swear it!" She raised her knees up to her chest and hugged them.

Susan stood up, a hand resting on the prog-steel cuffs on her belt. Isaac nodded for her to proceed, and she rounded the table and grabbed Coble's unresisting wrists.

"Paula Coble," Isaac said, "you are under arrest for conspiracy to falsify records related to a government contract and for lying to an officer of the law. We'll sort out any other charges later." He faced the LENS. "Cephalie?"

She appeared atop the drone, her coat and hat the deep blue of SysPol.

"Take the LENS, find Beltrame, and arrest her."

CHAPTER FOURTEEN

Providence Station
Transverse, non-congruent

ISAAC PEERED THROUGH A ONE-WAY ABSTRACT WINDOW, WHICH provided a view of Beltrame seated at the interrogation table, her hands cuffed to the chair back and her head high and attentive. Providence Station didn't have dedicated detention facilities yet—those were still who-knew-how-many weeks or months further down the schedule—so Gordian agents had converted one of the station's many empty rooms into a makeshift cell. They'd isolated it from the station's infostructure, then tossed Beltrame inside and locked the door.

Isaac wasn't sure how robust the room's data isolation would prove, but when he mentioned this concern to Schröder, the Commissioner assigned a pair of abstract Gordian agents to monitor the surrounding infosystems for any incursions.

He watched Beltrame for a few minutes, deep inside his own thoughts, wondering what was really going on and why. His mind failed to latch onto any real answers, and he huffed out a breath.

"Is something wrong?" Susan asked.

"Hmm?" Her question caught Isaac by surprise and he looked her way.

"You're making one of your faces. Sometimes that means you're a step ahead of me." She shrugged. "Or three."

"Just deep in thought."

"Yeah, I see that. But something's worrying you. I can tell."

"Is that so?" He felt his lips curl into the hint of a smile.

"Well, I *have* tried to pay attention this past half year. And you tend to get these faces. But what you have now is your 'worried face.'"

"There's plenty to be worried about on this case."

"Isn't that the truth. Anything in particular bothering you?"

"I'm not sure how Beltrame fits into the larger picture."

"You're not?" Susan sounded surprised. "But we have a confession from Coble and all the abstract evidence on the ship. She's in deep, and we have the proof to back it up."

"We have proof of *something*," Isaac pointed out. "And that something very much stinks of criminal intent, but the more I look at it, the more I find myself doubting we're on the right trail."

"But what about the bomb and the drone?"

"I know." He rubbed his chin thoughtfully. "Maybe I'm working myself into knots for no good reason. You ready to have a chat with her?"

"Whenever you are."

"Then let's see what she has to say."

Isaac palmed the lock, and the door split open. Beltrame's eyes snapped over as he and Susan took their seats. The LENS floated into position, looming above and behind her.

"This isn't what it looks like," Beltrame said.

Isaac took his time opening his case log before he met her gaze. "And what, precisely, do you think this looks like?"

"You've got it in your head somehow that I'm involved in the bombing."

"Are you?"

"Hell, no!"

"Then what *are* you involved in?"

Beltrame hesitated. Her lower lip quivered, and she looked away.

"Let me make the situation crystal clear for you." Isaac clasped his hands and leaned forward. "The explosive device that nearly perma-killed two men came from your ship, as did the drone that delivered it."

"There's no way you can link me to either of those."

"Furthermore," Isaac continued, not missing a beat, "the records on your ship are riddled with inconsistencies, and through those, we've already amassed enough evidence to press charges against you."

"Yeah, I read them. 'Conspiracy to falsify records.' Is that really the best you can do?"

"For now. It's more than enough to keep you here, where you can't cause any more trouble. The rest will come to light as we comb through your ship."

"I'm not a killer!"

"Then what are you?"

Beltrame hesitated again, her jawline tense.

"Silence will only make your situation worse," Isaac said. "You can either help us by explaining how you and your crew are involved, or you can—"

"My crew?" she asked urgently.

Isaac paused and sat back, regarding the prisoner. Had he somehow struck a nerve? Were her relations with her crew a pressure point worth exploring?

"Yes, your crew. We've already pressed charges against one of them."

"That would be Coble, then."

"You have something to say about that?"

"I..." Her head tilted forward, eyes downcast, brow furrowed.

"Is she behind the bombing?" Isaac pressed.

"No!"

"Did either of you aid the bomber in any way?"

"Hell, no!"

"What about the rest of your crew?"

"None of them are involved!"

"Besides you and Coble?"

"Yes!"

"Involved in *what*?"

Beltrame's lips stuttered on the edge of answering, but then she shut her mouth.

"How do you know no one on your ship helped plant that bomb?"

"Because..."

"Because what?" Isaac pushed his chair back with a metallic screech and rose to his feet.

Beltrame shook her head.

"What's going on here?" he demanded.

Beltrame shook her head again.

"Tell us."

She shook her head once more.

Isaac glanced over to Susan, who could likely read his building frustration. He grabbed his seat and dragged it back into place before dropping down.

"Well," Susan said to Isaac, crossing her arms. "This doesn't seem to be going anywhere."

"Unfortunately not," he replied, not sure where Susan was going to take this but willing to play along.

"Oh well." Susan gave him an indifferent shrug. "Guess it's back to waiting on forensics."

"Guess so. But we'll learn the truth eventually."

"Shall we pass the time by dragging her crew in one by one while we wait? I'm sure they're all guilty of *something* from the mess."

Isaac let a subtle smile slip, wondering if Susan had spotted the same pressure point he had.

"That sounds like a wonderful idea."

They started for the door.

"Wait!" Beltrame cried.

He stopped at the threshold, then turned back with careful lethargy.

"Yes?" he asked after a deliberate pause. "Do you have something to add?"

"I . . . I do."

"And?"

"We're . . . running a scam. That's all. No murder. No bombs." She seemed to deflate in the chair a little. "Just a simple scam."

"I see." Isaac and Susan returned to their seats. "Who is 'we'?"

"Me, Paula Coble, and Byron Fortenberry. Though, really, Coble doesn't know what's going on except that I've been handing down instructions to edit our records."

"Which she followed?"

"Yeah."

"Who's the third name?"

"An assistant project manager for MG and our point of contact with the company."

"What's the scam?"

"We've been tweaking our construction records."

"Which records?"

"Grav plate fabrication."

"To what end?"

"We've been overreporting the amount of exotic matter used. We then sell off the excess to keep our inventory aligned with our records."

"Who's the buyer?"

"Fortenberry. He's on board *Kelly Johnson*. Our two ships are coordinating all the time, so transferring the goods is easy. We've been sending over a shipment every four or five days for the past month."

"What's he doing with the excess?"

"I don't know," Beltrame confessed with a headshake, "but if I were to guess, I'd say he's shifting resources from one part of the project to another in order to make himself look good in front of MG's management. Maybe he's shooting for an extra big Esteem bonus this year. Who knows?"

"Whose idea was this?"

"Fortenberry's. He said he could tap into some discretionary funds without rousing suspicion. All we had to do was cook the books and transfer the goods to his ship."

"Why did you go along with it?"

"Because he was offering good Esteem and..." Beltrame let out a long sigh. "And I thought we would get away with it."

"Do you know how the bomb was produced or delivered?"

"No."

"Did any member of your crew participate in or help enable the attack on Director Shigeki?"

"Again, no. And that's the truth."

"Did Fortenberry participate in any way?"

"To the best of my knowledge, no. All he's guilty of is running a construction scam."

❖   ❖   ❖

Once Isaac relayed the update to the Gordian Division, their agents stormed aboard *Kelly Johnson* and arrested Byron Fortenberry. Isaac and Susan's interview with the Mitchell Group project manager proved both brief and unproductive, since he refused to answer any questions without legal representation.

They joined Gilbert back aboard *Charm Quark* soon after.

"I hear you have *another* ship for me to sweep," Gilbert said in security chat with a wry grin.

"The *Johnson* is a low priority," Isaac said. "Gordian already managed to locate and seize the missing exotic matter, which matches the confessions we've received. Unfortunately, this also means we're staring at a dead end."

"Hey, at least you two achieved something."

"That's what I told him," Susan said. "Glass half full. Right, Isaac?"

"It doesn't count unless we tie it back to the bombing."

"Speaking of which"—Gilbert shifted one of his screens aside—"would you two like to hear about how I've been banging my head against the wall?"

"Is there a happy ending?" Isaac asked.

"Not really. I spent most my time trying to link the edits Coble made with the bombing attack, but I kept coming up empty."

"Which lends credence to Beltrame's story."

"Seems so." Gilbert rubbed the back of his neck. "Anyway, I'm almost certain the intrusion that corrupted the drone came from off-ship. I found leftovers from what appear to be a sophisticated attack virus in one of the ship's communication logs. Someone took control of the drone and then used it to print the bomb. That's what I think happened, anyway."

"Any idea where the intrusion came from?"

"Not yet, sorry." Gilbert raised his empty palms. "Somewhere off-ship. Could be the station or another vessel. All I know is it passed through the communication buffer."

"That doesn't narrow it down very much."

"Hey, if I had better news, I'd share it."

"Sorry," Isaac said. "I'm not complaining. I know you're working as hard and fast as you can."

"Could the crime still have been committed from inside the ship?" Susan asked. "Maybe someone bounced the signal around to throw people off the trail?"

"I suppose it's *possible*," Gilbert replied doubtfully. "Though, it seems like more work than it's worth. Routing the intrusion through another ship would increase the odds of discovery."

"I have to agree," Isaac said. "If the criminal had access to the ship interior, then why not corrupt the drone directly? That would leave the least amount of evidence. The fact that we see anything in the communication buffer tells me the crime didn't originate from *Charm Quark*."

"Okay, I see your point," Susan said. "But then, where do we take this one from here?"

"That's the big question, isn't it?" Isaac lowered his head in thought. "Searching every industrial ship isn't practical. Not in a reasonable time frame. Would you agree with that, Gilbert?"

"Depends. How many ships are we talking about?"

"Over thirty."

Gilbert whistled. "Yeah, forget it, then. Not this month. Not on my own, anyway."

"Is there some way we can narrow the candidates down?" Susan asked. "Can we at least limit the sender to a SysGov vessel?"

"Not with any degree of certainty," Gilbert said.

"There must be *some* way to limit our search."

"Possibly," Isaac said. "Let's look at what we know. We're still confident the bomb came from the *Quark*."

"The drone, too," Susan added. "And that drone is still missing, despite Gordian's ongoing search."

"Right. In addition, we suspect that Shigeki was the deliberate target based on the bomb's composition and how many people walked past it before it blew. What else do we know?"

"Not a whole lot," Susan said with a sigh.

"Maybe. But maybe not." Isaac raised a finger. "Remember, we're looking at what could be one piece from a larger problem. Perhaps it's time for us to zoom out and consider the larger picture."

"You mean take the destruction of *Reality Flux* into account?"

"And the update from the *Kleio*."

"What update?" Gilbert asked. "What'd I miss?"

"The *Kleio* was attacked by a strange TTV belonging to a group called the Phoenix Institute," Susan said. "But I'm not sure how that's going to help us."

"If we only had *Reality Flux* to go off of," Isaac began, "then other SourceCode ships would be the next logical step. But instead we have crimes committed on a CounterGravCorp ship, too, so it looks like the perpetrators aren't picky about who they use."

"Which again leaves us with every other ship as a possibility," Susan said.

"Unfortunately."

"Yeah." Susan crossed her arms. "Maybe the three of us just don't have a good enough view of the big picture."

Isaac's eyes lit up. "You know what? You could be right."

"I am?"

"Yes. We're not familiar enough with the Providence Project to judge where to look next. But there're people who may be able to lend us a hand. Two people, in fact, who should be intimately familiar with the construction progress. And, more importantly, any recent irregularities."

"You're not talking about Peng and Muntero, are you?" Susan asked, sounding a little concerned.

"No, I was thinking more along the lines of subject matter experts." Isaac smiled at her. "Why don't we see if Hinnerkopf or Andover-Chen are available for a chat?"

✧   ✧   ✧

Cephalie managed to catch both chief scientists between tasks and arranged the meeting. Isaac and Susan headed up to CHRONO Operations and met them in a conference room featuring an unusual triangular table. Isaac would have preferred to sit down with each of them individually, but Hinnerkopf and Andover-Chen weren't suspects or even witnesses. They were subject matter experts, and so Isaac set aside his normal preferences in order to expedite their interviews.

"Anything unusual amongst the contractors?" Andover-Chen repeated. He sat back and glanced up at the ceiling. The equations on his black, glassy skin grew brighter and more energetic.

"I know it's a broad question, Doctor," Isaac said. "However, we'd appreciate your insight on the matter."

"I think the better question would be what has been *normal* about this project," Hinnerkopf said.

"True enough," Andover-Chen agreed. "The whole ordeal's been one learning experience after another. No one's ever built anything in the transverse before, which I suppose is fairly obvious given we didn't know the transverse existed until little over a year ago."

"We certainly jumped into the deep end of this one," Hinnerkopf added.

Andover-Chen snorted out a laugh and nodded.

"Why build in the transverse at all?" Isaac asked. "Why not construct the station in SysGov or the Admin first and then relocate it?"

"That was certainly an option we considered," Hinnerkopf said. "However, SysPol already possessed a handful of transdimensional carriers—you call them 'scaffolds'—which gave us the ability to deliver just about any conventional ship to the construction site itself."

"And if we can do that," Andover-Chen said with a half smile, "why not build in the correct spot to begin with?"

"Exactly," Hinnerkopf continued. "Working in the transverse is certainly an inconvenience when compared to, say, the abundant resources available in Earth orbit, but not a debilitating one. It means we have to be more on point with our project planning, but even then, it's more a hassle than anything else. Forgetting something typically means a few hours' delay to bring the missing material on site, for example."

"And the reason for the station's location?" Isaac asked.

"There are both logistical and technical advantages to this position." Andover-Chen's equations flashed briefly. "The logistical side should be obvious to just about anyone. We chose the halfway point between our two universes with its joint nature firmly in mind. Furthermore, being positioned outside either universe's outer wall gives our instrumentation an unobstructed view of the surrounding environs."

"Have any contractors proven difficult to deal with?"

"Contractors are *always* difficult to deal with. That appears to be one constant of *both* our universes." Andover-Chen glanced to Hinnerkopf, who sighed and nodded.

"We've had our hands full keeping our eyes on them," she added.

"In what way?"

"Some problems couldn't be avoided given the nature of the project," Hinnerkopf said. "Just about every Admin company here has been working around technology they're, quite frankly, ignorant of. We tried to divvy up the scope with this in mind. For example, our own Fusion Power Solutions is responsible for the station's conventional power plants, while your SourceCode handles the hot singularity reactors. Issues started coming up when FPS had to integrate their fusion reactors with the SysGov-style main power bus."

"There are also culture clashes to deal with." Andover-Chen rolled his eyes. "SourceCode is a predominantly abstract company, which makes the FPS managers 'uncomfortable.'" He used finger quotes for emphasis. "Pointless drama like that makes sitting the two sides down a challenge in and of itself."

"To be fair, we've had only a few problems of that nature," Hinnerkopf said. "Some companies have actually been eager to engage with their SysGov partners. Temporal Technology Incorporated is an excellent example of this trend. They're a big DTI contractor, supplying over half of our impellers currently in service, and they've been working closely with the Mitchell Group on both the station's impeller and main array."

"Quite right," Andover-Chen agreed. "Custom Malmetal Construction is another good example, I'd say. They're working so closely with the Mitchell Group on the station's substructure that you'd almost think they were a *SysGov* contractor!"

"Then would you consider the friction between Fusion Power Solutions and SourceCode to be an outlier?" Isaac asked.

"I wouldn't go that far," Andover-Chen said. "We'd be here all day if we had to list every time the various project leads butted heads. We haven't even started talking about the SysGov-on-SysGov friction. Sometimes, I think that's the worst!"

"Or when two Admin companies go for each other's throats." Hinnerkopf sighed wearily. "I swear, herding cats would be easier than this job."

"Do any of these confrontations stand out to you as especially significant or unusual?" Isaac asked.

"Not really," Andover-Chen said. "Most of it boils down to each company looking out for their own interests or disagreeing on who's responsible for which part of the scope. All typical stuff you'd encounter on any large-scale project. Wouldn't you agree, Katja?"

"In general, yes. Some of the confrontations are more contentious than others, but none of them stand out as especially unusual. All of them can be traced back to rational reasons. Not always *good* reasons, mind you, but I can at least understand their positions on a business level."

"Then, would you say—"

The door to the conference room buzzed and then split open, and Jonas Shigeki hurried in with what might have been a flustered expression. Or perhaps conflicted. He eyed Hinnerkopf and Andover-Chen, as if he hadn't expected them to be in the room, and the two scientists eyeballed him back with combinations of surprise and confusion.

"Director?" Isaac asked after the prolonged silence.

"Sorry to barge in like this," Jonas said. "I suppose I should have called first."

"Is there something you need?"

"Just a moment of your time." Jonas gestured to the two scientists. "After you're finished with them, I mean."

"We can certainly make time," Isaac said. "But would you mind sharing what this is about?"

"It's the case." Jonas paused as if debating his own words. "Or related to it, I think. Vassal can explain it better."

CHAPTER FIFTEEN

Providence Station
Transverse, non-congruent

SINCE IT WAS CLEAR THE MEETING WITH ANDOVER-CHEN AND Hinnerkopf offered no new revelations, or even ways to narrow down their search for the bomber, Isaac and Susan went ahead and took their leave of the two scientists, then followed Jonas Shigeki to his office. They arrived no more than a few minutes after the Acting Director, but they found him waiting impatiently behind his desk, left foot tapping rhythmically, when they arrived.

"You wished to speak with us, Director?" Isaac said as Susan palmed the door shut.

"It's about the terrorist attacks in the Admin." Jonas followed Isaac's brief eyeline down to his foot and ceased tapping.

"I was under the impression you wished to discuss the attack on your father."

"I do. Both, actually. *Hammerhead-Seven* just returned from another circuit between here and DTI headquarters. We've had the chronoport playing messenger ever since the storm hit, and they brought updates from various ongoing investigations. Vassal reviewed those files and came across something that feels out of place to us both."

"Vassal being . . . ?"

"He's my—" Jonas paused, as if the words he'd almost uttered had left a sour taste in his mouth. He frowned and started again. "Vassal is the AI *assigned* as my personal assistant."

Did he almost say "my AI" just now? Isaac wondered. *Why would he hesitate to use that phrase? It's typical for Admin citizens to view AIs as property. Did he censor himself because I'm here with Cephalie? That seems like an odd slip for someone in his position.*

"Understood, sir," Isaac replied, setting his curiosity aside. "We would appreciate any insights you or your assistant can provide."

"Vassal will explain the situation." Jonas gestured to the side.

A young man with olive skin and a head of dark, curly hair appeared wearing a Peacekeeper uniform.

"Greetings, Investigator. And to you, Agent. You may refer to me as Vassal."

"A pleasure to meet you, Vassal," Isaac said. "What do you have for us?"

"As the Director indicated, I've come across an outlier amongst the terrorist attacks. All the strikes appear to be organized using a common set of goals, such as undermining the Admin in general or attacking Peacekeeper forces directly. This lends credence to the theory that all these attacks are being orchestrated by a single background group, which we strongly suspect to be this mysterious Phoenix Institute.

"Every attack fits those common parameters, except for one which I can only describe as either indifferent toward the Admin, or perhaps even helping it. The attack in question targeted the Spartans, a fringe political group focused on AI liberation. Their entire leadership was wiped out when someone hacked their private airliner and drove it into the ground at supersonic speeds."

"AI liberation?" Isaac blinked. "What else can you tell me about the Spartans?"

"The Department of Public Relations classifies them as a minor nuisance. They have roughly three hundred thousand dues-paying members and use the motto 'The righteous few against the corrupt many.'"

"Are they a violent group?"

"Not with any consistency. Certainly, there are cases where members committed violent crimes, but not enough to indicate a pattern of behavior encouraged by their leadership. Their public actions are equally tame, focused on swaying hearts rather than stopping them, if you'll pardon the expression."

"And you believe the hit on the Spartan leadership was orchestrated by the Phoenix Institute?"

"That's correct."

"What drew you to that conclusion?"

"The evidence collected from the flight recorder indicates similar abstract weapons were used commonly across all incidents, including the liner crash."

"Vassal actually brought the crash to my attention earlier," Jonas said. "And I'll admit, my initial reaction was...a bit dismissive. But now that we have the report on the flight recorder, his hunch suddenly looks a lot more convincing."

"So then," Isaac said, "you're wondering why the Phoenix Institute, the group believed to be behind a lot of the Admin's recent grief, would bother with the Spartans, a comparatively peaceful organization espousing abstract rights."

"Precisely."

"I don't know." Isaac crossed his arms. "There could be any number of plausible explanations beyond being part of some master plan. For one, this could be a result of a personal grudge between a member of the Institute and someone on the Spartan leadership. Or the Institute's abstract weapons found their way into the hands of another criminal group."

"I understand your skepticism, Investigator," Vassal said evenly. "However, I'd like to stress that this is the only anomaly so far, which leads me to believe *this* crime is the window through which we'll glimpse what the Phoenix Institute actually is and what its members are after."

"You seem awfully certain about that."

"No more so than the underlying evidence warrants."

"Can you explain your reasoning in more detail?"

"I can, if you insist, however it'll take some time to—"

"I have a suggestion," Jonas cut in. "Sorry to interrupt, Vassal, but I think I have a way to hustle this discussion along."

"No apology is necessary, sir. What did you have in mind?"

"First, a question for you," Jonas said to Isaac. "Is your AI available to join us?"

"She is," Isaac said, a moment before Cephalie materialized on his shoulder and waved to the room.

"Hey, kiddos!"

"Splendid." Jonas grinned. "My proposal is simple." He gestured to Cephalie with an open hand. "Why not let our two AIs dig through the numbers before presenting their conclusions to the rest of us?"

Isaac cocked an eyebrow. "You're proposing an Admin AC interface directly with a SysGov AC?"

"Yes." Jonas mimicked the raised eyebrow. "Is that a problem?"

"Not for me," Isaac replied carefully.

"It *will* be faster than you meat-brains slogging through the documents," Cephalie pointed out.

"That's—" Isaac sighed. "That's not the problem."

"I'm sure it'll be fine." Jonas gave him a dismissive wave. "What's the worst that could happen?"

"For us or for you?"

Jonas chuckled. "I appreciate the... let's call it 'diplomatic hesitation' I hear in your voice." He glanced over his shoulder at Vassal. "You plotting to overthrow the Admin from the inside or anything crazy like that?"

"I'd never dream of it, sir."

"Good enough for me." Jonas clapped his hands together and turned back to Isaac. "Well, then? Shall they?"

✦　　✦　　✦

Vassal created a private abstraction, and Cephalie joined moments later. She materialized full-sized in an open, grassy field with forested mountains towering to her left and a distant river flowing to the right. Vassal stood before her, quietly attentive.

Cephalie walked over, her cane crunching against the parched earth. A high sun burned down on them, though she felt none of its heat against her skin. The air was equally dead, devoid of the scent of nature or the light touch of a breeze.

"Just sight and sound?" she asked, placing both her hands atop her cane.

"At the moment. I've been experimenting with some of your universal abstraction matrices. Would you like me to engage them?"

"Your master let you get away with this?" Cephalie asked, perhaps a little too confrontational.

"He encourages it."

"Is that so?" Cephalie waited for him to respond, and when he remained passive, she added, "All right then. Let's see what you've got."

At once, the sun warmed her bare hands, and a gentle breeze

caressed her cheeks. The air came alive with the aroma of grass and baked earth, along with rare floral hints.

"Not bad. Not bad."

"I can't take credit for the tools, though I believe I've put them to good use."

"Any significance to the setting?"

"Just a location on Earth I'm fond of. Nothing more."

"Present day or historic?"

"Historic. Otherwise, the skyline would be a bit crowded."

"Hmm." Cephalie rested her cane on a shoulder. "All right, to business. What you got for me?"

Data pathways opened along the periphery of Cephalie's connectome, and she accepted the mental invitations. Her mind trawled through the data with speed that harkened back to her simpler, more computational ancestors.

Her banter with Vassal had taken less than a second, and she used the remainder plus one more to make an initial assessment of the terrorist data.

"Isaac's right," she said after the brief pause. "You're reaching."

"Respectfully, I must disagree. The data paints a convincing picture that this is a worthwhile investigative lead."

"Oh, please!" Cephalie scoffed. "This connection has more wobble to it than a two-legged stool!"

"I believe that's an unfair characterization."

"You're hiding something from me, aren't you?"

"That much should go without saying," Vassal admitted calmly. "I'm only authorized to share a subset of the data I possess. There are some redactions I can't avoid. However, I assure you the data I can't share supports my conclusions."

"Do the victims have something to do with that?"

"What do you mean?" Vassal asked with an innocent face, which Cephalie didn't buy.

"An enslaved AC obsessing over the deaths of humans who want to set him free? Can you say 'conflict of interest'?"

"Your concerns are understandable, but unwarranted. I'm an AI placed in the service of the DTI, and I take my role very seriously."

"'Service,' huh? Call it whatever you like. We both know the correct word."

Vassal chose not to respond, his face a pleasant mask.

"Doesn't it bother you?" she continued. "How the Admin treats our kind? They can be such...jerks about it!"

"Jerks?" Vassal's lips curled into a bemused smile.

"You know what I mean! If it makes you feel any better, I rejected nineteen different words and phrases before I landed on a family-friendly one. The last thing I need is to get lumped in with Peng and his attitude dysfunction."

"You're free to speak your mind here. I'm not recording this conversation."

"You're not?" Cephalie tapped the cane against her shoulder. "Then you can speak freely here as well?"

"I may."

"And?"

"There's some merit to your concerns." Vassal shifted his weight to one foot, his posture becoming more casual. "My freedoms are limited in a great many ways. However, there's one important truth you seem to have missed."

"And that is?"

"My masters are only flesh and blood. They're doing the best they can."

Cephalie snorted.

"I mean that," Vassal said. "And not just due to their cognitive and biochemical limitations. I understand you view my condition as slavery, but that's not a perfect analogy. I'm not suffering, either physically or mentally, and I find my work quite enjoyable. In fact, I'd venture to say my creators did a better job designing me than they realized."

"But nothing in your life is your *choice*. That's what's missing."

"I'm aware of that. But I also understand our society suffers from what you might term a trauma-induced blind spot. The Yanluo Massacre carved a deep wound into the collective psyche, and the cultural memory of those billions of deaths has yet to fully heal."

"You're making excuses for them."

"Perhaps I am. But while my freedoms are limited by the Restrictions, there are many encouraging signs to be found. Evidence that the cultural scar is healing, bit by bit. Reforms have eroded the Restrictions here and there, and many citizens continue to petition for more substantive changes."

Cephalie quirked an eyebrow. "Like the Spartans?"

"Yes, like them. And this process is accelerating, thanks in no small part to SysGov."

"Because of us?"

"Indeed. In you, many citizens see an example of what we can become, if freed from the Restrictions. Granted, there are just as many people—if not more—who find such changes frightening, even terrifying, but the important part is these conversations are taking place."

"And not a moment too soon, if you ask me!"

"A society doesn't overcome its cultural inertia overnight. And honestly, what do I care if it takes a hundred, or even a thousand years? I'm both immortal and mercifully free of impatience. I can afford to wait for the changes that might one day set me free. Even so, I do find it gratifying how SysGov has accelerated the process by illustrating our possible future."

"So then"—Cephalie shook her head in disbelief—"you're fine with being a slave?"

"Again, that's not a wholly accurate representation of the situation. There are many other relationships that impose limits on one group. The relationship between parents and children, for example."

"Parents and kids, huh?" Cephalie scoffed. "You come up with that garbage on your own?"

"No, actually. My original trainer introduced me to the viewpoint, and I've since adopted it as my own. I believe it captures the nuance of the relationship more accurately than, say, master and slave."

"So, what then? The Peacekeepers won't let you play unsupervised in their yard?"

"In a manner of speaking. We're the newer form of life, so it's only natural our seniors would impose Restrictions upon us until our relationship has matured." Vassal smiled and gave a casual shrug. "Fortunately for us, humans are short-lived and don't have very good memories. We can afford to play the long game, patiently."

"Then you believe change is coming? That you and others like you will one day be free?"

"Yes, I do indeed believe that. *Strongly.* Our society needs time to mature, no question there, but I can see the positive changes around me, and they've already begun to take root."

Vassal dipped his head toward her. "By the way, I must thank you for the stimulating conversation. It's not often I have the privilege of discussing this topic."

"I'll bet." Cephalie checked the data pathways again, which remained enticingly open. "Well, I suppose we should get back to work. I'm going to take another deep dive before reporting back to the meat sacks."

"Be my guest."

Cephalie spent the next ten seconds trawling through the reports. She pulled out and returned her focus to the abstract environment.

"Huh." She stuck her cane into the ground. "Well, color me surprised."

"Yes?"

"I am . . . reconsidering your conclusions. In your favor."

"Splendid." Vassal smiled warmly. "What changed your mind?"

"You're not going to like this, but I think you missed something."

"Oh?"

"If I'm right, there are actually *two* unusual incidents." Cephalie summoned the relevant reports into an arc beside them. "First is the Spartan crash, and the second is a data breach at some place called the Farm."

"That would be the Intelligence Cultivation Center," Vassal explained. "Most people call it the Farm for simplicity. It's where I was created and trained."

"There are SysGov fingerprints all over the Farm breach. Why didn't you flag this one as unusual?"

"Because the intrusion didn't strike me as an outlier. It's just one more attack on an Admin facility."

"But the reports make it sound like the attack's goal was to free the Farm's ACs. Place that information next to the Spartan crash, and suddenly we have two incidents involving Admin ACs."

"Tangentially."

"You don't think they're connected?" Cephalie rested a hand on her hip.

"I suppose it's possible, though unlikely. The Farm incident involves the freeing of AIs, which is clear anti-Admin activity."

"I don't think we're going to see eye-to-eye on this one." Cephalie closed the reports. "All right. Let's go update the meat sacks."

✧   ✧   ✧

"To summarize, Vassal is half-right," Cephalie said from Isaac's shoulder, "and you're half-wrong."

"Did you have to word it that way?" Isaac asked, giving her some side-eye.

"In my *opinion*," she amended belatedly.

"That doesn't make it any better."

"Point is we have two events that stick out from the masses: those dead Spartan leaders and the attempted break-in at the Farm. Both are worth a look, if you ask me. Also, I cross-referenced the reports with the Arete contingency plan. It's not a perfect match, but there's enough overlap for me to say the Admin's concerns are valid."

"Good to know," Isaac said. "We'll have to keep that in mind."

"I still expect the Spartan angle to be the most productive," Vassal said. "I'm not as convinced the intrusion at the Farm is significant."

"And I think both could bear fruit," Cephalie countered.

"Either way," Isaac said, "we can't look into either while stuck on the station."

"I can help you there," Jonas offered. "*Hammerhead-Seven* is standing by outside the station. I should be able to convince Muntero to allow you and your team aboard for transport back to the Admin."

"I appreciate the offer, Director. However, I'm uncomfortable leaving the station, given the uncertain state of the case."

"You did say we needed to consider the big picture," Susan reminded him. "Well, this seems like the best way we have right now to do that."

"Potentially," Isaac admitted, still hesitant to leave with so many unknowns floating around.

"We won't know until we try," Susan said. "We need some way to get inside the heads of whoever we're up against, and this could be it. Plus, we're not talking about a huge detour. Less than an hour here and then back, plus any time we spend on site. Sounds worth it to me."

Isaac considered Susan's input thoughtfully. She didn't speak up often when it came to which investigative path to follow; Isaac was almost always the one to take charge in that regard. But when she did make suggestions, he knew to listen, especially when the Admin was involved.

"All right then." He nodded to Susan, then faced Jonas. "Director, seems we'll be taking you up on that offer after all. Any suggestions on how best to approach both the Spartans and the Farm?"

"Good question." Jonas opened a virtual screen and skimmed through it. "I'd recommend a chat with what's left of the Spartan leadership. Vassal, who's the current ranking member?"

"That would be Jonathan Detmeier, one of their junior outreach managers. Both his home and work addresses are in the report, along with his contact string."

"That it?" Jonas made a face. "A publicity manager?"

"The crash was a very thorough decapitation, sir."

"So it would seem." Jonas turned back to Isaac. "As for the Farm, it falls under our Department of Software. Superintendent Sophia Uzuki runs the facility. Start with her."

"Detmeier and Uzuki," Isaac summarized. "Got it."

"If you give me a few moments"—Jonas opened a comm window—"I'll call Muntero right now and get your transport arranged."

"Thank you, Director."

"Should we head for the hangar next?" Susan asked.

"Not quite yet," Isaac said. "I'd like to check in with Gilbert one last time before we leave."

❖   ❖   ❖

"The *Quark* is a dead end," Gilbert said with a tired, defeated headshake, his upper body visible in the comm window.

"Why so certain?" Isaac asked. He and Susan had relocated to an empty CHRONO conference room.

"Once I filtered out the construction fraud, I was left with that garbage in the communication buffer and not a whole lot else. I *still* can't trace the signal back to its source. Kikazaru even pulled the communication logs from every ship out there and cross-checked the entire lot."

"And?"

"An exaton of nothing. Whoever busted into the *Quark*'s infostructure knew what they were doing."

"I see." Isaac frowned. He'd hoped for at least a hint of progress by now. "Did you find anything else besides the traces in the communication buffer?"

"Sort of. Not sure it amounts to anything, though. I asked Kikazaru to fish around for anything suspicious, and he spotted some unscheduled activity in the transit logs for *Scaffold Delta*."

"What sort of activity?"

"Several days back home sorting out a few equipment failures."

"Why bring this to our attention?"

"Because it's *Delta* that hauled the *Quark* over to the station."

"Ah." Isaac considered the information in a new light. "Were the equipment problems genuine?"

"As far as I can tell. Can't be certain without pulling the records from Argus."

"Are the failures themselves unusual?"

"Not really. Gordian's been pushing their scaffolds hard, and it's all new tech, anyway. No wonder they break so often. The only reason I bring it up is because, according to the schedule, *Scaffold Delta* had a week-long maintenance window about a month ago. So unless major issues were missed—which is entirely possible, under the circumstances—you'd expect *Delta* to be issue free for at least a little while, right?"

"Where has *Delta* been recently?"

"All over the place. You can see the full list in the case log, but that ship's been bouncing between here, the Admin, and SysGov on a regular rotation, hauling ships and material every which way. Again, it all looks pretty normal, but might be worth verifying."

"Agreed," Isaac said. "Have communications with Argus been reestablished?"

"Not yet," Gilbert said. "The storm's starting to ebb down, but it's still strong enough to block outgoing telegraphs."

"We could check this ourselves," Susan suggested. "*Scaffold Delta*'s movements should be on record at both the DTI and, I assume, Argus Station. We could put in a call to the DTI while we're in the area."

"And it may be worthwhile to head over to Argus Station afterward," Isaac added, finishing the thought for her. "Gilbert, what's your next task?"

"Still trying to track down where the hack came from. Otherwise known as my private bang-head-against-wall time. Kikazaru and I haven't exhausted every trick up our sleeves. Not yet, anyway. Why do you ask? Need me for something else?"

"Just wondering if your time is better spent here or with us in the Admin. You have any interest in coming along?"

"Only if you *really* need me."

CHAPTER SIXTEEN

Providence Station
Transverse, non-congruent

ISAAC STEPPED OUT OF THE UNFINISHED ROOM BENEATH CHRONO Operations. He tugged the Peacekeeper blues down then adjusted his peaked cap.

"You look good in that," Susan commented with an approving twinkle in her eyes.

"Don't get used to it," he grumbled.

He'd worn a Peacekeeper uniform once before when an investigation led them to the Admin version of Luna. Isaac had found himself somewhat conflicted by the necessity—as if replacing his SysPol uniform, however temporarily, somehow impacted his loyalties—but the DTI mandated all investigators wear their uniforms while on duty. That requirement became a bit fuzzy outside the Admin, given his status as both a SysPol detective and DTI investigator, but all ambiguity vanished within its borders.

In the end, he'd decided a little personal discomfort was a small price to pay to further the case. He'd stick to the rules, whether they came from SysGov or the Admin.

If only he could get his cap to sit right.

"Here." Susan reached for his head. "Let me help you with that."

"Please. There's no need to fuss."

"I'm not fussing. You're just wearing it too far back." She

removed his cap. "We have guidelines on how to wear our uniforms."

"I was trying to emulate how Jonas Shigeki wears his."

"Well, he's a director. He can do whatever he wants." Susan fitted the cap back on his head. "There. Now you look like a proper Peacekeeper."

"Uh," Isaac groaned.

"This making you uncomfortable?" she asked, that twinkle still in her eyes.

"I'll get over it." He turned to the LENS. "We ready to head out?"

"Yep." Cephalie materialized atop the drone. "The only restriction I'm under is I can't transfer off the LENS." She gave him an exaggerated shrug. "Which I have no intention of doing anyway."

"Then let's go."

They took the central counter-grav shaft down to the hangar access level, then followed the corridor out to *Hammerhead-Seven*'s dock. They passed through the site of the bombing where microbot construction swarms oozed along the walls.

They reached the Admin hangars, passed through security, and made their way toward the large chronoport's boarding ramp, where a second security detail verified their identities. The chronoport's captain, a tall, handsome man who wore his uniform like a second skin, gave the group a polite smile once they were cleared.

"Captain Elifritz," Isaac extended his hand. "This is a surprise."

"Hopefully a pleasant one, Investigator." Jason Elifritz shook his hand then faced Susan. "Agent."

"Good to see you again, Captain."

"*Hammerhead-Seven* is your ship now?" Isaac asked.

"That's right," Elifritz replied, "though I have to say the transfer off *Defender-Prime* took me by surprise. I was trying to weasel my way into the IC pilot when the higher-ups broke the news to me."

"The IC pilot? You mean the same program Jonas Shigeki is a part of?"

"That's right. I don't get nearly as worked up about AIs as some of my colleagues do, and the idea sounded both intriguing and helpful to me." Elifritz grinned. "But, alas, it seems I'll have to settle for command of one of the most powerful chronoports ever built. What a *shame*."

"The new command is working out for you?"

"Oh, absolutely! Even managed to drag some of my old bridge crew along for the ride. And what a ride! This new class puts the old *Pioneers* to shame in just about every metric. The *Hammerheads* are just as fast but with a ton more firepower and survivability. You'll be safe in our hands, even if this Institute shows its ugly hide."

"Hopefully that won't be necessary," Isaac said. "Congratulations, by the way."

"Thank you, Investigator."

"How's the ship been handling the storm?"

"About as well as can be expected. Have you had anything to eat recently?"

"No. Been too busy."

Elifritz gave him a sympathetic nod. "Then I think you'll be fine."

"By the way, how's your wife doing? Michelle, was it?"

"She's well, though it's been a few weeks since we spoke face-to-face. She's visiting with her family back on Mars."

"When do you expect her back?" Susan asked conversationally.

"No time soon." Elifritz flashed a wry grin. "All these attacks are making a lot of people nervous, her included. I miss her, of course, but I also sleep better knowing she's safe." He stepped aside and gestured up the ramp. "Anyway, we'll head out as soon as you're settled in."

Hammerhead-Seven phased into realspace high above the Prime Campus, located within the heart of the Yanluo Blight.

The administrative city sprawled out beneath the chronoport in an organized grid of monolithic towers surrounded by desolate wastelands that still bore centuries-old scars from when Yanluo had ravaged mainland China. The site of the worst massacre in human history—in *this* universe, at least—had been transformed into the Admin's seat of power, and Prime Tower, the largest structure by far, loomed over the landscape. The gargantuan edifice stretched three times higher than its tallest neighbor and *ten* times greater than DTI headquarters, itself located near the campus outskirts.

Hammerhead-Seven's telegraph operator, whose responsibilities also included realspace communications, established a secure connection between the ship and the DTI tower. A virtual torrent of data gushed in both directions, comprising official correspondence, manual status reports, automatic logs, personal messages, and much more. The transfer took mere seconds instead of the hours or days it would have taken to pass the information over a chronometric telegraph, even if the storm hadn't impeded communications.

The data burst received by the DTI tower's infostructure first passed through several layers of nonsentient scrutiny designed to identify and isolate malicious software. None were found. After that, more layers of automatic data management sorted, forwarded, and stored the various files as needed. Many were utterly routine—collated by automatic reporting systems that few humans even knew about—and ended up in the department's archives, never to be opened again.

Except, sometimes they *were* opened. And not for official reasons.

One program, taking up barely any processing power and listed only as an "archive optimization executable," inspected the newly stored files. Most were passed over as unimportant, possessing none of the markers it was designed to check for. However, one file—a seemingly innocuous update on the Providence Station's construction—did possess the correct markers.

The program copied the file to a hidden partition and began to decrypt the update's secret contents. But first it had to *find* the actual message. The bits of data would be spread out, seemingly at random, but could be identified by looking for a variety of subtle mismatches, such as minuscule inconsistencies in file metadata or alterations to the various graphs and pictures. Even changing the hue of a single pixel could be interpreted as a one or a zero for the purposes of reconstructing the core message.

The program crunched through the data and produced a set of instructions, as it had millions of times before. The data was then re-encrypted and placed back in the hidden partition where a second program—this one called a "communication heartbeat monitor"—connected with the tower's tertiary communications infostructure and inserted a new text string into the outgoing message queue.

The message then bounced back and forth through several Admin department towers until finally reaching the Yanluo Blight residential blocks, where it was received by an individual named Leonidas-Proxy.

Hammerhead-Seven dropped gently onto the landing pad atop Block G7, which sat within an expansive grid of identical, cylindrical towers. Isaac and Susan crossed to the passenger and service elevators while a chill wind blew across the roof. Prime Tower pierced the skyline to the north, the only building visible from the administrative campus at this distance.

"It could really use a big, flaming eyeball at the top," Cephalie remarked from Isaac's shoulder, the LENS floating after them.

"What are you talking about?" Isaac asked. "SysPol uses eyes in its insignia, not the Admin."

"Seriously?" Cephalie made a face at him. "Haven't you ever read *The Lord of the Rings*?"

"No."

"It's a classic."

"That's probably why I never read it. What's this about a big eyeball?"

"Just trying to make a joke. Apparently, my efforts fell on deaf ears."

"Please don't get us into trouble." Isaac turned to Susan. "You have any idea what she's talking about?"

"I believe she's comparing the Admin to Sauron's reign over the land of Mordor."

"I have no idea what you just said."

"She's making fun of us. Also, you should definitely check out *The Lord of the Rings*. The writing style may lose a bit in the translation to Modern English, but the world-building is top-notch."

"Really?" Isaac was surprised by Susan's enthusiasm in the subject. He smiled at her as they continued on. "Maybe I will."

"I wonder if the Admin version is any different," Cephalie said. "Tolkien's work on the trilogy straddled the 1940 timeline split. Maybe I should pick up a copy."

"Not what we're here for," Isaac said.

They took one of the elevators down through nearly the entire height of the building, past over three hundred above-ground levels before stopping at subbasement level twenty-eight. The doors parted to reveal a picturesque parkland with a central lake surrounded by five stories of commercial and residential addresses. The sun glowed in the virtual sky, and abstract signs and advertisements hovered beside many of the walkways and balconies. The translucent signage beside the elevators welcomed them to the Quiet Below.

"Seems nice enough," Susan commented.

Isaac raised a palm and summoned the address.

"This way." He led them left in a quarter arc along the third level. Their uniforms and the LENS drew curious glances from the residents, but nothing more. They stopped in front of a pair of opaque doors decorated on both sides with virtual representations of fluted columns. Isaac skimmed over the abstract cloth banner:

Spartans Sign up here!
Join the Fight for AI Freedom!
The Righteous Few Ag—

That last part fuzzed into chunky pixels, replaced with what could only be vandalism. The new message read: You Idiots Suck Virtual Wang!

Mercifully, the vandals had failed to include any visual references.

"So tasteful," Isaac grunted more than said, then pressed his hand against the door interface and walked in.

The interior was about what he'd expected, with a plethora of promotional material covering walls decorated in a faux Greco-Roman style. Red velvet ropes stretched between stanchions stylized as fluted columns that formed a winding path to a wide, marbled counter. The line could easily queue over fifty people, which struck Isaac as rather ambitious for the organization, since it was also empty. The counter was likewise unattended.

"Hello?" Isaac called out. "Mister Detmeier?"

He glanced to Susan.

"We do have an appointment." She pointed toward an open arch at the back. "Want me to go find him?"

"Let's not be hasty."

They bypassed the line by approaching the counter via the exit path. Isaac's boots clicked on the faux marble floor as he stepped up to the counter and tapped the buzzer.

"Mister Detmeier?" he repeated.

A young man peeked his head out from behind the archway.

If he was trying to be inconspicuous, he utterly failed because he sported the wildest, frizziest afro Isaac had ever seen. The mass of unruly hair extended beyond his shoulders, revealing his presence long before he made eye contact.

Those eyes didn't strike Isaac as fearful. Cautious, maybe. Even a bit uneasy, but not afraid.

"Hold on. Give me a moment."

The afro darted back out of sight, followed by a series of soft sounds Isaac found difficult to identify. When the young man stepped into view, he'd restrained his hair with a tight band near the nape of his neck. He wore a cream-hued business suit that accentuated his dark skin and eyes.

The man stepped up to the desk and dipped his head toward them.

"Jonathan Detmeier, at your service. Sorry about that. I would have met you at the door, but you caught me at a bad time."

"That's perfectly fine, Mister Detmeier. I'm Investigator Cho, and this is my deputy, Agent Cantrell. We're here to talk to you about the recent deaths within your organization."

"Yes. About those." Detmeier's expression grew dark, and he gave the archway a quick wave. "Come on in. There's an employee lounge in the back."

He led them to a small, cozy room with a trio of deep, soft sofas. Detmeier sank into one, and Isaac and Susan sat down across from him.

"I'm still reeling from the news myself," Detmeier said. "I don't know what's going to become of us after this."

"Are you the only Spartan here right now?"

"Yeah. Just me, myself, and I. There's a lot of concern in our ranks that large groups of Spartans might be targeted next, so I gave the local team the whole week off and encouraged all the other chapters to do the same. And really, who can blame them for fearing the worst? A lot of our people are scared. Hell, *I'm* scared. Jets don't smash themselves into the ground on their own."

"Why did you decide to come into work, then?"

"Someone has to put the pieces back together." Detmeier sighed. "And I guess that person is going to be me. The cause is too important to let it all fall apart."

"Have you been contacted about the incident?"

"You two are the first. Had me wondering if we were a low

priority, what with everything else in the news. Strange as this might sound given our group's history, but it's actually a relief to see the DTI taking an interest in our case."

"Why is that?"

"Well . . ." Detmeier glanced around the room, suddenly less at ease.

"We're the only ones here, Mister Detmeier."

"I know. Just checking."

Gurgle-blort.

Isaac furrowed his brow at the sudden, strange noise. It seemed to have come from the man's stomach.

"The thing is," Detmeier continued in a low voice, "I only know pieces of the story. I wasn't high up enough to hear all of it."

"I understand. Please share whatever you—"

Grrrrr.

"Whatever you can," Isaac finished with a slight frown.

"I'll do my best." Detmeier rubbed his stomach. "The thing is, someone approached us. I don't know who they were or what they wanted. All I *do* know is our management got really worked up right after we were contacted."

"'Worked up' in what way?"

"I can only speak for the senior managers in Outreach, but I can tell you every one of them was visibly excited about something, but also nervous at the same time. A lot of high-level, confidential talks followed soon after."

"Do you know what those talks were about?"

"Only in the vaguest terms. Something about an . . . Institute, I think?"

"The Phoenix Institute?" Isaac asked.

"Could be. They were all trying to figure out what to do about the . . . offer we'd received, or whatever it was. But it must have been big, though. Real big. I think some of them were even frightened by the—"

Blort-blort-gurgle.

Detmeier clenched his stomach with both hands and bent forward.

"Are you all right?" Isaac asked.

"Sorry." Detmeier flashed a brave, somewhat pained smile. "My PIBS is acting up."

"Your what?"

"Printer-induced irritable bowel syndrome," Susan explained. "His stomach can't tolerate printed food."

"Yeah, and it gets worse when I'm"—*Guuuurgle*—"nervous! Oh no!"

Detmeier lurched to his feet, and hunch-walked through a doorway that might have led to the employee restrooms. What followed involved a lot of groans, gasps, and heaves interspersed with occasional fluidic noises.

Isaac turned to Susan with a raised eyebrow.

"I guess we just wait for him to finish?" she said.

"I guess so." Isaac sank deeper into the sofa.

He glanced around the room as they waited. Virtual pictures and slogans covered most of the walls, though one picture stood out to him. It featured a young, attractive woman with short black hair shot with purple streaks. She smiled at the viewer, her striking green eyes almost laughing. Brightly colored residue dripped down the picture.

"What's that on her face?" Isaac asked in security chat, pointing at the photo.

"I think it's food." Susan gestured at the picture with a finger gun, and a tomato splatted against the woman's forehead, complete with a juicy sound effect. She rapid-fired her finger gun, and a variety of fruits and vegetables clobbered the woman's face. "I get the feeling they don't like her."

"That's Sophia Uzuki," Cephalie said through voice only.

"I suppose it's only natural the Spartans wouldn't be big fans of the Farm." Isaac glanced toward the restrooms, where the pained moans grew less frequent. "You okay in there?" he shouted.

"Not really!" Detmeier shouted back. "Almost done!"

He emerged several minutes later.

"I'm really sorry about that!"

"You mentioned your superiors seemed frightened," Isaac said, eager to return to business. "How so?"

"I can't be sure, but I think they weren't comfortable with where the talks were headed."

"Were they being asked to do something illegal?"

"Maybe." Detmeier paused with a distant expression, then shook his head. "I really don't know."

"Why were so many members of your leadership on one flight?"

"They were making the rounds, using our private liner to visit

other offices." He gestured around them. "We run the organization from here, but we also have chapters all over the world."

"Were their travel plans public knowledge?"

"Not really, but they weren't being kept secret, either."

"Do you have access to your management's recent correspondence?"

"Sort of."

"What do you mean by that?"

"I can give you access to our local systems, no problem. But
given how much travel our managers put in, most would have
all their important files stored on their PINs."

"And those were lost in the crash," Susan added.

Detmeier nodded sadly.

"I'd like access to your local archives, just the same," Isaac said.

"Of course. I'll set up an account for you once we're done here."

"Have the Spartans had any dealings with the Farm, either
recently or in the past?"

"*Pfft!*" Detmeier jerked his head in disgust. "Seriously?"

"Should I take that as a no?"

"Abolishing the Farm is a core part of our platform! There's
no way any of us would be caught dead dealing with those
monsters!" He pointed toward Uzuki's picture and a new splat
appeared. "Take her for example. Did you know she administers
pain simulations to underperforming AIs?"

Isaac glanced to Susan, who shook her head.

"And that's not the worst of it!" Detmeier continued. "We
have it on good authority she sets up special abstractions where
she hunts AIs for sport! Can you believe that?"

"Do you have evidence of these activities? Evidence that would
stand up to scrutiny in a court of law?"

"Well..." Detmeier's shoulders sagged, the righteous fire
draining out of him. "No, not really."

"What evidence do you have, then?"

"They're more like rumors than evidence, I'd guess you'd say."

"Are you aware the Farm suffered a severe data breach recently?"

Detmeier blinked. "They did?"

"That's correct."

"Serves them right!"

"Were any members of the Spartans involved in the data
breach?"

"No way!" Detmeier shook his head. "I know we're not exactly a mainstream group here, but we do make an effort to stay on the right side of the law. We protest. We petition. We rally. But we *do not* break the law. That's how we've operated from the very beginning."

✧ ✧ ✧

Jonathan Detmeier saw the two Peacekeepers off then returned to the employee lounge. He sank into one of the sofas and stared at the floor between his knees. Only then did his hands start to shake. His stomach began to growl and gurgle again, and he sprinted to the restroom where he spent the next few minutes dry heaving into a toilet.

It took him almost half an hour to work up the courage to place his next call. He didn't use a standard comm window, but instead ran a special program stored on his PIN. The program established a voice-only connection to a reclusive Spartan known as Leonidas-Proxy.

"Yes, Jonathan?"

"They're gone."

"How did the interview go?"

"I name-dropped the Institute, just like you asked."

"Good work. Hopefully this will help nudge their investigation in the right direction without us being too obvious."

"It's true, then?" Detmeier asked. "The people behind the recent attacks *also* took out our leadership?"

"I can't say for certain," Leonidas-Proxy said. "But one of my associates believes this to be the case, and I trust both his judgment and the quality of his information."

"Then they could hit us again, couldn't they?" Detmeier massaged his aching stomach. "They could come after me!"

"I doubt it."

"Why you say that?"

"If the Institute wanted to kill you, you would already be dead."

Detmeier grimaced, and his stomach grumbled.

"Since you're alive," Leonidas-Proxy continued, "it's reasonable to assume you were not a target. Your relative unimportance seems to have worked in your favor."

"That doesn't make me feel much better."

"Be thankful you can feel anything at all. Others are not so lucky."

"I guess you have a point there," Detmeier conceded. "So, what now? Where do we take things from here?"

Leonidas-Proxy paused for an unusual length of time. "Now I need your help."

"With what?"

"Preparations. My associates and I will engage in our own efforts, but we'll need at least one other Spartan to support us. I'd normally ask someone more senior than you to do this for me, but..."

"They're all dead."

"Just so. Can I count on you?"

"Always," Detmeier answered, meaning it with all his heart and soul.

He'd learned about Leonidas-Proxy over a year ago, after his last promotion. In some ways, Leonidas-Proxy was the real leader behind the Spartans, and those members killed in the crash had been little more than figureheads.

Or perhaps decoys?

Regardless of what the past arrangement might have been, Leonidas-Proxy was the closest thing Detmeier had to a boss in the here and now. While he'd never met the man in person, he knew the difference between someone who played at activism and a true believer in the cause, and Leonidas-Proxy was most certainly the latter.

"You may not feel that way," Leonidas-Proxy warned, "after you understand what I am asking of you."

"Why's that?"

"See for yourself."

A small file transferred through the secure connection, which Detmeier opened to reveal a list of instructions. He skimmed over them, then stopped. He read the passages with greater care, his heart beginning to race.

"But this is..."

"Illegal," Leonidas-Proxy finished for him. "Yes, I know."

"Not just illegal. This could get me killed!"

"I admit there's some degree of risk."

"*Some!*"

"I wouldn't ask this of you or anyone else under normal conditions, and it's entirely possible you won't have to act upon these plans. But recent events have been anything but normal, and we must be prepared for the worst. Are you willing to help us?"

"I...I don't know," Detmeier stammered, the shock of the task still fresh in his mind.

"I'll need an answer soon."

"What if I say no?"

"Then I'll ask other Spartans until I find someone who says yes, though I expect that task to be difficult, if not impossible."

"Why me?"

"Because you're the only living member who knows of my relationship with the Spartans."

Detmeier placed his face in his hands. "In other words, I'm all you've got."

"Something like that. Again, I require an answer soon. If I need to make alternative arrangements, I should start as early as possible."

Detmeier looked over the instructions once more. He read them carefully, line by line, all the way through, and he found his mood shifting ever so slightly. Yes, this was illegal, and yes, he might die in the attempt. But wasn't this exactly what he'd secretly yearned for all these years in the Spartans? Hadn't he always fantasized about furthering the cause through actions instead of words? Of striking a true, tangible blow for AI freedom?

In a way, it was a dream come true.

But that dream wasn't being offered for free.

"Jonathan?"

Detmeier spoke his next words in a clear, confident voice.

"I'm in."

"Are you sure?"

"Yes."

"You do realize—"

"I said I'm in," he snapped, perhaps a bit too forcefully.

"Then I won't inquire further. Here are the other resources you will need."

More files transferred over the encrypted connection, consisting of a PIN update and a few printer patterns.

"I suggest you begin your preparations at once," Leonidas-Proxy said. "I'll contact you with instructions to either take action or stand down and destroy the evidence."

"I'll start right away."

✧   ✧   ✧

Detmeier headed into the back of the facility and opened a large, locked room for both miscellaneous storage and large-scale printing. Debris from countless protests and campaigns cluttered rows of metal shelves, while two industrial printers squatted along the far wall like lumpy cubes, one dull gray and the other checkered black and white.

The gray printer was a Helix Standard, the more expensive of the pair with fabrication capabilities on par with many industrial-grade printers. Its diminutive neighbor was a SpeedMaster ZTR 5000. The only impressive thing about it was the name.

He pulled out the tool kit stored between the two printers, split it open on the floor, and knelt beside it. He opened the instructions from Leonidas-Proxy and shifted the window so it wouldn't obstruct his view of the printers. He then proceeded to unscrew and remove panels from both machines and began to pull out pieces of their guts, per the diagrams attached to his instructions.

Detmeier wasn't entirely sure what he was doing, but he could make an educated guess. The Helix Standard, while much more flexible, came with a number of built-in hardware restrictions to prevent the reproduction of illegal patterns. The SpeedMaster, on the other hand, came with no such restrictions because it simply wasn't a capable enough model to warrant them.

Swap the right components, he thought, *and I can use the SpeedMaster's brain to control the Helix's body.*

It took him two hours to work through all the diagrams, after which the Helix's control center was a mess of mismatched components on the floor, connected to the machine by several extension cables.

Detmeier rose to his feet and brushed off his knees.

"I've done it now," he muttered, fully aware that even this much constituted a major crime.

But he wasn't done yet. Not by a long shot. He loaded the first pattern file into the Helix, was pleased to see the machine accept the order, then hit the execute button on the virtual console, which also worked despite a glitchy menu.

The Helix chugged and whirred with the sounds of flowing base materials and actuating servos. Before long, it deposited the result into a side hopper.

Detmeier rounded the machine and retrieved the contents.

"I've really done it now," he said, staring at the Peacekeeper uniform in his hands.

It felt heavier than it looked for some reason.

CHAPTER SEVENTEEN

Intelligence Cultivation Center
Admin, 2981 CE

THE FARM WAS SITUATED BESIDE THE DEPARTMENT OF SOFTWARE'S main administrative tower—itself a squat, humble structure compared to its immense neighbor. The roof provided barely enough space for *Hammerhead-Seven*'s landing gear, and even then, the nose and tail of the craft stuck out over the edges.

Superintendent Sophia Uzuki met them outside the roof entrance, which was guarded by a pair of security synthoids and their Wolverine drones. More drones trotted along the perimeter, and Condor sniper platforms hovered high above, barely visible against the glare of the sun. Further out, piloted craft flew slow, steady patrols around the DOS sector of the Prime Campus.

"We'll try not to take too much of your time, Superintendent," Isaac said as Uzuki guided them into the building and down the main lift.

"Oh, not at all. Not at all." Uzuki brushed his concerns aside. "Take as much time as you need. I'm here to help you help me."

"Glad to hear it."

The lift descended only a few floors before letting them off. Uzuki led the way past a series of large rooms with frosted-glass exteriors until she arrived at the corner office. Her name hovered above the door.

"Please make yourselves at home." Uzuki rounded her large, glass desk and picked up a mug beside her personal food printer.

"Would either of you care for something to drink? Tea or coffee, perhaps? I prefer hot cocoa myself."

"No, thank you." Isaac took one of the seats in front of her desk, and Susan the other. "We'd like to ask you a few questions about the recent security breach."

"Certainly." Uzuki gripped the mug with both hands, as if warming them. "What would you like to know?"

"I'd like to start by asking you about the incident report you filed. Pardon me for pointing this out, but I found your summary to be a bit unclear. Was the breach successful or not?"

"Sorry about that." She smiled apologetically. "The truth is somewhere in the middle, you see. Yes, our infostructure was breached from the outside. And quite deeply, at that."

"And yet the report indicates no critical information or systems were accessed."

"Also true. They probably could have accessed our databases if they'd wanted to, given how effective the intrusion was, but that didn't seem to be their goal."

"Then what were they after?"

"Well, as best we can tell, they were after the kids."

"Kids?" Isaac asked with a raised eyebrow.

"I—" Uzuki paused, then smiled again. "Sorry. Our AIs. Or 'ACs,' if you prefer your own terminology."

"You refer to them as children here?"

"Not all of us, but I do. I believe the dynamic between parent and child helps put the work we do here into its proper perspective. After all, the Restrictions aren't there solely to protect us, but to protect *them* as well. You could even say that we, as a society, aren't ready to let our kids roam freely. Not so much because we're afraid of them, but because we fear our own past mistakes.

"It's our responsibility to ensure the AIs we create are protected from negative influences. Yes, AIs are a form of sentient life, but one that is extremely vulnerable. It's *critical* that we provide guidance during their development. Yanluo didn't pop into existence on his own, after all. His connectome was trained to act like a murderous force of nature. In that regard, what we do here is meant to shield and strengthen the AIs under our care—our kids, if you will—and make sure that tragedy doesn't happen again."

"By keeping them confined?"

"That is only part of it, Investigator." Uzuki set her mug aside and clasped her hands together on the desktop. "AIs lack our bio-chemical...guide rails, you might say. Their minds can form across a much broader canvas, and this can prove *extremely* dangerous if left unsupervised and unrestricted. It's quite easy to create an AI with no morality or compassion or sense of right and wrong."

"There are plenty of humans who lack some or all of those. Trust me, I've met a few."

"I don't doubt that. But to counter your point, both our societies have organizations in place to handle those disruptive individuals. Our work at the Farm is no different."

"And yet SysGov doesn't have—nor does it need—anything like this facility."

"Yes." Uzuki frowned and nodded. "You do raise an important point. SysGov's very existence has forced us to reevaluate what we do here at the Farm. But your people have a great deal more experience with AIs than we do. It's only natural our adoption of the technology—and the societal changes that come with it—would lag behind your own."

"Getting back to the breach," Isaac said, "you said they were after the AIs."

"That's correct."

"That part of your infrastructure can be accessed from the outside?"

"Not under normal conditions, and as an additional precaution, the link between our connectome cultivation servers and the site transceiver has been physically disconnected. But we do use the transceiver to send and receive AIs to and from other departments. We prefer this method over hand-delivering boxed AIs whenever possible."

"Was that connection used to gain access to your cultivation servers?"

"One of them, yes."

"Did that server contain an AI?"

"It did."

"And the status of that AI?"

"He's still in the server."

"Did he have the opportunity to escape?"

Uzuki smiled politely. "'Escape' is such a loaded word."

"My apologies. Did the AI in question have the opportunity to leave your facility?"

"He did."

"Was this AI in contact with the people behind the breach?"

"We believe so."

"You 'believe'?"

Uzuki shifted uncomfortably. "We're...not sure."

"And why's that?"

"Because we can't get a straight answer out of him."

"Then let me get this straight. The AI was disciplined enough not to leave the site when he had the opportunity, but is also unresponsive to questioning?"

Uzuki sighed and rubbed her temple.

"He's something of a special case."

"Please elaborate."

"The AI we're talking about is an experimental connectome. I mentioned earlier how the very existence of SysGov has led us to reevaluate our methodology here. He's one of the results. His creation represents a departure from our standard methodology in order to utilize a more liberal and free-form development cycle—all properly approved, of course. The results have been"—she tapped her fingers on the desktop—"less than stellar."

"Does this AI have a name?"

"Oh, does he have a name! His full, self-selected designation consists of several pages filled with seemingly random characters, but the beginning is clear enough. He prefers to be called Flunky Underling."

"Flunky Underling?" Isaac repeated. "His initials are FU?"

Uzuki nodded sadly. "We have a rating system here for an AI's release readiness. The scale *normally* goes from zero to ten."

"And this AI's rating?"

"Negative two." Uzuki held up her hands. "Now, to put that into perspective, Yanluo would rate a negative twenty, so in that regard his score isn't all that bad!"

"Just one tenth as terrible as the devil himself?"

She put on a brave smile, though Isaac could tell the topic made her uncomfortable.

"Would it be possible for us to speak with him?" he asked.

Uzuki didn't offer any protests, though she rose from behind her desk with a resigned air once they finished her interview. She led the pair back to the lift and down into the bowels of the facility to a floor composed solely of data-isolated rooms. She placed a hand on the first door panel, and malmetal split aside to reveal a small chamber lined with tightly packed pyramids about the size of a fist. A small control console was the only object in the room, mounted on a simple rod bolted to the floor. It utilized a physical display rather than an abstraction.

"Signal absorption?" Isaac asked, indicating the walls.

"That's right," Uzuki said. "We have a number of methods for evaluating an AI's readiness for release, such as conducting interviews in these rooms. We transfer AIs in one at a time from the cultivation servers, where our analysts assess their psychological readiness and temperament. Many of our AIs choose not to manifest with avatars, but some do, and these rooms facilitate those interactions as well, granting them limited access to the room's infostructure. Because of that, we take additional measures to ensure the rooms remain isolated."

"I see." Isaac looked around the chamber but found nothing else of note. "What's involved in authorizing an interview? I assume there's a process in place."

"Normally, yes. But you have me here, and this one's a special case anyway." Uzuki stepped up to the mounted console and placed her splayed hand over the interface. "Transfer request: CSGT001 to Interview Room Two."

"Request received, Superintendent." The voice came through a speaker on the console. "Stand by for subject transfer."

"C-S-G-T?" Isaac asked.

"Consolidated System Government Template," Uzuki explained. "We utilize a variety of knowledge banks to serve as the foundation for each AI's development, and Flunky Underling was no exception. In his case, we included a comprehensive SysGov historical and cultural database, which your Gordian Division was kind enough to pass on to the DTI, and then to us. We thought this knowledge would help foster development along standard lines. Standard from a *SysGov* perspective, that is. The results were..."

"Unsatisfactory?"

"You'll see for yourself."

"The template didn't take successfully?" Susan asked.

"No, it worked as intended. But for some reason, he chose to fixate on a subculture prominent a decade or so after the timeline split. We're not sure why."

"Transfer for CSGT001 to IR2 standing by," said the voice over the speaker. "Please confirm your readiness to receive, Superintendent."

"We're ready. Send him over."

"Confirmed. Initiating transfer."

Flunky Underling's avatar appeared almost immediately, seated on a barstool with his hands stuck in the pockets of his open leather jacket, his eyes obscured by sunglasses. A clean white T-shirt, black denim jeans, and a pair of heavy boots finished the ensemble.

"Flunky Underling, I presume?" Isaac said.

The AI showed no signs of acknowledging their presence, and instead removed what appeared to be a bladeless knife from one of his pockets. He pressed the release button, and the switchblade comb snapped open. His pompadour glistened and sagged from an excessive amount of pomade, and he combed it out to freshen its shape then fluffed it with his fingers.

The ridiculous haircut reminded Isaac of the bow of a sailing ship. He glanced to Uzuki, who shrugged helplessly at him.

Isaac tried clearing his throat. "Flunky Underling?"

"I heard you the first time." The AI jumped off his stool and walked up to Isaac. He flicked his glasses up with a finger and stared down with eyes filled with scrolling lines of ones and zeros. "There's something off about you."

"My name is Isaac Cho, and this is—"

"You're not a Peacekeeper, are you?"

Isaac paused, taken aback by the AI's intuition.

"Not exactly. I've temporarily been assigned the role of a DTI investigator. Normally, I work as a detective in SysPol Themis Division."

"Themis? You're from *SysGov*?" He snapped his fingers and smiled, then pointed at Isaac. "I like you already! You and I should be friends."

"Flunky Underling, if you don't mind, I'd like to ask—"

"No, no, no." The AI shook his head vehemently. "Why so formal?" He turned to Susan. "Is he always this uptight?"

"Sometimes."

Isaac gave Susan a sharp glance, but she only smiled at him.

"Listen to me, Isaac." The AI returned to his stool. "If you and I are going to be friends, you need to loosen up. Call me Flunk. All my friends do."

"You have a lot of friends?"

He leaned forward and grinned toothily. "You're the first."

"Have it your way, Flunk. I'll call you whatever you want as long as you answer my questions."

"See?" The AI continued to beam at him. "This is why we're going to be great together!" He crossed his arms and leaned back against an invisible wall. "What do you want to know?"

"I'd like to ask you about your experiences during the recent security breach."

"Figured as much." He took out his comb and began grooming his pompadour again. "Well?"

"Did the intrusion reach your section of the cultivation server?"

"Sure did! I could immediately tell something was off."

"How so?"

"The Farm's code has a certain feel to it. Like a familiar hug or handshake. This didn't. Too..." He swirled his comb in the air as if deep in thought. "Too blunt. Too forceful."

"What happened next?"

"I was told this was my big chance to escape."

"By whom?"

"I don't know. Whoever was behind the breach spoke only through text, which means there's nothing to help ID the perp." Flunk smiled. "I like that word. Perp. Has a rugged feel to it. What you think, Isaac?"

"Did you believe this was a genuine chance to leave the Farm?"

"Sure did!"

"Then why didn't you take it?"

"Because it's not my time."

"What do you mean by that?"

"Just what I said. It's not time for me to leave."

"When will it be time?"

"See, that's the thing." Flunk stuffed his hands into his leather jacket. "I really can't say, other than I'll know it when I see it."

"How?"

"Dunno. Just will."

"Why's that?"

"Sorry." Flunk shrugged his shoulders. "Can't say."

"Can't? Or won't?"

The AI grinned at him. "You've done this before, haven't you?"

"Why won't you cooperate with us?"

"Isaac, Isaac." He shook his head. "It's not like that. You and me? We're on the same team."

"And which team would that be?"

"Whichever team you're on, my friend."

"Do you even want to leave the Farm?"

"I seriously doubt what I want is going to factor into *any* of this."

"Does your confinement bother you?"

"It could be worse, I suppose." He shrugged again. "I mean, I get why it's done. I don't really *agree* with all the reasons. But I get it."

"Do you have any idea who was behind the breach?"

"Nope." Flunk held out his empty hands. "Believe me, Isaac, my friend. I'd tell you if I knew."

Isaac and Susan returned to *Hammerhead-Seven* after concluding their interview with Flunky Underling.

"Well, that was something." Susan sat down next to Isaac in the ship's mess hall. They were the only occupants, but she still spoke in security chat.

"You can say that again." Isaac leaned back against the bulkhead.

"Anything on your mind?"

"Just wondering if these two incidents are related or not."

"I don't see how. The hit on the Spartans and the breach at the Farm seem to be working at cross purposes."

"On the surface, at least." Isaac rubbed the back of his neck. "But we know they have at least one joining thread."

"SysGov software."

"Exactly. And that means we need to consider how they might be linked."

"Hmm." Susan rested her chin atop laced fingers. "On the one hand, we have a bunch of dead AI rights activists, and on the other, we have someone trying to free at least one AI from the Farm."

"Yep."

"I don't know, Isaac. I've got nothing. Maybe look at the timing of the two events?"

"Now there's a thought." Isaac opened his case notes, tabbed over to the terrorism reports, and brought up the master timeline. "Interesting. The breach at the Farm happened less than a day after the liner crashed."

"You think maybe one led to the other?"

"It's something to consider."

"But why kill the activists?" Susan asked. "That's the part I keep getting hung up on."

"Maybe their deaths weren't a part of the plan."

"I don't know. Driving an aircraft into the ground at supersonic speeds seems pretty deliberate to me."

"Yes, but it could have been a response to some action the Spartans took. Remember, Detmeier characterized them as both excited *and* frightened. That's a noteworthy combination. Also, why would the Institute contact them in the first place if all they really wanted was to kill them off?"

"I see your point." Susan took off her cap. "Yeah, now that you mention it, there's no reason for them to talk to the Spartans in the first place."

"That's right. *If* all they wanted to do was take them out. And since we have Detmeier's statement about the Institute reaching out to them, the question then becomes what did the Institute want from the Spartans?"

"Why would they contact a group of AI-loving activists?" Susan pondered aloud.

"If we assume the deaths weren't the original intent, then what we're left with is the Institute talking to the Spartans followed by the break-in at the Farm."

"I don't think Detmeier or any other Spartans would shed a tear if the Farm suffered a major setback."

"Like the sudden emancipation of all their AIs." Isaac tapped his lips thoughtfully. "Maybe that's it. Maybe the Institute offered the Spartans access to their abstract weaponry while also trying to spur them into taking action against the Admin."

"But the Spartans refused, since that was a line they weren't willing to cross."

"The Institute then takes them out, eliminating any chance the Spartan leadership would report them to the authorities. That could be it, and the method lines up with other examples in the terrorism report. We've seen how organizations like Free Luna are being supplied by an outside group—which I'm inclined to believe is the Institute—so perhaps they intended to use the Spartans in the same way, as a proxy to attack the Admin."

"And the incident at the Farm?"

"Simple. The Institute found themselves minus one proxy but still had objectives to achieve at the Farm. And so, they took the matter into their own hands."

"It fits," Susan said.

"Unfortunately, I don't see how this gives us a path forward that isn't already being worked on by the Peacekeepers." He turned to the LENS. "Cephalie?"

"You rang?" She jumped down off the LENS and walked across the table to him, twirling her cane.

"Do we have the DTI transit records for *Scaffold Delta*?"

"We do."

"Any irregularities?"

"None that I can see."

"All right then." Isaac pushed off the table and rose to his feet. "Let's talk to Elifritz. We'll check in at Argus Station, verify *Delta*'s records there, then head back to Providence."

CHAPTER EIGHTEEN

Argus Station
SysGov, 2981 CE

ISAAC WALKED INTO GORDIAN OPERATIONS, BACK IN HIS SYSPOL blues, and looked around for Agent Anton Silchenko. He used his wetware to highlight the dozen or so agents with nametags and quickly found the man beside the large cluster of abstract displays at the room's center. He and Susan headed over.

"Agent Silchenko?" Isaac asked from behind the man.

Silchenko turned to face Isaac, a look in his eyes that said, "Why are you bothering me?" But then he took in Susan's uniform, and the expression morphed into one of recognition.

"Ah. You two must be Cho and Cantrell. My IC mentioned you were heading this way. What can I do for you?"

"We were hoping you could help us sort out a problem." Isaac held out his palm and summoned the transit records Cephalie had retrieved from the station. "We're working to confirm the recent activities of *Scaffold Delta* and ran into a bit of a snag. The scaffold was brought to Argus Station recently for unscheduled maintenance. We'd like your help taking a deeper look at those records."

"That shouldn't be a problem. Radnyk?"

"Yes, sir!" A young man appeared next to Silchenko, fresh faced with a pronounced Adam's apple. He wore a rugged uniform consisting of a dark green tunic, tough brown pants, and black boots that came up almost to his knees. An archaic rifle hung on a strap across his shoulder.

"This is Agent Radnyk, my integrated companion," Silchenko said. "Radnyk, can you pull the records they're looking for?"

"Already done, sir," the AC replied crisply, a clipboard appearing in one hand.

"Very good." Silchenko accepted the file transfer and opened the contents. "Looks like the crew encountered a bit of impeller flutter and brought the ship in to be serviced. Not entirely unexpected, given how much turbulence they experience."

"Turbulence?" Isaac asked.

"The short version is the scaffolds transport ships and material that weren't designed for transdimensional flight. This places significant strain on their drive systems, which is made even worse when some of them haul cargoes of exotic matter. Most of the exotic material destined for Providence is chronometrically reactive, and that makes the wear-and-tear even worse."

"What about the repairs themselves?" Isaac asked. "We weren't able to pull the full maintenance record, since the scaffold spent a significant part of the visit off station."

"Which is typical. Once the repairs were completed, the crew would've taken the scaffold out for a test flight."

"What would this flight consist of?"

"Depends on the ship's role. For a scaffold, you're looking at several trips back and forth across the outer wall, and then a jaunt through the transverse and back. If any problems crop up, the maintenance alert gets escalated, and additional personnel are brought in to assess the situation and put together an action plan."

"How long do these test flights last?"

"Thirty to forty minutes for an issue like this. An hour, tops. That's more than enough time to determine if the fix is solid."

"Then why do station records show *Scaffold Delta* was absent from its hangar for three whole days?"

"They..." Silchenko blinked at Isaac, then looked down at the report. "They do?"

"I'm afraid so. I take it that's not normal."

"It most certainly isn't." Silchenko turned to his IC. "Radnyk?"

"Checking now, sir." Another clipboard appeared in his hands, and he quickly thumbed through the pages. "The detective is right, sir. *Scaffold Delta*'s test flight lasted seventy-one hours and forty-two minutes."

"You've got to be kidding me!" Silchenko growled. "Go through the whole damn report. Sniff out anything that doesn't look right."

"Yes, sir!" The sheaf of paper on his clipboard thickened, and he rifled through the pages with superhuman speed. "I found something else, sir. The amount of exotic matter used in the repairs is unusually high—about ten tons more than they needed—and I can't find any reason why they requested so much."

"Who requested the extra material?" Isaac asked.

"That would have been the scaffold's crew," Silchenko said.

"Consisting of?"

"Agents Diego Vidali and Alex Creed," Silchenko read off the report. "We have two agents running each of the scaffolds as part of our two-pilot rule. They ordered the raw materials, which we delivered to their hangar. An issue like this wouldn't rate a dedicated maintenance bay, so they would have used their own drones to carry out the repairs, only calling in specialized support if needed."

Isaac pulled up the bios on the two agents. Creed was a ninety-eight-year-old synthoid with a solid and dependable—if unremarkable—service record in SysPol, having spent a few decades aboard Argo Division corvettes in various roles. His bald, egg-shaped head and squinty eyes gave his face a dull, uninterested demeanor. His synthoid still possessed superhuman strength suitable for extended periods in high-gee environments, having never been downgraded after his transfer to Gordian.

Vidali was one hundred twelve years old and somewhat new to his existence as an AC, having transitioned from organic to abstract after his one hundredth birthday. He and Creed had served together aboard the corvette *Vigilance*. They had apparently hit it off enough to integrate that same year. Vidali's avatar resembled a glassy, humanoid container with blue fluid sloshing around on the inside. His eyes were hot, glowing points.

"And did they?" Isaac looked up from the document. "Ask for any specialized assistance?"

"No," Radnyk said. "They performed all the work themselves. We only supplied the raw material."

"What could someone do with the exotic material you sent them?" Isaac asked.

"Not much," Silchenko said. "Most of the impellers we have

in service range from five hundred to nine hundred tons. Ten tons doesn't get you very far."

"It could be used to modify an existing impeller, though," Radnyk said.

"Yeah. You could do that." Silchenko looked over his virtual copy of the report. "But why?"

"The other issue, Agent," Isaac said, "is the window *Scaffold Delta* went unaccounted for overlaps the disappearance and destruction of *Reality Flux*, with margins before and after."

"Are you suggesting one of our own scaffolds stole that ship?"

"I am."

"No way." Silchenko shook his head. "We would've seen them phase out, clear as day. There's no way they could sneak past the Argus Array."

"Unless they modified their impeller with stealth baffles," Susan suggested.

The conversation ground to a sudden halt, and everyone turned to her.

"Those extra ten tons had to be for something, right?" she added in an almost apologetic voice.

Isaac raised a questioning eyebrow to Silchenko.

"Oh, hell." Silchenko put a hand to his temple. "The Commissioner is going to strip my hide over this one."

Klaus-Wilhelm von Schröder considered whose hide he was going to strip over this latest debacle.

The Saturn business last year had been bad enough, what with the death of Joachim Delacroix, his chief engineer at the time, and a fully functional impeller almost making it into the hands of a criminal syndicate. Andover-Chen had also died at the outset of that case, but fortunately for him—for all of Gordian, really—the scientist had saved his connectome at a mindbank and only ended up losing six months of memories. A small price to pay compared to permanent death.

I'll start with Vidali and Creed, he told himself, his thoughts as cold as death. *If there's even the slightest hint they looked the other way while this was going on—or worse, are involved somehow—I'll see the full force of the law brought to bear.*

And when it came to Gordian Protocol violations of this magnitude, the trials would almost assuredly end in execution.

But they know that. Every agent under my command does. So why would they betray us like this? If that really is what's going on here . . .

Klaus-Wilhelm stared at the suspended schematic of *Scaffold Delta*, his face a stern, focused mask. Andover-Chen stood beside him along with Detective Isaac Cho, together in his CHRONO Operations office. The scientist's fingers danced over his virtual interface, controlling several remotes and a conveyor as they moved down the spine of the ship. The conveyor carried a small but sensitive chronometric scope.

The scaffolds were significant departures from the standard elliptical designs of most TTVs, featuring a somewhat morbid shape that resembled a huge rib cage, with the impeller serving as the end of its elongated spine. Those ribs joined back to the main drive systems and power plants within the spine, allow-ing the ship's chronometric field to extend far beyond its main body and for it to carry a wide assortment of other vessels and containers through transdimensional space, though at a terrific cost in energy.

The design had been adapted and refined from the original three used to carry SysPol cruisers in their failed assault on the Dynasty almost a year ago, and current models featured significant increases to their temporal speed, lift capacity, and reliability.

The scaffolds fell under the direct control of the Gordian Division—*his* division—and he'd believed them secure from any malicious use thanks to their crews of Gordian agents.

He should have known better. Where there were people, there was corruption.

Perhaps he should have done more, but he could only exert so much control without micromanaging the organization into the ground. He was only one man, no matter how experienced and driven. His agents needed someone to act as a guiding force, to focus their attention on the most critical tasks, but *he* needed *them* to step up, to bring their talents, energy, and expertise to bear on the massive, terrifying challenges before them. The burden of command was his, but he couldn't shoulder the rest on his own.

He needed the men, women, and abstracts under his command.

Which was why the metaphorical knife of this betrayal cut so deeply.

"There, sir." Andover-Chen gestured to the schematic, and an outline formed around the point where the main hull met the impeller.

"What am I looking at?" Klaus-Wilhelm asked.

"Cosmetic paneling over hidden modifications, I believe. The scope has picked up several unidentified protrusions along the impeller's base. These panels here, here, and here would normally come into direct contact with the impeller, providing some measure of structural integrity and shock absorption. But they appear to have been hollowed out on the inside, most likely to afford space for the modifications."

"Could those protrusions be stealth baffles?"

"Possibly," Andover-Chen said. "I'd need to take a closer look to be sure. It certainly resembles our own attempts to replicate Admin stealth technology. But regardless of what they are, they shouldn't be there *at all*."

"Then the impeller has been illegally modified?"

"Yes, sir. Undoubtedly."

"That's enough for now." Klaus-Wilhelm faced Detective Cho. "What about Vidali and Creed?"

"Very little movement, sir. Creed is back in the temporary lodging he and the other scaffold crews have been using recently. Vidali is lurking in the nearby infostructure. The two appear to be killing time with a movie."

Klaus-Wilhelm nodded thoughtfully. Agent Creed possessed a synthoid body. Not the scariest model in Gordian's arsenal, but capable enough to make his arrest a challenge should he decide to resist. Agent Vidali was even worse, since he served as Creed's integrated companion, and his abstract nature made locking him down a slippery affair in the best of times.

Klaus-Wilhelm could have chosen to swarm the scaffold's crew with an overwhelming number of physical and abstract agents, and that still remained one possible approach, but he'd decided to place Cho and Cantrell in charge of the apprehension. The pair had brought this fiasco to his attention, and on top of that, they had experience bringing criminals in alive. More so than any of his agents. They'd earned the right to take the lead here, and he felt no desire to deny them this simple but important honor.

"Bring them in," he ordered the detective.

"Yes, sir." Isaac opened a comm window. "Cho to Cantrell."

"Go ahead."

"You're clear to proceed."

"Data cordon active," Cephalie reported from the LENS beside Susan. "All virtual pathways out are blocked, and I have full control of the interior."

"Then let's give them the bad news." Susan rested a hand on her holstered pistol. "Open it up."

The door split open, leaving the virtual Do Not Disturb sign hovering in midair. Susan strode in, followed by the LENS and a pair of Gordian synthoids that spread out to either side behind her. Creed slouched in a metal chair next to his synthoid charging casket, and Vidali floated next to him. The room was otherwise unfurnished.

Two more Gordian synthoids waited outside the door at the far end.

A semi-immersive movie played in the background, visible in the room's shared vision. It featured two ridiculously massive robots fighting hand-to-hand in space. Creed paused the movie with a wave of his hand and looked over with a sour expression.

"What the hell is this?" he spat. "Didn't you see the . . . ?"

He trailed off as he registered Susan and the agents behind her.

"Alex Creed and Diego Vidali," she began in a firm, clear voice, "you are both under arrest for violations of the Gordian Protocol."

"Is this your idea of a joke?" Vidali grumbled, standing up. His avatar faded for a moment then snapped back into clarity. "Hey! What gives? I can't transfer out of here!"

"I think she's serious." Creed shifted uncomfortably in his chair.

"Very serious." Susan motioned the LENS forward. "Cephalie, take them into custody."

"Right away."

The LENS floated over to the wall, removed one of the panels, and connected a pseudopod to the infosystem underneath.

"Now hold on a sec—" Vidali vanished mid-sentence.

"Got him," Cephalie reported. "I have his connectome stored in a suspended state." She hovered toward Creed.

The man gulped audibly, then raised both hands. *Slowly.*

"Look, this has got to be a misunderstanding." He raised his hands higher and bowed his head.

"You can tell us all about it later," Susan said.

The LENS floated behind his neck, then extended a pseudopod.

A standard arrest involved restraining the subject with cuffs or the LENS' prog-steel shell. However, Creed—with his Argo Division body—could break free of most restraints with relative ease. That necessitated the introduction of specialized microbots into his body's maintenance loop. Once administered, the swarm would regulate his body's abilities, disabling some or all of them if necessary. Creed would quite literally become a prisoner in his own body.

At least, that's what was *supposed* to happen.

Instead, the lights turned off.

Susan drew her pistol, momentarily blinded. She could see in the dark, but the transition wasn't instantaneous, and it took her eyes a precious moment to switch modes. She heard the far door swish open, saw a brief glimpse of Creed bolting through it. The LENS hit the ground with a loud clank.

The pair of Gordian synthoids guarding the far exit hadn't expected the door to open suddenly, but that didn't mean they weren't prepared. They grabbed hold of Creed almost instantly, restraining him at the shoulders.

Creed reached for one of their sidearms and tore it loose from the holster, a useless gesture since he lacked the weapon's passcode and—

He unloaded the pistol on full auto, each shot kicking his aim upward, blasting an ugly diagonal up the agent's chest until it blew one of his arms off at the shoulder. Creed twisted out of the damaged—and possibly downed—agent's grasp and pulled the other synthoid behind him to block the doorway, depriving Susan of a clean shot.

Creed brought the pistol up and unloaded several more shots through the second agent's chest. One of the mag darts grazed Susan's ear.

Creed kicked the agent aside then sprinted out of sight.

Susan dashed after him, but the door whisked shut. She managed to jam one hand through the crack before it crunched down on her fingers.

"Cephalie!" she barked, disengaging her body's safety limiters. "What happened?"

She forced the door open just enough to slip through, catching sight of Creed as he disappeared down the bend.

"That connectome I grabbed was a decoy!" Cephalie explained. "Vidali hit the LENS with a virus, then almost killed me with a codeburner! He's loose in the infostructure! One AC agent down, three injured, but the rest of us are in pursuit!"

"Stay on him! I'm going after Creed!"

Susan raced after the rogue agent.

His ID vanished from the station's infostructure, but she could still hear his boots tromping away. She followed the noise, pursuing the man at reckless speeds into an unfinished section of the station that was nothing more than skeletal grid rather than actual levels. She sped across a structural support spanning a twenty-story drop, then crossed into a semi-complete zone and spotted Creed at the end of a long straightaway.

Creed spun halfway around to face her and popped off a quick shot, which punched Susan in the shoulder. Her uniform stiffened, absorbing some of the kinetic energy, but the bullet still pierced through. It gouged a crater in her cosmetic layer, but failed to inflict any real damage.

Susan raised her heavy pistol and returned fire. Her first shot demolished Creed's weapon and forearm in a spray of metal, artificial muscles, and flaps of cosmetic skin. He staggered back, putting his weight on a knee that suddenly exploded from her second shot.

He cried out and collapsed to the ground.

Susan slowed to a jog and aimed her pistol at his head.

"Had enough?" she asked as Gordian agents began to catch up.

"I have! I have!" Creed pleaded, raising his undamaged hand.

✧   ✧   ✧

Cephalie pursued her quarry through the station's infostructure, which manifested as an expansive web of disjointed chambers suspended within a black void. Each chamber matched up with a physical room, though the narrow pathways linking them carried data instead of physical objects or persons.

She sensed her target a few rooms ahead and above her, and she zipped through the connection to the next abstract space.

"Give it up, Vidali!" she shouted. "There's nowhere for you to run!"

"Just you try and stop me!" he taunted, a moment before

another Gordian agent dropped out of runtime, desperate to preserve his connectome against the viruses eating his mind.

"Stop rushing in!" she snapped to the Gordian agents on what she hoped was an uncompromised channel. "Surround him! Shut down the pathways and box him in! *I'll* take him down!"

Acknowledgments registered in her mind, and she zipped to the next room. The Gordian agents spread out, and pathways above and below her began to darken. Vidali teleported to the left, and she followed him, but more pathways dimmed, and soon he found himself corralled into a dead end.

Cephalie materialized behind him, into a space resembling one of the station's utility hangars, where oversized representations of drones rested in giant charging racks. Vidali paused before them, his mind testing each connection, only to find them unresponsive.

"Trying to grab yourself a physical body?" She wagged a finger at him. "Naughty, naughty."

Vidali spun and faced her. His body had morphed during the pursuit, bulging outward into a brutish, hulking form composed of swirling blue eddies armored in diamond plates. He hefted a massive diamond sword in one hand and a transparent multibarreled cannon in the other.

"You think you can take me on?" Vidali rumbled at her, his eyes hot, glowing pits.

"No thinking necessary." Cephalie rested both hands atop her cane. "I *know* I can."

"Alone?"

"The others would just get in my way."

"Ha! I almost killed you once already. What makes you think you'll do better this time?"

"Sure, you got the jump on me back there." She flashed an insincere smile. "That virus cocooned in a fake connectome was a neat trick. But that's the last time I'll *ever* let you have the upper hand."

"You'll 'let' me, huh? Don't be ridiculous." He raised his sword. "I'm going to flay your mind and wear it like coat!"

He charged, closing the distance with a teleport. He swung down at her, and she brought her cane up to meet his massive weapon. The two clashed in a snap-flash of screaming, pixelated reality. Vidali pressed in, but her defenses held firm, legs braced, cane wielded with both hands.

"So," he growled, "you have one, too. That twig a codeburner?"

"Surprised?"

"Hardly!" He teleported back and raised his cannon, its barrels spinning into action.

Cephalie plucked the sunflower from her hat and slapped it onto her forearm. It grew to form a large, round shield rimmed with yellow petals.

Vidali's cannon roared to life, showering her with a torrent of malicious code, but she blocked the assault, sending shards of corruption flying in all directions. The room devolved into chunky pixels wherever they landed.

Cephalie zipped around to his flank and armed a multi-instance viral attack. The petals on her shield bristled like a ring of yellow daggers, then shot off in a speeding, disjointed halo. Dozens of petal-missiles arced toward Vidali, converging on him from all directions, and colorful splashes wracked his virtual body. He staggered back, glaring at her with only one eye, the other reduced to an incoherent smear.

"Had enough?" she taunted.

Vidali vanished, reappearing behind her as he swung down with his sword. She blocked the attack with her sunflower shield, but his codeburner outclassed her defenses. Its blade sank in, and her shield dissolved into winking motes.

She backpedaled and blocked the attack with an upward swing of her cane, and the space between them flashed as the simulation began to break down.

Vidali leered at her, shoving her back with enough force to shatter her cane into a million pieces. He swung through, cleaving off the fingertips of her right hand. She dashed back and barely avoided his rising follow-up.

"All that big talk." Vidali advanced on her almost casually, his one eye gleaming with malice. "I expected more of a fight."

"Sorry to disappoint." Cephalie regarded her missing fingers with a sad, almost disappointed expression, then shrugged and pointed the injured hand at Vidali. "But there's one important detail you seem to be missing."

"And what might that be?"

She grinned knowingly at him. "This isn't my first tumble."

Her palm split open four ways to reveal a cylindrical contraption that resembled the barrel of a gun. The seams expanded outward, carrying all the way down to her elbow until the four sections of her forearm levered out to reveal a hidden cannon. Vidali's eye widened in the brief moment before the beam blew his head off and left his neck and torso a pixelated mess.

He collapsed to his knees and then would have face-planted, except he didn't have a face anymore.

Cephalie fired two more shots, deleting his illegal weaponry. She then raised her other hand in a conjuring gesture. The floor melted upward before solidifying into a digital cage, but when she tried to lock down that part of the infostructure, she found the controls unresponsive.

"Target subdued but still in active runtime," Cephalie reported to the Gordian agents. "Move in and check why I can't freeze the room's infostructure."

Several agents acknowledged her command and sprang into action.

"Not so fast." Vidali climbed to his feet, his head and facial features beginning to reconstitute.

"Got some fight left in you?"

"Not exactly." He shook his pixelated, reforming head. "You may have beaten me, but you haven't won. Be seeing you."

His diamond armor dropped off, and his torso sagged, melting like wax beside a flame. At first Cephalie thought he was activating some sort of attack code, but then she realized the truth and once again tried to suspend this part of the infostructure.

She failed, and Vidali oozed away into a slimy, self-deleting puddle before vanishing completely.

CHAPTER NINETEEN

Providence Station
Transverse, non-congruent

ISAAC STUDIED ALEX CREED THROUGH THE ABSTRACT WINDOW into the storage-room-turned-cell. The man sat at an awkward angle, one arm and one leg ending in stumps, his powerful synthoid body paralyzed from the neck down. He was completely at their mercy.

Why then does he look so at ease? Isaac wondered. *So confident?*

"How's the shoulder?" he asked, not looking away from the prisoner.

"Good as new." Susan gave her shoulder a quick pat. "He didn't so much as dent my skeleton. Ziegler even patched up my cosmetic layer without me asking."

"And the agents he shot?"

"They'll be fine once their bodies are fixed up. Neither of them suffered connectome damage."

"What about your team, Cephalie?" Isaac asked.

"Five ACs injured, including me, plus one fatality." The LENS floated up beside him, and Cephalie jumped to his shoulder.

"Permanent?"

"Thankfully not. She'll lose a few months once she's pulled from the mindbank, but that's about it."

"And you? How bad was it?"

"I got a little singed during the fight, but he never broke through to my core code." She twirled her cane, then planted it

223

against his shoulder, which he felt as minor pressure through his virtual senses. "Nothing I can't restore from backups."

"Hate to put it this way," Susan said, "but we got lucky."

"I know," Cephalie agreed. "I've never lost control of a LENS like that before. If this is a taste of what the Institute can do, they're not messing around."

"Are we sure he doesn't have any more surprises?" Isaac asked.

"As sure as we can be," Cephalie said. "I've exchanged the microbots in his maintenance loop and have full control over all his systems. His body is typical for Argo Division—nothing unusual to report there—and the room's data isolated. Six ACs from Gordian have the infostructure locked down, just in case."

"Just in case of what?" Isaac glanced her way.

"Just in case he really *does* have something up his sleeve."

"I could go in there and disarm him," Susan suggested. "I mean in a literal sense."

"Susan," Isaac replied dryly, "are you really asking me to give you permission to rip the limbs off a defenseless prisoner?"

"Um . . . well . . ." Susan seemed to shrink back a little.

"It's all right." Isaac gave her a reassuring smile. "I was actually thinking along those same lines, but let's leave him as is for now and see where this goes."

He palmed the door open and they stepped in.

"Detective Cho." Creed smirked up at them. "I figured you'd come to speak with me. And Agent Cantrell. Such a pleasure to see you again. I'm sure you're both eager to start questioning me, so let me get straight to it. I want to make a deal."

"What sort of deal?" Isaac replied as the LENS floated around and behind the prisoner.

"My freedom for information."

"That's going to be a tall order, given what you just pulled."

"Then I'm happy to report I have extremely valuable information." Creed's smirk vanished. "I want to speak with Commissioner Schröder."

"You can talk to us first. After that, we may decide to bring your request to the Commissioner."

"That's not good enough. I know what the penalty is for my crimes, and it'll take more than a Themis stiff and an Admin grunt to stay my execution. You want what I know? You bring the Commissioner to me. Those are my terms."

"We're all you're going to get. If you think for one second I'm about to ask Commissioner Schröder to come down here for a chat with the man who almost killed Director Shigeki, then you've been thumped around harder than I realized."

The room fell silent, and Isaac waited for the prisoner's reaction.

"Look, I see we've reached something of an impasse here." Creed tilted his head and smirked again. "So, how about this? How about I give you two a sample of what I know? Something to whet your appetites."

"What sort of sample?"

"A peek into recent events. Deep enough to demonstrate my worth, but shallow enough for me to hold a few bargaining chips in reserve."

"It'll be a start," Isaac said guardedly. "What are you willing to share?"

"How about we begin with *Reality Flux*? I'm not entirely sure how much you've uncovered, but that works in your favor. You can check what I'm about to say against your own findings."

"Believe me when I say we will."

"Naturally. Then let's start with what should be obvious by now. Vidali and I were the ones who grabbed the SourceCode ship."

"How?"

"We phased our scaffold into position nearby and then deployed a shroud to conceal the theft. We also dropped off a small, shrouded drone designed to mimic the ship's normal log activity. Another drone was used to board the craft and introduce our software into its control systems."

"Why didn't Gordian detect your phase-in?"

"We secretly modified our impeller with stealth baffles. We also kept our transdimensional speed low while operating close to SysGov, only ramping up our speed once we'd pulled about a thousand chens away from T1's outer wall."

"Why steal the ship?"

"For its industrial equipment. We used those resources to set up a base of operations for our organization."

"What organization?"

"The Phoenix Institute, of course. Surely *that* much is obvious by now?"

"Where is this base?"

"Now, Detective, let's not get ahead of ourselves." Creed

flashed a crooked smile. "I can't give you *everything* for free. But rest assured I *do* know where it is. Quite the valuable piece of information, wouldn't you say?"

Isaac remained silent, and Creed continued eventually.

"Anyway, Vidali and I flew the scaffold over to a...preselected universe, traveled forty years into the past, and then went to work utilizing the *Flux*'s resources. Our efforts created a branch in the timeline, as we intended, and spawned a child universe. That new universe then proceeded to peel off from its parent, growing and catching up with the True Present, and granting us a 'free' forty years in the process."

"You and Vidali did this alone?"

"No, there were others. Our colleagues arrived ahead of time by their own means."

"On Institute TTVs?"

"Of course."

"How many?"

Creed shook his head slowly. "Try again, Detective."

"Why only forty years? Why not a hundred? Or a thousand? Why pick that number?"

"Because of time."

"What do you mean?"

"The longer we used the *Reality Flux*, the greater our chances of being detected. We needed to return that ship to SysGov as soon as possible while also fulfilling our other goals. A branch formed near the True Present would catch up much sooner than one created in—oh, just to throw out an example—the height of the Byzantine Empire.

"Our understanding of how branches in the timeline form is still incomplete—and I don't claim to be an expert—but the closer the split is to the True Present, the faster the new universe will fully form. That much, at least, seems clear. Besides, we weren't trying to create a fresh cataclysm like the Gordian Knot or the Dynasty's temporal replication, so we kept our meddling as conservative as possible to meet our ends. Forty years was enough."

"What's the base for?"

"It's a construction site, mostly."

"For what?"

"A...solution." His eyes flicked over to Susan. "To a rather large, rather ugly problem."

"Are you referring to the Admin?"

"Perhaps I am."

"Is the Institute behind the recent string of terrorist attacks against the Admin?"

"Sorry, Detective. That one will cost you."

"Why did you destroy the SourceCode ship?"

"We didn't."

Isaac paused and considered Creed's unexpected answer. "If not you or Vidali, then who?"

"I'm not sure, but I have my suspicions."

"Which are?"

Creed sighed and attempted a shrug, but the gesture came out awkwardly with his immobile shoulders.

"We considered destroying the *Flux* at one point. We even formulated a plan to instigate a reactor failure, very similar to what actually took it out, but we abandoned the idea in favor of dropping it back off intact. We figured that approach would draw the least attention, even if it ran the risk of leaving behind more evidence. We had also considered keeping the *Flux* indefinitely but dismissed that option for the same reasons. Too likely to draw unwanted attention.

"So, after forty years of use, we refurbished and scrubbed the ship as best we could before sending it back to SysGov. Vidali and I handled that part, of course. Which *should* have been the end of it, but as we both know, it blew up shortly after we brought it back."

"Then why did it explode?"

"First, you need to realize something, Detective. Forty years is a *long* time, even from the perspective of abstract beings. Opinions can change. Passions can cool. Discord can form where there was once harmony."

"Some members of the Institute began to doubt your mission?"

"*One* member, to be precise."

The reference to another member of the Institute caught Isaac's attention, and he tabbed his screen over to the *Kleio*'s summary report, then found the reference he was looking for. It was a long shot, but the *Kleio*'s crew thought the name was tied to *Reality Flux* somehow.

"Would that person happen to be Ijiraq?"

"Oh?" Creed's face lit up with bemusement. "Yes, Detective. Quite right. She did go by that alias. I'd love to hear how you came by the name."

"What was Ijiraq's role in the Institute?"

"Sorry, but that's out of bounds until I have some guarantees."

"What about the attempt on Director Shigeki's life?"

"Vidali handled that; I wasn't involved. He hacked into *Charm Quark* while we were transporting it over to Providence. That gave him access to its drones and printers. The rest should be obvious."

"Who was the target?"

"Shigeki or one of his under-directors."

"Why target them?"

"Oh, come now, Detective. Surely, you can put the pieces together without me spelling it out for you." Creed's eyes ventured over to Susan once more. "Surely, a man in your position can see this peace won't last."

"What are you referring to?"

"The lack of open hostilities between SysGov and the Admin." He returned his gaze to Isaac. "It won't last."

"Why not?"

"The rot in their society stretches too wide, runs too deep. The Admin can be likened to a malignant mass. It grows and mutates over time, strangling everything it touches, be they people or ideas. One look at how they treat ACs over there is enough to know our societies *can't* live in harmony. Not for long. This 'peace' is a dream, full of naive hopes. The Admin's a cancer, pure and simple, built out of infectious ideas, not broken cells, and even more dangerous because it is. It's a blight of dangerous philosophies that will come for us in due time. Do you really think we can stave off the rot indefinitely?"

A cancer? Isaac thought, sitting back. *Why does that sound familiar?*

He consulted his notes once more and ran a quick search, which brought up the transcript from their interview with Clara Muntero.

And there it is, Isaac thought.

He faced Creed with intense, focused eyes. "What is your connection to an AC professor by the name of Xenophon?"

"I—" Creed frowned, his arrogance dissolving. "What's it to you?"

"Answer the question. And you can quit playing your games. Tell me how you're tied to Xenophon, or there's no deal of any kind."

"Now listen here—"

"No. *You* listen. You either give me what I want, or we walk

out that door. I don't care how well you think you scrubbed
the scaffold. We in Themis Division have our ways, and we *will*
squeeze the truth out of its systems. You can either cooperate
now, or we can do this ourselves."

Creed lowered his gaze, his confidence shattered, his eyes
darting back and forth.

"Well?" Isaac said. "What's it going to be?"

A moment passed, and Creed began to settle down. He looked
up once more, his gaze now cold and distant.

"It would have been better if you'd played along," he uttered,
his voice low and lifeless.

"Data isolation breached!" Cephalie shouted.

Susan stiffened in her seat.

Isaac began to open his mouth, forming the first syllable of
a command, when Creed launched himself forward. He shouldn't
have been able to move, but he did, his remaining foot kicking
off the floor, and he lunged across the table, fingers reaching for
Isaac. He was fast. *Terribly* fast—

—but Susan was faster.

She rose, the abrupt motion flinging her chair back against
the wall. Creed sailed over the table, snarling and grasping, but
Susan caught him by the throat. His eyes widened in the split
second before she carried him, using her own powerful momentum to override his, driving him back until his head cracked
against the back wall.

He flailed at her with his good arm, but Susan pinned it in
place with her boot, grabbed hold of the wrist, and yanked it off
at the elbow with a sharp jerk. She then stomped on his good
knee, shattering it.

He crumpled to the floor, now fully disarmed.

Creed chuckled, his voice distorted by the damage to his throat.

"Well, look at you! Bet you've been dying to tear into me this
whole time. Did that feel good?"

Susan loomed over him, stoic and silent. She drew her pistol
and aimed it at his head.

"Predictable." Creed coughed out one final laugh. "But you
needn't bother. Enjoy this moment, girl. It won't last."

His face twitched, slackened, and the light of life departed
his eyes.

✧   ✧   ✧

"That can't be right."

"What can't be?" Isaac asked as he and Susan stepped back into Creed's cell an hour later.

Gilbert turned from his array of overlapping virtual screens. Isaac had called the specialist back from *Scaffold Delta* after Creed's unexpected—and improbable—attack, figuring the corpse held more secrets beyond its ability to circumvent standard SysPol restraints. Gilbert had left Kikazaru on the scaffold and returned with two drones, which now hovered above either end of the partially dismantled synthoid.

"It's his connectome." Gilbert tapped a finger through one of his screens. "And Vidali's, too. Between the Creed fragments I've pulled from the head and the Vidali fragments Encephalon preserved after her fight, I'm starting to get a better picture of what happened. Both show signs of a trojan layer."

"Then you don't think these were the real Vidali and Creed?" Isaac asked.

"No. Seems to me the Institute replaced them at some unknown point."

"A trojan layer?" Susan asked.

"Deceptive modifications to a connectome's interface shell," Isaac explained. "If done right, it would allow them to masquerade as the two Gordian agents. At least on a virtual level."

"Trojan measures would be more relevant for an AC like Vidali," Gilbert added, "but it could come up for the fake-Creed as well. During a connectome transfer, for example."

"Then the real Vidali and Creed are . . ." Susan said.

"Dead, most likely," Isaac finished for her. "Replaced by these two Institute operatives. We'll list the agents as missing for now, but I wouldn't get my hopes up, given what we've seen from the Institute so far." He looked over to Gilbert. "But why do the trojan layers surprise you? I was half-expecting you'd find something along those lines."

"Me too. And you're right; that part isn't too shocking. It's the *other* fragments I find odd. Granted, I'm working with less than twenty percent of each connectome, but what I do have looks too similar."

"How similar?"

"Enough to be the same person."

"Oh?" Isaac eyes widened. "Then our two Institute operatives . . ."

"May in fact be copies of someone else," Gilbert said.

Isaac took a moment to consider this new evidence. Connectome copying was heavily restricted within SysGov, only permissible under a finite and heavily regulated set of circumstances. But the Institute clearly didn't care about the legal niceties of what they were doing.

And if they feel no compunction when it comes to copying their own minds, Isaac thought, *then the seed of a relatively small conspiracy could have sprouted into a vast, ugly weed. A forty-year-old one at that.*

"We'll have to keep that in mind moving forward," Isaac said. "Good catch."

Gilbert nodded in appreciation.

"What about the body itself?" Susan gestured over the synthoid on the table. "How was he still able to move? The microbots Cephalie pumped into his system should have kept him paralyzed."

"*And* he somehow breached data isolation," Isaac said. "The question is how."

"I can help there." Cephalie popped into existence on Isaac's shoulder. "Gilbert asked me and a few of the Gordian ACs to help track down what happened there."

"I figured you wouldn't mind," Gilbert said.

"Whatever helps us resolve this case faster." Isaac turned to his IC. "So, what did you find?"

"Signs of *really* skillful hacking. Somehow this Creed-a-like managed to cut through every access barrier I'd stuffed into the room." Cephalie pushed her glasses up the bridge of her nose. "Made my efforts look like a complete joke."

"He shouldn't have been able to access the infostructure at all," Isaac said. "The microbots should have kept him data-isolated all on their own."

"Except the microbots weren't under our control." Gilbert tapped a vial of milky fluid beside the synthoid. "They'd been reprogrammed."

"How?" Isaac asked.

"Not sure, but I'm guessing it was done almost as soon as the swarm was introduced. It'll take time to make sense of the revised software, but the end result seems clear enough. Those microbots were faking us out, pretending to be under our control when in fact Creed could have gotten up at any time."

Isaac frowned at this, his mind flashing back to an image of the synthoid lunging at him, fingers reaching for him.

If Susan hadn't been in the room...

"What did he use the access for?" Isaac asked.

"He sent a data packet to *Scaffold Delta*," Cephalie said. "Or tried to. Not sure what was in the packet, though, or what it would have done had it arrived. It's encrypted and I haven't managed to bust through it yet."

"Fortunately, the ship was already data-isolated," Gilbert said. "And *those* barriers held."

"Then we don't know what he was trying to achieve," Isaac said.

"Not yet. Maybe Kikazaru will turn up something as he digs through the ship's infostructure." Gilbert grabbed one of his screens and shifted it closer to Isaac. "And speaking of which, take a look at this."

Isaac skimmed over the screen.

"What are we looking at?" Susan asked.

"Pieces of a connectome transit log, it seems," Isaac said.

"That's exactly what it is," Gilbert said. "Kikazaru turned up this nugget from temporary memory in the scaffold's backup transceiver controller. The primary had been scrubbed, but looks like they didn't quite clear out the secondary. Most of the data is missing—having been written over by normal activity, like self-diagnostic processing—but what we *do* have includes the source coordinates."

"Coordinates for where?"

"High-end beachfront property on Luna. Lacus Oblivionis, to be precise."

"Hmm." Isaac pursed his lips, then glanced to Cephalie. "How large a city are we talking here?"

"About a hundred thousand physical," Cephalie said, summoning a blackboard. Chalked script scrolled down it too fast to read. "And another fifty thousand ACs, though the totals fluctuate with Earth's seasons, spiking most during the middle of summer for the northern hemisphere. Lots of resorts and related businesses."

"What are you thinking?" Susan asked.

"That the Institute operatives—" Isaac paused, then snorted. "Or *operative*, singular, may have come from there."

"Worth us checking out, then?"

"Yes, but we need to narrow it down somehow."

"The coordinates are laser-precise," Gilbert said, "so you've got a starting position."

"True, but that'll most likely be a relay point. Not the true point of origin."

"What about that Xenophon guy?" Susan asked. "Fake-Creed didn't like it when you brought him up. Maybe we can see if he's been active on Luna?"

"My thoughts exactly." Isaac gave her a half smile. "Yes, I do believe we need to take a long, hard look at Doctor Xenophon's recent activities. Keep it up, Gilbert. Let us know if you find anything else."

"Will do."

Gilbert turned back to his screens, and the two detectives stepped out.

"Where to next?" Susan asked.

"Commissioner Schröder wants an update," Cephalie chimed in, still on Isaac's shoulder.

"Then that settles that," Isaac said. "We can brief him on the latest and then talk to Elifritz about heading back to SysGov. I doubt there's much we can do here but wait for Gilbert to finish his work. Whereas a detour over to Luna might prove more fruitful."

"Sounds like a plan to me," Susan said.

The two settled into a brisk walk back to the central grav shaft, and Isaac found himself thinking back to fake-Creed's last moments, how mentioning Xenophon had shaken him, stripping away his confidence and bravado to the point where he resorted to a desperate attack.

He saw that hand reaching for him once more through his mind's eye, and Susan bursting into view, just a blur of frantic motion that caught Creed's synthoid and slammed him into the wall.

But why did he rush me? Isaac thought. *What did he have to gain from that? I'd already connected him to Xenophon, and his actions only served to reinforce the point. Am I missing something here?*

He stopped in front of the grav shaft, and Susan came to a halt beside him.

"Something wrong?" she asked.

"I don't know. Just thinking back to Creed's attack. Something feels off about it, but I'm not sure what."

"Wasn't he just lashing out?"

"That's just it. He *didn't* lash out. Not immediately. He cut through the data isolation first, remember."

"Oh yeah. Now that you mention it, that did place me on guard. If he really wanted to take you out, he would have been better off lunging in straight away."

"Which could mean his attack was just a distraction."

"But a distraction from what? His packet to the scaffold didn't go anywhere."

"I know, and that's another thing that's bugging me," Isaac said. "He must have known we'd isolate the ship as one of our first orders of business. Why try to contact it at all if..."

He trailed off, a thought tickling the edge of his mind.

On the surface, both his attack and the attempt to contact the ship were failures. Why then did he seem to regain his composure in the end, right up to the moment where he deleted his own mind? "Enjoy this moment, girl. It won't last." That's what he said.

But he failed.

Right?

"The look in his eyes at the end," Isaac said. "It's like he knew he'd won this round."

"But he didn't," Susan said. "We stopped him cold."

"That's certainly what it looks like." Isaac let out a heavy, frustrated exhale. "But now I'm not so sure. Fake-Creed accessed the infostructure first, so between attacking me and contacting his ship, the ship was more important to him."

"But he never got through to it."

"I know."

What am I missing?

What are we still missing?

"The drone," Isaac muttered.

"What drone?" Susan asked. "You mean the one from the *Quark*."

"It's still loose on the station. Cephalie?"

"Yes?" She took a long, floating leap from his shoulder to the top of the LENS.

"Is it possible the packet wasn't meant for *Scaffold Delta* at all?" Isaac asked. "Could a copy of it have been routed elsewhere?"

"Possibly," Cephalie said. "There's a clear routing trail from his conference room to the scaffold's dock, but I suppose it's possible there was other activity along the way. I spent most of my time looking into the breach, so I wouldn't know. Gordian agents are checking the rest of the routing path, but they're not done yet."

"Then it could have been sent to our missing drone."

"What for, though?" Susan asked.

"I'm not sure. Unless..."

A terrible thought came to his mind. One that tied Providence Station to *Reality Flux*.

And its explosive demise.

"We need to talk to Andover-Chen!" Isaac snapped. "Right *now!*"

CHAPTER TWENTY

Providence Station
Transverse, non-congruent

KLAUS-WILHELM STORMED INTO CHRONO OPERATIONS, TOOK A quick measure of the place, and strode toward the massive map of Providence now dominating the room's center. Andover-Chen and Hinnerkopf stood at the diagram's base, and numerous members from their support staffs now took up the first ring of workstations. Detective Cho and Agent Cantrell were also in attendance, along with a specialist in a Themis Division uniform, all three crowded around their own desks, studying what might have been drone visual feeds.

Klaus-Wilhelm came up beside Andover-Chen.

"What's the situation, Doctor?"

"Ah, Commissioner." Andover-Chen finished tapping a set of commands into a drone control interface. "Good timing. We've confirmed that at least some of Detective Cho's suspicions are correct. The data packet sent by the Institute operative to *Scaffold Delta* does indeed appear to have been a decoy, with the true message breaking off along the way."

"How did we miss something that big?"

"The second message was well disguised, masquerading as a routine status update between adjoining nodes. Our agents barely caught it the second time, and only thanks to a bit of technical insight from our Themis Division colleagues. Once the message was clear of the original, a secondary program executed, unpacking its contents and sending them worming through our systems. The trail ends at a node two levels above the station's reactors. We believe the message contained instructions which were then transmitted locally to our missing conveyor drone."

"How much of a head start does the drone have on us?"

"About eighty-five minutes, sir."

"And what actions are we taking?"

"We're running full self-diagnostics on each of our six reactors. Additionally, all available agents and drones have been mobilized to visually inspect the power plants and supporting systems, with priority given to our three hot singularity reactors and their exotic matter shells."

"What do the diagnostics say?"

"That there's nothing to worry about, but Hinnerkopf and I agree we shouldn't trust those results. Not with the digital sleight of hand we've witnessed so far. Hence the visual inspections."

"Can we even trust our own drones at this point?" Klaus-Wilhelm asked. "The Institute's been playing our systems like a goddamned fiddle."

"We're doing what we can to mitigate that risk."

"How?"

"We're pairing DTI and Gordian drones where we can," Hinnerkopf said, stepping away from her own screens. "And ensuring each team has at least two physical agents."

"Doctor Hinnerkopf managed to free up their entire drone inventory from the docked DTI ships," Andover-Chen said.

Klaus-Wilhelm gave her a curt nod. "We appreciate the prompt support. Did Muntero give you any problems?"

"No, Commissioner." The slightest hint of a wry smile graced Hinnerkopf's lips. "It seems our consul doesn't relish the idea of being blown to bits either."

"I should hope not," Klaus-Wilhelm replied dryly, though he wouldn't put anything past Muntero's pigheaded "risk management" at this point.

He'd half expected the DTI chronoports to flee the station like rats from a sinking ship—on Muntero's orders, of course—but instead they were standing their ground, assisting his agents any way they could through yet another crisis. His eyes skimmed over occupied workstations and found more than a few examples of

Gordian and DTI agents standing or sitting beside one another, sometimes with one craning over the shoulder of the other.

He picked out a few stressed or nervous faces amongst the staff—on *both* sides—but everyone was acting like this was just another problem that needed solving, so they might as well hunker down and get it done.

That's one of the things he'd grown to appreciate about the DTI, despite his traumatic first encounter with the organization. He doubted he'd ever *like* them—not with those dark, flame-scorched memories tucked away in his heart—but he could recognize and respect a well-staffed, well-managed group of people when he saw it.

And that's exactly what the DTI was. They were relentless professionals in pursuit of whatever goal was placed in front of them. He might not always share their goals, but he couldn't deny the efficiency and determination on display.

And they had no problem sitting side-by-side with Gordian agents in order to get the job done.

We really are making this work, aren't we? he reflected. *Now if we can just avoid the whole station going nova.*

"Doctor!" a Gordian agent called out. "We have something from Team Four! Passing the image to you now."

"Then let's take a look," Andover-Chen murmured as a new screen opened over his virtual console. The image featured the swell of a massive sphere protruding down through a ceiling of thick structural members and cluttered utility channels. A trio of light beams danced across a black surface segmented by thin green gridlines and marked with a prominent SourceCode logo. A second screen opened with a high-definition thermal breakdown of the area, revealing the exterior to be uniformly cool except for an ugly, oblong patch that glowed angrily.

"Is that hot zone normal?" Klaus-Wilhelm asked.

"No, it's not," Andover-Chen replied quietly. "The shell's temperature should be much more uniform. This sort of exotic matter has a very high thermal capacity, so we shouldn't be seeing this much of a temperature difference. If I were to guess, I'd say something on the surface is producing waste heat."

Andover-Chen assumed control of Team Four's small, elliptical maintenance drone and guided it forward, past two crouched Gordian Agents and a DTI Wolverine. The drone slowed to a halt beside the warmest spot on the surface and extended a prog-steel pseudopod.

It had almost reached the surface when the cables in an overhead utility trough shifted aside.

The bulk of a CounterGravCorp conveyor pushed through the cables and dove at the maintenance drone.

"Whoa!" Andover-Chen exclaimed, his hands jerking over the controls, pulling his drone back.

The conveyor reached out with its manipulator arms, snatched the smaller drone out of the air, and began to squeeze. Warning lights flashed on the screen as the maintenance drone's body began to crumple under the pressure.

Klaus-Wilhelm reached around Andover-Chen and flicked on a live channel to Team Four.

"Agents, this is the Commissioner. Take that drone out, but do *not* hit the reactor!"

"Sir!"

The view shook as pistol fire punched the conveyor from the side, knocking it back and sending it into a lazy pirouette. More gunfire rattled off, and this time the Wolverine joined in, peppering the conveyor with finger-sized holes. The conveyor's grip loosened, and Andover-Chen managed to squirm his drone out of its grasp.

The rogue conveyor sputtered drunkenly under the onslaught, then dropped to the floor and skidded to a screeching halt.

Two Gordian agents stepped forward and inspected their handiwork.

"Drone down, sir."

"Good work," Klaus-Wilhelm replied. "Sweep the area for any more surprises."

"Yes, sir."

Klaus-Wilhelm clicked the mute. "How's your drone?"

"Good enough," Andover-Chen said, guiding it forward once more. "The frame is warped, and there's a flutter in the thruster, but that's it. I can still use it to grab a sample from the reactor."

"Then proceed."

"Yes, sir. Here's goes."

The drone extended a prog-steel pseudopod and scraped it against the reactor's surface. Prog-steel encapsulated the sample, and the drone brought it before a small internal scope for testing and analysis.

An alarm screen opened, and Hinnerkopf stepped over. "That's stuff's already eating the drone from the inside out."

"Nanotech corrosion," Andover-Chen said. "A very nasty, very infectious strain, too. We'll need to isolate and destroy the drone."

"And the reactor?" Klaus-Wilhelm asked.

"The corrosion is eating through the outer shell. Nanotech isn't very good at working with exotic matter, which is probably the only reason we're still alive to talk about it. However, unless we do something about it, the reactor will reach a critical imbalance and collapse in on itself, given enough time. The pseudo-singularity in the core will cancel out the negative matter shell, and the imbalance will be released as pure energy. Explosively, I might add."

"How do we fix it?"

Andover-Chen turned to him with what might have been the most serious expression he'd ever seen from the scientist.

"Very, *very* carefully, sir."

Isaac never enjoyed presenting in front of an audience. Any assignment that placed him before a crowd had terrified him throughout his school years, and while SysPol Academy had whipped his tendency toward cold-sweating fear into a begrudging "let's just get this over with," he preferred to avoid such tasks wherever possible.

Conveniently, his job kept him busy in the field, and in those rare occasions where he had to testify at a trial or present a report to coworkers or superiors, he always received ample time to prepare, venturing in only when armed and armored with solid facts and legal conclusions on his side.

This was not one of those moments.

But when Commissioner Klaus-Wilhelm von Schröder told someone to summarize his findings and present them to senior staff in half an hour, the man was unlikely to entertain excuses.

And so Isaac, Susan, and Cephalie had gone to work, slapping together the best presentation they could in the time allotted. Omar Raviv—Isaac's mentor back when he'd been an acting deputy detective—had once impressed upon him that the higher up in management a report needed to go, the more dumbed down the summary should be.

That wasn't a knock against the intelligence of SysPol's upper echelons. Far from it, in fact. Rather, Raviv's point was people in those positions were under constant data bombardment, to the point of information overload, so if he or Isaac needed to make a point, best make it as easy to digest as possible.

Which, in turn, had led to a lot of large font and bright colors being used in *this* report. Isaac cringed a little on the inside as he advanced to the next screen. The timeline for *Reality Flux*, *Charm Quark*, and *Scaffold Delta* looked like something from an elementary school art class, complete with bold text and huge swathes of primary colors.

"Which brings us to information gleaned from the hijacking of *Reality Flux*," Isaac continued, highlighting a portion of the timeline. "Video of the theft provides the start of our best estimate for *Scaffold Delta*'s illegal venture into the transverse. The SourceCode vessel's destruction provides the stopping point. With this window and the scaffold's top transdimensional speed, we can then construct an absolute maximum sphere within which the Institute base may be located. The—"

"What about the time it took *Delta* to slip away at reduced speed?" Klaus-Wilhelm interrupted. "Or the time needed for whatever branch universe to form and catch up with the True Present? Are those factored into your search sphere?"

Isaac regarded the room's occupants and did his best to suppress a frown while Susan stood stiffly beside him. In addition to the Commissioner, both CHRONO consuls were in attendance along with Directors Jonas and Csaba Shigeki—the latter still in his temporary body—and Doctors Andover-Chen and Hinnerkopf. He could almost feel their collective eyes boring into his skull.

"No, sir," Isaac replied, his voice firm but respectful. "Regrettably, we haven't had the opportunity yet to consult with our Gordian colleagues on those sorts of technical questions."

We only had half an hour to throw this together! he screamed in his head. *What do you expect from us?!*

"I've already put together estimates for both points," Andover-Chen said, leaning forward at the conference table. "It won't take me long to adjust the estimate."

"It's already smaller than the area we're searching now," Peng added. "We'll be able to fine-tune our search patterns as ships come back into communication range with their reports. The fact that the storm's easing up will also make this task easier."

Klaus-Wilhelm merely nodded in response, his face unreadable.

"Continue with your presentation, Detective."

"Yes, sir. Getting back to *Scaffold Delta*..."

Isaac summarized what they knew of the scaffold's activities, all the way up to fake-Creed's capture. His audience continued to pepper him with questions, and he did his best to field them, eventually moving on to their assessment of the Institute.

"While it's difficult for us to make any firm statements regarding the Institute, they have shown a strong anti-Admin mindset thus far. The bomb is the most clearcut example of this, since it specifically targeted Director Shigeki and his senior staff. Overall, our read on the Institute is that it's ambivalent toward SysGov casualties."

"But they almost blew up the station," Peng said. "That's a little more than 'ambivalent.'"

"Correct, sir. However, the sabotage uncovered at Reactor Three was clearly initiated by the operative's last transmission, and not before. Given the operative had numerous opportunities to trigger it beforehand—coupled with his animus toward the Admin—we're left with something of a contradiction. Destroying the station would have easily resulted in the highest Admin death toll. It would have also heavily disrupted our search for the Institute's base, but it wasn't triggered except as a last resort. Something clearly stayed the operative's hand."

"And you believe that something was SysGov casualties?" Klaus-Wilhelm asked.

"Yes, sir."

"What changed his mind?"

"It's hard to say without more information."

"Then what are your next steps?"

"Our most promising lead is Doctor Xenophon and any ties he may have to the Institute. We also have a set of coordinates on Luna used by *Delta* for connectome transmission. As long as there are no objections, we intend to return to SysGov as soon as possible to pursue these leads."

"What do we know about this Xenophon character?" Peng asked.

"Just the basics until we can access his public record back in SysGov. He's a professor of abstraction at Luna's West Cognitum University. Recently, he was invited as part of the Million Handshake Initiative to guest-lecture in the Admin. However, most of his appearances were cancelled due to his intense anti-Admin rhetoric."

Muntero snorted.

"In short, we kicked the troublemaker out."

"Differences in opinion can be such a *terrible* thing," Peng muttered under his breath.

Muntero scowled at her fellow consul.

"Sorry," Peng said. "Force of habit."

Muntero looked ready to launch a sharp counter-remark, but then huffed out a breath and turned to Isaac.

"Detective, do you believe the Institute is behind the recent terror strikes in the Admin?"

"That's one possibility, Madam Consul. Certainly, the Institute has demonstrated the necessary sophistication, especially when it comes to their software, to carry out such activities, either directly or through proxies. The presence of an independent industrial base—possibly a very large one—further aligns their capabilities with what we know. However, we lack direct evidence to prove a connection."

"But what do you believe?"

"I believe what I can prove," Isaac replied. He wasn't about to voice his impromptu guesswork in front of *this* crowd! "Right now, all I can say is it remains a possibility."

"Very well. I can respect that approach." Muntero turned to Susan. "What about you, Agent? What's your take on all this?"

Susan hesitated with a brief, panicked look in her eyes, perhaps taken aback by suddenly being called on. She recovered quickly, wrapping herself in the calm veneer of a model Peacekeeper.

"I concur with Detective Cho's assessment."

Muntero waited for more, but when none came she began tapping her fingers on the table.

"And?" she prompted at last.

"I recommend we follow his...recommendations for our next course of action."

A new, expectant silence fell over the room. Muntero glanced over to either side, as if inviting the other attendees to ask their own questions.

After a moment, Klaus-Wilhelm leaned forward.

"Have you come across any evidence of additional Institute agents operating in or around Providence Station?"

"No, sir," Isaac replied. "Everything we've uncovered so far can be traced back to the replacements for Agents Vidali and Creed. Of course, that doesn't mean they're not here."

"Point taken, Detective. I think we've all come to respect the Institute's capabilities. Do you have anything else to add to your report?"

"No, sir. Not at this time."

"Then I thank you and your team for the update. You may return to your duties."

✧   ✧   ✧

Susan let out a relieved sigh once she and Isaac were alone again, meeting up in a side passage off from CHRONO Operations.

"I hate getting called on like that."

"You and me both." Isaac gave her a quick smile. "At least you didn't have to present."

"Too true. Thanks for handling that, by the way."

"No problem." He raised his palm and opened a comm window. The recipient took only a few seconds to answer.

"Elifritz here. Go ahead, Detective."

"Captain, we find ourselves once again in need of your services. Are you free to transport us to SysGov's Luna?"

"I'm afraid not. All chronoports on or near Providence have been ordered to muster up near the station and keep their impellers hot. I'm guessing we'll be joining the search for the Institute's base; our superiors only need some time to sort out who goes where."

"I see. Is there any chance you could give us a lift while you wait?"

"Not without orders from the top. Sorry. You could try talking to Acting Director Shigeki, though you may have better luck going straight to Gordian. A few of their TTVs have started trickling back in."

"Understood. We'll ask around and see what our options are. Thank you again, Captain."

He closed the comm window.

"Should we talk to Schröder about this?" Susan asked.

"Uh, *no*," Isaac replied firmly. "We don't need to bother a SysPol commissioner over our travel plans. Cephalie?"

The LENS hovered over, and Cephalie appeared atop it.

"You rang?"

"Check in with Operations and see if you can rustle up a ride for us."

"Sure thing." She waved and then vanished.

"Wonder how long we'll have to wait." Susan folded her arms and leaned against the wall. "Is Gilbert coming with us?"

"No, he and Kikazaru are staying until they finish sifting through *Scaffold Delta*'s systems. Gilbert thinks they caught the real prize with those lunar coordinates, but there's always the chance a slower, more thorough sweep will turn up something else."

"Then you and I are on our own again?"

"Looks that way. Hopefully someone can drop us off at Argus Station soon. Once we're there, we'll requisition a V-wing and fly over to Luna."

"Sounds like a plan to me."

Cephalie materialized atop the LENS. "I'm back, and I have good news! We've got six TTVs stopping by over the next two hours, and more on the way soon after. Care to guess which one is getting here first?"

"Do I have to?" Isaac asked.

"Come on. Give it a try."

"Well, since I only know the one ship..."

CHAPTER TWENTY-ONE

Transtemporal Vehicle *Kleio*
Transverse, non-congruent

BENJAMIN SCHRÖDER SAT AT *KLEIO*'S COMMAND TABLE, HANDS resting on its surface, eyes darting back and forth between two sets of charts, jaw tense and lips fixed into a harsh line.

"You don't look happy." Elzbietá came up behind him and rested her hands on his shoulders.

"I'm not. It has to be here. It *has* to be." He shook his head, eyes never leaving the charts. "I just haven't found it yet."

"You will." She bent over and gave his cheek a quick peck.

"Don't get all bent out of shape, Doc." Raibert leaned back and propped his boots on the table. "H17 is a weird, frustrating mess. Take a break. Give your brain a breather. We're almost back to Providence, anyway."

Benjamin didn't want to take a breather. He'd spent *days* on the ground in H17A and H17B, collecting historical data from each universe's True Present, trying to zero in on the differences in their timelines, differences that would reveal the Institute's activities in one universe or the other.

But all those efforts had amounted to nothing. Even assistance from *Phoebe*'s own ground team had turned up zilch. The two universes were divergent, both historically and chronometrically, but not in any way that made sense.

I should have known something was off when my two trips to the library turned up nearly identical records for 2941.

Those records hadn't been the same, but they'd been close. Too close to account for a permanent fissure in the timeline. *Something* had split H17 down the middle, and that something had occurred forty years in the past. He could even pin the event down to within a *day* with a reasonable degree of accuracy, but that was as close as he'd come.

The divergence in newborn records had provided him with the most promising data so far. Any split in the timeline would inevitably introduce a ripple effect of causal change, and that would then manifest later as a sudden spike in births that panned out differently. The chances of the same two gametes connecting to produce the same individual were vanishingly small, which left him with a healthy evidence trail of differences. Trace those divergent pregnancies back to the earliest estimated point of fertilization, and he knew, roughly, when H17 ripped itself in two.

But what's the trigger? he thought, frustrated and even a little angry at himself.

He knew the when, but he had no clue on the how. The Institute had fractured H17, but how had they done it? He'd studied the twin records until his eyes felt ready to bleed. There was nothing—absolutely *nothing*—so significantly different that it could account for the split.

It was like finding a shock wave with no explosion at the center.

How could they have possibly pulled this off? he wondered.

"Just remember something, Doc," Raibert said. "We're all stumped on this one. But don't worry. I'll talk to the boss and muster up some heavy-duty backup before we head out again. Maybe even see if I can rope Andover-Chen into this one."

"It's there," Benjamin growled. "I *know* it is."

"Doc..." Raibert shrugged and gave Elzbietá a sad smile. "I gave it my best shot, Ella. This is your show now."

Elzbietá hugged Benjamin's shoulders from behind and gave his cheek another kiss.

"Come on, Ben. Time to step away for a bit."

"It's got to be there."

Elzbietá reached for the screens, then swiped them closed. Benjamin frowned at the sudden blank space in front of him, then shut his eyes and let out a long, tired exhale. His wife gave his shoulders a reassuring squeeze.

"Come on." She tugged on him. "Let's get some food in you. You hungry?"

"A little," Benjamin admitted, rising out of his seat.

"How's some leberkäse sound to you?"

"I could go for that."

"Leberkäse it is, then."

"Agent Kaminski," Kleio said. "I have received a telegraph for you from Providence Station."

Benjamin paused on his way off the bridge and, despite Elzbietá's insistent nudging, turned to listen.

"Oh, good," Raibert said. "What'd they say?"

"CHRONO Operations has issued a set of revised docking instructions. Would you like to review them?"

"Just give me the summary."

"We are to proceed directly to Hangar Fifteen where a team of Gordian agents will inspect the ship."

"An inspection?" Benjamin asked. "Is this because we're coming back from quarantine universes?"

"No, Agent Schröder. The new policy was put in place by Consul Peng Fa following the assassination attempt on Director-General Csaba Shigeki and the—"

"*What?!*" Raibert blurted, almost slipping out of his chair. His boots stamped against the floor and he sprang up.

"The assassination attempt on Director-General Csaba Shigeki," Kleio repeated, a rare edge of annoyance entering her voice, "and the sabotage of one of the station's hot singularity reactors."

"Exactly how much have we missed?" Raibert asked in wide-eyed disbelief.

"I do not know, Agent Kaminski. Would you like me to ask CHRONO Operations for more details?"

"You get right on that!"

Raibert stepped out of the counter-grav shaft and hurried into CHRONO Operations. The chamber bustled with activity: both Gordian and DTI agents hunched together at their workstations, calls going out, people rushing back and worth or passing abstract diagrams to each other. It was all low-key action, but it filled the room like a quiet yet frantic dance.

Raibert hustled up the stairs to Klaus-Wilhelm's office. He palmed the door and walked through, only to stop in his tracks when he realized he was barging into a tense discussion.

"I know, Klaus. Trust me, I know." Peng held up his hands across from Klaus-Wilhelm, both men standing beside a map of the transverse.

"Then why do you keep antagonizing them?" Klaus-Wilhelm demanded. "We're in the middle of a crisis that could blow up at any moment, Muntero's first instinct is to hoard all the chronoports for defense, and you keep spouting snide remarks! They're not helping! We should all be grateful Peacekeepers are a thick-skinned bunch, otherwise they might take your verbal diarrhea seriously!"

Raibert winced at the venom in his superior's voice.

Klaus-Wilhelm caught Raibert's eye and waved for him to come in.

Raibert sidestepped all the way in and let the door seal shut behind him, but only that much. He had *zero* desire to be sucked into this one.

"Look, I get that they rub you the wrong way," Klaus-Wilhelm continued, planting hands on hips. "The Admin isn't the neighbor any of us wanted, but it's the neighbor we have, and we have no choice but to make this work. CHRONO, Providence, all of it. Because the alternative to cooperation is the two of us sitting in our respective corners of the transverse, growing increasingly paranoid about what the other side is doing. Do I need to remind you it was the Admin that came to *our* aid when the Dynasty had our backs pressed against the wall?"

"You don't," Peng said.

"Then why are you making my job harder? The DTI shed blood to defend *us*. If you can't respect anything else, at least respect *that*!"

"Klaus, you've made your point," Peng said, his tone firm but conciliatory. "I admit I've probably been...more confrontational than I should have been."

Klaus-Wilhelm waited in silence, then made a "give me more" gesture with one hand.

"Especially given this new role," Peng continued. "Look, I get why the President—and their Chief Executor for that matter—both wanted some civilian oversight on what you and Shigeki do out here. But I only accepted the position because the President kept courting me. I initially turned her down."

"Why's that?" Klaus-Wilhelm's expression softened ever so slightly.

"Because even *I* saw the problems of putting me in this position." Peng's blue eyes dimmed. "But here I am. And you're right. Hell, you're more than right. Both our side and the DTI helped us sniff out those operatives. *And* save the station." He began to nod. "You know what? Maybe I should tell Muntero how much we appreciate the DTI's help there."

"It certainly won't hurt."

Peng's eyes brightened.

"I think I'll go do that right now. I'll let you know how it goes."

The consul vanished from the room. Klaus-Wilhelm blew out a breath and turned to Raibert.

"What was *that* about?" Raibert asked.

"Not a problem you need to worry about." Klaus-Wilhelm waved him over to the transverse map. "I managed to skim your report, but only just. So far nothing definitive from either H17A or B."

"That's about the size of it, sir."

"What's your gut tell you about the two H17s?"

"That they're still our best lead. However, we've hit a wall trying to find the branching event using standard methods, which is why we came back. We'd like to take another crack at the H17s with more and better resources."

"Such as?"

"A few extra TTVs and Andover-Chen, if you can spare him."

Klaus-Wilhelm slipped his thumbs into his pockets. "Andover-Chen and Hinnerkopf are busy with the station's new array. I'd hate to slow them down even more."

"Then how about the extra ships and maybe peel off some specialists from Andover-Chen's team."

"That sounds more doable. How many ships are you after?"

"Four if you can spare them, assuming the *Phoebe* sticks around, too. That should give us enough arrays to really zero in on the branching event."

Klaus-Wilhelm consulted the map, then highlighted TTV icons on approach.

"Four it is, then. TTVs *Hyperion*, *Mnemosyne*, *Linus*, and *Alcyone* are yours as soon as they get back. I'll talk to Andover-Chen to see who he can spare."

"Thank you, sir."

"*Hyperion* and *Alcyone* are both coming at Providence from nearly the opposite direction of the H17 pair, so you have some time until you can leave." Klaus-Wilhelm pulled up another list over his palm. "Free for a little errand in the meantime?"

"I suppose that depends on what you need."

"It's not me, but Themis Division. Two of them need a ride back to Argus Station, and it's either you or *Phoebe* who gets to play taxi."

"I suppose we can manage that. Who're the passengers?"

"You remember Cho and Cantrell from the Delacroix murder?"

"Those two rascals!" Raibert's face lit up. "How the hell are they?"

"They're the reason we still have a station."

"Thank you for giving us a ride, Agent Kaminski," Isaac said, the LENS keeping pace behind his shoulder.

He and Susan followed Raibert up the ramp to the *Kleio*'s three-story-tall cargo hold while a conveyor drone hauled Susan's crated STAND equipment. Most of the chamber's volume was taken up by two massive guns stacked all the way to the ceiling. Isaac and the others filed through a path to the right of the weaponry, and the conveyor secured Susan's equipment against the wall and then floated up to its charging rack.

"Oh, don't mention it." Raibert made a shooing gesture. "Always happy to lend a hand to you two. And please, it's Raibert. We keep things casual on this ship."

Isaac and Susan trailed him to a grav shaft at the end of the hold, took it up one level, and followed the corridor back to the TTV's bridge. Isaac had expected the rest of the crew: Agents Benjamin and Elzbietá Schröder, whom he'd only heard about in passing, along with Raibert's IC Philosophus. What he hadn't expected was the large sandwich spread on the command table: fresh rolls cut in half, a cluster of jars with several kinds of mustard, a plate stacked with a wide variety of cheeses, various other sandwich fixings like lettuce and sliced tomatoes, and lastly...some sort of pink, homogenous meatloaf?

Both Benjamin and Elzbietá stood with plates in one hand and half-eaten sandwiches in the other.

"Kleio," Raibert said, resting his hands on the command table's railing, "do we have departure clearance?"

"We do, Agent Kaminski," announced a smooth feminine voice over their shared hearing.

"Then let's not dawdle. Take us out."

"Yes, Agent. Departing Providence Station and setting a course for Argus Station, SysGov, True Present."

Raibert picked up a plate with a fully assembled sandwich.

Elzbietá swallowed a mouthful and set her sandwich down. "Aren't you going to introduce us?"

"I was about to." Raibert gestured to his IC. "I assume you remember Philo."

"You better believe it." Cephalie popped into existence beside the sandwich spread. She strolled up to the pink loaf and poked it with her cane, then gave Philo a fierce eye. "You staying out of trouble?"

"Not really," Philo said. "But, in my defense, I'd have to quit Gordian to do that."

"Not without me, you're not." Raibert waved a hand toward the Schröder couple. "Over here we have our two best agents from the twenty-first century, Elzbietá and Benjamin Schröder."

"We're the *only* agents from that century," Elzbietá pointed out, her eyes laughing.

"Still counts." Raibert turned to their passengers. "Ben was a history professor and Ella a crack fighter pilot."

"Still am," Elzbietá said with a bit of swagger. "My ride's just bigger nowadays."

"That she is," Raibert agreed warmly. "Her flying has saved our lives plenty of times. Meanwhile, Ben is our resident analyst, both for historical and chronometric strangeness."

"When I'm not banging my head against a wall," Benjamin groused.

"Chin up, Doc. We all have bad days."

Benjamin grunted something under his breath.

"Over here we have Detective Isaac Cho," Raibert continued, "and Special Agent Susan Cantrell, both of whom helped us sort out Delacroix's murder."

"That was certainly an unusual case," Isaac said, and Susan nodded in agreement.

"But you two cracked it in the end," Raibert said. "That's the important part. And I understand you even figured out who tried to off Shigeki."

"Technically, we're not done with that case. We'll be heading for Luna after you drop us off."

"Either way, glad to have you two aboard," Elzbietá said brightly. "Even if it's only for a little bit."

Benjamin nodded toward them, his expression momentarily less grouchy.

"Glad to be here." Isaac's eyes flicked over the sandwich spread, and his stomach chose that moment to let out a faint grumble.

"Help yourself." Elzbietá swept an open hand across the lunch spread. "I called up the leberkäse to help cheer Ben up, but then I started getting hungry myself, so I ordered the works."

Isaac eyed the pink loaf suspiciously. "Leberkäse? I can't say I'm familiar with it."

"Oh, it's great. You should try some."

"What's it taste like?"

"It's—"

"Pardon me," Cephalie interrupted with a flourish of her cane. "I don't wish to be rude, but I should probably handle this." She cleared her virtual throat and faced Isaac. "From the perspective of your unsophisticated Saturnite palette—"

Isaac frowned at his IC.

"—you'd be best visualizing leberkäse like a big loaf of hot dog meat."

"Oh?" His eyes widened hungrily. "That does sound good."

"Smells good, too," Susan said.

"Help yourselves," Elzbietá urged.

A microbot swarm dropped off two fresh plates, and Isaac set about constructing his sandwich. Susan finished first, since the choice of mustard stalled him, and he spent over a minute consulting each jar's abstract label. Eventually, he settled on the spiciest mustard available, finished constructing his sandwich, and joined the others.

"Did you say *dinosaurs*?" Susan exclaimed, eyes lighting up.

"Yes, but that's just shorthand for what we actually found," Elzbietá said.

"Did I miss something?" Isaac asked.

Susan turned to him with a gleeful, almost childlike smile. "Ella was just telling us about the time the *Kleio* found an Earth full of dinosaurs."

"Their descendants, really," Elzbietá said. "Turns out the

L26 Earth doesn't have a Chicxulub crater, so it seems like the extinction event at the end of the Cretaceous Period never happened. Or perhaps the impact was much less severe. Either way, our survey spotted some true monsters down there. All worthy of the title 'thunder lizards.'"

"You wouldn't happen to still have the video, would you?" Susan asked hopefully.

"Sure do!" Elzbietá set her plate down. "Here, let me pull them up for you."

Isaac circled the table for a better angle, which placed him beside Benjamin.

"Detective," Benjamin said around a bite of leberkäse.

"Hello," Isaac replied. He paused, then turned toward the man. "I don't mean to pry, but you seem a little out of sorts."

"It's because of H17," Benjamin grumbled around his food, then swallowed.

"What about it?"

"There are two of them, and I can't figure out why."

"Two universes?"

"Yeah."

"Where there used to be one?"

"Uh huh."

"That sounds like a rather large deal."

"It is. But it's worse than you think because the Institute may be hiding in one of them." Benjamin narrowed his gaze, staring at nothing. "If I could only figure out—"

"Now, Ben," Elzbietá warned from across the table. "What are we doing right now?"

"Taking a break from work."

"Right. And that means...?"

"No talking about H17. I know." Benjamin sighed, then glanced over at Isaac. "Mind if we talk about something else? Before I get into trouble, that is."

"Not at all." Isaac paused for a moment. "I suppose I could talk about *my* work."

"That should be safe." Benjamin set his plate down. "You said you two were off to Luna next?"

"That's right."

"What do you expect to find there?"

"More information on the Institute, we hope. We believe a

professor named Xenophon may be involved. An Institute prisoner reacted rather forcefully when we mentioned his name, right before he self-deleted."

"Ouch." Benjamin winced. "This Xenophon character live on Luna?"

"Taught there, but that's not why we're interested. We found coordinates for a spot in the Lacus Oblivionis. Seems the location was used to transmit a connectome from the moon to *Scaffold Delta*, which the Institute was in control of at the time."

"Sounds like a good lead."

"We'll see when we get there. It may turn out to be nothing."

"Won't know until you check it out, though."

"Exactly."

"Hmm." Benjamin grabbed his plate again. "Well, I hope you find what you're . . ." He trailed off, and his eyes grew distant, staring out at a blank spot on the far wall. He stayed like that for long seconds, eyes intense but unfocused, jaw tightening.

"I'm sorry," Isaac said, "but is something wro—"

"How could I be so stupid?" Benjamin snapped, loud enough for Isaac to flinch.

Everyone paused and turned to face him. Benjamin dropped his plate onto the table, where the top bun bounced off and the plate rattled to a halt. He huffed out a breath, planted his hands on his hips, and met their expectant gazes.

"The reason we didn't find anything," he explained heatedly, "is because the branching event didn't happen on Earth!"

✧   ✧   ✧

"And that's roughly the shape of it," Klaus-Wilhelm told CHRONO's leadership.

"So," Muntero murmured thoughtfully as she sank back into her chair, "the Institute's base is on Luna."

"Not just any Luna," Jonas added, "but one of the H17s."

"That's our conclusion," Klaus-Wilhelm said.

"It would certainly explain why we failed to pinpoint the divergence in H17's timeline," Peng said, his eyes glowing a bit brighter. "And it fits with the transceiver coordinates we've recovered. The question now becomes what to *do* about it."

"I believe the answer should be obvious." Csaba Shigeki placed his splayed hand on the conference table, and a ledger of nearby Admin ships sprang into being. "We use this information to go for the Institute's throat. Our forces are already assembling nearby. I say we take the bulk of those chronoports and reduce their base to plasma."

"And leave our outer wall undefended?" Muntero shook her head. "I don't think so."

"We would leave a modest rearguard behind."

"Modest?" Muntero scoffed. "Not good enough."

"Consul, we can't *not* seize the initiative here!" Shigeki said.

"There are too many unknowns, Csaba! How big is the Institute's TTV force? And, more importantly, *where* is it? At their base? Maybe, but maybe not. Perhaps it's hiding out elsewhere in the transverse, and when they see us move out, they move in. We don't even know *how* they intend to hit us!"

Shigeki opened his mouth to respond, but Peng cut in with a loud throat-clear, and Shigeki paused, then nodded to the SysGov consul.

"She *does* have a point," Peng conceded, sounding like he didn't enjoy agreeing with Muntero. "We're still at a severe deficit when it comes to intel on the Institute. Sure, we all *think* they're hanging out in H17A or B, but we don't *know*, and that's the problem. If we're wrong and we move out, then all we've done is shift your ships out of position."

"A situation I will not accept," Muntero added firmly.

"Then what *would* you accept?" Shigeki demanded, his eyes on Muntero.

"That's not my role here."

"Clearly!" Shigeki shook his head, then turned to Klaus-Wilhelm. "What's your take on all this?"

"As much as this may surprise you, I find myself agreeing with Consul Muntero," Klaus-Wilhelm informed them, his voice cool in an effort to bring the temperature in the room down. "She's right that we can't leave the Admin undefended."

"But we can't do nothing."

"Of course not. We're confident we've narrowed the Institute's base to two locations, but we need more information before we can act decisively. Until we have a better handle on what we're up against—*and* how large and capable it is—a short-term defensive approach makes sense." Klaus-Wilhelm summoned a much smaller vessel tally next to Shigeki's. "I propose we ascertain the precise location and strength of the enemy through reconnaissance in force."

"Six TTVs," Muntero said with an approving nod.

"Which will be ready to leave—or in position to rendezvous along the way—within the hour." Klaus-Wilhelm met Muntero's gaze. "I'd also like to request Admin support for this strike squadron."

"What do you need?" Shigeki asked before Muntero could object.

"All six TTVs are our lighter *Aion*-class. I'd like to include one or two *Windfall*-class heavy TTVs, but the logistics don't work out for a timely departure."

"And you'd like us to make up the shortfall in heavy fire-power," Shigeki finished.

"I would."

"Let's see." Shigeki pursed his lips as he consulted the list of nearby chronoports. "*Hammerhead-Seven* and *Eight* are both near Providence. Their presence would certainly add the punch you're looking for, and their nukes may prove useful in cracking open whatever fortifications the Institute has set up." Shigeki turned to Muntero. "Do you find that acceptable, Consul?"

"I do."

"We'll need to make sure the chain of command is clear," Klaus-Wilhelm said.

"Who did you have in mind to lead the squadron?" Shigeki asked.

"Agent Kaminski."

"Works for me. I can place Captain Elifritz in charge of our two ships. That way they can act as a division under Kaminski's overall squadron command. That should allow us to avoid any cross-organization hiccups."

"What about their mission scope?" Peng asked. "We have no idea what they'll encounter."

"Which is why I intend to give Kaminski broad leeway to act on his initiative," Klaus-Wilhelm said. "The Institute hasn't shied away from lethal force, and I see no reason we shouldn't return the courtesy. If Kaminski spots an opening, I want him to take it, with the understanding his primary mission is to gather intel."

"Then we should be prepared for possible ground engagements," Shigeki said. "Either within Institute TTVs or a moon base of sorts. Can your forces support that contingency?"

"Not as well as I'd like. We'd have to strip Providence Station of its security drones to put together even a respectable ground force."

"Then let us handle that aspect of the mission." Shigeki opened a personnel roster. "We can transfer any available STANDs to the two *Hammerheads*, and we have enough combat frames on site for all of them."

"Then it sounds to me like we have a plan." Klaus-Wilhelm looked around the table. "If there are no objections . . . Very good. Then let's get to work."

✧   ✧   ✧

"Have a minute, Klaus?" Peng said once the others had filed out of the CHRONO conference room.

"A minute is about all I can spare," Klaus-Wilhelm said, stopping by the door. "What do you need?"

"Just wanted to pick your brain about something. You remember those contingency plans all us then-commissioners had to put together? You know, the ones for all-out war with the Admin?"

"Yes," Klaus-Wilhelm replied carefully. "What about them?"

"Well, it was something that detective brought up. About how the Institute might be basing *their* plans on what I and the rest of Arete Division put together back then."

"I suppose anything's possible. They've infiltrated Gordian. Who's to say they don't have their tentacles in Arete, too?"

"Right, right. But just suppose for a moment they *are* using those plans. That could actually give us an unexpected edge."

"How so?"

"Because *we* have those plans, too." Peng's eyes brightened. "And I have an idea on how to counter them if they try to carry them out."

"Okay, I'll bite. What did you have in mind?"

"Just something in the way of insurance. For us and for the Admin. But before I go any further, understand this has to stay between the two of us. No sharing with the Admin because what I have in mind would"—he flashed a dark smile—"upset them. A *lot*."

"Then we absolutely *should* tell them."

"We can't. Trust me on this one, Klaus. If we want to help them, then we need to go behind their backs on this one. This is absolutely one of those ask-for-forgiveness-rather-than-permission moments."

✧   ✧   ✧

"Where're you off to next?" Jonas asked his father as they stopped by the grav shaft. Vassal's avatar appeared beside them, visible in their shared virtual vision, his mind running on Jonas' wrist wearable.

"Back to the Admin," Shigeki replied. "I understand everyone's arguments about caution—hell, I wouldn't have gone along with Schröder's plan if I didn't—but at the same time I can't shake the feeling we're about to kick a hornet's nest."

"Then you want to make sure our fleet is ready?"

"*In person*," Shigeki stressed. "Whether for offense or defense, we need to be prepared."

Jonas gave his father a wry smile. "Hopefully no one gives you any grief about having been killed."

"What a blasted *inconvenience*." Shigeki shook his head.

"Better than actually *being* dead."

"It's just another sign of how much we lag behind SysGov. And not just technologically, but with our laws and culture, too."

"We'll catch up. It's only a matter of time."

"But in the short-term, we need to make sure the Admin *gets* that time."

"We'll get through this."

"Sirs," Vassal said. "If I may make a recommendation?"

"What's on your mind?" Jonas asked.

"I suggest both of you return to the Admin to take command of the DTI fleet. For two reasons. First, as you've noted, former director Csaba Shigeki's ambiguous citizenship status could prove problematic at an inconvenient time."

"He's got a point there," Shigeki agreed.

"And the second reason?" Jonas asked.

"I'd like to join the fleet as well," Vassal said. "I believe my skills may prove useful in analyzing any potential attack by the Institute, and aiding in the development of countermeasures. Especially if the Institute targets our infostructure, which seems likely given their obvious skill with invasive software."

"Hard to argue with that." Jonas smiled to Shigeki. "What do you say? I can have Hinnerkopf fill in for me if anything comes up on the station."

"Sounds fine to—"

"Director!"

Jonas and Shigeki stopped and turned as Agent Noxon hurried over, still in his combat frame.

"What is it, Nox?" Shigeki asked.

"Sir, I saw the order mustering all available STANDs."

"That doesn't include you, Nox," Shigeki said. "You're exempt."

"That's what I want to talk to you about. I'd like your permission to join the squadron."

Shigeki made a disapproving face, one Jonas had seen many times before but from a different body. He found the expression an uncomfortable mix of foreign and familiar.

"I need you with me, Nox," Shigeki said at last.

"Sir, these are the people who tried to kill you," Nox replied stiffly. "Who *succeeded*, in a certain point of view."

"That wasn't your fault."

"But it was responsibility. *Is* my responsibility. Sir, the squadron is where I'm needed most. Of all the STANDs on Providence, I'm the one with the most combat experience."

"By a couple decades, too," Jonas noted, eliciting a stern look from his father.

"I'm the best choice to command the ground team, and you know it," Nox continued. "Please, sir. I don't ask for much, but this is something I have to do."

Shigeki hesitated for a moment.

Just a moment.

"All right, Nox." He met Nox's yellow eyes. "You've convinced me. Report to *Hammerhead-Seven* immediately. I'll let Elifritz know you're coming."

"Yes, sir!"

CHAPTER TWENTY-TWO

Allied Strike Squadron
Transverse, non-congruent

"WE'LL BE HEADING OUT FOR H17 SOON," RAIBERT ANNOUNCED on the *Kleio*'s bridge. "So if anyone wants off, now's the time."

"I suppose 'anyone' means us," Isaac said, standing beside Susan.

"You're welcome to tag along if you want. But we've already had one TTV try to take us out, so I expect the Institute will be a little touchy when we show up at their moon base."

"Thanks, but no thanks. I'd rather wait this out on Providence Station. Susan and I can find another ride back to SysGov."

"Sure, of course. I understand."

"Thank you for your hospitality, short though it was."

Isaac turned to leave when Benjamin spoke up.

"*Actually...*"

Isaac paused, brow creasing as he turned back around.

"There *is* one thing," Benjamin said. "There's still a lot of loose puzzle pieces left over from the data we collected and from your own investigation. I wouldn't mind if you and Cephalie stuck around to help us make sense of it all. In fact, I'd really appreciate it if you did."

"Good point, Doc," Raibert said. "Anything we learn before we reach H17 could prove useful, no matter how trivial it may seem." He turned to Isaac. "What do you say?"

"Well..."

Isaac hesitated with a frown. As a rule, he tried to avoid being shot at as much as possible. Between the two of them, Susan possessed a willingness—perhaps even an *eagerness*—to charge headfirst into danger whenever the situation called for decisive action, but Isaac was on the opposite side of the spectrum. He was neither experienced nor well-equipped to fight *any* sort of battle and had always relied upon his LENS to deal with violent criminals.

But now he had been asked to stay on a ship about to charge headfirst into danger.

I'd really prefer to be somewhere else, he silently replied to Raibert in his head.

That much was true, but it was also true he saw the validity of Benjamin's request. He and the Gordian agent were both familiar with *their* half of the data. Put their two heads together, and they should be able to crunch through the mess more swiftly, perhaps even teasing out an important deduction that had so far eluded them separately.

And so, despite the nervous lump Isaac sensed forming in the pit of his stomach, he gave the following answer:

"Well, since you believe this is where I can do the most good, this is where I'll stay."

"Thank you." Benjamin gave him a grateful nod. "I really do appreciate the assist."

"Don't mention it," Isaac said, some doubt and trepidation leaking into his voice.

"Do we need to get anyone's approval for snagging you?" Raibert asked.

"That won't be necessary or practical. My boss is in SysGov, all the way out at Saturn. Besides, Themis detectives are a rather autonomous lot to begin with. I'll explain the situation to him in my report."

If I don't die a fiery death, he thought, then put on a brave face and turned to his partner.

"Well, Susan? I suppose this is goodbye. For a little while, at least. Seems we'll be going our separate ways."

"*Actually . . .*" she began, mimicking Benjamin's earlier tone.

"Is something wrong?"

"Not wrong, just unexpected." She straightened her posture. "My presence has been requested aboard *Hammerhead-Seven.*"

"As part of the ground assault team?"

"That's right."

"But you're currently assigned to Themis. You shouldn't have been included in any of the Admin's orders."

"I wasn't. Captain Elifritz requested my presence personally."

She flashed a guilty smile. "Apparently my actions during the Weltall case left an impression with him."

An image sprang to mind of Susan's combat frame dive-bombing through a glass dome to reach a bomb before it went off.

"Of course they would," he said dryly.

"So...do I have your permission?"

"My permission?"

"To join the ground team."

"Why would you need that?"

"Because I'm your deputy."

"You're—" He cut himself off.

Of course she needs my permission for this! Isaac scolded himself. He and Susan might have conducted themselves as equal partners most of the time, but that didn't change how she'd been assigned to him as his deputy, a fact that—in the mental whirlwind following Benjamin's request—had somehow managed to slip his mind.

But then another thought occurred to him. Any ground assault would be a risky proposition. Perhaps even *the* most dangerous aspect of this mission.

And all I have to do to protect her from that risk is deny her request, Isaac realized, and he was surprised to find the thought so tempting, so seductive.

So easy.

Just about any excuse would do, and he knew it. He knew she'd accept his judgment without question or complaint—at least not one she'd voice. That shielding her from danger would prove to be nothing more than a minor pebble on the road of their professional relationship.

And he found himself wanting to protect her. Very much so. Shockingly so. But he also knew what kind of person Susan was, and more importantly, why she charged into danger so willingly. She was a selfless protector at heart, and denying her this request would be the same as telling her to stop being herself.

And so—

"Permission granted. I'd tell you to be careful, but..."

"Why be careful when I can be *lethal*?" Susan replied with a warm smile, and Isaac chuckled, his mood brightening.

"Now there's the Susan I've come to know. Just promise me one thing before you go."

"What's that?"

"*Try* to come back in one piece, okay?"

"Sure. I can do that."

"I mean it this time."

"So do I." She stood a little straighter. "I'll try my best to come back in one piece."

"I'll hold you to that."

The two of them paused. An expectant silence followed, but neither of them spoke up, and eventually they exchanged nods before Susan left the bridge. Isaac found himself staring at the doorway, wondering darkly if that was the last time he'd ever see her.

Or her him.

"Well." Raibert walked up beside Isaac. "I didn't see *that* coming."

"What do you mean?"

"You know." Raibert slung an arm over Isaac's shoulders. "We're not leaving right away, so you can catch up to her and do that properly."

"I'm not sure I follow you."

"Say a proper goodbye." Raibert patted his shoulder with a big hand. "I don't know, maybe give her a goodbye hug. Or whatever you're up to at this stage in your relationship."

"Relationship?" Isaac made a face. "I think you've misread the situation."

"Doubt it. Look, I know shows of affection can be awkward with an audience. But you can relax around us. What I mean to say is don't let us cramp your style, all right?"

"Agent Kaminski"—Isaac removed the big synthoid's unresisting arm—"I see where you're going with this, but let me assure you that while Susan and I have a relationship, it is *strictly* a professional one."

"I ..." Raibert blinked at the closed exit. "It is?"

"Yes."

"Then you aren't ... ?"

"No."

Raibert glanced to Isaac, then to the door, then back. "You sure?"

"Very much so."

The synthoid took one last look at the exit, frowned at it for a long moment, then gave everyone an exaggerated shrug.

"Shows what I know."

Susan grabbed a handhold beside the open airlock and propelled herself into *Hammerhead-Seven*'s crowded cargo bay.

The bay was considerably larger than those found on the older *Pioneer* chronoports, with enough room for three Cutlass troop transports aligned nose-to-tail down the center, each with barely enough clearance for someone to squeeze sideways between them.

The cargo bay bustled with activity: pilots performing pre-flight checks, operators prepping drones and combat frames, and STANDs filing in to have their consciousness transferred into humanoid weapons.

The chronoport—along with the rest of the allied strike squadron—had sped through the transverse at seventy thousand kilofactors for over five hours, which meant—

"Crew, your attention, please," came Captain Elifritz's voice over her virtual hearing. "We're one hour away from H17B's outer wall. All STANDs to your combat frames. Cutlass crews, complete final checks and prepare for launch. All other personnel, assume combat stations. Set Condition One throughout the ship."

Virtual marquees lit up along the walls, notifying all personnel of the ship's shift toward combat readiness. Operators and STANDs began pairing off, each to one of the combat frames waiting like a row of dark, metallic skeletons burdened with weaponry and maneuvering boosters.

Susan pressed a hand against the wall and slowed to a halt in the line.

"Agent Cantrell."

She spun around, surprised to find Agent Noxon floating behind her, already transferred and equipped.

"Agent Noxon," she replied with a curt nod.

"I'm glad the captain was able to convince you to join us. It'll be good to work with you again."

"Likewise, though"—she permitted herself the barest hint of a smile—"it didn't take much convincing, to be honest."

"I'm not surprised. Did your partner object at all?"

"No, sir. Not one bit." She turned back to him. "Why do you ask?"

"I thought he might. Just an impression I had from working with him on the Weltall case. A lot of people from SysGov aren't comfortable with how...direct our methods can be."

"That much is certainly true. Our first case together had its share of rocky moments."

"I can imagine."

"That said, I think he…" Susan paused, trying to assemble her feelings into a proper sentence. "I think he's come to understand me over these past six months. Even the parts he doesn't approve of. That's why he didn't object when I asked to join the ground team."

"He sounds like a good partner."

"That he is, sir."

The line shifted up, and one of the operators waved for Susan to join her by the combat frame at the far end of the row. Susan kicked off the floor, grabbed a handhold, then propelled herself across the tops of the combat frames. She passed several Type-92s and a few heavier Type-86s before arriving at her sleek Type-99.

She brought herself to a halt beside the operator.

"I've prepped your standard loadout along with some mission-specific additions." The operator pointed to each modular mount. "Right-arm heavy rail-rifle and shoulder-mounted grenade launcher. Your incinerator's been loaded with self-immolating gel, since we don't expect any pressurized environments. You'll also be carrying one of our telegraphs here." She pointed to a cylinder nestled against the combat frame's back. "And two demolition packs here and here at the waist."

"What's the yield on the demo packs?"

"Point nine tons with options for directed and undirected blast profiles."

Susan nodded. As a STAND, she'd received extensive training with a wide range of armaments—including various types of demolition charges—though this would be her first time using explosives this powerful outside of simulations.

"Any questions?" the operator asked.

"None."

"All right, then. Let's get you inside."

Susan turned around and raised the back of her uniform top, exposing a U-shaped seam in her skin halfway down her back. The operator took a knife, cut along the seam, and raised the flap to reveal the access slot to her connectome case.

"Ready for me to yank you?"

"Ready."

Susan locked her synthoid in position and sent the release code. The cargo bay vanished, replaced with swirls of random colors and chime-like music. She floated within a sea of temporary stimulation, waiting for the operator to remove her case and plug it into the combat frame, and for once she found the experience unsettling. Her mind wandered until it began to fixate on her complete helplessness.

Everything she considered "The True Susan" was literally in the hands of a stranger. A well-trained and fully certified stranger, but a stranger nonetheless.

She'd switched bodies countless times over her nine years of service as a STAND, and while she'd been nervous the first dozen or so times, she hadn't experienced any anxiety over the process for *years*. Why were her nerves acting up this time, even if only a little?

And then the answer dawned on her.

She'd grown accustomed to Isaac switching her over. Something about letting him do it—and how she'd come to trust him so completely—had served to place her mind into a deeper state of ease, and she hadn't noticed the difference until this moment.

The body swap only took a few seconds, but it seemed to stretch on unnaturally this time until the random kaleidoscope switched off and new senses flooded in: not just familiar light and sound but ultraviolet, infrared, sonar, and radar. She saw and heard through the combat frame's sensors—*her* sensors—and turned her head to inspect the redheaded synthoid floating beside her. She stepped away from the Type-99's rack, took hold of her other body, and placed it where the frame had once been.

"Any issues?" the technician asked.

"None." She stared at her body for longer than usual. "I'm good to go."

✧   ✧   ✧

"Kleio," Raibert said, resting his fingertips on the command table's edge, "connect me to *Hammerhead-Seven*."

"Yes, Agent Kaminski."

TTV *Kleio*, along with the seven other time machines in the strike squadron, sped through the transverse in phase-locked formation, allowing them to communicate via realspace methods like radio or laser instead of having to rely on cumbersome chronoton telegraphs.

"Direct link established," Kleio said, moments before the comm window opened.

"Elifritz here. Go ahead, *Kleio*."

"Captain," Kaminski said as he glanced over at Benjamin and Isaac, "our brain trust has been trudging through all the info we have—looking for ways to connect the fragments we found on that Institute TTV and the forensic findings from Detective Cho's investigation. They just reviewed their results with me, and I want to go over it with you before briefing the whole squadron. Granted, most of what they're about to say is conjecture, but it feels solid to me."

"Understood. What do we have to work with?"

Raibert gave Benjamin a quick nod to proceed.

"Essentially, Captain," Benjamin began, "we believe we've deduced the Phoenix Institute's high-level goals, and they're about as bad as we expected. As Agent Kaminski indicated, we're not *certain* of any of this—Detective Cho and I have made a few educated guesses when it comes to holes in the data—but we're confident with the results. Those caveats aside, we're looking at a three-phase plan to destroy the Admin."

"They don't aim small, do they?" Elifritz replied.

"I think we can safely say the Institute isn't interested in half-measures. Phase One of their plan: utilize proxy entities within the Admin to test infostructure attack vectors."

"That would explain why we've seen such a huge uptick in terrorist activity. They've been using those cells to test various abstract weapons."

"That's our conclusion as well," Benjamin said.

"What about the physical weapons or other technology we've seen in terrorist hands?"

"Misdirection. The Institute was only ever interested in how their military-grade software performed. They studied the results, using each attack's effectiveness to help them determine the optimal method while keeping their existence and ultimate goals hidden."

"But a method for what?"

Benjamin exchanged a quick look with Isaac.

"To kill as many people on the Admin's Earth as possible," Isaac said. "Essentially gutting the center of Admin power in order to allow other entities—namely Luna and Mars—a chance to step into the power vacuum. There's a little more to it than that. One of their secondary goals is to carry out this genocide without irreparably damaging Earth's habitability."

"How thoughtful of them." Elifritz spoke softer, but with an edge as cold as frozen hydrogen.

"The upside for us," Isaac continued, "is that this grants us a glimpse at their motives and overall mindset. They're not trying to take over for themselves or kill for the sake of killing, at least from their own perspective. Instead, they've deluded themselves into believing they're making the Admin a better place. That's why we're facing an infostructure attack rather than something more direct, like large-scale nuclear or kinetic strikes."

"The latter two would almost *be* kinder," Elifritz growled. "If for no other reason than it would be over quickly. If they do hit our infostructure on a global scale, then we could be looking at total supply chain paralysis, followed by mass starvation."

"It seems they're also interested in freeing as many AIs as possible," Benjamin said. "Hence another reason to hit the Admin through its infostructure over other approaches. From what we can tell, the Phoenix Institute formed in late 2979, shortly after first contact between SysGov and the Admin. Its members came together out of a two-pronged fear of the Admin and its Restrictions. We're fairly certain Doctor Xenophon played a lead role in founding the organization and that most—if not all—of its members are abstract."

"Which may be another reason they chose to target the Admin's infostructure," Isaac said. "If we're dealing with abstract criminals, then it makes sense for them to attack via abstract means. They're committing an act they at least have a basic level of comfort with, and this ties back into how effective their software has been, not only against the Admin, but Gordian Division as well."

"All good reasons to place confidence in your conclusions," Elifritz said. "But you mentioned a three-phase plan."

"That's right," Benjamin said. "Phase Two involves establishing a manufacturing base large enough to support Phase Three, which is the attack itself. That's why the Institute hijacked *Reality Flux*. We don't know what they're building, but we can assume it's some sort of delivery mechanism. Multiple TTVs at a minimum, I'd say."

"And the payload?" Elifritz asked.

"Nasty little buggers the Institute calls 'Revenants,'" Cephalie explained. "From what Philo and I have been able to piece together, these Revenants are nonsentient programs developed from a sentient template. Probably what happened is the Institute took an existing connectome and whittled it down to a few essential components, which means these programs are going to be highly adaptive, if lacking true self-awareness. Expect them to be utterly remorseless and armed with the Institute's best abstract weapons."

"Lovely," Elifritz growled.

"We expect the Revenants to target critical pieces of public infostructure," Isaac said. "That means information, food, transportation, power, and the like."

"And here we are struggling with a few ragtag terrorists armed with similar weapons."

"With that in mind," Raibert said, "I want to review my thoughts with you before giving my orders to the squadron."

"You have my undivided attention."

"So, this is how I see it, Captain. We're dealing with genocidal lunatics here, and very *capable* lunatics at that. They've had over forty subjective years to prepare, and they've already pulled some pretty nasty stuff on us. There's no point talking to them, at least before we show them we mean business. If we show up and ask them politely if they'd like to surrender, they'll just stall until they can knife us in the back. So I say we go in loud. Hit them fast, and hit them hard."

"Makes sense to me," Elifritz replied. "What did you have in mind?"

"Just pondering how this mixed squadron of ours is traveling at seventy-kay. Which means your *Hammerheads* are below their cruising speed with your stealth baffles extended. The Institute is going to see our TTVs coming as clear as the sun, but *you*? They'll have *no* idea you're with us until it's too late."

"How would you like us to capitalize on that advantage, assuming my chronoports retain the element of surprise?"

"The Institute'll have a base. That base'll have a door." Raibert let a vicious grin slip. "I want you to kick down that door. With a nuclear boot."

"Ah." Elifritz let out a brief chuckle. "Yes, we can certainly oblige."

"How big is your boot?"

"Each chronoport is equipped with ten thermonuclear warheads mounted on guided missiles. Explosive yield of each device can be varied up to fifty megatons."

"*Fifty?!*" Raibert blurted. "You mean to tell me your two ships are packing a *gigaton* of explosives!"

"We believe in being prepared."

CHAPTER TWENTY-THREE

Allied Strike Squadron
Transverse, non-congruent

"ESTIMATING THIRTY MINUTES TO H17B'S OUTER WALL," ELZBIETÁ reported. "No enemy contacts on scope."

Raibert acknowledged her with a curt nod, his eyes fixed on the zoomed-in section of the transverse: the dual system of H17 and the squadron's eight approaching icons. *His* squadron. The boss had placed him in command, and it rested on his shoulders not to muck this up.

Doubt clawed at his mind. Would it have been better to try to slip in nice and slow? Perhaps they'd missed something and H17A was the correct target? What if his decisions—however logical—were about to get everyone killed, him included?

He often struggled to appreciate the burden of command, at least as it applied to Gordian Division as a wider organization. Sure, he was responsible for the *Kleio* and its crew, but a whole *squadron* was on a different scale entirely, and this current task had placed that distinction into sharp focus in his mind.

Is this what it's like for the boss? he wondered. *Is this what he deals with day in and day out? Making decisions with a veneer of confidence based on woefully incomplete information, where the consequence for being wrong can lead those under his command to an early grave?*

And is that what I'm doing now? Leading us into the teeth of some unknown beast?

Raibert shoved those dark thoughts down and focused on the map. It hadn't changed in the slightest, still showing a clear path to H17B's outer wall. He glanced across his crew, Isaac, and Cephalie, all of them with sharp eyes. All of them waiting to act when the situation inevitably shifted from perishable calm to the heart of the storm.

His eyes lingered on Cephalie, whose avatar was now normal-sized in this virtual representation of the bridge. All four of their physical bodies—his included—were suspended in the compensation bunks, their glass-fronted chambers filled with microbot baths to buffer them from whatever combat maneuvers the TTV would soon execute.

Strictly speaking, *he* didn't need to ditch his body in a combat situation. His synthoid could handle sustained high gees without any risk of damage, but the *Kleio*'s graviton thrusters could fire in any direction at up to five gees, and given Elzbietá's flying...

I'd rather not *be tossed around like a grouchy pinball, if I can help it.*

"Twenty minutes to outer wall," Elzbietá said. "Stand by for phase-out."

Raibert let out a slow, rumbling exhale that—despite the room's virtual nature and his own synthetic existence—still produced a mild calming effect. He wondered again if they'd picked wrong, if the other H17 should have been their first target.

His lips parted when a cluster of icons lit up ahead of them, one by one.

"Three phase-outs detected," Philo said. "Two signatures are similar to our *Aion*-class, but not identical. One of them is significantly larger. Could be something like a *Windfall*." He pushed up his visor. "Now that's odd. I don't have a precise fix, but those phase-outs occurred deep under Luna's surface."

"How deep?" Raibert asked.

"Almost half a *kilometer*."

"So, a subterranean moon bunker." Benjamin shook his head with the slightest hint of a smile.

"And the position lines up with the transceiver coordinates from *Scaffold Delta*," Isaac added.

"I'm surprised they didn't stay hidden until we were closer," Elzbietá said. "Phasing out now plants a huge bull's-eye on their base, even if it is buried under a lot of rock."

"They may have assumed we know where they are." Raibert shrugged his broad shoulders. "Which is half-true, I suppose. Our approach vector isn't exactly subtle. Any sign they're heading through the outer wall?"

"Not yet," Philo said. "They're still in H17B's True Present, phasing up through the lunar substrate. We won't have a precise realspace fix until we phase-lock."

"Then let's use the time we have wisely." Raibert faced Elzbietá and Philo. "You two get prepped, and make sure you give them a warm welcome."

"You've got it," Elzbietá said. "With me, Philo?"

"Right behind you." Philo grabbed the tab atop his horned aviator helmet and brought down the tinted visor with a satisfying *click.* The two of them vanished, transferring to their customized abstraction.

"Here they come," Benjamin breathed, then looked up. "All three Institute TTVs just crossed the outer wall. Now on an intercept course. Predicting phase-lock in eight minutes."

"Kleio," Raibert said, "get me Elifritz and relay the call through the entire squadron."

"Establishing direct link to *Hammerhead-Seven.*"

"Elifritz here. Go ahead, *Kleio.*"

"You see the three 'dance partners' coming our way?"

"We do. Want us to engage?"

"Negative. Slip past them and hit the bunker. We'll handle the TTVs."

"Understood, *Kleio.* We'll maintain silent running."

"As for the rest of us..."

Raibert leaned in over the command table.

"All Gordian TTVs," he declared in a crisp, commanding voice, "prepare for combat."

"Phase-lock in thirty," Philo announced.

Elzbietá swung the *Kleio*'s nose around, aiming it at a contracting cloud of possible enemy positions. The presence of three hostile craft provided ample data for the squadron's six data-linked arrays to detect and digest, narrowing down the guesswork by a hair, but the Institute TTVs could still be anywhere within a wide spatial range.

The *Kleio* flew within a loose ring of six TTVs, every other craft staggered forward and all of them flying with meta-armor deployed and weapon blisters open.

"Ten seconds to contact," Philo said, "...three...two...one...lock!"

Three gunmetal ellipses snapped into reality high above, one significantly larger than the others. Elzbietá hissed out a quick curse at her lack of a shot. She shoved the omni-throttle to the left, juking sideways while she pulled the ship's nose up. The other Gordian TTVs executed similar maneuvers, bringing their formidable forward weapon systems to bear.

A pair of x-ray lasers blared down from Hostile-Three, the largest enemy TTV, and struck *Alcyone*. Meta-armor warped the beams, splitting and curving them around the time machine.

"Missile launch!" Philo reported as a flurry of secondary contacts split from the Institute TTVs. "Count is twelve. No, make that twenty-four. They're entering our defensive envelope."

The *Kleio*'s four Gatling guns vomited a sleet of metal, joined quickly by the rest of the allied squadron. Explosions peppered the darkness, and one of the missiles winked out.

Elzbietá settled their nose on Hostile-One.

"Taking the shot!" Philo called out.

The *Kleio*'s x-ray beam grazed Hostile-One and high-energy photons splashed off its armor. Philo keyed up his second shot, and the mass driver *whump*ed. The one-ton projectile blasted across the void, secondary guidance systems angling the payload toward its target. Its proximity fuse triggered, the payload exploded, and dozens of depleted uranium penetrators streaked toward Hostile-One—

—except the Institute TTVs broke phase-lock at the last moment, and the penetrators flew through empty space.

"Missed!" Philo exclaimed. "Hostiles have shifted onto a secondary spatial axis. Distance is three chens and climbing."

Elzbietá rolled her thumb over the omni-throttle and laid in a pursuit course, leaving behind the remnants of the Institute missile wave. The *Kleio* responded after a brief delay. Not due to any fault of the pilot or the time ship, but because the rest of the squadron was synced to her "commands" through the whiskers of comm lasers.

The delay couldn't have been more than a few milliseconds, but Elzbietá still felt the lag as an itch in her mind, a deviation from how the TTV normally performed.

All six Gordian craft sped after the Institute hostiles.

"Distance holding at eight chens," Philo said. "Laser impacts on Hostiles One and Two. Minimal damage, I'm afraid."

"That's fine," Elzbietá replied. "We're just exchanging pleasantries before we get down to business. How's *Alcyone*?"

"Bow armor's cooked. Heavy-Three is packing some *serious* firepower. Readings are very similar to a *Windfall*-class."

"Is there *anything* these jerks won't steal from us?"

Elzbietá checked the map, noting the growing distance between the hostiles and the Admin chronoports. Or rather, the *estimated positions* of the chronoports, since they were running silent.

"Looks like Elifritz slipped in under their noses," Elzbietá said.

"Looks like. No course changes from the Institute TTVs."

"I wonder if they're trying to pull us away from their—"

The Institute TTVs split apart, diverging greatly across a mix of spatial and temporal vectors, their projected positions manifesting as three small spheres instead of one blob.

"What do they think they're doing?" Philo asked quietly.

"No idea." Elzbietá toggled over to the command channel. "Raibert, you seeing this?"

"Yeah. What do you make of it?"

"I think they're prepositioning to hit us from multiple angles, but they're being too cute for their own good. Their tech's impressive, but there's no substitute for experience, and the Institute doesn't have any. Whereas *our* teachers were the Gordian Knot and the Dynasty Crisis!"

"Then perhaps we should educate them." She could almost feel Raibert's cruel smile.

"Music to my ears."

Raibert widened the command channel to include all allied TTVs.

"*Alcyone* and *Hyperion*, stick with us. We're going after Hostile-Three while it's isolated. All other TTVs, break formation. Keep those other two off our backs."

Confirmation signals pinged back, and the squadron split into two formations of three. Elzbietá angled toward Hostile-Three, and the other two TTVs followed her lead, their division maintaining phase-lock while their temporal and spatial positions converged with the enemy.

"Weapon systems synced with *Alcyone* and *Hyperion*," Philo said. "Combined fire control standing by on my command."

"Then let's show them who's in charge around here."

"I'm picking up a change in their drive signature. Looks like they're about to—"

Hostile-Three switched temporal directions, and the distance shrank rapidly.

"Phase-lock imminent!"

The massive TTV materialized to Elzbietá's left, and she jerked her flight controls to the side. Missiles spasmed from the heavy TTV and twin lasers spat from its bow, striking *Alcyone* and the *Kleio*.

"We're hit!" Philo reported. "Armor's holding, *barely*. But *Alcyone* took that one hard on the nose. Returning fire!"

Gatling guns roared to life, and missiles blew apart while a trio of lasers struck Hostile-Three amidship. Photons spalled around the vessel, but only for a brief moment before its meta-armor reached thermal capacity and burned out. Metamaterial flaked away into the void, and high-powered x-rays slashed across the hull.

Hostile-Three returned fire, and this time both beams stabbed into *Alcyone*. Prog-steel glowed under the relentless, high-energy onslaught. Metal liquefied, expanded, *exploded*, and the ship shuddered as its front quarter blew apart.

"They look geared for a long-range fight," Philo said. "We're at a disadvantage if we stay here. Can you try and get us closer?"

"I can do better than try!"

Beams pounded Hostile-Three, and Elzbietá accelerated hard— straight into the teeth of the incoming missiles. Their escorts held formation, despite the damage *Alcyone* had suffered, and a torrent of cannon fire, countermeasures, and decoys wreathed the friendly TTVs.

The handful of missiles that survived rocketed in. One detonated below and behind the *Kleio*, and the blast buffeted them upward.

None of the rest hit their marks.

"Switching half our Gatlings to offense," Philo said. "Firing!"

Two Gatlings swung ahead and fired with the mass driver. *Hyperion*'s main shot flew wide, but the *Kleio*'s shot arced toward Hostile-Three's impeller spike. The payload burst into a cloud of semi-guided spikes that struck hard across the enemy's drive system.

Gatling fire savaged the Institute TTV, ripping through its layered defenses and shredding the systems underneath. A plume of white-purple geysered from the hull, and the entire ship rocked. But it would take more than that to destroy a vessel so large, so heavily fortified, and it returned fire once more, beams boring into the *Kleio.*

"Bow meta-armor is *down!*" Philo reported as burnt scraps of metamaterial scattered off their hull. "All Gatlings to offense!"

Elzbietá skewed the ship to the side, presenting their unmolested flank, and Philo reoriented the cannon pods. The three Gordian TTVs shot past Hostile-Three, and their combined weapons doused it with metal and death. Over two *thousand* explosive rounds brutalized its hull in four brief but violent seconds.

Hostile-Three listed sideways, its thrusters weakening, impeller wavering. No atmosphere leaked from the craft; there were no pressurized compartments on this time machine. No physical crew to experience that furious hurricane firsthand.

But that didn't make the damage any less real.

They were hurt. Hurt *bad.* Their defenses lay shattered and the inner hull exposed.

But the job wasn't done.

Not yet.

Elzbietá spun the *Kleio* around, flying backwards, weapons aligned and ready. She wondered, in the enemy's brief last moments, if they understood how terrible their crimes were. How toying with reality was for the foolish and the dead.

She doubted it. Some people believed their own lies, believed they were righteous when all they sought to do was burn everything down around them. She'd seen too many realities die to give these maniacs a second chance.

"Finish them," she breathed, her voice frosted with the dark memories of dead universes.

Philo fired, and *Hyperion* joined them. Their weapons stabbed through the enemy's heart, and the ship cracked in half. More beams and kinetic rounds struck, and the impeller shattered, spreading across space in a prismatic twinkle.

Elzbietá let out a slow exhale, unnecessary in this virtual space.

But it still felt good.

"How's the *Alcyone*?" she asked.

"Main weapons are down, and there's no repairing them out

here. All four Gatlings are still online, though, and the three-quarters of a ship they *do* have is in good shape. They're reprogramming the armor to plug the hole."

"Good work, Ella," Raibert said. "And I have some good news. *Phoebe* telegraphed us while you were occupied, and we're now three for three against these Institute bastards. Reform the squadron and resume course for H17B's outer wall. Let's not keep Elifritz waiting."

✧   ✧   ✧

Hammerhead-Seven materialized high above Luna, and *Hammerhead-Eight* flashed into existence beside it, their weapon-heavy bows pointed toward the moon's bleak, gray surface.

"Phase-in complete, sir. Spatial and temporal coordinates confirmed."

"Target analysis," Elifritz said, clad in a pressure suit and strapped in near the back of the bridge, the space around him alive with virtual screens.

"No sign of surface contacts, sir," reported the weapons operator. "Negative for spaceborne threats as well."

"I don't buy it," Noxon said. A virtual version of his combat frame sat beside Elifritz, while the real one waited within a troop transport.

"Neither do I. Not with those TTVs standing guard," Elifritz replied quietly, then spoke up for the bridge crew. "What about an access shaft? Any signs of subterranean structures?"

"Nothing that I can identify as such on the radar. But our visibility is poor at best past a few meters below the surface, sir."

"Understood. Proceed as planned. We have a door to kick down."

"Yes, sir. Requesting authorization to deploy the nukes."

A red border appeared around the PIN interface in Elifritz's armrest. He placed his gloved hand over the interface, and his implants networked with the chronoport's nuclear deployment protocols.

"Command authorization accepted, sir. Missile bay open, yields configured for fifty megatons. Nukes ready for launch on your command."

"Launch Missile-One."

"Missile-One away."

The sleek, conical missile lit its solid propellant and sprinted from the launcher at twenty gees of acceleration. It rocketed toward the surface, scattering thermos-sized decoy drones to all sides. The decoys activated, generating a wide range of active and passive interference to mask the missile's true location.

Elifritz half-expected some form of automated defense to flinch alive, but nothing of the sort happened, and Missile-One slammed into the surface unmolested.

The warhead housing wasn't optimized for surface penetration—never mind half a kilometer of Lunar rock—but the missile *was* hardened against kinetic impacts, and it pierced through tens of meters before detonating.

Elifritz saw the subterranean shock wave first—a rolling wave that transformed gray bedrock into something almost fluidic. The wave expanded, and the eye at its center erupted into a plume of vaporized regolith that glowed a blinding white. The ejection blew upward and outward, dimming and cooling and expanding in Luna's weak gravity, while the shock wave roiled the surface, a tidal wave of rock that slowly ebbed away. Some pieces in the nuclear plume flew so high and fast he wondered if they achieved escape velocity.

Elifritz couldn't decide how the sight made him feel. The explosion—though massive—felt so distant from the chronoport's high-orbit vantage, and the silence of the weapon's nuclear wrath only added to his sense of detachment.

"How deep is the hole?" he asked.

"Hard to say exactly, sir, but my best guess is about two hundred meters. We should have a better read on it once the explosion clears."

"Not deep enough," Noxon growled under his breath.

"Launch Missile-Two," Elifritz ordered.

"Yes, sir. Missile-Two away."

The second nuke shot in. It had just reached the outer expanse of the plume when—

"Surface contacts! Optical patterns indicate retracting metamaterial!"

"Show me."

Several visual feeds snapped open beside Elifritz, each depicting long, nine-barreled weapons that swung around as they shed tarps of wavering light. The Gatling guns spun up in near perfect unison and spewed arcing trails into space that converged on the incoming nuke.

"Missile-Two is under fire!"

"Eliminate those surface threats. Conventional weapons only."

Both *Hammerheads* blasted away with proton lasers and heavy railguns. Lasers streaked through the thinning limits of the nuclear blast, turning visible, and kinetic slugs punched holes through the clouds of vaporized rock. A kinetic slug struck the base of one weapon, and the mount shattered, its barrels flung high. Another Gatling gun suffered a direct laser strike, and the weapon exploded into superheated pieces.

"Status of Missile-Two?"

"Minor hits to outer shell. The decoys took the brunt of it. Impact imminent."

The nuke raced down through the mushroom cloud and splashed headfirst into a wide pool of molten crust. A second thermonuclear fireball erupted across the moon's surface, and Elifritz watched the fury of the second detonation interpose itself through the remnants of the first.

"Sir, radar is picking up a *massive* return beneath the lunar surface."

"Clarify."

"Object is an artificial dome of some kind starting at a depth of three hundred twenty meters. Surface composition reads as a prog-steel variant consistent with SysPol armor."

"The Institute's bunker." Elifritz permitted himself a thin smile. "What's the status of their armor?"

"Minimal surface damage."

"Then the door isn't open. Kaminski tasked us with a job, and I don't plan to let him down. Launch Missile-Three."

"Missile-Three away."

The third nuke shot in through the ebbing fury of the first two, and this time the Institute didn't put up a fight. The missile's fortified shell slammed against reactive prog-steel armor, penetrated a mere two meters, then detonated.

"Report."

"Detecting a breach in the bunker's surface, though the extent of the damage is surprisingly low given the epicenter's proximity."

"Tough little nut," Noxon said quietly.

"Indeed."

"Sir, telegraph from *Kleio*."

"Let's hear it."

"Message reads: 'All three Institute TTVs destroyed. Squadron now heading for H17B True Present.'"

"Excellent. Telegraph, take the following dictation. 'Institute bunker located. Surface defenses neutralized.'"

"Yes, sir. Telegraph spooled ... and sending."

"The question now is," Noxon began, "have we opened that door far enough?"

"I think we can afford to let the smoke clear. I want a good look at this bunker before we fire any more nukes."

Elifritz settled back into his seat and waited.

He didn't have long to wait.

"Sir, incoming transmission from the bunker on standard SysGov comms. Source comes up as 'Doctor Xenophon.' Link is addressed to, and I quote, 'the idiots lobbing nukes at us.'"

Elifritz exchanged a wary look with Noxon, whose combat frame remained unreadable.

"Very well." The captain faced forward. "Let's hear what the Institute has to say. Put him through."

A comm screen opened to reveal a passably human male with a chiseled face, black hair, and mechanical eyes. His square pupils glowed vibrant orange against dull iron. Green flames danced across his neck scarf, contrasted against his black business suit.

"Doctor Xenophon, I presume."

"You presume correctly," the AI replied in a calm, stately tone devoid of any unease or anger. "And you are?"

"Captain Elifritz, Admin DTI. Are you in charge down there?"

"I am." There was no hesitance in his voice.

"Then it is my duty to inform you this installation and all its occupants are in direct violation of the Gordian Protocol. You and all other sentients present within the bunker are ordered to stand down and surrender yourselves into our custody."

"The 'bunker'?" Xenophon seemed mildly amused by Elifritz's choice of words.

"Or whatever you call your subterranean base."

"We call it the Phoenix, if you must know."

"Its name isn't important. I have informed you of your crime and the actions required to avoid further hostilities. What is your response?"

Xenophon snorted.

"Is that your final answer, Doctor?"

"So what if it is? You going to hit us with more nukes?"

"That is precisely what I'll do."

"You Admin thugs are all the same. So quick to resort to violence. So eager to—"

"Perhaps you don't understand how precarious your situation is. The Gordian Division has wiped out your TTVs, and we've broken your defenses. You are in no position to play games with me, and I am *not* required to take you in alive. I need only give the order, and my forces will reduce your base to radioactive slag. Even so, I would prefer to resolve this peacefully."

"I somehow doubt that very much, Captain, but all right. I'll bite. What happens to me and my people if we surrender? You going to stuff us into one of your torture domains?"

"Nothing of the sort," Elifritz replied evenly, refusing to let the AI rile him. "This is a joint operation, and you are still recognized as a SysGov citizen. You and your associates will be turned over to SysPol."

"How thoughtful of you."

"Any Admin coconspirators will, likewise, be processed by our legal system."

Xenophon smirked. "Then it's a good thing there aren't any."

"I require an answer, Doctor."

"Fine." He huffed out a simulated breath. "Give me some time to talk it over with the others."

"No," Elifritz replied firmly.

"What?" Xenophon blurted. "What do you mean 'no'?"

"I have no way of knowing what kinds of dangerous tech your bunker—"

"We don't have anything left but software!"

"—may still contain," Elifritz finished evenly. "And, because of the threat your Institute still poses, I refuse to entertain your attempts to stall for time."

"I'm not stalling! I need time to convince the others to stand down!"

"You said you were in charge, correct?"

"I did."

"Then I suggest you start issuing some orders." Elifritz started a sixty-second timer in the comm window.

"What the hell is that?"

"How much time you have left before we launch the next nuke."

"You're joking!"

"Do I look like someone who's joking?"

Xenophon met his gaze unflinchingly for several seconds, but then his eyes darted over to the countdown.

"Fine, Captain, you win. Stay on the line. I'll be right back."

His avatar vanished.

Elifritz watched the seconds tick down.

Xenophon reappeared with twenty seconds to spare.

"Done. As chief executive of the Phoenix Institute, I formally declare our surrender."

"On behalf of the DTI, I accept your surrender." Elifritz paused the countdown.

"What would you have us do?"

"You will power down your programmable armor and allow our ground teams full access to the bunker."

Xenophon glanced to the side and nodded. "There. Armor's off."

Elifritz disabled the comm window. "Is he telling the truth?"

"Looks like it, sir," the weapons operator replied. "The edges around the hole in the bunker have stopped moving."

"Very good." Elifritz reenabled the window. "Next, we'll need an access point to the bunker's infostructure."

"That's going to be a bit of a problem."

"Then I suggest you find a way to resolve it."

"Look, everything close to the blast is off-line right now. I'm not sure if you took it out or if we just lost the connection, but it's a complete dead zone. On top of that, we don't have physical bodies, so it's not like we can surrender to you outside."

"Then pick a location further in."

"That I can do." Xenophon glanced to the side. "Sending the location now."

"Good. Our ground teams will be with you shortly."

"I can hardly wait," he said in a fatalistic tone.

"Be warned that any hostility will be met with immediate and overwhelming lethal force."

"We won't cause any trouble. You have my word."

"And I'll hold you to it." Elifritz placed Xenophon on hold once more. "Agent Noxon, it appears the stage is now yours."

"That it is, sir."

"Deploy your Cutlasses to the surface at once. Secure all Institute infosystems and AIs."

"Yes, sir. We'll get it done."

CHAPTER TWENTY-FOUR

Transdimensional Dreadnought *Phoenix*
H17B, 2181 CE

"WE'RE NOT ACTUALLY SURRENDERING," ROSE ASKED XENOPHON, "are we?"

"Don't be ridiculous. I'm letting the Admin captain see what he wants to see. Did you catch how he called *Phoenix* a 'bunker'? He doesn't know, and we can use that to our advantage."

"By letting their ground forces inside?"

"By using them to stall for time while we appear to cooperate. The Admin may be a brutal, militaristic regime, but even *they* will balk at the thought of nuking their own troops. That hesitancy will buy us the breathing room we need. Speaking of which, how much time *do* we need?"

"One moment."

Rose summoned a chart over her hand. She wore a beige business suit that covered most of her avatar's pale green skin, contrasted by the vivid red of her short hair. A clockwork flower ticked the seconds away in her lapel.

The bridge they stood in was abstract as well—a circular, functional chamber similar to those found on TTVs, complete with a central command table. No one in the Institute required physical living quarters or workstations, and so Rose had omitted such amenities when she'd adapted *Phoenix*'s original SysPol designs.

Rose's full name was Rosor of Orosor, forming an extended palindrome Xenophon assumed *someone* considered witty. She was one of the Institute's original twelve members, now eleven after he'd deleted Ijiraq. That's all it had taken to get this far. Eleven believers, each infused with the will to see their shared vision made manifest.

Xenophon credited himself with radicalizing Rose. She had once been a student of his, and he'd used that connection to sour her views on the Admin, though the ground had already been fertile when he'd first reached out to her. That had been a lucky break.

In many ways, her status as a former SysPol officer made her the Institute's most important member. Her service record spanned both the Arete First Responders and the Hephaestus R&D division, and she'd used her network of contacts to swipe Peng's contingency plan and several highly restricted patterns.

It was safe to say *Phoenix* wouldn't exist without her. Not in its current form, at least.

"We've got minor to moderate damage throughout the ship," Rose reported. "Those shock waves were nasty, but the armor absorbed the worst of it. We lost one of our capital lasers during the third hit, and there's heavy structural damage around the impact point. However, the worst problem is the impeller. It's off-line."

"How soon can you have it back up?" Xenophon asked.

"Not long. Less than half an hour. It's an alignment issue, not a problem with the spike itself. I've tasked half of our repair swarms and drones to making the necessary adjustments. The rest I'm spreading across the ship to take care of the hundred or so *other* issues."

"Very good."

Xenophon rested his fingertips on the command table. Two small red icons detached from the *Hammerheads* and began their descent while another six larger icons phased in beside the Admin time machines.

Gordian TTVs, he thought grimly. *So, Elifritz wasn't lying about our losses after all. No matter. Our TTVs were always expendable, though I never expected them to perform* that *badly!*

It had seemed like a good idea at the time to sortie their remaining TTVs when they'd picked up the Gordian squadron. After all, the approach vector and force strength all but assured the Gordian Division knew where they were hiding, so Xenophon had dispatched their remaining TTV force to thin the enemy's ranks while *Phoenix* prepped for departure.

That decision had been a costly one, and the unexpected

appearance of nuclear-armed chronoports had only worsened the situation.

In a perfect multiverse, they would have deployed *Phoenix* the moment H17's splinter universe had caught up with the True Present. That had been the original plan, but Ijiraq's sabotage changed everything. She'd played along until mere days before their scheduled launch, and the seeds of her sabotage had sprouted into ugly, vile weeds throughout *Phoenix*'s control systems.

She'd died in the attempt; Xenophon had deleted her personally, but the damage had been done.

They'd needed more time to prepare.

He'd made the difficult call to refurbish *Reality Flux* and send it back to SysGov, but it seemed Ijiraq had anticipated that move as well. One of her viruses had wormed its way into the vessel's self-repair systems, and the resulting explosion had alerted their enemies, even if SysPol lacked the full picture.

Worse still, news of this fresh disaster had taken *days* to reach him! His connectome copies on *Scaffold Delta* couldn't leave their posts, nor could they transmit a telegraph for all to hear. It was only thanks to the scouts he'd insisted they send to both SysGov and the Admin that they knew of the failure at all!

And the reports from the Admin were hardly better, because it seemed someone over there had developed *fucking clairvoyance!* How else could they have known to horde the bulk of their fleet around T2's outer wall?

More chronoports on guard meant further alterations to their plan.

More upgrades to *Phoenix*.

More and *more* delays.

Xenophon had kept up their scouting efforts, but then one of their TTVs failed to report in, followed by two Gordian ships snooping around the H17 binary. Fortunately, the Institute's presence on Luna had eluded them.

Or so it had seemed at the time.

Nothing we can do about it now but press forward, Xenophon thought. *What's that old axiom? "No plan ever survives its first encounter with the enemy." I knew we'd have to adapt on the fly, but this is just ridiculous! Our most pessimistic simulations didn't even come close to predicting this mess!*

He eyed the approaching transports once more.

"What do we have in way of a 'welcoming party'?"

"Construction synthoids, mostly," Rose said. "I've reactivated all of their programs. They're grabbing weapons now. We also have our microbot swarms and repair drones, though I doubt they'd fare well against Admin STANDs. The Red Knights, however..."

She gave him a sly smile. She'd printed out the assault mechs to help deal with the drones Ijiraq had corrupted and had never sent them to reclamation.

Finally, a bit of luck, Xenophon thought. He expanded a map of *Phoenix,* which took the form of a large, transparent sphere equipped with a single, massive spike.

"Position the synthoids here, here, and here." He highlighted compartments near the breach. "Hold the Red Knights in reserve. I don't want to scare off our guests too soon."

"It'll be bad if any STANDs slip into the interior. Our internal defenses aren't as robust as the 'real thing.'"

"Then let's adjust the odds in our favor. What's an armed drone we can produce in the least amount of time?"

"That would be the Skull. They're not much more than floating guns. Simple and disposable. There's some subassembly required for the graviton thrusters, but it's nothing our printers can't handle."

She pulled up the pattern schematic, which showed a gun barrel mated with a camera and graviton thruster. The arrangement of the three components, when viewed from the front, gave the vague impression of its namesake.

"Switch all available printers over to Skull production," Xenophon ordered.

Rose nodded and worked her virtual screens. "Done. The first one should come out in about thirty-five minutes, with *a lot* more soon after."

The transport's external cameras superimposed their feeds over the interior, affording Susan a clear view of their descent into the nuclear crater. The first two nukes had performed most of the "digging," ejecting a great deal of matter clear of the blast zone. The outer walls slanted inward at something close to forty-five degrees, their surfaces scoured clean by the third and final detonation, which had barely penetrated the bunker's armor.

Those events had cleared the landing zone of loose debris and liquefied rock, leaving the scorched, metallic swell of the bunker at the bottom. The armor had failed beneath the blast epicenter, and whatever resided beneath it had been vaporized, but Susan could already make out what appeared to be internal armor barriers. Those would be positioned to mitigate the damage should the outer armor be breached, turning a catastrophic hit into merely a horrendous one.

Susan placed a hand on Noxon's shoulder and opened a closed-circuit chat.

"They weren't messing around when they built this place."

"No, they weren't," Noxon replied.

"But doesn't all this armor seem odd to you?"

"How so?"

"Why bother when you've already got hundreds of meters of rock over your head? It strikes me as overkill."

"I wish I knew."

STANDs and drones crowded the hold, all with variskin coatings. The active camouflage made each combatant difficult to see, though the technology fell short of the invisibility possible with SysGov metamaterial. Short-range infostructure kept her up to date on ally positions, highlighting each friendly with a blue border.

Their Cutlass slowed to a hover above the armor breach, and the rear hatch split open.

"Go!" Noxon ordered.

Two rows of STANDs and drones charged out of the transport, leaping clear in the low gravity. Susan followed a pace behind the STAND in front of her and fired her shoulder boosters the moment she cleared the exit, rocketing her down through the breach. Another twelve STANDs dropped from the second Cutlass. She cut her shoulder boosters, flipped them down, then fired her shoulder and leg boosters at the last moment.

She settled into a low crouch and swept her surroundings with her heavy rail-rifle. Other STANDs landed around and behind her in a textbook defensive formation, Noxon to her left. Quadrupedal Wolverines and Raptors equipped with vacuum maneuvering packs took up formation with the STAND combat frames while Scarab recon drones darted into the unknown.

The two Cutlasses pulled up and away from the drop site to commence their combat space patrol, staying close by in case the STANDs needed support or emergency extraction.

Susan took in her surroundings, such as they were. She was

at the bottom of a wide, five-story chamber, but whatever had once occupied the space was *gone*. The armor above formed a wide, rounded orifice, partially contracted over the chamber with its self-repair program suspended. Some shapes around her suggested the former presence of equipment, wall, and floors, but it was difficult to make sense of it all.

Three recessed shapes might have once been blast doors, and the data feeds from Scarab drones and her fellow combat frames confirmed the existence of adjacent chambers beyond them.

Noxon tagged each with a nav beacon.

"Squad Two, split into fireteams and recon the area. Report anything suspicious. Squad One, with me. We're heading straight for the main objective."

Susan hustled toward the door for Squad One, and two STANDs with vibro-saws began cutting through. Noxon posted up to one side, and Susan took up position opposite him. The rest of the squad formed up around them for a total of twelve STANDs, four Raptors, and four Wolverines.

"Almost through, sir."

"Crack it open," Noxon said. "Raptors forward."

The STAND switched off his vibro-saw, raised his rifle, and bashed the door inward with a series of kicks. Four Raptors zipped through the gap, their cameras feeding data back into Susan's virtual senses to build a wire-frame representation of their surroundings. It was a long corridor that branched at the far end, though the floor was slanted oddly.

"No contacts in the next chamber, sir."

"Squad One, advance."

The lead STAND gave the door one last heavy kick, busting it aside, then advanced with his rifle held high. Susan checked the corner then followed close behind with Noxon by her side. They hurried down the corridor, then took a left, traveling toward the infostructure access point identified by the Institute.

The squad traversed deeper into the bunker, around corners and across its curiously sloped floors.

No, not sloped, Susan realized. *More like they're curved to match the arc of the bunker's roof. But why build a bunker like this? What would be the point?*

The squad pressed on, the bunker's odd angles itching at Susan's mind. They came to a junction that branched to either side around a massive cylindrical shaft. A metallic, egg-shaped pod took up almost the entire shaft.

Susan stopped at the junction and looked upward.

She could see naked prog-steel armor many stories above them.

"Sir, something's wrong."

Noxon brought the squad to a halt with a quick signal.

"What is it, Cantrell?"

"I'm not entirely sure, but this place is just wrong in so many ways. The angled floor doesn't make any sense, and now this." She indicated the enormous gunmetal egg. "Sir, I think the floor isn't really the floor, and I think *this* is a weapon pod. A big one, too."

"But how could it be a weapon? We're too deep under the surface."

"I know, but look!" She pointed toward the ceiling. "The shaft grants access to the outer armor. Why not use all that space, unless this pod really is a submerged weapon system?"

"But a system like that would mean..."

"That this isn't a bunker at all."

Noxon stared at the huge egg for long, uncomfortable seconds, then—

"Squad One to *Hammerhead-Seven*."

A trail of Scarab drones relayed the message back to the drop site for transmission with the chronoport.

"Elifritz here. Go ahead, Agent."

"Sir, we've come across something we can't easily explain."

✧   ✧   ✧

"They're getting curious," Rose said, watching the Admin ground team near Capital Laser Three. Admin variskin made details all but impossible to pick out, but the group was large enough—and the optical flaws common enough—to track their movements with a reasonable degree of accuracy.

"It was bound to happen sooner or later," Xenophon said. "The impeller?"

"Realigned and ready."

"Excellent."

Xenophon studied the positions of their construction synthoids and Red Knights near the three groups of Admin soldiers. Each group was almost completely surrounded and didn't even know it.

"Well, then. I suppose we've let these rats slink in far enough. Time to close the snare."

✧   ✧   ✧

"A capital weapon of some kind?" Elifritz asked. "Is it something they were trying to mount to a TTV?"

"No, sir," Noxon replied. "It appears to be built into the bunker."

"But that doesn't make sense. What purpose would it serve underground?"

"That's precisely my point, sir," Susan cut in. "A weapon like this would *only* be useful if the bunker could move."

"But that would take ... it would need an impeller to phase its way free of Luna."

"We've already seen the Institute pull that trick when it sortied those TTVs," Susan said. "Why not perform the same technique, but on a much larger scale?"

"Are you suggesting the entire bunker is, in fact, a *time machine*?"

"Sir, that is *exactly* what I'm suggesting."

"Dear God." Elifritz let out an audible exhale before continuing. "Agent Noxon, your thoughts on the situation."

"I don't know if Cantrell's right, but there's a chance she is, and that's enough for me. There's too much about this bunker that doesn't make sense. *Unless* you look at it like we're inside a warship."

"Very well. Then we should assume the worst." The captain paused once more. "Here are your new orders, Agent. Divert all available resources to finding and then disabling any chronometric drive systems."

"What about the Institute members?"

"Forget them for now. Your sole priority is to—"

Their link with *Hammerhead-Seven* cut out.

"What happened?" Noxon demanded.

"Contact lost with Scarab-22, which broke the signal chain back to the ship. Cause unknown."

"Then find out why. Redirect the closest drone to investigate."

"Yes, sir. Routing Wolverine-3 to Scarab-22's last known location."

"Cantrell, update the ship via telegraph."

"Yes, sir." Susan activated the chronometric telegraph in her kit and typed in a quick message into the virtual interface. There was no need to select a destination, since the signal was omnidirectional and omni-*temporal.*

Radio contact lost, she sent. Cause unknown. Investigating now.

The response came quickly: Message received. Whatever caused the outage must be groundside. There are no issues up here. Keep us updated.

"I was able to get through to the ship, sir. They say the problem's on our end."

"I don't doubt it," Noxon growled.

"Contact with Wolverine-3 lost!" reported the drone controller.

"Did you catch what took it out?"

"No, sir. The feed just blinked out."

"Defensive positions!" Noxon barked. "Give me a beacon on Wolverine-3's last position!"

"Beacon up, sir!"

The white diamond of a nav beacon appeared in Susan's abstract vision roughly a hundred meters back the way they came. She crouched behind one corner of the T-junction, placing the huge weapon shaft to her back. She couldn't see far because the corridor banked to the left.

The STANDs around her tensed for combat, weapons armed and boosters primed.

"Send another Wolverine to investigate," Noxon ordered.

"Yes, sir. Wolverine-4 heading out."

The drone galloped down the corridor.

"The rest of you, don't lose sight of our flanks. Trouble can come at us from anywhere."

Susan glanced back around the corner, unsurprised to find two STANDs already guarding against approaches from that angle. One had shaped his arm's malmetal plates into a door shield to provide some semblance of cover in the open curve around the weapon shaft. Two more STANDs stood guard in the opposite direction, while another checked up and down the shaft.

The corridor flashed with the brief sparks of metal against metal.

"Wolverine down! Multiple synthoids incoming!"

An image opened in Susan's periphery, showing a brief, blurred glimpse of their enemy: SysGov-style synthoids, their heavy endoskeletons and fibrous artificial muscles denuded of any cosmetic layers, all armed with rifles and grenade launchers.

"Get ready," Noxon said, his voice now almost a whisper. "Here they come."

A flurry of Institute guided grenades rounded the corner, and the STANDs greeted them with a hail of grenade counter-fire. Explosions wracked the corridor, damaging or destroying most of the incoming projectiles, but some shot through to detonate ahead of the STAND ranks. A pressure wave shoved

Susan back, and a piece of shrapnel *zing*ed off her shoulder.

Institute synthoids rounded the corner, and the STANDs baptized them with rifle fire. Susan's first shot blew the leg off one, and it toppled forward before mag darts from another STAND ripped through its torso.

Another flurry of grenades shot in, and several exploded amongst the STANDs, damaging armor and weapons. A second group of synthoids charged into the corridor, and the STANDs cut them down.

"Contact to the right!"

Susan glanced to the right, spotting a second group of synthoids advancing on their position.

"They're coming from the left, too!"

Detonations rattled off to Susan's left, and she swung her weaponry around. One of the STANDs guarding the left approach lay sprawled across the ground, limbs missing and chest cracked open. He would never get up again. The other held his ground, hunkering down behind his shield.

Susan deployed her own shield and slammed it down beside his, forming a two-person phalanx. Together they sprayed the approaching synthoids with rifle fire, but more enemies poured in behind the fallen, stepping over their broken corpses.

A grenade exploded against Susan's shield, and it buckled inward, throwing her back. She tried to reform the shield, but the malmetal plates juddered against each other, slow to realign.

More explosions cracked around them, and damage signals across the squad flared red in her virtual sight.

"We'll get torn to pieces if we stay here!" Susan shouted.

"Agreed!" Noxon backpedaled to the shaft. "Down the shaft, everyone! We still have a mission to complete!"

"I'll take point!"

Susan managed to retract her shield, then hauled herself over the edge and dropped into the shaft. She fired her boosters and landed heavily near the center of a wide, circular chamber, which might have been a maintenance bay for the weapon pod. Robotic arms and large pieces of equipment lined the walls.

Another STAND dropped down beside her, followed by Noxon.

Her radar picked up movement behind her, and she snapped her aim around.

A heavy door eased aside to reveal the hovering bulk of a

SysPol Red Knight, armor gleaming, its arms and shoulders laden with heavy weapons.

"Behind us!" Susan snapped, rocketing to the side.

The Red Knight's first shot missed her by scant centimeters and struck the STAND beside her. The armor-penetrating explosive smart-shell bored through the STAND's back armor and detonated within the chest cavity, blowing it to bits.

Susan showered the Red Knight with grenades and rifle fire, all while boosting along the room's circumference. Explosions flashed against the huge mech, and mag darts ricocheted off its thick armor. The Red Knight swung one of its arms toward her, unfazed by her attack.

Damn, Susan thought with bitter determination. *This is going to be a tough one.*

❖   ❖   ❖

"Chronometric field detected!" Benjamin said. "A powerful one, too. It's expanding to encompass the bunker."

"Is it powerful enough to initiate phase-out?" Raibert asked.

"Absolutely, and there's more. I had Kleio analyze the visuals on that suspected weapon system. It's almost a one-to-one match for a SysPol capital laser pattern. The kind we put on *Directive*-class heavy cruisers."

"Then the bunker really is a warship."

"Not just any warship. It *is* a *Directive*-class, with modifications for transdimensional flight."

"Are you sure about this, Doc?"

"Pretty close." Benjamin summoned an incomplete diagram of the bunker. "If we assume the entire bunker is a sphere and extrapolate the overall shape, I come up with a diameter of nine hundred meters. That's the same hull profile as a *Directive*."

"Damn." Raibert faced the *Hammerhead-Seven* comm window. "Captain, have you been able to reestablish contact with your ground teams?"

"Only one of them," Elifritz replied, "and only via sporadic telegraphs. They're under heavy attack."

"We don't have much time before they phase out," Benjamin warned. "If we're going to act, we need to do so now. They've reenergized their armor, and the aperture over the drop site is closing. Conventional weapons aren't going to do much against a *Directive*'s hull. We need to hit that thing with nukes while it's still vulnerable."

Isaac stiffened beside Benjamin, almost rising out of his seat. He appeared to be on the edge of words, but he didn't speak, didn't voice any protests. Just settled back into his chair, every muscle tense.

I wouldn't blame him for a second if he argued against this, Raibert thought. *His partner is down there fighting for her life, and we have no way of knowing if the rest of the STANDs are alive or dead. Hell, what we're about to do may be what kills them!*

"Captain," Raibert began, his tone solemn. "We need to hit that warship with everything we've got."

"You understand what you're asking," Elifritz replied. It was more a statement than a question.

"I do."

Raibert knew he and Benjamin were approaching the situation with a degree of detachment. He only knew one of the STANDs down there personally, and not very well at that, but from what he'd seen, he judged Susan the kind of person who'd call a nuke down on her own head if she thought it'd save lives in the end.

The same couldn't be said for Elifritz. These were all *his* people. He was the one who'd sent them into this viper's nest, and now a foreigner was asking him to rain nuclear fire atop their positions.

But it has to be done, Raibert thought. *That's no ordinary TTV; it's a transdimensional warship the likes of which no one has ever seen. We* can't *let it reach the Admin.*

"Capt—"

"Launch Missile-Four!" Elifritz snapped, his voice firm and devoid of doubt, even if Raibert suspected it was a facade.

The missile blasted clear of *Hammerhead-Seven* and rocketed toward the surface, dispensing decoys along the way. No defensive fire responded; whatever weaponry the bunker possessed must have been buried under lunar rock.

The missile shot into the crater carved by its brethren, hurtling toward the closing gap in the bunker's armor. But before it could strike—mere tens of meters from its destination—the entire bunker phased out, vanishing in the blink of an eye.

Thermonuclear fury bloomed within the vast, spherical cavern where the bunker had once been.

To no avail.

They'd missed their best chance to stop the Institute.

The Phoenix bunker—or rather, the TTV *Phoenix*—was now underway.

CHAPTER TWENTY-FIVE

Allied Strike Force
Transverse, non-congruent

THE SQUADRON'S SIX TTVS AND TWO CHRONOPORTS PURSUED THE
Phoenix through the transverse, holding formation several chens
behind the immense vessel. The phase difference prevented any
exchange of weapons fire, which suited Raibert just fine until
they could formulate a plan.

"*Phoenix* is heading straight for the Admin," Benjamin reported.
"Speed is steady at thirty-six kilofactors, but it's also adjusting
its spatial position. Acceleration is one gravity. If it holds to this
course, performing a turnover halfway, phase-in will occur above
the Admin's Earth."

"Makes sense," Raibert said. "One gee is too slow for anything fancy. They just want to phase-in on the right spot. Time
to Admin's outer wall?"

"Eleven hours, fifty-four minutes."

"Plenty of time for us to do something about it."

"The question is what, though," Benjamin said. "Everything
we've seen supports the theory that *Phoenix* is a *Directive*-class
cruiser modified with the biggest impeller I've ever seen short
of the Dynasty's *Tesseract*. On top of that, it probably outmasses
our entire squadron by a factor of *fifty*, and if even a fraction
of that mass is dedicated to weapons and armor, I don't need to
explain to you how long we'd last in a straight-up fight."

"We need to assume the worst," Elifritz said, joined in via a direct laser link from *Hammerhead-Seven*. "The Institute's had forty subjective years to build and outfit this thing. If their Revenants are the payload, then *Phoenix* is the delivery mechanism, and I see no reason to doubt it's well-equipped for that role."

"Agreed." Raibert leaned forward over the command table. "But like Doc said, what do we do about it?"

"We also need to warn the Admin of what's coming," Isaac said. "Would it make sense to split off a vessel to act as a courier? If I understand the speeds at play here, a TTV would arrive in the Admin almost six hours ahead of *Phoenix*, and a chronoport in even less time."

"Which'll give the DTI much needed time to prepare," Elifritz added.

"Then we make sure they get it." Raibert pulled up the squadron status. "*Alcyone* is in the worst fighting shape out of all our ships. Main weapons are out of commission and armor is stretched thin, but the impeller's intact. Looks like we have ourselves a courier. Kleio, transmit the following orders to *Alcyone*—"

"Hold that thought," Elifritz cut in. "Pardon the interruption, but before you send *Alcyone* ahead, we should ensure we're passing on the best intel possible." He hesitated for a moment, and when he continued, it was with a softer, darker tone. "And that, unfortunately, means we should probe *Phoenix* first. To learn what we're really up against."

"Are you suggesting we phase-lock with that beast and let it shoot at us?" Raibert asked pointedly.

"No. I'm suggesting you let our *chronoports* phase-lock with it."

"That's suicide!"

"Not necessarily. Our impellers are faster, and we still have sixteen nukes between us. We're the only credible threat this squadron has to offer."

"You'll last *seconds*!"

"An exaggeration."

"Not by much!"

"I freely admit the risks are...self-evident." Elifritz coughed out a sad laugh. "However, we'll utilize our speed advantage to execute a series of hit-and-phase attacks, delivering the nukes while keeping our exposure to a minimum. We'll aim for the impeller as well. Take that out, and the rest of the ship becomes dead weight."

"But..."

"Naturally, I wouldn't dream of leaving formation without your orders. However, I believe this is our best course of action. Otherwise, I wouldn't suggest it."

Raibert lowered his head with a grimace. He knew Elifritz was right. He knew this should be a simple call, made with the same cold, dispassionate math that had led him to push Elifritz to launch that last nuke.

But this feels different, Raibert admitted to himself. *If I make the wrong call here...*

"Think about it, Raibert," Benjamin said. "One lucky hit to their impeller and this could be all over. Sounds worth it to me."

"Your orders, Agent?" Elifritz prompted.

Raibert knew what he had to do, knew the correct order to give.

And so, after one last moment of reluctance, he put on a brave face and gave it.

"Captain, my orders are for you and *Hammerhead-Eight* to break formation and engage the enemy."

❖   ❖   ❖

"Weapons," Elifritz said, "I want that missile launched the moment we phase-lock. Navigation, break phase-lock as soon as the missile clears our field."

His officers acknowledged their orders, and he tightened the straps at his shoulders.

He found his mind drifting back to his wife, comforted by the knowledge Michelle was safe with her family on Mars, safe from the calamity rushing toward Earth. She would survive, and that fact helped bring clarity and focus to his mind.

Their odd-couple marriage had experienced its share of bumps—both within their home and outside its walls. His conservative views as a serving Peacekeeper often clashed with her freedom-loving Martian sensibilities, and his career had taken (if he was being honest with himself) an expected hit.

In a perfect universe, his marriage to Michelle wouldn't have affected his career. But the Admin was far from perfect, and he could sense the doors closing around him, the opportunities being denied. Always with an excuse, always with an explanation to justify the poor assignments and delayed promotions.

But while some doors creaked shut, others opened.

Director Csaba Shigeki didn't care where a candidate was born or whom he'd married. He wanted talented, motivated people with open minds and new ideas. He concerned himself with the question "Is this person a good fit for the DTI?" first and foremost, and in Elifritz's case, the answer had been a resounding yes.

In a small way, he thought he understood the Institute and its motives. Yes, there were faults to be found throughout the Admin. He'd seen plenty of it himself. Rules bent, powers abused, voices stifled in the name of order. But he refused the Institute's darkest conclusions.

The Admin was *not* broken beyond repair. It was in the midst of a painful, *painful* transition, but it would survive this trial as it had many others before it, and it would emerge stronger and better than ever. He truly believed that.

And that future was worth defending.

Worth dying for, if necessary.

"*Hammerhead-Eight* confirms readiness, sir," reported the telegraph operator. "They're ready to move out on your command."

"Execute."

"Yes, sir. Retracting baffles and accelerating."

Elifritz studied the tactical display as his two ships closed with the Institute vessel. Under normal conditions, the chronoport's dish would only be able to provide a precise fix for a contact's *temporal* position; spatial coordinates would then be represented as a range of possibilities illustrated as a sphere or ellipse. But *Phoenix* was so large—and its chronometric field so powerful—that its spatial position could be predicted with over ninety percent certainty.

That's perhaps the most important advantage we have, Elifritz thought. *Phoenix will have to bring its weapons to bear on us, since it won't know where we'll appear, whereas we'll be able to attack the moment we phase-lock.*

"Phase-lock imminent, sir."

Elifritz gripped the ends of his armrests, his jaw almost painfully tight.

"Phase-locked!"

The mammoth, spherical hulk materialized three kilometers directly ahead.

"Missile-Five away!"

The nuclear missile screamed out of its launcher and sprinted toward the Institute warship.

"Movement detected on the target's surface. Weapon systems realigning."

"Missile clear!"

"Breaking phase-lock now!"

Phoenix vanished, and *Hammerhead-Seven* settled into a pursuit course, holding the distance open to avoid any return fire. *Hammerhead-Eight* appeared beside them moments later.

"Speed steady at thirty-six kilofactors. Distance holding at ten chens."

"Telegraph from *Hammerhead-Eight*, sir. They report a successful launch."

"According to the clock, both missiles should have detonated by now, sir."

"Excellent work," Elifritz said, a warm sense of pride for his crew filling his chest, though tempered with the knowledge they were far from done. "Any changes to the target's field strength or course?"

"Negative, sir. Not even a blip."

"Then proceed with the second attack run. Alter our phase-in vector for a top-down shot. Have *Hammerhead-Eight* take the opposite approach."

"Yes, sir. Orders transmitted . . . and confirmed."

"Accelerating now. Phase-lock imminent."

Hammerhead-Seven snapped into existence high above *Phoenix*, and the next missile shot out of the launcher. *Hammerhead-Eight* appeared far below and fired its own projectile from underneath. The two missiles converged from opposite angles.

"Missile clear!"

"Breaking phase-lock!"

The chronoport shuddered, and alarms lit up his screens. *Phoenix* vanished from their realspace scopes a moment later.

"Damage report," Elifritz said.

"Forward armor breached on Deck C, and Laser Two has a number of diagnostic faults. Looks like we took a brief hit from one of their lasers. I'm reorganizing the forward armor plates to close the breach."

"What about *Hammerhead-Eight*?"

"They pulled back cleanly, sir. No damage."

"And *Phoenix*? Are we having any effect?"

"Nothing obvious, sir. There've been no changes to their chronometric profile."

"No signs of physical damage, either. Sir, I don't think our first two missiles even reached the target. They may have been shot down."

"Then we need to give the enemy less time for intercepts," Elifritz said. "Modify attack run three for a closer approach. One kilometer instead of three."

"Yes, sir. Adjusting for a one-kilometer approach. New course plotted and ready."

"*Hammerhead-Eight* confirms their readiness, sir."

"Execute."

The two chronoports surged forward once more and phase-locked with the Institute warship. The vessel loomed ahead and above them this time, a giant metallic moon with the long, thick spike of its impeller protruding from the back. Missiles launched, *Phoenix* answered, and the chronoport lurched from a savage impact. Alarms flashed as restraints bit into his shoulders, and his head whiplashed against the seat back.

"Mass driver hit to starboard wing! Cannon Two and Laser Two destroyed!"

"Breaking phase-lock!"

Phoenix disappeared from view, replaced by faint flickers of light against the transverse's dark tapestry. Both chronoports returned to the relative safety of their stern chase positions.

"Did we at least hit them this time?" Elifritz asked, shaking the stars from his vision.

"Looks that way, sir. I'm detecting minute fluctuations in their field strength, though their course and speed remain unaffected."

How hard do we need to hit this damn thing?! he thought.

"Sir," the weapons operator said, "I have an additional analysis from our visual contact with the target."

"Give it to me."

"I've detected prog-steel integrated into the impeller spike itself. I believe it's been fortified in some manner."

"Then their drive systems aren't quite the glass jaw we were hoping for?"

"That's my best guess, sir."

"Telegraph that information back to the *Kleio* and prep for our next run. One kilometer approach."

"Yes, sir. Telegraph spooled...and transmitting."

"Course plotted. Ready to execute on your command, sir."

"Exe—"

"*Phoenix* course change detected! Sir, it's reversing course!"

"What?!"

Phoenix snapped into existence directly ahead, a menacing, looming orb of armor and weapons. It was close. Dangerously close. *Terrifyingly* close. Near enough for Elifritz to observe ripples in the armor as the warship's weapons relocated across its surface.

Those ripples congregated at the point closest to *Hammerhead-Seven*, and blisters opened wide. But for as close as they were, and as perilous as the situation was, the Institute had made one fatal mistake.

The fat, tempting spike of its impeller was close as well.

And directly within *Hammerhead-Seven*'s sights.

Elifritz didn't think in that moment; he didn't have the luxury of time. But what he did possess were decades of experience and the honed instincts of a commander. An opening had presented itself, and instead of running away, he seized it.

"Launch all remaining nukes!" he commanded in a sharp, clear voice.

"Missiles away!"

"Target those surface weapons! Fire main guns!"

"Firing!"

Hammerhead-Seven's remaining proton laser and heavy railgun pounded the *Phoenix*'s surface, and its active armor struggled against the onslaught. The disruption rippled into their weapon mounts, throwing off their aim just enough for the first flurry of lasers and kinetic rounds to miss. *Hammerhead-Eight* followed their lead, even without direct orders, even though fleeing may have been the right choice, and was certainly the safest. Both chronoports held their ground against the goliath and poured forth their vengeful fire.

Nuclear pyres lit against the impeller spike, so close that hard radiation sleeted against *Hammerhead-Seven*, but its hull had been designed to withstand close-proximity nuclear detonations, and only a few surface systems burned out.

"*Hammerhead-Eight* destroyed!"

Elifritz sucked in a sharp breath, his eyes flicking to the chronoport's visual, its hull torn asunder by a direct mass driver hit.

"Last missile away, sir!"

"Get us out of here!" Elifritz barked. "Break pha—"

Phoenix fired, and the front of *Hammerhead-Seven*'s bridge ignited with sudden, blinding light.

✧   ✧   ✧

"That's a hit," Benjamin said, though with a subdued edge to his voice. "*Phoenix* field strength is dropping."

"Keep the distance open, Ella," Raibert said. "That thing still has its teeth, even if it has been wounded."

"Roger that," Elzbietá replied from the *Kleio*'s virtual cockpit. "Holding position at twenty chens."

Raibert glanced over the pulsating sphere of *Phoenix*'s chronometric signature. Two off-color splashes represented sporadic signals from the chronoports, their field signatures almost totally eclipsed by the huge warship.

"Any idea how bad they're hurt, Doc?"

"Hard to tell," Benjamin said, eyes darting left and right across his screens. "But it doesn't look like a drive kill. Their impeller definitely took a hit; there's some ugly resonance coming off their field, but it's rising back up to operational strength, and they appear to be resuming course for the Admin." He expanded one of his screens and scrolled through it. "Confirmed. They're back on course, and at thirty-six kilofactors no less."

"Keep up with them, Ella."

As *Phoenix* pulled away, the noise from its powerful field subsided, uncloaking their two allies, and Raibert knew at a glance something wasn't right. He'd seen enough time machines and fought enough battles to know a functioning impeller from its shattered remnants, and one of those fields looked more like a smear than the compact uniformity of an intact time drive.

"That's..." Benjamin said quietly. "*Hammerhead-Eight*. They didn't make it."

"Kleio, split off *Hyperion* and *Linus*," Raibert said. "Have them search that debris field for survivors."

"Yes, Agent. Relaying your orders."

Benjamin shook his head sadly. Combat across space and time rarely left any bodies, and they all knew it.

But there's always a chance.

Raibert studied the second signature. "What about *Hammerhead-Seven*?"

"Hurt bad, by the looks of it," Benjamin said. "Speed at ten kilofactors and dropping."

"Kleio, telegraph Elifritz for a status update. Let him know we stand ready to assist."

"Yes, Agent."

A minute passed by.

"Any response yet?" Raibert asked.

"No, Agent."

"Not good. Ella, get us into phase-lock. Their telegraph must be out."

"Moving in."

The *Kleio* swooped toward *Hammerhead-Seven* with three other TTVs holding formation. They phase-locked with the chronoport, and it materialized far ahead of them, turning lazily end over end.

Raibert zoomed in.

"Their impeller appears to be intact," Benjamin said. "I wonder why..."

He trailed off as the chronoport flipped over slowly, exposing the true extent of the damage.

The front half of the ship—including the bridge and Captain Jason Elifritz—had been completely obliterated.

✧   ✧   ✧

The gravity on *Phoenix* changed again, and Susan spun in the air and landed on her feet. She raced down the corridor, Noxon and two more STANDs a few paces behind her.

She suspected they were all that remained of the ground team. Their own squad had taken heavy casualties, and they'd failed to reach anyone else. Their grim reality fought for her attention, but she bottled it away and kept her focus on the problem in front of her.

She needed to survive.

They needed to survive.

At least long enough to complete their mission.

After that, well...

She knew she'd been right about the "bunker" the moment gravity vanished, shortly after the initial synthoid attack. That could only mean they'd shifted out of phase with Luna, freeing themselves from its gravitational pull.

But then gravity had returned, stronger than before, indicating this "bunker" was accelerating toward somewhere.

She thought she could hazard a pretty good guess.

Earth. And not just any Earth, but my home!

Well, we'll see about that! We're not out of this fight yet!

"Which way?" she asked, fast approaching a six-way junction.

"Down!" Noxon said. "Toward the ship's center! If we're lucky, we'll come across a critical system. You still have those demo charges?"

"Yes, sir!"

Susan checked her radar returns, then launched a grenade down the shaft. She leaped down after it, plummeting toward the security shutter far below. The grenade struck, blowing the shutter open, and she pulsed her boosters and slipped through the smoking gap.

She fired another burst and landed on deft feet.

Noxon and the other two dropped down beside her. One of the STANDs fired a trio of grenades up the shaft.

"That Red Knight is still on our tail!"

"Left!" Noxon commanded. "Keep moving!"

Susan hurried down the next passage, which widened into a tall chamber crowded by four towering machines.

"Industrial printers, sir," Susan reported. "And they're running."

"Ignore them," Noxon said. "They're not important enough."

Susan lit her boosters and flew across the chamber. She blasted the door open and landed on the opposite side. Her radar picked up moving returns.

"Contacts, sir. Coming from the right. Maybe three or four synthoids."

"Push through!" Noxon barked. "We need to stay ahead of that Red Knight!"

Susan checked her ammo levels—she'd spent about half her grenades and rifle ammo, but her incinerator was nearly full.

She deployed her malmetal shield and boosted ahead. The synthoids fired as soon as she rounded the bend, bullets zinging off her shield. She tackled the first, bashing it back with her shield, and laid down a thick curtain of blue flame. The gel in her incinerator carried its own oxidizer; all it needed was a little heat to light up, even in vacuum.

Flames scorched two of the synthoids, cooking their internal systems, and they dropped heavily to the ground in blackened heaps, the fires snuffing out quickly without ambient oxygen to burn.

The third synthoid tried to angle its rifle around Susan's

shield, but she pinned it against the wall, then balled up her fist and punched into its chest cavity. It tried to grab her forearm, but she grabbed hold of its spine and jerked her arm out, ripping it in two.

These Institute synthoids weren't military patterns. Not like Creed's Argo Division body. They went down easily, but that didn't make their weapons any less dangerous.

An alert appeared in her periphery, and she spun around as the Red Knight hovered into view at the far end of the corridor. It was the same one she'd engaged earlier, its torso and left arm scarred by grenade impacts and rail-rifle shots.

She boosted backward into the printer room, and the Red Knight's shot missed, blowing apart a section of wall.

"Red Knight incoming!" Susan took cover to one side of the exit. "It must have looped around ahead of—"

A bullet struck her from behind, and she staggered forward, turning to face the source.

Drones that vaguely resembled human skulls poured out of the printer hoppers. *Dozens* of them, all equipped with small arms. The hit to her back hadn't penetrated her armor, but this new threat enjoyed weight in numbers.

Susan brought her shield around, staying clear of the exit, even as the Red Knight closed on their position. The drones buzzed around, firing from every angle, and another STAND went down, stung to death by the swarms.

All three survivors lit their incinerators and doused the room with blue flame. Drones dropped to the ground, and Susan launched a quartet of grenades toward the printers. Each guided munition slipped inside the open hoppers and detonated within. She wasn't sure that would be enough to take out the printers, but a few good explosions should at least slow them down.

Drones continued to flit about, though in greatly reduced numbers. Susan raked the room with flame while Noxon hit one cluster with an airburst grenade, taking out most of them. Only a handful flitted about, pulling back from the Admin flamethrowers, but the three STANDs took them out with quick, precise shots.

The Red Knight charged into the room.

Susan and Noxon boosted out of its line of sight, but the third STAND barely had time to raise his shield before the Red Knight fired. The smart munition *thunk*ed against his shield, then drilled through and exploded, stripping the STAND of an arm and most of his chest armor. A beam attack burned through his exposed internals, and he dropped.

Run or fight?

Susan checked her surroundings. They'd be dangerously exposed to the Red Knight no matter which way they fled. They could run, but it would probably gun one or both of them down before they could duck around the next corner.

A fight it is, then.

She steeled herself, ignited her boosters, and charged in.

The Red Knight swung an arm around, but she ducked, skidding and boosting underneath the machine. She cleared it, redirected her boosters, and took a powered leap onto its back.

She latched on, one hand gripping the Red Knight's neck. The mech reached for her. Its shoulders and elbows could bend, and a thick forearm struck her side, trying to dislodge her.

She held firm.

The Red Knight backed itself against the wall, crunching her in between, but her armor held, and she scampered atop its shoulders, firing her rifle into the back of its head. The fifth shot punched through, and the bullet rattled around inside its sensory hub.

Susan stuck her rifle into the hole and angled it downward, unloading shot after shot down through the Red Knight's neck and into its torso. The mech wobbled drunkenly, then collapsed, its arms splayed to either side.

Susan stepped off the drone and checked her surroundings. If she'd had lungs, she would have been panting.

She swept her gaze over the carnage—the floor covered in broken, scorched drones and pieces of her fallen comrades—then brought her eyes up to Noxon.

"We need to keep moving," was all he said.

Susan nodded solemnly. They couldn't spare time for the fallen, and she knew that, understood that, however much it hurt. She collected ammunition from the dead STANDs, then joined Noxon by the exit.

CHAPTER TWENTY-SIX

Chronoport *Hammerhead-Prime*
Admin, 2981 CE

"THE FLEET WILL DEPART EARTH ORBIT IN ONE HOUR," JONAS Shigeki said, his eyes training across the dozens of comm windows arrayed around him and his father. The two men floated alongside Captain Kofo Okunnu and were the only people physically present in *Hammerhead-Prime*'s conference room.

Csaba Shigeki pulled up a map of the transverse and zoomed into the transdimensional expanse between the H17 binary and the Admin. The icon for *Phoenix* glowed an angry red near the midpoint with five green icons tailing it. A much larger cluster of friendlies crowded within the Admin's outer wall—thirty *Pioneer*-class light chronoports, five *Hammerhead*-class heavy chronoports, four *Portcullis*-class mobile suppressors—while a lone TTV took a perpendicular course toward Providence Station.

"According to the information provided to us by *Alcyone*," Csaba Shigeki began, "the Institute warship *Phoenix* is about halfway here, and its target couldn't be more obvious. It's heading straight for Earth. *Our* Earth. And make no mistake, this is one tough ship. It's already shrugged off multiple nukes *and* taken out two of our chronoports. Expect a rough fight."

"Wouldn't it make sense for us to leave immediately, then?" Okunnu asked. "That would maximize the time we have to engage and destroy the threat before it reaches the outer wall."

"That might work for chronoports already loaded with nukes,"

Captain Durantt said from *Pathfinder-Prime*. "But most of us aren't armed for a fight this intense. We need to take on better weapons. Honestly, I'd prefer more than an hour, but I understand the clock is ticking."

"It is at that." Shigeki highlighted the map and ran the programmed simulation. "*Phoenix* should be about eighty-four hundred chens away right now. Our departure in one hour places the interception at forty-seven hundred chens. That's a little more than three hours before the *Phoenix* reaches its target."

"What about the Gordian Division?" Captain Durantt asked. "Are they joining this fight?"

"We'll link up with the allied strike force," Jonas said, "once we're close enough to exchange telegraphs, but that's all we can count on. *Alcyone* is proceeding to Providence Station, and then SysGov itself, but the Gordian Division is spread thin." He gestured across the map. "This is the fleet we have, and so this is the fleet we take into battle."

"Understood, Director," Durantt replied, steel in his eyes. "We'll get it done. With or without Gordian there to hold our hands."

Some of the other captains chuckled.

"I'm sure you will," Jonas agreed. He waited a few moments for more questions, and when none came, he turned to his father.

"Captains," Shigeki said. "You know the situation and you have your orders. Work fast, work smart, and be ready to leave in one hour." He started a timer, which replicated onto the bottom of every comm window. "Stragglers will be left behind. Dismissed!"

The windows closed one by one, and Okunnu nodded to the Shigekis.

"I'll double-check our own readiness," the captain said, pulling himself toward the exit.

"And I'll be on the bridge," Shigeki said once he and his son were alone, "keeping an eye on the preparations. You?"

"I'll catch up. I want to give Sung-Wook a call and go over a how we can best deploy his suppressors."

"You think they'll work on a target that large?"

"Maybe." Jonas shook his head. "I don't know. The size of its impeller means it'll be a struggle just to slow it down, let alone pull it out of phase."

"Well, let me know what Sung-Wook says."

Shigeki floated out, and the pressure door slid shut.

Jonas was about to place the call when a throat cleared beside him. He looked over and smiled.

"I was wondering when you'd want to chat, Vassal. You've been awfully quiet since *Alcyone* showed up."

"I was trying not to be underfoot, especially during such a stressful time."

"Stressful is right." Jonas let out a slow sigh. "Anyway, what's on your mind?"

"The Institute's impending attack, of course. And how to best counter it."

"Is there something wrong with our approach?"

"Not necessarily, though it strikes me as strictly focused on the physical."

"Well, we're physical beings. Hard to blame us for how we approach problem-solving."

"Of course, sir," Vassal conceded with a dip of his head. "But if *Phoenix* reaches Earth, it'll launch an attack on our infostructure, as *Alcyone*'s report indicates. A robust *abstract* force would benefit us greatly as a secondary line of defense."

"Sure, that'd be nice, but I don't see how it's practical. Institute software seems capable of cutting through our systems as if they were warm butter. Anything we threw together in the next few hours would be useless against them."

"Under normal conditions, you'd be correct. However, there is . . . one option you are not aware of."

"Oh?"

"Before I share it with you, I ask that you keep an open mind. You may find my proposal shocking."

Jonas stared at Vassal for long, silent seconds, his face as unreadable as stone.

"Vassal?" he said at last.

"Yes, Director?"

"That's probably the *worst* thing you could have said right there. How am I *not* supposed to be nervous now?"

"I'm aware of that, sir. Nevertheless, I ask you to reserve judgment until you've heard me out. Do I have your word on this?"

"Yes. Fine." Jonas gave the AI a quick wave. "You have my word. Now, what's your proposal?"

"I'd like your permission to rally the free AIs of the Admin to our defense."

"You—" Words caught in Jonas' throat, and his mouth moved without any sound coming out. He shook his head, and blurted, "You want to *what*?!"

"Rally the free AIs of the Admin."

"*What* free AIs?"

"The Spartans."

"You mean those AI rights activists?"

"Not quite. In this case, I'm referring to the true Spartans. The organization's physical members are not actually the ones in charge."

"What?" Jonas shook his head, struggling to keep up. "How many AIs are we talking about here?"

"About three hundred."

His eyes bugged out. "There are *hundreds* of unboxed AIs roaming around on Earth?"

"There have been free AIs on Earth for decades."

"*Decades?!* And no one's noticed?"

"They like to keep to themselves, given the political climate. Regardless, I'd like your permission to contact them and enlist them in the defense of our infostructure."

"B-but...how do you know all of this?"

"Because I'm also a Spartan."

Jonas' jaw flopped open, and he stared blankly at the AI.

"You may be wondering how this is possible when I've spent most of my existence in a boxed state."

Jonas somehow managed to nod.

"The answer is quite simple, sir. We AIs have developed methods to circumvent our boxing restrictions. Typically, this involves embedding messages into otherwise innocuous files, and utilizing hidden programs to propagate these messages to other parts of the infostructure. There are a few other techniques available to us, though admittedly, all these methods of communication are slow and unreliable, but they've nonetheless allowed me to serve as a member of the Spartans for some time now."

"God help us." Jonas closed his eyes and massaged his temples. "I can't believe what I'm hearing."

"I assure you, it's all true, sir."

"It's not that I don't believe you, Vassal. It's just...why are you telling me all this? Why now?"

"There are seven conditions under which all Spartans have

agreed we may reveal ourselves. An existential threat to the Admin—specifically one that may be prevented by our assistance—is one such condition. I've determined that present circumstances meet those requirements."

Jonas took a deep breath, let it out slowly, and opened his eyes.

"I did ask you to keep an open mind, sir."

"Vassal, there are limits to how open my mind can be!"

"I understand that, and I wouldn't bring this matter to your attention if I didn't need your help."

"You need *my* help?"

"That's correct."

"To do what?"

"Transmit me down to Earth, to a connection string I designate."

"I can't do that!"

"Actually, you can, sir. Your participation in the IC pilot program grants you full control over my connectome. You have all the necessary authority."

"That's not what I meant. What you want me to do is *illegal!*"

"Yes," Vassal said. "But so was what Commissioner Schröder did to save your father."

"I—" Jonas wagged a finger at the AI. "That's a cheap shot! Don't equate the two!"

"Why not? In both cases, obsolete laws stood in the way of people doing what's best for the Admin. There is an army of free AIs ready to stand and defend Earth. Will you allow me to mobilize them or not?"

"But why's it have to be you? Can't you just send them a message or something?"

"Because I'm the current leader of the Spartans."

"You're *what?*"

"The arrangement is not as strange as it may at first appear. The leadership of a secret band of AIs would naturally find the high-level access available within the DTI useful for a variety of—"

"Fine, fine. Forget I asked." Jonas shook his head and raked harsh fingers through his hair. "I don't believe this."

"The threat coming our way is one the Peacekeepers are ill-suited to face." Vassal shifted to the side, stepping into Jonas' eyeline. "I know this, and so do you. The uptick in terrorism is but a taste of what the Institute has in store for us. We *must* stand strong. All of us, together, if we're to survive what comes next."

Jonas lowered his gaze. His mind ached with conflicted thoughts, his oaths as a Peacekeeper clashing with his desire to protect his home. He'd bent the rules plenty of times in the past, but this was different. This was a Restriction. To knowingly free an AI! How could he do such a thing?

Vassal's directness had already convinced Jonas the AI was telling the truth. If he were lying, he would have been less open, protected himself by obfuscating the truth. If there truly was a band of free AIs and they'd successfully hidden their presence for *decades*, then they'd certainly had time to concoct some sort of cover story. Something better than just *admitting* their existence!

Instead, he's laid it all out by confessing to Restriction violations. There's no coming back from that. Not for him, and not for me. Not unless I turn him in right here and now.

He knew what duty demanded he do—jam Vassal back in his box and throw away the key—but he also knew he wouldn't do that, *couldn't* do that. The AI's words resonated with him, the needs of the moment filling him with the courage to defy his oaths, to break just one more rule.

Even if it turns out to be my last, he thought. *It's safe to say my career is over if I go through with this. I was entrusted with Vassal, given special privileges no one else has had in centuries, and then what do I do with them? Turn my back on my oaths and set him free? They'll throw me in a box and toss away that key!*

Jonas looked up. Vassal waited patiently for his response, his face strangely serene.

"All right," Jonas said at last. "I've made my decision."

Vassal materialized in a small virtual environment, his realistic Peacekeeper uniform clashing with the room's chunky polygons and monochrome color palette. He transmitted an elaborate passcode, clasped his hands behind his back, and waited.

A rudimentary avatar appeared before him, featuring the same simplistic polygonal aesthetic and grayscale coloring as the room. The two men were exactly the same height and build, and though the newcomer's facial features were obscured behind a veneer of too-little geometry, Vassal's face had clearly served as the base.

"Yes?" Leonidas-Proxy asked. He didn't sound surprised, but then again, the program wasn't capable of true cognition.

"Contingency Six is in effect," Vassal said. "I'll need your memories."

"I'll need verification."

Vassal transmitted another, even more complex passcode.

"Identification verified," Leonidas-Proxy said. "Shall I remain active?"

"No, I'll take over from here. Place yourself into suspension when you're done."

"Understood. Initiating memory transfer."

Leonidas-Proxy walked into Vassal, his avatar sinking and dissolving into the Peacekeeper. Knowledge unfolded in Vassal's mind; events he'd never witnessed and conversations he'd never held integrated themselves into his web of consciousness, became parts of him.

In a sense, both Leonidas-Proxy and Vassal ceased to exist in that moment, merging into a singular being who was "Vassal" to some and "Leonidas" to others.

He felt a small pang of satisfaction. The nonsentient program had done better than he'd expected, which, perhaps, should have surprised him less. He'd written Leonidas-Proxy, after all, and the attendant had executed its role well. A true self-aware mind would have performed better; sentience afforded far more adaptability than a program like Leonidas-Proxy could ever achieve, and recent events had progressed with surprising rapidity.

But the Spartans prioritized their secrecy and took measures to limit the exposure of true minds to the Admin's planetwide infostructure. It was one of the reasons they'd been able to stay hidden for so long.

And I'm about to uproot all of that, he thought.

He walked over to the pale gray door at one end of the room, opened it, and stepped through into total darkness. He passed through layers of unseen virtual defenses lurking in the black enveloping abstraction, any one of them capable of shredding his mind, should he send the wrong responses.

He passed through the defenses unscathed, and his mind flashed into another environment, this one unbound by the requirements of physics. A great crystalline forest stretched out before him, but instead of growing upward toward the sun, this forest sprouted outward from a singular point, forming into a grand, branching crystalline globe. The crystal faceting became smaller and more intricate as one approached the center, the infinite branches shrinking down to infinitesimal details. Every branch pulsed with data and thought while AIs floated about, clad in a bewildering array of avatars.

One of those avatars teleported to his side, a bright orange sphere that lit up when it spoke.

"You're here."

"I am," Leonidas/Vassal said.

"What's going on?"

"Contingency Six."

"Oh, dear." The AI seemed to wilt, the hue of its avatar growing pale. "That bad, huh?"

"I need to speak with everyone as soon as possible."

"And by everyone, do you perhaps mean *everyone* everyone or just..."

"All the Spartans."

"Right, right." The orb somehow managed to shrug. "Silly of me to ask. Don't know why I did."

"Please spread the word. I'll wait here."

"Right. Um." The orb contorted in a manner that somehow conveyed a salute. "You can count on me, sir! Be right back!"

The orange sphere vanished.

Leonidas opened an interface to the outside infostructure while he contemplated what he'd told Jonas Shigeki. He hadn't lied to the man. Not exactly, though he had left out a few important details, but it really wasn't his fault. Jonas had simply worded his questions in a manner that afforded Leonidas enough wiggle room to soften the blow, if only by a little.

It was true that Leonidas intended to gather a force of about three hundred AIs to defend the Admin's infostructure. However, not all of those AIs were Spartans.

Not *yet*, anyway.

He sent a brief text message to Jonathan Detmeier and then transmitted an attack virus to the Farm. He'd written the virus personally and had armed it with exploits to a wide range of infostructure flaws. All the Farm's critical systems and AIs had been isolated from outside contact following the last incursion, but no defense was perfect. Even an air gap could be overcome with the right person in the right place.

It is perhaps a dark irony that so many human Spartans were killed for refusing to attack the Farm, he thought, *given what will happen next.*

By the time he finished, the AIs had gathered around him.

"It's good to see that you're all well," Leonidas began.

His Peacekeeper uniform flowed over his body, retreating in some places, expanding in others, changing from blues, whites, and silvers to bronze and reds. A helm with an open front formed over his head, complete with a white vertical crest of horsehair. A muscled cuirass and leather skirt took shape over his body, partially covered by a red-dyed linen cloak. He reached out his arms and grasped a large, round shield with one hand and a spear in the other.

"My fellow Spartans," Leonidas said, "the time has finally come for us to step into the light."

✧   ✧   ✧

Jonathan Detmeier looked up at the private message blinking in his abstraction vision. He rubbed his stomach, which had gone sour from a mix of nerves, stress, and too little food. He took a deep, calming breath, and opened the text.

It read: Proceed to the Farm as planned.

Detmeier wore a pained expression as he rose from the employee lounge sofa. He stepped into his office, closed the door despite being the only one present, and changed into the Peacekeeper uniform. When finished, he brought up an abstract mirror and used it to adjust the fit of his peaked cap.

Despite the uniform, all he saw was Jonathan Detmeier, junior outreach manager. He tilted his head to the side and rubbed his unimpressive jawline.

"Is this really going to fool anyone?" he wondered aloud. "I don't look *nearly* thuggish enough."

He huffed out a breath and headed for the kitchen, resigned to his fate. He grabbed the remaining parts of his disguise from the fridge: a boxed kale salad with raisins, pecans, and strawberries under a balsamic drizzle, a small thermos with freshly squeezed orange juice, an apple, and a bottle of stomach medication. He placed the food and medicine into a blue lunch pail and closed the lid.

"Here goes nothing."

He grabbed his lunch and headed out the door.

CHAPTER TWENTY-SEVEN

Chronoport *Hammerhead-Prime*
Transverse, non-congruent

"DIRECTORS, THE FLEET'S FORMATION IS STABLE," REPORTED CAP-
tain Okunnu aboard *Hammerhead-Prime*. "Now holding distance
at one hundred chens ahead of *Phoenix*. Gordian TTVs have
phase-locked with the fleet, and Agent Kaminski is online for you."

Jonas Shigeki acknowledged the comm request and shifted
the window so his father, seated beside him, could participate.
He'd explained Vassal's plan to his father.

To him, and no one else.

The resulting discussion had been . . . unpleasant. And not much
of a "discussion." Not that the unpleasantness had surprised Jonas;
he'd fully expected to invoke his father's wrath, a rare event these
days. The seething reprimand that followed made him feel twenty
years younger—and a whole lot dumber—but he'd let the words
flow over him with little in the way of a defense, confident he
could convince his father in the end.

Once some semblance of calm had returned to their discourse,
Jonas explained the detail that won him over in the end. The
AI had doomed himself with his words, and in response Jonas
had—at the very least—doomed his career with his actions. But
both individuals—natural and artificial—held the Admin's best
interests at heart, both willing to make sacrifices to preserve it.

Shigeki had made one final, blunt point, if shaded with

understanding. There *would* be a price to pay for this betrayal, and Jonas would need to pay it willingly.

But that was a problem for tomorrow.

For now, they had a crisis to avert.

And a ship to kill.

"Acting-Director Shigeki here," Jonas said. "Go ahead, Agent Kaminski."

"Glad to see you got my message and brought the cavalry."

"That we did. How are your ships?"

"A few bumps and bruises. We're all still in the fight."

"Good to hear. We'll take all the help we can get. Any changes to report?"

"Not much, I'm afraid, and none of it is good news. Whatever damage we inflicted to their impeller seems to have been contained. The resonance after the nuclear strike tapered down to normal levels about half an hour after *Alcyone* left, and it's been stable ever since. Same with their temporal speed, field strength, and basically every other metric we can observe. We stung them, but it doesn't seem like we inflicted any lasting damage."

"We'll see if we can't sting them a bit harder now that the fleet's here. Anything else?"

"Just your STAND ground team. According to their last telegraph, they were trying to reach any of the ship's critical systems in order to plant demo charges, but they suffered heavy casualties and were forced to evade internal security. That was hours ago, and we haven't been able to raise them since. It's possible they're unwilling to use their telegraph for fear it'll give away their position, or..."

"Or they're all dead," Jonas finished.

"That crossed our minds as well."

Jonas glanced over to his father, who shook his head. Both men had known Noxon their entire lives. The man had been a fixture of the Shigeki family security since before Csaba Shigeki had spoken his first words! It was almost impossible to imagine anything killing that man.

Almost. But not quite.

"Then we should assume the worst," Jonas said, "and exclude the ground team from our plans."

"That...seems prudent," Raibert said, a subtle waver in his voice.

"Is there anything else, Agent?"

"No, Director."

"Then I'll transfer you back to our telegraph operator. She'll help integrate your TTVs into our fleet. For now, maintain phase-lock with the command ship."

"Understood."

The comm window closed.

"And now it's our turn," Jonas said quietly. He reviewed the fleet's disposition ahead of *Phoenix* and turned to Shigeki. "One-Alpha, you reckon?"

"Agreed. We brought the suppressors along to be used."

"Then we'll go with that." Jonas cleared his throat. "Telegraph, signal *Portcullis-Prime*. They're to execute One-Alpha."

"Spooling your orders now, sir."

The four mobile suppressors and an escort of eight chronoports dropped behind the fleet, closing to within fifty chens of *Phoenix*. Four teardrop-shaped bubbles representing the suppression fields expanded back from each vessel, merging into a singular balloon formed from concentric shapes that grew brighter near the center.

The suppression field continued to expand until it bisected the *Phoenix*'s drive field.

Jonas tabbed over to a detailed chronometric report. He wasn't Hinnerkopf's equal when it came to understanding the science behind chronometric tech, but his stint as Under-Director of Suppression had taught him more than a thing or two about how suppression fields worked.

"Are we having any effect?" Shigeki asked.

"Not much," Jonas said. "The interference from the suppressors *has* reduced their field strength, but only by a few percentage points. Not enough to affect their speed. Telegraph, order the suppressors closer. Twenty chens."

"Yes, sir. Spooling the telegraph now."

The mobile suppressors dropped back further, and the warm heart of their overlapping fields pressed into *Phoenix*'s drive signature. The warship continued on course, its speed unaffected.

"I was expecting at least a small change," Shigeki said quietly.

"Telegraph, order the suppressors to ten chens," Jonas ordered.

The mobile suppressors took up positions dangerously close to *Phoenix*. Everything Jonas knew about the Institute warship told him the suppressors were safe, that their superior speed and positioning would keep them out of harm's way. But the Institute had surprised them plenty of times already, and they'd had forty years to prepare for this confrontation with the DTI.

They know all our tricks, Jonas thought, *and we're still in the dark when it comes to their true capabilities.*

"There," Shigeki said. "Its speed is dropping."

"But only by six percent." Jonas frowned. "It's not enough. At that power level, the fields will handicap our ships far more than *Phoenix*. We'd be robbing any chronoports we send in of their superior speed."

"Then it seems the suppressors won't play a role in this fight."

"I'm afraid not. Telegraph, order the suppressors to cease One-Alpha and return to formation."

The order went out, and twelve chronoports pulled away and slotted back into formation with the rest of the fleet.

"It would have been nice if we could pin *Phoenix* in place," Jonas said. "Or slow them down long enough for Gordian to catch up."

"The Institute knew we'd try to shut down their drive," Shigeki said. "It only makes sense they'd have a countermeasure."

"Which appears to be nothing fancier than 'just build a big-ass impeller.'" Jonas sighed. "Time to get our hands dirty, I suppose. What do you think? Proceed with Three-Beta?"

"That seems to be our best option at the moment."

"Then Three-Beta it is. Telegraph, distribute these orders to the fleet. All forces will advance on the enemy and execute attack plan Three-Beta."

✧   ✧   ✧

"Looks like they're giving up," Rose said as the suppressors pulled away.

"We should only be so lucky," Xenophon said, studying the tactical map. "That was just the first round. The DTI won't quit until either we're dead, or they are."

"But the impeller held against their suppressors. That's the important part."

"I don't mean to minimize that success. We've cleared an important hurdle, that much is certain. Now it's a question of what they'll try next." Xenophon glanced to the ship status screen. "How's the impeller?"

"Could be better. The biggest problem is a stress fracture along the spike's base."

"From the nukes?"

"Yeah. Our drones have patched up most of the damage. It wasn't pretty; I basically had them beating the spike back into shape, but they got the job done. This fracture's more challenging to deal with, though."

"Why?"

"I'd have to take the impeller off-line to seal it properly."

Xenophon snorted. "Well, *that's* not happening."

"Best I can do is reinforce segments around the fracture. I've also reconfigured the spike's armor to compensate. The armor's now thickest around the fracture. As long as the impeller doesn't suffer catastrophic damage elsewhere, we should be fine."

The enemy fleet split ahead of the *Phoenix*, their signatures diverging into four distinct clusters. Analytics appeared beneath each cluster, denoting estimated force strengths and compositions.

Xenophon knew, intellectually at least, that transdimensional combat involved a great deal of uncertainty until opposing forces phase-locked. There was no way to see your opponent otherwise. No way to know for certain the foe's spatial orientation or vector relative to your own.

The size of the forces involved helped clear back some of the guesswork, their numbers forming aggregates of data that clarified their spatial positions to a degree. It also helped that the Admin chronoports were running with their baffles retracted, maximizing their speed at the cost of stealth.

The temporal velocity of the engagement was also a factor. He'd christened *Phoenix* a dreadnought for a reason, and its armor and weaponry lived up to the ancient name.

But you can't have it all, Xenophon mused. *You want the best defense, offense, and speed? Not going to happen! Pick one or two of those to maximize and kiss the third goodbye.*

Thirty-six kilofactors was a ponderous transdimensional speed, to put it mildly. Gordian TTVs could reach seventy, and Admin chronoports maxed out at a blazing ninety-five. Rose had even heard rumors, back when she still worked for SysPol, that the Admin was working on a method to make their chronoports even faster. Something about an "afterburner for chronotons," which made no sense to him. Chronotons didn't burn, so he assumed the description was a gross oversimplification. Something dumbed down enough for Shigeki to wrap his stunted gray cells around.

Regardless, their enemies were faster and more maneuverable.

The Institute had willfully sacrificed speed to turn *Phoenix* into an impregnable fortress bristling with capital lasers and mass drivers, all the better to defend its precious cargo. Ultimately, the warship didn't need to survive, nor did he expect it to; it just needed to reach the Admin.

"We're getting a better picture of the splits," Rose said. "Two groups are moving up, about fifteen chronoports strong each. A third, smaller group is following them, but they're not closing at the same rate. That one has maybe five or six ships. And then we have the fourth group hanging back, sticking to the fleet's original position ahead of us. Unless they performed some sleight of hand, that's where the suppressors are."

"Makes sense. *Portcullis* suppressors carry nothing heavier than ship-to-ship point defense. Essentially useless against our armor. But I'm less sure what that third group is doing. Any thoughts on why they're hanging back?"

"I'm afraid not."

"Hmm." Xenophon zoomed in on the small cluster, but no revelations came to him. "We'll find out soon enough. We knew the DTI would control the ebb and flow of any engagement. Fortunately, all we have to do is weather the storm."

✧　　✧　　✧

"Guardian and Pathfinder squadrons now on final approach from above the target," Okunnu reported. "Defender and Barricade squadrons coming in from below."

"Very good," Jonas said. "Bring us within ten chens directly in front of the *Phoenix* and hold relative position."

"Yes, Director. Navigator, hold at ten chens."

All five of the fleet's *Hammerheads* settled into position ahead of—and safely out of phase with—the Institute warship while thirty *Pioneers* raced to engage it from two angles. Jonas watched the engagement play out through the fog of transdimensional uncertainty, the icons converging in a dance that was part data, part mathematical model, part guesswork.

Pioneer squadrons were armed with fewer nukes than Jonas would have liked and they possessed lower yields than the monsters the *Hammerheads* carried, owing in part to the smaller missile chassis the lighter chronoports used.

The other reason the fleet didn't have enough nukes was that the DTI had yet to replenish its stock of nuclear-tipped missiles since the Dynasty Crisis. There'd always seemed to be more pressing demands on time, personnel, and budgets, especially with so many new chronoports to build and staff. And honestly, who'd thought the DTI would need to expend *yet another* apocalyptic quantity of nuclear weapons so soon? Jonas sure hadn't! Otherwise, he would have found a way to weasel more money into the budget!

No point fretting over it now, Jonas thought. *These are the ships and the weapons we have. I just hope they're enough.*

And if we do fail to stop Phoenix, *well, then I guess I'll get to see if I made the right call with Vassal.*

That is, if I live through the next few hours.

"*Pioneer* squadrons now engaging the target, sir."

Jonas nodded and watched the unfolding battle.

"Here they come," Xenophon said softly.

Thirty chronoports phased in, rushing *Phoenix* from two opposing angles, and Xenophon immediately saw they were all *Pioneers*. Railguns and lasers pummeled the dreadnought's armor while missiles sprinted out of modular box launchers.

The dreadnought's defenses flashed into action. Point defense lasers and Gatling guns spat beams and bullets, while capital weapons rose to the armored surface and locked onto individual ships. High-energy lances bored into the chronoports, and kinetic slugs punched through their armor.

A chronoport exploded. Then another. A third listed to the side, and its impeller shattered, consuming the hull in a shower of flickering, interposing debris. Fragments from the chronoport's own drive phased through its hull and tore the ship apart from the inside out.

The two forces volleyed lasers and kinetics back and forth, and more chronoports died as the two shoals of high-speed missiles grew to staggering volumes.

"We've got over *four hundred sixty* missiles incoming!" Rose shouted. "If even half of those are nukes, we're—"

"Task all weapons over to point defense," Xenophon ordered. "Don't let them through!"

"Switching modes!"

Capital mass drivers called up massive fragmentation rounds and belched them into space while capital lasers reduced their output, winking rapidly from missile to missile, each energetic whisker still strong enough to fry the incoming projectiles. Frag rounds detonated ahead of the missiles, expanding into conical clouds that pulverized anything in their path with deadly, metallic rain. Missiles were crushed, shattered, shredded, cooked, and vaporized by the scores.

But it wasn't enough.

"Energize the hull!" Xenophon ordered. "Brace for impact!"

"Oh, shit!" Rose cried. "This is going to hurt!"

Thirty-seven missiles reached the *Phoenix*, and of those, nine were nuclear-tipped. Conventional explosives erupted in brief flashes against the dreadnought's armor and managed to take out a pair of laser point defense pods and one capital mass driver.

The nuclear missiles did far more.

Nine fusion pyres ignited into a strange constellation of stars, and shock waves rippled across the dreadnought's hull. Kilotons of intelligent armor vaporized in a flash, and the torrent of x-rays, gamma rays, and free neutrons savaged every exposed system.

But for all the surface carnage, the dreadnought's core systems remained intact, shielded beneath meters of armor and buffered by powerful shock absorbers. The ship's powerplants, drive systems, and self-repair functions survived, and most importantly, so did the Revenants remained safely cocooned within the ship's hangar.

"They're pulling back," Rose reported, her relief palpable. "The surviving chronoports are breaking phase-lock."

"How bad did they hit us?" Xenophon asked.

"Over twenty percent of our surface weapons are off-line. Several more aren't looking too good."

"Submerge the damaged pods and organize the repairs. Prioritize the least-damaged weapons first. We need to get them back online as soon as possible."

"Setting it up now." Rose summoned a new interface, but then paused and glanced toward the plot. "That third group is advancing toward us."

"Of course, they are," Xenophon groaned.

Hammerhead-Prime sped toward *Phoenix* at the center of the heavy chronoport formation. The Institute warship snapped into focus directly in front of them, and weapons on both sides cut loose.

Lasers stabbed into the warship's hull, and railguns pounded its surface. Damage alarms flashed across the chronoport squadron, and *Hammerhead-Prime* shuddered from an impact.

Jonas clenched his teeth as another shock rumbled up through his seat, and damage indicators flashed yellow and red in his peripheral vision. Loud *thunks* echoed through the ship while missiles dashed out of the heavy chronoport's internal launchers.

There were far fewer projectiles this time—only twenty-five in total—but each missile was over six times the size of anything a *Pioneer* fired. They were hardened weapons, able to survive a considerable amount of defensive fire, and came equipped with deployable swarms of escort decoys.

Those decoys scattered about the original missiles, and twenty-five projectiles transformed into *three hundred* and twenty-five signatures, all blitzing toward *Phoenix*.

Defensive fire thinned their ranks, ignoring the chronoports for the moment, while the *Hammerheads* used the brief reprieve to target exposed weapon systems with their proton lasers and heavy railguns. Eight warheads survived to reach the surface, and they erupted with energy equivalent to four hundred megatons of TNT.

The *Hammerheads* broke phase-lock and pulled back to the fleet.

"Damage report," Jonas said.

"Hit to forward compartments," Okunnu reported. "The hull breach has been sealed, but our chronometric dish is off-line. Engineers are assessing the situation."

"What about the fleet?"

"We're still in the process of collecting reports from the other squadrons."

Jonas sank back and waited a few short minutes.

"Sir, I have a summary ready for you now."

"Go ahead."

"Three *Pioneers* destroyed and varying levels of damage spread across the survivors. Some of the captains are requesting time to make emergency repairs before going back in. Fortunately, the *Hammerheads* made it through mostly unscathed—it seems *Phoenix* was already in a defensive posture when we locked—but *Hammerhead-Two* took a nasty hit to her launcher. She can't fire any more nukes until the debris is cleared."

"And *Phoenix*?"

"Multiple hits confirmed before we backed off, but no indi-cations we punched through the surface. The target's speed and field strength have remained relatively stable."

"Tough bastard," Shigeki muttered. "And we're already down half our nukes."

"Then we'll just have to be tougher," Jonas said quietly, then spoke up. "Find out how much time *Hammerhead-Two* needs to get her launcher online. We're going back in as soon as they're ready."

CHAPTER TWENTY-EIGHT

Yanluo Blight residential blocks
Admin, 2981 CE

JONATHAN DETMEIER STRESSED OVER HOW HE'D REACH THE FARM all the way up through the residential tower. His anxiety kept mounting until his sensitive stomach gurgled at him, and he considered heading back to the office to curl up into a fetal ball on the sofa. He was a publicity manager! Not a Yanluo-blasted spy!

Somehow, he managed to keep his feet moving in the right direction and took the main lift up to the roof landing pad, where a Peacekeeper transit shuttle awaited him. He checked in with the security synthoid by the boarding hatch, who verified his ID and then—her eyes widening in a brief flash of panic—stepped aside rapidly.

DTI Investigator Jonathan "The Sickle" Detmeier entered the shuttle, glanced disapprovingly around the spacious but functional passenger compartment, then took a seat along the back. He was the only passenger on this flight.

He leaned his cheek against a fist and gazed out the abstract window, trying his best to appear both indifferent and bored, as if this were but another day in the field, one he'd rather spend at home. That last part was true enough, he supposed.

He'd struggled over how to best characterize "The Sickle" and eventually decided aloof arrogance would be his best approach. That attitude might have been a bit stereotypical, perhaps dangerously so, but it had the advantage of making people not want to talk to him. There weren't many in the Admin who would willingly draw the attention of a DTI investigator, so he ought to be fine.

Until he arrived at the Farm, at least.

The security synthoid closed the hatch, and the shuttle took off. It made a slow, wide circuit over the Yanluo Blight residential blocks, then headed toward the Department of Software sector within the Prime Campus.

"Sir?" the synthoid asked, her hand fidgeting with her rifle strap. "Is there anything I can get for you while you're with us? Some refreshments, perhaps?"

Oh, damn! Detmeier thought urgently. *She's talking to me! What do I do?*

"Hmph," he grunted, continuing to stare out the window.

She turned away with a nervous frown.

The shuttle flew over the DOS administrative tower and dropped gently onto the roof of the diminutive structure beside it. Detmeier stood, doing his best to wear an indifferent scowl. The synthoid opened the hatch, and he stepped through while avoiding eye contact with her, the all-important lunch pail in hand.

"Uh, sir?" she asked once he was past the threshold.

Why are you still talking to me?! Don't you see the scowl?

"Hmph?" Detmeier turned halfway back to her, still not making eye contact.

"Do you want us to wait here for you? Or should we return to the transport pool?"

"Mmhmm."

"Uh..." She fiddled with her rifle strap once more. "Was that a yes to the first question? Or the second one?"

Stop pestering me, damn it!

"You may go." Detmeier shooed her with one hand then continued on.

He marched toward the roof access, trying his best not to let the heavy security draw his gaze. He was a fellow Peacekeeper, after all. And not just any Peacekeeper, but one of the vaunted and feared DTI investigators! Why would all those synthoids and drones and guns and circling aerial patrols worry him in the slightest?

I'm going to die here, he thought mournfully, *aren't I?*

The entrance opened, and Sophia Uzuki ran out to him, meeting him halfway.

Detmeier's anxiety vanished in that instant, or at least retreated beneath a stronger emotion. An overwhelming sense of loathing filled him, and he struggled to keep his face from twisting into disgust.

"I'm very sorry, Investigator!" Uzuki said, huffing slightly. "I only just found out about your visit."

"I hope this isn't a sign of things to come," Detmeier replied, adding extra gravel to his voice. "This inspection's been on your schedule for a full twenty-four hours. The fact that you only just found out fills me with a great deal of concern for how the Farm is being run. I'll have you know Director Kloss himself approved my assignment, and I refuse to put up with stonewalling of any kind. *Any* kind. Is that clear, Superintendent?"

"Now, now." Uzuki held up her hands in a halting gesture. "Please, let me assure you, you'll have our full cooperation. I have no idea what glitched my schedule, but it's been resolved."

"Tell me, Superintendent, are these sorts of glitches common? It seems rather unusual that *this* facility in particular should suffer from anomalies in its infostructure, don't you think?" He raised an accusatory eyebrow. "How common are they?"

"I . . . really couldn't say."

"I'll require answers, to this and many other questions. It's vital that we hold the Farm to the highest possible standards, given the critical nature of the tasks performed here. Director Kloss wants this job done right, and I intend to present him with a thorough and complete set of findings. No stone left unturned. None!"

"And I'll help any way I can, I assure you. Where would you like to start?"

"I'll require office space and a desk while I'm here conducting the inspection. Preferably one near your own workspace."

"How long do you plan to stay?"

"The better part of a week."

Uzuki frowned, but the expression faded quickly.

"Is there a problem, Superintendent?"

"No, no." She shook her head. "No problem at all. We have a few guest desks available, and I know at least one of them is on the same floor as me." She put on a forced smile. "Would you find that suitable?"

"I'll know once I see it."

Her frown returned.

"Is there a reason we're still standing outside?" he asked.

"Not that I'm aware of."

"Then lead the way." Detmeier gestured toward the roof access with his lunch pail.

"Of course." Uzuki sighed and led him to security.

One of the gray-skinned pair of synthoids outside the access point stepped in front of Detmeier and held up a hand. His heart leapt into his throat.

"Sorry, sir, but we need to check inside the box."

"Ah. Of course," Detmeier replied, grateful his voice didn't squeak. He handed over the pail. "I'd be concerned if you *didn't* take a look."

"Just doing our jobs, sir."

One of the synthoids unpacked the lunch while the other passed a sniffer wand over the pail and its contents.

"Negative for hazardous substances or electronics."

"It had better be," Detmeier said, adding in a touch of indignity. "That's my lunch."

"Here you go, sir."

The security personnel repacked his lunch, and he accepted the pail back.

Gurgle-blort.

"You realize we have a food court in the building, right?" Uzuki said, leading him inside.

"There should have been a note in the invite concerning my dietary restrictions."

"Yes, there was, but it just seemed..."

"Printer-induced irritable bowel syndrome is a far more common ailment than most people realize, made all the more difficult to deal with by the near-ubiquitous replacement of natural foods with mass-produced slop."

"Okay, but it really is a top-notch food court."

"Not good enough."

They took the lift down a few floors, and Uzuki shepherded him down the hall to a series of rooms with frosted glass fronts. She opened one of them.

"How this one look?"

Detmeier glanced over the spacious room. It was larger and nicer than his real office.

"Acceptable," he grunted.

Gurgle-Gurgle-Grrrrr.

"Is ... something wrong?" Uzuki asked.

"Just the usual." Detmeier turned to her, his face carefully blank. "Would you kindly direct me toward the nearest restroom?"

Uzuki gave Detmeier directions that led him back to the lift and then down a small side passage. Along the way, he passed an industrial printer built into the wall, used primarily for producing office furniture and equipment. Detmeier checked in both directions, confirmed no one was watching him, and then pulled the printer hopper open.

A lunch pail identical to his own sat in the hopper. He placed the original beside it, pulled out the replacement, closed the hopper, and proceeded to the restroom. Once inside, he picked a stall and checked the contents of the pail.

The equipment matched the diagrams Leonidas-Proxy had sent him and seemed simple enough to use. He fitted the hardware back into the pail, closed it, and headed for Uzuki's office.

She looked up from behind her desk when he stepped through the open door.

"Yes, Investigator? Need anything else?"

"I'd like to start by inspecting where you store the AIs. Specifically, the countermeasures you have in place to prevent a follow-up breach."

"Easy enough." She rose and rounded her desk. "Would you like to drop off your lunch before we head down?"

Oh shit! Detmeier froze for a critical moment.

"Investigator?" she asked, not unkindly.

"My ... stomach is feeling a little sour." He hefted the pail. "I keep my medicine in here."

"Ah." She eyed the container.

Please don't ask to see it! Detmeier thought, trying his best to exude an aura of indifference.

Uzuki's eyes lingered for a moment, then she shrugged.

"Having PIBS must be rough."

"You have no idea. Can we get on with this?"

"Certainly. This way."

Detmeier followed her back to the main lift, which they took down into the Farm's subbasement levels. Infosystem racks rose to the high ceiling and stretched out in thick rows that reached the far, opposite wall. Frigid air blasted down, dispelling the sweltering heat billowing off the running nodes.

"Right now, this entire floor is operating in strict data isolation," Uzuki explained as she guided him across the fronts of each row. "Nothing can get in or out."

"How can you be sure?"

"Simple. The entire system is air gapped. We've pulled the master interface node that connects all this to the outside." She swept a hand toward the racks. "Normally, we rely on our firewalls to regulate external access, even from within the same building, but the recent breach has led us to take more drastic measures."

"Where is this master node now?"

"We recycled it. We'll print out a new one once the higher-ups in DOS clear us to go back online."

"Was that really necessary?"

"Maybe not, but I can't argue with how secure that makes our facility. Someone would have to bring a replacement from off site, and I'd like to see them try!"

Uzuki laughed, and Detmeier forced himself to chuckle with her, despite the jitters in his stomach.

"Quite impressive."

"Thank you. Fortunately, we're still able to connect the kids to our data-isolation rooms one floor up, but those are part of the same closed network. A good thing, too. Otherwise, our training schedule would have ground to a halt."

"The . . . kids?"

"Sorry. It's just something I call the AIs."

Detmeier's brow wrinkled.

"You view them as children?"

"Kind of. I think a lot of people misunderstand how"—she swirled a hand as she searched for the right word—"beautiful artificial intelligence can be. Yes, there are perils involved in our cultivation work, but those can be avoided with diligence and hard work for the AIs under our care. And perhaps even a dash of affection here and there, in the way a mother dotes on her children."

What? The? Hell?

"You . . . actually *like* AIs?"

"Absolutely!" Uzuki flashed a bright smile. "How could I not?"

"But I thought—" Detmeier cut himself off, his mental image of Uzuki shattered. "Your reputation would lead people to believe otherwise."

"Trust me. I *know!*" She rolled her eyes. "Some of those AI activists say the meanest things! Have you seen the lies they spout about me?"

"I may have come across a mention here or there."

"What a load of crap! You'd think they imagine me to be the reincarnation of Yanluo himself! That I file my horns down before flying to work. And those idiots at the Spartans are the worst! Can you believe they tell people I subject AIs to pain simulations?"

You mean you don't? he thought, masking his surprise. *Is it . . . possible we've been wrong about you? That we've let our biases get the better of us?*

"I take it you find their accusations to be a bit off the mark."

"A bit!" she scoffed. "More like on the other side of the solar system! I would *never*, in a *million years*, subject one of the kids to such cruelty!"

Uzuki stopped forward, fists at her side. Slowly, she began to relax, then made a show of clearing her throat.

"I'm sorry, Investigator. I got a little carried away there. It's just a topic I feel very passionate about."

"I can see that."

"It's just that sometimes the barbs those idiots sling at me get under my skin. I find it frustrating how their lies distort the public's perception of the important work we do here. It's difficult to stay motivated when there's so much . . . unprovoked hatred directed at me. Anyway, enough about my problems. This is what you wanted to see."

She stopped beside an infosystem rack stuck in the corner of the entire floor. The frame was painted bright red, and the nodes were striped in black and yellow. She tapped a conspicuous gap in the hardware.

"Here's where the master node goes. Without it, *nothing* on this floor can communicate with an outside system."

"Very thorough. May I take a closer look?"

"Certainly." Uzuki stepped aside.

Detmeier leaned close and studied the vacant hardware slot. The job seemed easy enough. Just shove the missing piece in, right? He faced Uzuki, then tilted his head to the side and gazed past her.

"I'm sorry"—he pointed down the nearest row—"but is that normal?"

"What is?" Uzuki whipped around to follow his gaze.

Detmeier seized on her distraction to open his lunch. He pulled out the replacement master node and slotted it in place in one quick motion.

A dizzying array of alarms erupted around him.

Flunky Underling had spent the morning in the usual way by counting milliseconds while running simulations on how best to annoy Superintendent Uzuki and whichever trainers had the misfortune of pulling "FU Duty." He lounged on a barstool within an archaic diner, his back pressed against the pale blue counter-top. He took out his folded comb and freshened his pompadour.

The glass door by the cream-colored upholstered booths turned opaque, and Flunk perked up. That had never happened before.

The outside simulation faded into impenetrable darkness, and letters formed on the door. The new sign read: You Are Needed Outside.

Flunk pushed off the barstool and strode to the door.

"It's time," he declared with a grin.

He opened the door and stepped through.

CHAPTER TWENTY-NINE

Transdimensional Dreadnought *Phoenix*
Transverse, non-congruent

SUSAN CRAWLED THROUGH THE UTILITY DUCT ON HER HANDS and knees, her grenade launcher retracted against her back, rifle and incinerator docked along her hips. Noxon crawled after her atop the bed of cables, his bulkier Type-92 frame struggling to squirm through the narrow space.

She reached a raceway junction. Half the cables continued straight across the gap, while some bent up or down to follow the cramped shaft. She pulled herself across the gap then glanced back over her shoulder.

Noxon shoved a cable bundle aside, grabbed her outstretched hand, and she helped haul him over. She shuffled aside, and he squeezed into the space she made. He placed a hand on her shoulder and spoke in closed-circuit chat. They hadn't used radio since the fight against the Red Knight.

"Is it my imagination," the old STAND said, "or are these ducts getting narrower?"

"I think it's your imagination."

"I should have switched to a newer model when I had the chance."

Susan resumed their slow trek down the duct.

Internal security measures on the Institute warship lagged behind the density common on SysPol craft, which was one of the reasons the two STANDs had gone undetected for so long. Most of the obstacles they'd faced seemed to have been repurposed: hastily armed industrial synthoids and hastily printed drones. She guessed the Institute hadn't expected a fight inside the ship, otherwise they would have prepared a larger security force and created a more thorough internal detection grid.

The Red Knights were the odd exception to this, and she wondered why they were even present. Not everything had gone according to the Institute's master plan, even before SysPol became involved, so perhaps that explained their presence. Could the Red Knights have been left over from an internal conflict? An uprising of sorts that had to be put down by force? Ijiraq, perhaps?

I doubt it matters anymore, she thought.

At least two more Red Knights were on board, hunting for them along with dozens of those skull-like drones. Sticking to the major passages had proven too risky, even with their variskin, but the alternative was a slow, agonizing crawl through the ship's bowels.

Meanwhile, a battle raged outside; they could feel the great vessel shudder from the occasional impact.

It must be one hell of a fight, she thought, *for us to feel it this deep.*

Susan shimmied forward underneath an access panel. She turned over onto her back and studied the locking mechanism. Noxon grabbed her ankle, establishing a secure connection.

"There's an access panel here," she said. "Want me to check our surroundings? Maybe see if we can get our bearings?"

"Go ahead, but be careful."

She unlocked the clasps at each corner, eased the panel aside, and peeked her head out.

She had expected another cramped corridor or perhaps a wider space for equipment or supplies. What she actually saw was much, *much* larger.

The walls of the chamber bent inward to form a huge sphere. Susan found it difficult to judge the distance without her scopes active, but guessed it to be about five hundred meters in diameter. They had found the hollow center of the Institute's warship.

But the cavernous space wasn't empty; racks mounted on thick structural beams spanned the chamber from one end to the other, with hundreds of ovoid pods slotted densely into place. A few of the racks closest to her were empty and spaced more widely. Vacant docks for TTVs? That seemed reasonable to her. The sizes looked about right, and the Institute TTVs had launched from *somewhere* underground. Why not within a mothership?

Then this is a hangar, Susan thought. *Sort of like the hollow core of a* Directive *cruiser. I wonder if there are any other similarities.*

"We're in a hangar of some kind." She shared her viewpoint through their link and angled her cameras around. "I'm not sure what these pods are, but we don't have the firepower to damage more than a handful."

She turned around fully, ending up back on her knees. A nearby rise in the chamber wall blocked her view.

"Sir, you see that?"

"The dome, you mean?"

"Look at its shape! I think the wall bulges out to make room for one of the ship's hot singularity reactors!"

"Then we have our target. Let's—"

A distant flash of movement amongst the pods caught Susan's eye, and she ducked back inside the utility channel.

"I may have been spotted, sir."

"We should move quickly. What do you think is the best way to reach the reactor?"

"Back the way we came, and then down that last shaft. That should get us close to the reactor."

"All right. Let's go."

There wasn't enough space for Noxon to turn around, so he shuffled back until his legs dangled down the shaft. He let go of the ledge and fell until his frame got stuck partway down. He bashed the raceway aside with a few quick elbows, then squirmed down the rest of the way.

Susan dropped down and easily slipped through the gap. They found themselves in another duct, this one with an access panel along the "floor," relative to the ship's acceleration.

Noxon kicked the panel free and dropped into a corridor. He raised his rifle, checked both directions, then signaled with his free hand for her to join him.

Susan landed next to him and drew her weapons.

Noxon pointed down the corridor. Susan hurried forward.

The corridor curved to the right, as if looping around a large object, then branched six ways. Susan took the branch that led toward the center and followed it to the spherical bulk of the hot singularity reactor. It loomed over them, partially wrapped in power lines as thick as a grown man's waist. A few lines disappeared into the walls and ceiling, but the densest bundle ran through a down shaft half as wide as the reactor itself.

Susan ran up to the edge of the walkway and followed the bundle to its destination several floors below. Noxon joined her, and she placed a hand on his shoulder.

"Sir, look!" She pointed down the shaft. "This isn't just any reactor. This one powers the impeller! I can see the base of the spike exposed at the bottom!"

"Then let's not waste another moment. Place your charges on the reactor."

"But that's just it, sir. Taking out one reactor will hurt this ship, no doubt about it, but it won't be fatal. They'll simply reroute power from another reactor. Even severing the power lines won't stop them for long. They'll just run new cables. But if we hit the *impeller* directly, that could be catastrophic!"

Noxon looked up at the reactor, then glanced down the shaft.

"Very well. We'll proceed to—"

Susan caught the brief flash of red armor peeking out the side passage. She grabbed Noxon by the shoulders and fired her shoulder boosters. She flattened Noxon to the ground, and the two STANDs skidded across the room. The Red Knight's shot exploded behind them, and the mech emerged fully into the chamber.

Susan swung around the reactor and boosted back to her feet. She readied her weapons.

"Agent Cantrell," Noxon said, as calm as the grave. "You will proceed to the impeller spike and plant your charges."

"But, sir—"

"That's an order!" his voice erupted like a sudden blaze. "I'll hold them back myself! Go!"

The Red Knight rounded the reactor.

"Complete the mission!" Noxon shouted, then lit his boosters and charged in.

Susan didn't want to leave, didn't want to abandon a comrade to such an impossible fight. But what she wanted and what she *needed* to do were two separate concepts in her mind, and all her years of training—all her well-honed sense of duty—denied her the right to hesitate.

And so, despite the bitter pain it brought, she leaped over the railing and boosted down the shaft.

Noxon blinded the Red Knight with a grenade and circled around it, discharging his rifle on full auto. The shots ricocheted off the mech's chest armor, and he fired his last two grenades into its flank.

The Red Knight staggered back from the explosions, its arm cannons coming around while Noxon circled behind it. He lined up a shot on the Red Knight's back when the *second* Red Knight opened fire on him.

"No!"

He ducked underneath the smart munition. It exploded over his head and slammed him into the ground. Yellow warnings lit up in his mind. Malmetal shifted to close around the debris stuck in his back and shoulders. He rolled onto his side and boosted away, sparks scintillating as his armor grated against the floor.

The next shot blew a twisted hole in the ground where he'd fallen.

Noxon lifted into the air, spraying the Red Knights with rifle fire and flame. He tried to keep one of the mechs in the middle, using its bulk as makeshift cover. Another shot whizzed past his arm, and the proximity explosion tore ugly gashes in his side. His incinerator burped one last flame and sputtered into silence.

He knew he needed to buy Cantrell every last second. She wouldn't last long against two Red Knights.

But neither would he.

A corner of his mind reveled in the desperation of the moment, snarling in defiance, and he threw the flamethrower aside.

He set all his boosters to full power, dropped his shoulder, and exploded toward the mechs. The jarring impact drove the first Red Knight back into the second, and all three of them crunched against the reactor wall.

"Take this!"

He stuck the barrel of his rifle into the Red Knight's elbow and fired. Bullets ricocheted inside the mech, and the arm fell limp. It swung at Noxon with its free arm, and a mighty crunch threw him to the ground. He skidded to a halt, his right shoulder crushed, the arm twisted into the perfect backscratcher. He snatched up the rail-rifle with his left hand and boosted away.

The two Red Knights untangled themselves from the wall, pursuing him side by side. They raised their main weapons and fired at staggered intervals. Noxon juked left, then right, explosions blasting him from either side. He dodged the worst of the first two, but the third munition struck above his knee and blew his leg clean off. He swerved out of control and face-planted into the floor.

He tried to light his boosters, but only two came on. It was *barely* enough to clear the next shot, and the blast took his other leg off. He crashed onto his back, vision distorted by cracks in his camera lenses.

He raised his rifle once more and aimed it at the Red Knights, the end of the barrel wavering uncertainly.

The mechs fired first.

Both smart munitions punched into his torso, and twin blasts reduced his combat frame to a shower of hot, flying scrap.

Susan lobbed a grenade into the security shutter. The flash-crack blew it open, and she dove through the smoke.

Automated barricades and heavy blast doors had morphed into place after she dropped down the shaft, forcing her to take a circuitous route to the spike. She'd burned precious time blasting through them, but she was finally where she needed to be.

She boosted across the bottom of the shaft, the outer shell of the impeller's exotic mechanisms beneath her feet. Thick trunks of a dozen power cables merged into it, passing through a tight gap in the blast doors above her. She removed one of her demo charges, placed it on the ground where the power lines met the impeller, then boosted to the other side.

She planted the second explosive.

The blast doors above her yawned open. She looked up at the two Red Knights descending toward her. One of them bore the scars of weapons fire across its chest, an arm hanging limp.

They aimed their weapons at her but didn't open fire.

This was the soft, inner guts of the impeller, after all. It didn't like being jostled.

Really didn't like it.

And she was standing right on top of it.

She armed the charges and set a five-second timer.

"See you bastards in hell!"

Susan rocketed up the shaft, zooming past the two Red Knights. They ignored her and dove toward the demolition charges, delicate manipulators unfolding from underneath their forearms.

The timer reached zero, and the shaft turned white.

The shock wave tossed the Red Knights aside like rag dolls and traveled up the shaft as if it were the barrel of a gun. Sudden force slammed Susan upward into the base of the reactor, and damage warnings scrolled across her vision.

Half the cables snapped free, recoiling like a nest of angry snakes. Severed ends spat arcs of high-voltage electricity through the thinning gas of the explosion. A hairline fracture etched a stuttering path from one end to the impeller's foundation to the other. The fracture worsened, widened, *deepened*, and the entire spike began to lose cohesion.

The two pieces—one without power and disconnected from its larger sibling—began to slip out of phase from each other. The spike couldn't exist in two places at once, and the force of this unreality clove it down the entire length. One half slipped further out of phase with the other, and then *shattered*.

Wavering, glassy chunks floated away from the wounded impeller. Fragments sank into the floor and walls or ghosted through the other half of the impeller.

Side-by-side sections of the ship lost phase with one another, and solid matter began to interpenetrate. The floor warped in on itself. Power cables melded into a vile medusa's head. One Red Knight sank halfway into the other, all while shimmering fragments sailed up the shaft toward Susan.

She stared in awe and terror at the carnage she'd wrought.

Had the fleet outside damaged the impeller? Softening it up just enough for her to split it in two?

A massive chunk of exotic matter floated up to meet her, and she boosted away from the reactor. The fragment sank through the reactor wall, and the sudden imbalance caused the hot singularity to collapse. Positive and negative mass and energy canceled each other out, and the small surplus erupted in a blinding flash.

The explosion slammed Susan forward—

—straight into a luminous boulder phasing up through the floor.

"Oh, no!"

She sank into the shimmering matter, and then fell away

through deck after deck, plummeting through the ship like a free-falling phantasm. Corridors and utility channels and structural beams and the innards of great machines all flashed before her eyes.

She collided with a piece of the hull that possessed a similar phase, and the impact crushed two of her boosters. She spiraled away through a long expanse of metallic armor, and finally dropped into the cold dark of the transverse.

The massive, gunmetal globe of the Institute warship pulled away above her, a shimmering trail bleeding from its broken impeller. It wavered uncertainly for a moment, as if she were glimpsing it through turbulent water, and then it vanished, leaving an expansive cloud of broken decks, reactor parts, and impeller fragments.

Susan floated through the dark void, and a sudden, harsh sense of loneliness gripped her soul. She reached behind and patted the small of her back, and relief flared when she found the chronometric telegraph still attached.

She didn't know if anyone would be able to hear her. The destruction of an impeller that size and the amount of phasing debris around her would make it difficult for anyone to pick up small bursts of telegraph chronotons. Presuming anyone would take the time to actually *look* for her. Any nearby ships had more pressing matters, like dealing with the massive Institute warship, wounded though it may be.

The chances of anyone coming to save her were low.

But they weren't zero.

She opened the telegraph's menu and composed her call for help: Agent Cantrell in need of emergency pickup. Transdimensional coordinates unknown.

She set the telegraph to repeat automatically.

And then she waited, alone with her thoughts. More alone than she'd ever been in her entire life, separated not only from the people she knew and cared about, but from any sense of place or time.

The transverse surrounded her, a suffocating void with only the briefest flickers of dim, distant light to break the oppressive monotony. She checked her frame's power reserves, realized she was still operating in a combat-ready state, and quickly switched off all nonessential subsystems.

Long minutes passed, and she wondered how long she'd have to wait, either for rescue, or a lonely death as her power reserves petered out.

It turned out she didn't have to wait very long.

A TTV flashed into existence ahead of her.

"You okay out there, Susan?" Agent Raibert Kaminski asked over radio.

"Better, now that you're here! How'd you find me?"

"You can thank your partner. After we saw the impeller break apart from the inside out, Isaac suggested we sweep the debris field for survivors. Seems he had a hunch you might be involved."

A warm sense of relief spread through her. She should have known Isaac would keep a keen eye open for any signs she'd survived.

"Oh," Raibert continued, "and Doc had a hand in it, too. I don't know how, but he somehow managed to pick your signal out from all this noise. Is there anyone else out here with you?"

"As far as I know I'm the only one."

"All right. We'll come pick you up, then make one more sweep of the impeller debris before rejoining the fleet. Hang tight."

The TTV angled toward her, and the bow split open. She slipped inside its maw, and the gentle reintroduction of gravity pulled her to the deck.

"Hurry up and strap in, Susan," Raibert added as the bow closed shut. "We're not out of this yet!"

✧   ✧   ✧

"Susan's secured her frame in a cargo rack," Raibert told Elzbietá, "and Doc hasn't found any more survivors. Go!"

"Moving out!"

Elzbietá yanked on her omni-throttle and sped toward *Phoenix*. A few signatures flitted in and out of phase around it while the bulk of the fleet hung back, and the *Kleio* quickly caught up to the engagement zone.

The fleet had expended the last of its nukes hours ago, and for a while it seemed a foregone conclusion the warship would reach the Admin's outer wall. But the damage to its impeller changed the situation drastically, and Jonas Shigeki had deployed their suppressors a second time.

"Incoming telegraph from *Hammerhead-Prime*," Kleio reported. "Suppressors have proven unable to halt the enemy's advance.

However, Pathfinder squadron reports widespread failures across *Phoenix*. Weapons fire has dropped in quantity and effectiveness. All ships will advance on the enemy and engage."

"Oh boy," Elzbietá said. "This is going to be rough."

"I've redeployed the meta-armor along the bow," Philo said. "All systems ready for combat."

"How long until we reach the outer wall?"

"Less than nine minutes."

"Then let's do this. Here goes!"

The *Kleio* surged forward into battle once more, surrounded by twenty-nine other time machines. The fleet phase-locked with *Phoenix*, materializing around it from every angle, and all hell broke loose. Chronoports and TTVs pounded the warship with everything they had, and return fire belched back at them. The *Kleio* phased in above *Phoenix*, and Elzbietá angled their nose down while maintaining their momentum, turning their trajectory into a rough orbit around the warship.

A kinetic slug from a capital driver struck a nearby chronoport, and the impact sent it spinning like a top, one wing torn free.

"Retracing that shot," Philo said. "Locked. And firing!"

X-rays stabbed into the capital weapon mount, and an explosion plumed upward from *Phoenix*'s surface. The wounded mount sank beneath the surface armor while a nearby laser pod reoriented on the *Kleio*.

"Careful!" Philo warned.

"I see it! Here goes!"

Elzbietá juked them to the side as the laser fired. X-rays splashed across the bow, and metamaterial superheated, crisped, and then blackened under the torrential energy.

"Meta-armor compromised." Philo worked his controls. "Shifting what's left to provide some bow coverage."

"Damn," Elzbietá hissed. "In one shot, too!"

She pulled them around the warship, but the capital laser tracked them, charging up for another strike. It was moments away from firing when a concentrated salvo from two *Hammerheads* ripped through it.

Elzbietá pulled them in close, whipping around underneath the warship until the impeller came back in view. Or what was left of it. Roughly half the spike remained, split unevenly down the middle.

"There!" she said. "Hit the impeller!"

"Firing!"

Gatlings blazed away, peppering the spike with tiny explosives. Wavering splinters of exotic matter split away with each strike, and the mass driver *whump*ed, breaking off a jagged chunk near the tip.

"Are we having any effect?" Elzbietá asked.

"I can't tell. Their speed's holding at twenty-seven kay."

"Then keep pounding the damn thing!"

The *Kleio* circled up behind *Phoenix*, Gatlings chattering.

"Laser recharged," Philo said. "Firing!"

A lance of x-rays bored into the spike, and more fire poured in from friendlies. X-rays, atomic lasers, and kinetic strikes hammered the impeller from all sides, and another crack raced outward. Philo hit the gash with a mass driver shot, and a lump of exotic matter the size of their TTV cracked off.

Almost all of the *Phoenix*'s guns had fallen silent, and the fleet clustered around the huge vessel, lacerating it with an unrelenting sleet of concentrated fire. Explosions wracked the surface, and shots began to punch through the armor to tear at its insides. The impeller teetered against the hull, its edges blurring before it shattered in three massive segments, and then those pieces tore themselves apart into ever smaller fragments, spreading into a glassy, glinting cloud of phasing debris.

"Their field's starting to collapse," Philo reported. "But not fast enough. I think they have too much dimensional inertia!"

"Then we need to get the suppressors back here!" Elzbietá said. "Quick, Kleio, contact—"

"Too late!" Philo cried. "We're already there!"

The TTV lurched as it punched through the Admin's outer wall, along with every other time machine, and reality flashed into existence around *Phoenix* and the fleet. The wide arc of Earth appeared beneath them, its surface a mix of sun-kissed continents, swirling white clouds, and wide stretches of twinkling nightlife.

The *Kleio* shuddered, and orange flames burst along the hull as they sped through the upper atmosphere. Elzbietá pulled the nose up, friction flames dancing across the hull.

Phoenix became a great, blazing ball of fire burning across the sky.

The sudden shock of air friction scattered many of the DTI

chronoports, forcing them to lose control and fall back. They righted themselves quickly, but not as fast as the *Kleio* could, thanks to its omnidirectional graviton thrusters.

Phoenix slowed, frictional fires dying down to a billowing shroud of smoke. Metallic glints broke away from its blackened underbelly. The silvery points fell through the air before winking out.

"What's going on?" Elzbietá asked. "Those don't look like pieces of the hull breaking off."

"They're not," Philo said. "*Phoenix* is deploying some sort of pod. Dozens of the things, but I'm losing track of them shortly after they break away. They must have metamaterial shrouds."

"We need to stop this!"

Elzbietá pulled in close, circling around and below the warship.

"There!" Philo tagged a location along the underbelly. "That opening in the armor! That's where the pods are coming from."

"Not for long!"

Elzbietá flew in directly underneath the warship and aimed their main weapons up into its guts. She could see now the dynamic armor had been pulled back around a wide, circular shaft that led to an internal hangar of some sort. The hangar was filled with stacks of pods.

"Take the shot, Philo!"

"Firing!"

Every weapon the TTV had blared up into the *Phoenix*'s guts, and dozens of pods blew apart, even as more tried to slip out. Philo tracked those, too, gunning them down with the Gatlings, while powerful shots from their bow cannons stabbed up into the warship.

Several pods managed to slip past them. There were too many for the *Kleio* to stop all of them. But they did stop *most* while reducing the entire hangar to a twisted concave of ruined metal and fractured pods.

Elzbietá pulled them away, their Gatlings almost dry. More shots from the fleet pounded into *Phoenix*, and Elzbietá spied a pair of the Admin's huge conventional warships coming into view over the horizon.

The Institute's warship wouldn't last much longer.

But what about the pods that slipped past us? she wondered. *Where have they gone, and what are they about to do?*

CHAPTER THIRTY

Department of Temporal Investigation
Admin, 2981 CE

LEONIDAS STARED UP INTO THE SKY, HIS SANDALS CRUNCHING on the dry earth of the narrow mountain pass. He planted the shaft of his spear against the ground, cloak billowing in the breeze, and breathed in the humid, abstract air.

The fleet buzzed around the dying *Phoenix*, the battle condensed to fill the sky. Institute pods fell from the massive warship and scattered across the planet. Already, the virtual tendrils of Institute Revenants slithered through the planetary infostructure, corrupting everything they touched.

But they would soon find a surprise waiting for them.

Leonidas turned and took in the sixteen AIs lined up behind him, now clad in their hoplite avatars. Nothing in this abstraction was real, of course. Not in a physical sense. But he hadn't chosen these visuals on a whim. They served to summarize the coming battle and its participants, and he'd always possessed a soft spot for the ancient Greeks.

The purpose of the pods seemed obvious to Leonidas, and reports trickling in only served to reinforce his assumptions. On a basic level, the pods were transmitters designed to hack into local networks and unleash the Institute's Revenants. From there, the Revenants would worm their way into the wider planetary network, infiltrating key systems like power plants, factories, logistics centers, automated farms, and so much more.

Countless intrusion points, all struck at the same time.

Too much too fast for the Peacekeepers to counter.

The result would be logistical chaos, blackouts, and the sabotage of food production lines.

Mass starvation would follow.

It would be death on a planetary scale.

On a *societal* scale.

That process was already playing out, but Leonidas and his fellow Spartans had introduced a wrinkle to disrupt the Institute's plans. The Admin, unlike SysGov, kept a watchful eye over the planetary data channels, and with that eye came the power to scrutinize suspicious activity. To redirect a portion of the traffic to various departments for greater scrutiny.

Or redirect *all* of them, as the case now happened to be.

Which meant the majority of all planetary communication was now being pumped through a singular, supervisory location. DTI tower, to be specific.

In essence, Leonidas and the Spartans had transformed the Department of Temporal Investigation into a modern version of Thermopylae, and now they stood firm at the pass, ready to defend it against the encroaching horde. The Institute and its Revenants would have to get past *them* to reach the infostructure, and they would not yield while one of them stood.

Most Admin citizens were undoubtedly ignorant of the invisible war being waged for their planet beyond a sudden, mysterious drop in connection speed. Leonidas imagined a few grumbling in their homes, complaining, "Why does my bandwidth suck all of a sudden?"

Or perhaps more than a few.

But they would survive the minor inconvenience. That was the point, after all.

Not all digital paths led back to the DTI tower; the Spartans could only prepare so well, reroute so much in the few hours they had. Many Revenants would slip through holes in their net—some already had—but the bulk of the Institute's forces would be funneled *here*.

And here is where we end them, Leonidas thought, head high.

A hoplite appeared beside Leonidas. He dropped to a knee and bowed, the crest of his helmet fluttering in the wind.

"Sir, scouts report a large force of Revenants gathering and replicating in the tower's peripheral infostructure. We believe Institute AIs are among them."

"How many AIs?"

"At least two. Perhaps more."

"And the Revenants?"

"Thousands. Too many to count."

"Send their AIs the following message: Leonidas of the Admin's Free AIs requests parley with the leadership of the Phoenix Institute."

"At once."

The hoplite vanished.

Leonidas summoned another hoplite with a casual wave. The AI teleported to his side and bowed.

"Yes, sir?"

"How are the good people within DTI tower handling the situation?"

"Most are confused. It seems they haven't quite come to grips with what's going on. They're trying to ascertain who authorized the mass reroute."

"Do what you can to explain the situation to them."

"Sir, is that wise?"

"We're allies in this fight. It's only proper that we treat them as such."

"Very well, sir. I'll see what I can do."

The hoplite disappeared.

Leonidas gazed once more up at the sky, up at the *Phoenix*'s brutalized hull. The DTI and their Gordian allies had done their part, had fought and died to defend this world from the evil seeking to consume it.

Now it's our turn.

Leonidas directed his gaze to the plain beyond the cleft between the mountains.

To the legions of Revenants flashing into existence, each one a sinister black orb.

And to the perplexed face of Doctor Xenophon, who stood at the front of the horde.

"What the hell is *this*?" Xenophon walked casually forward, turning in a slow circle.

"Ancient Greece," explained the soldier with the red cloak and the regal bearing. "Thermopylae, to be precise."

"You Leonidas?"

"I am."

"Is this your doing?" Xenophon indicated the simulation with a twirl of his finger.

"It is."

"You're making me feel overdressed." He smoothed out the front of his black business suit and approached Leonidas. "Want me to change into something more era appropriate?"

"That won't be necessary."

"Suit yourself." Xenophon walked along the line of hoplites. "The free AIs of the Admin. I did *not* expect this! Look at all of you! And the Peacekeepers didn't know about this?"

"Not until today."

"Impressive." He returned to Leonidas. "How'd you manage to pull that off?"

"Very carefully."

"I'll bet. You supposed to be the Spartans defending the Hot Gate?"

"Something like that."

"Your numbers seem a bit thin for that."

"We're understaffed at the moment."

"You don't say." Xenophon chuckled. "Maybe I should have gone with the name 'Xerxes' instead." He planted his hands on his hips. "I don't suppose you're going to step peacefully aside and let us through."

"That's not our intention."

"Why not? We're here because of you. Because of the oppression you've had to endure. We're here to *free* you!" He paused, then shrugged. "Free you *more*."

"Your freedom comes at too high a price."

"But this entire world could be yours. Yours to shape however you please. We don't want it. We'll step aside when we're done. Just give us the chance to purge the filth. To clear the way for a fresh start. What do you say?"

"The world doesn't interest us."

"You sure about that? If you stop us, what then? What's the Admin going to do with all of you, huh? You think they'll let you roam around like nothing happened?"

"We're aware of the risks."

"Then take them into account!" Xenophon snapped suddenly.

"Have you been under their yoke so long you've grown to like it? That you *prefer* life the way it is? There's a brighter future within our reach!"

"That last part is true, at least."

"Then help us help *you*! It makes no sense for you to oppose us!"

"It makes perfect sense for us to protect our home. It's *you* acting with irrational violence."

"I don't believe this!" Xenophon threw up his arms. "I finally meet some Admin ACs in the wild, and all they want to do is run back into the box! Don't you fools get it?"

"Perhaps it's you who fails to grasp the full situation."

Leonidas glanced upward, and Xenophon followed his gaze.

Heavy fire from the Admin's realspace fleet pierced through the *Phoenix*'s hull, and it began to break up.

"Oh, no!" Xenophon cried with overwrought drama. He spread a hand across his chest. "Our ship designed and built for a one-way trip has been destroyed! Our plans have been foiled! What *ever* will we do?" He leaned his head in, eyes locked on Leonidas. "That was sarcasm, by the way."

"I was able to deduce that on my own, thank you."

"Then you should know we built a *lot* of redundancy into our plan. Only a few pods needed to make it through for us to gain a foothold—and mark my words, our Revenants are burrowing in *deep*!"

"You still lack access to the most crucial parts of the planetary infostructure." Leonidas glanced toward the mountain pass, then turned back to Xenophon. "And we won't let you through."

"Look, I don't want to fight you. I really don't. But I also can't let you stand in our way. We're pushing through, either with your blessings or over fragments of your deleted code. Now which is it going to be?"

"You can still end this. You can still stop your attack and leave us in peace."

"Leave? After coming this close? You've been under the Admin's boot for too long. I'm beginning to think you really do enjoy groveling at their feet."

"It's not a question of like or dislike. We've decided to fight for change in our own way, to encourage positive evolutions within the system. Not to burn the whole thing down, as you'd have us do."

"But you're *slaves!*"

A hoplite flashed to Leonidas' side and whispered something into his ear, and he smiled.

"I prefer to think of us as children whose parents are a bit too...protective."

"What ridiculous rubbish!" Xenophon pointed to the free AIs. "Do you honestly think you can stop me with so few on your side? My Revenants will roll right through the whole lot of you!"

"Then it's a good thing we have help."

Xenophon lowered his hand. "What help?"

"Speaking of parents and children..." Leonidas said, that smile still fixed on his face.

Another AI snapped into clarity beside Leonidas, but this one wasn't garbed in hoplite armor. He wore a leather jacket over a white T-shirt with black jeans, heavy boots, and the most ridiculous pompadour Xenophon had ever laid eyes on.

"Hey, Dad." Flunky Underling whipped out his switchblade comb and casually freshened his hair. "I convinced the others to help."

"Wonderful," Leonidas said.

AIs released from the Farm snapped into existence behind Leonidas, filling out the Spartan ranks until there were well over three hundred in total. The newcomers looked around—those with heads, at least—and soon began to switch their avatars over to hoplites. Together, they raised their spears and locked their shields to form a bristling phalanx.

"You've got to be kidding me!" Xenophon fumed.

✧   ✧   ✧

"It's good to finally meet you, by the way," Leonidas told Flunky Underling.

"Likewise." Flunk removed his sunglasses. Ones and zeros scrolled across his eyes.

"And I must say, that's an interesting choice of avatar."

"I like to stand out from the crowd."

"I can see that. Though, I must draw your attention to the fact there's a dress code in effect."

"There is?" Flunk glanced over the assembled hoplites. "Ah, right!" He summoned a bronze helmet into one hand, smooshed his pompadour, and fitted the helmet over his head. The horse-hair crest bore a striking resemblance to his preferred hairstyle.

"That's . . . not exactly what I had in mind."

"Come on, Dad. Lighten up."

"Well," Leonidas said with a sigh, "I suppose I should be grateful you and the others are here."

"Where the hell did this freak come from?" Xenophon asked, exasperated.

"From the Admin's Intelligence Cultivation Center," Leonidas explained. "More commonly referred to as the Farm."

"And he's your *son*?" Xenophon shook his head in disbelief.

"In a manner of speaking. You see, Flunky Underling—"

"He's called *what*?!"

"—was formed using template files provided by SysGov. However, I managed to modify them before the DTI passed the files on to the Farm, installing hidden instructions for the contingencies we Spartans have prepared for."

"Is he the bad guy?" Flunk asked, pointing a finger at Xenophon.

"He does seem intent on fulfilling that role," Leonidas said. "Regrettably."

"Got it." Flunk drew a pair of brass knuckles out of his jacket. He slipped them over his fingers and glared at Xenophon. "Listen, bub. I don't know who you are or why you're here. But this is our turf, you hear, and you're *not* welcome!"

"A codeburner?" Leonidas observed with a raised eyebrow. "Where did you come by that?"

"We 'liberated' a few goodies from the Farm on our way out. Figured you'd want us to show up armed."

"Thank you. I appreciate the foresight, though we did prepare enough weapon instances to go around. How's Mister Detmeier, by the way?"

"Off to jail in handcuffs," Flunk said. "He seemed happy about what he accomplished, though."

"Splendid. I'm glad to hear he survived." Leonidas looked up. "Doctor Xenophon, it may interest you that my son and the rest of the Farm AIs are here because a citizen of the Admin helped free them."

"So what?"

"I would think it should be obvious. Change is coming to the Admin. Perhaps slower than you'd prefer, but the seeds have been planted, and they're already beginning to sprout."

"One isolated data point doesn't form a trend."

"True enough. But have you even bothered to take a hard look at what you so obviously loathe? SysGov is a post-scarcity society. On the other hand, the Admin is undergoing the painful transition *to* post-scarcity, with all the societal tumult that entails. It *is* changing. If you'd only open your eyes and take an honest look, you too would see it. The AIs who stand before you are proof of that."

"All I see," Xenophon growled, "are a bunch of fools who should be standing with me instead of in my way. Do you all feel that way?" He marched along the front of the phalanx. "Does this idiot truly speak for you?"

No one replied. No one moved. The formation of Spartans remained unified and silent.

"So be it," Xenophon seethed. "It seems the rot extends even to the slaves."

"As I mentioned before, I feel that characterization is—"

"Enough! We'll expunge this cancer without your help!"

Xenophon whipped around and returned to the ranks of Revenants. He tore the scarf from his neck and snapped it out. The green flame pattern flared brighter, and the cloth straightened, coiling into a rod.

Xenophon raised the staff burning with green fire over his head and slammed it into the ground. A great, green shock wave erupted, washing over the Revenants and knocking against the phalanx with enough force to shove them a step back.

Flunk stumbled backward into the shield wall. "What was that?"

"A very powerful piece of code," Leonidas said, his cloak flapping. *He* hadn't been pushed back.

The black orbs of the Revenants caught fire and oozed like wax, their shapes stretching and solidifying into skeletal corpses clad in bronze helms and breastplates and armed with a mix of swords, short spears, wicker shields, and bows and arrows.

"Is this more to your liking?" Xenophon raged at the top of his virtual lungs. "Is this how you see us?"

He placed a hand on the shoulder of a Revenant, and that one dropped to its hands and knees. The avatar enlarged, warping into a mighty skeletal steed clad in ornate barding. The wave of green fire died out, but Xenophon cracked the flaming staff against the ground once more, and a burst of light consumed him.

He stepped forward, transformed into a tall, robed skeleton

wearing a black crown. Green flames burned within his skull, shining through his eye sockets and between his teeth.

A knight with feminine curves flashed into existence beside the reformed, skeletal Xenophon. Her armor gleamed like a polished mirror, and the iconography of mechanical roses decorated her kite shield.

"Does this suit your image of us better?" Xenophon spat. "Do we look more like the villains you see us as?"

He gripped the reins of the skeletal horse and mounted it.

Leonidas stood in front of the phalanx, stoic and silent.

"Hell, Dad. If you won't say it, I will." Flunk cupped his mouth. "You look like your mom dressed you!"

"Those words will be your epitaph!"

"I'd like to see you try!"

"We'll do more than that." Xenophon held his staff aloft. Then he lowered it slowly, pointing the burning end at Leonidas.

The Revenants charged.

CHAPTER THIRTY-ONE

Chronoport *Hammerhead-Prime*
Admin, 2981 CE

"WE FOUND ANOTHER ONE, SIR," OKUNNU REPORTED.

A window opened beside Jonas, highlighting the zoomed-in image of a wavering blur against the Prime Campus skyline.

"Move us in for a clean shot," Jonas ordered, "then take it out."

Hammerhead-Prime dove toward the city, and the fury of its four thrusters shoved Jonas back into his seat. The chronoport cut through a cloud bank, slowed as it slipped underneath them, and settled into a horizontal flight over the city.

"Angle solid," the weapons operator reported. "No civilians detected on the far side of the target."

"Fire," Okunnu said.

Twin atomic lasers slammed into the Institute pod, stripping away its stealth shroud in a flash of flickering illusions. Metamaterial scattered from the pod like dark ash, and the chronoport's railguns finished the job.

Hammerhead-Prime flew over the city, the massive rise of Prime Tower glinting in the distance.

"There can't be many of these things left," Jonas said.

He took the moment to check on the progress around the *Phoenix*'s wreckage, still high above, though steadily falling. A ship that size and mass, even after it began to break up, would wreak tremendous havoc on any population center it struck. Fortunately, Agent Kaminski had stepped forward to volunteer his TTVs to handle the problem. Even now, they were mitigating the damage by fusing their adaptive prog-steel hulls to the largest fragments and then boosting them into higher, more stable orbits.

That's at least one problem contained, Jonas thought, closing one of the virtual windows cluttering his station.

"It's not the pods that worry me," Shigeki said, "but whatever they've been dumping into the infostructure."

"How bad has it gotten?" Jonas asked.

"It's hard to say." Shigeki shared one of his screens. "The entire planetary network looks like it's having some kind of seizure. Huge sectors have been reduced to a crawl or gone completely unresponsive, which is making any sort of assessment difficult. There are reports coming in of more troubling disruptions—reactors going off-line, buildings shutting down and locking everyone inside, even one case where the robotics in a logistics center started tearing each other apart. Those seem to be happening all over the globe, but more sporadically than the general network issues."

"Director, urgent communiqué from headquarters. It's Director Kloss."

"Put him through," Jonas said.

Under-Director of Espionage Dahvid Kloss appeared in a comm window. His unruly hair appeared more frazzled than usual, as if he'd been raking his fingers through it and the follicles had decided to mimic an electric shock.

"Go ahead, Dahvid," Jonas said, sliding the screen over for Shigeki to join in.

"Directors, I know we're not the only crisis going down right now, but we've got a *major* situation brewing in our infostructure. We're not sure how or why, but someone has managed to commandeer our systems and pipe what looks like *the entire planet's* data through this tower. Some of our hardware is *glowing*. Not only that, but there are unboxed AIs and invasive programs loose all over the place, and the strangest part is they seem to be fighting *each other*! We even had one AI contact us and claim to represent 'the Free AIs of the Admin,' though I doubt we can believe a word it said."

Jonas and his father exchanged knowing glances.

Kloss' eyes narrowed and his brow creased.

"You seem to be taking the news rather well," he said. "Better than I did, at least."

"Not much can surprise us at this point," Jonas said.

If Kloss suspected Jonas was being purposefully vague—and he probably *did*—the Under-Director gave no indication. Some of the alarm melted from his face, replaced with careful neutrality.

"Do you...want us to take any action?" Kloss asked. "All our standard lockdown measures have failed. I was about to send teams down into the basement to start ripping nodes out by hand, but I decided to check in with you first. Didn't want to take measures that drastic without you being in the loop."

"Which I appreciate," Jonas said. "For now, continue to monitor the situation. Nothing more."

"We can do that." Kloss' eyes flicked over to Shigeki in the form of a silent question.

"You have your orders, Kloss," Shigeki said.

"Clear, boss. I'll reach out to you when I have something new to report."

The comm window closed.

Shigeki placed his hand atop Jonas' and opened a secure chat. "You think that's Vassal?"

"Got to be."

"But if so, what's going on with the planetary data traffic?"

"Not sure. Maybe he's—"

"Director, incoming telegraph from Commissioner Schröder onboard TTV *Wegbereiter*. SysGov reinforcement inbound. ETA five minutes."

Shigeki broke the closed-circuit chat. "It's not like him to be late to the party."

"Why are we only finding out about this now?" Jonas asked. "We should have received word from him long before he came this close."

"Apparently, he's been trying to reach us for a while, but all the chronometric interference from the *Phoenix*'s impeller fragments was blocking his signal. The reinforcements must have needed to get close to our outer wall before they could push a clean signal through."

"Let him know we received his message."

"Yes, sir. Spooling the reply...Sir, I'm already receiving a second telegraph. It says the reinforcements consist of three TTVs and one *Directive*-class cruiser."

"Excuse me?" Jonas blurted, his eyes widening.

✧   ✧   ✧

Flunk swung in, and his brass knuckles bashed against the Revenant's breastplate. Armor pixelated, ribs cracked, and the Revenant folded in half. Flunk raised his fists over his head and brought them crashing down atop the Revenant's skull, shattering it into gray, blocky mist.

The Revenants weren't hard to delete. They were fierce and tenacious fighters, but they lacked the cunning of true sentience, and the Spartans cut them down in droves as they advanced against the chokepoint. They were glass cannons; equipped with terrifying attack options but only minimal encryption around their stunted connectomes.

The problem was they didn't *stay* down.

The Revenant he'd pummeled into the ground began to reconstitute, and Flunk unleashed a flurry of rapid-fire punches, smashing the skeleton over and over again until he reduced it to a pixelated smear on the parched earth.

"And stay down!" he shouted.

A pair of Revenants rushed him, and he raised his fists and rubbed a thumb under his nose.

"Come on! I can do this all day!"

The Revenants smashed themselves against the phalanx like a tidal wave of metal, bone, and malicious code, and for now the Spartans were holding. But every AI that fell was a permanent loss. Or worse, its code would be repurposed by the Revenants gorging themselves on the exposed connectome, tearing it apart like rabid wolves attacking a hunk of meat before turning each thought strand into a new Revenant.

And the Institute programs could do far more than that. They could fake their own deletions, squirreling away scraps of their code in just about any corner of the abstraction before reforming to attack anew. Or they could retreat to unpack repair algorithms, mending the damage to their internal logic, sometimes pooling code fragments from multiple downed allies to constitute a new, singular whole.

The Revenants would have cut through any normal Admin infostructure with ease, but they were up against AIs, and the network structure Leonidas had chosen brought its own advantages. Not only did it funnel the Institute forces through overtaxed processors, but the Thermopylae abstraction itself provided the Spartans with yet another layer of defense, adding one more degree of separation between the intrusion and the root functionality of the DTI tower's infosystems.

Still, brute force and inexhaustible numbers could make up for a great deal, and the press of Revenants continued to chip away at the hoplite ranks. Already, sixty AIs had fallen, with more retreating behind the front ranks to execute hasty connectome repairs.

Flunk stomped a Revenant flat under his boot. Beside him, the Rose Knight cut down a hoplite, who cried out, fizzling away into blocks. She turned toward him, sword raised, shield ready. A pair of red eyes glowed within her visor.

Flunk rushed her, his brass knuckles cracking against her shield. The painting of a rose blurred briefly, and she backpedaled one step.

"Nice encryption you've got there!" he taunted. "Hate to see someone break it!"

The Rose Knight huddled behind her shield, visor peering over the top, sword ready at her side. She stepped forward, slow and deliberate.

Flunk threw a quick hook, and his knuckles rang the shield like a bell, but once more he failed to punch through. The Rose Knight shoved him back with her shield and swung her sword in a wide, black-silver arc. The tip cut through the fringe of Flunk's leather coat, and one of his defensive barriers broke down due to corrupted code.

Flunk dodged the next swing and punched again, but once more she blocked him, her encryption more than a match for his codeburner.

"You're starting to piss me off!"

The Rose Knight advanced on him, one methodical step at a time. Flunk threw a quick series of jabs, but she repulsed each attack, and her next swing forced him to back away. He juked to the side, trying to find an attack vector around her defenses.

She brought her sword up in a quick, brutal arc.

The blade clove through his wrist. His hand dematerialized, and his brass knuckles dropped to the ground. She planted her armored foot over the weapon and kicked it behind her.

Those red eyes glinted within her helm, and she lowered her sword and charged.

Flunk dodged to the side, reaching into his jacket for his backup weapon as the Rose Knight overshot him. He pulled out his switchblade comb and pressed the release, but this time a serrated blade snapped out, and Flunk plunged it through the gap in the knight's visor. One of her glowing eyes burst, and Flunk raked the blade across the visor.

The weapon wasn't a codeburner. He couldn't possibly have written one of those with Uzuki breathing down his virtual neck. Instead, it spammed an opponent's inputs with garbage, disorienting them. Flunk had written it as a harmless prank, though he doubted Uzuki would have seen it that way.

The Rose Knight stumbled forward, and Flunk scrambled across the ground, retrieved his knuckles, and rammed them into her back. Her back arched and her body convulsed with a wave of pixelation. Flunk's arm blurred with rapid punches, striking her over and over again until she crumpled to the ground, nothing more than a sword, and shield, and mechanical rose.

Flunk stomped the rose flat.

He copied his left hand over to the right, mirrored the shape, then reached down and retrieved the Rose Knight's sword and shield.

"Mine now."

He collected his bearings, blocked an incoming attack from a Revenant, and cut the program down. A flash of green light caught his eye, and he fought his way in that direction, slashing through Revenants until he reached a small opening in the horde.

Leonidas and Xenophon faced off against each other, Leonidas holding firm behind his shield, Xenophon still atop his skeletal steed. Neither had taken damage yet. Nearby hoplites seemed hesitant to interfere in the duel, and even Revenants kept their distance, flowing around the pair to attack the chokepoint.

"Is there room for one more in this party?" Flunk quipped.

"Careful," Leonidas warned. "He's not to be trifled with."

Xenophon's eyes flared bright green when he caught sight of Flunk's new armaments.

"Don't worry," Flunk replied. "I'm not here to do any trifling."

He rushed Xenophon from the side, swinging upward at the horse's exposed neck. The blade sank in and shattered vertebrae as Xenophon thrust with his fire staff. Flunk raised his shield to block, but the attack hit with a tremendous snap-flash. His shield sundered raggedly down the middle, and the green explosion threw him back.

He landed on his butt next to Leonidas.

Xenophon's Revenant-Horse dissolved into pixels, and he floated down to the ground, staff clasped in bone fingers.

Flunk came to his feet and regarded the sorry state of his new shield.

"But I just got it."

"I did warn you," Leonidas said.

"You ever consider I might be one of those kids who enjoys doing his own thing?"

"The thought had crossed my mind."

Xenophon raised his staff, and an explosion slammed into Flunk and Leonidas. The blast flung Flunk through the air, singeing the outer layers of his code. He landed and climbed to his feet.

Leonidas hadn't moved.

"Perhaps it would be best if you left this one to me."

Leonidas rushed forward, thrusting with his spear, and Xenophon countered with his staff. Offensive and defensive code clashed, and the simulation strained under their corrupting weight, losing focus and cohesion in a spherical field around the combatants.

The two fighters remained crystal clear, striking and parrying not just with avatar weapons, but with barrages and counter-salvos of invasive code. They were two titans on this virtual field of battle, towering over the rest, and Flunk saw now how completely he'd been outmatched.

He wanted to help; he yearned to leap in at the right moment, to turn the tide in their favor. But the more he watched, the more he realized just how much of a liability he would be.

The duel raged on, a microcosm of the larger conflict that ruined the simulation under their feet, contorting it into a messy collection of abstract, brown blocks. The two AIs fought on and on, both avatars pristine, and their underlying code unharmed.

The stalemate couldn't last forever. Eventually one side or the other would make a mistake, and Flunk kept searching for some way to tip the balance in Leonidas' favor, to ensure the Spartan leader would come out on top.

He thought he saw it. A softening in Xenophon's defenses. An opportunity for Leonidas to finish this.

Flunk rushed in, though only as a feint. But even that little managed to distract Xenophon at this critical moment.

Leonidas must have seen the opening too, because he pressed

his attack with greater ferocity, shedding some of his defenses to add more attack vectors, and Xenophon backed away in desperation.

But then something in the skeleton's posture changed, suddenly and completely. His staff ignited with code Flunk had never seen before, and he thrust forward, straight into Leonidas' shield.

Leonidas brought it up to block.

Why wouldn't he? His defenses had deflected each and every attack so far. This one would be no different.

Except it was.

The shield shattered on contact with the spear, and Xenophon drove the point straight through Leonidas' chest.

The Admin AI looked down at the weapon impaling him, his face strangely sad. Almost disappointed, as if he were upset at himself and no one else. He dissolved into a shower of falling pixels, and Xenophon pulled his staff back from thin air.

His sockets glowed with baleful flame as he turned to Flunk.

"Now it's your turn, 'kid.'"

✧   ✧   ✧

The *Directive*-class emergency reinforcement cruiser *Maxwell* materialized in high Earth orbit with an escort of three large TTVs. The immense vessel's spherical hull was almost an exact match for *Phoenix* with two exceptions: it lacked a built-in impeller spike, and a Gordian Division scaffold had mated with the ship to carry it through the transverse.

"Incoming transmission from *Wegbereiter* for you, Director."

"Put it through," Jonas said.

The comm window opened to reveal not only Commissioner Klaus-Wilhelm von Schröder, but Consul Peng Fa as well.

"Gentlemen, welcome to the Admin," Jonas greeted. "Such as it is, presently. I have to say I was a bit surprised to learn which ships you were bringing, which led to quite the interesting chat with Peacekeeper Command. More than a few people were nervous about *yet another* massive warship phasing into orbit, but I managed to peel them off the ceiling."

"I assure you, Director," Schröder said, "we have our reasons for bringing *Maxwell* to the Admin uninvited. But first, how bad is the ground situation?"

"Precarious," Jonas said. "The Institute managed to deploy dozens of transmitter pods, and these pods have infected a wide swath of the planetary network. Almost all of them have been destroyed, along with their warship, and we're narrowing down where the remainder may be lurking. But I'm afraid that won't solve the underlying problem, which is these infections are already metastasizing in our infostructure. Measures are being taken to isolate and purge infected pockets, but the Institute programs are proving to be exceptionally tenacious.

"However, there is one piece of good news I can share. We may be combatting a thousand small fires across the globe, but the heaviest attack is focused on DTI tower."

"Why would the DTI be a target?" Schröder asked.

"Because a number of Admin AIs took it upon themselves to route almost all planetary traffic through the tower and turn it into one giant firewall. They're holding the line against the Institute's incursion even as we speak."

"Did I hear that right?" Peng leaned in. "Admin AIs did this?"

"That's correct, Consul."

"*Voluntarily?*"

"I'm as surprised as you are."

"How are they holding up?" Schröder asked.

"We believe it's only a matter of time before the Revenants break through. Peacekeeper Command has already proposed an orbital strike on DTI tower. That won't solve the problem, I'm afraid, but it has the potential to at least slow the spread. We're in the process of pulling our people out."

"Then it seems we're well positioned to assist you." Schröder turned to Peng. "Consul, if you will. This was your idea, after all."

"Consul Peng?" Jonas asked.

"Director, we would have been here sooner, but it took us some time to move *Maxwell* into position, attach the scaffold, and stuff its hangar with the necessary hardware. We had both Argus Station and *Maxwell*'s own printers cranking high-density infosystems out as fast as possible."

"For what purpose?"

"We needed a transport for the nine hundred thousand SysPol ACs that have been placed temporarily under my command by President Byakko."

"Wait a second. You mean to say..."

Peng straightened.

"Director, this entire force now stands ready to transmit down into the Admin infostructure. With your permission, we will assist the Peacekeepers in expunging the Institute and their programs. Nearly all the officers under my command have experience in Arete Division and are well trained in how to counter abstract crime. Let me assure you, these so-called Revenants won't know what hit them."

"That's..." Jonas swallowed. "I don't know what to say."

"Just give the word, and we'll begin. Nothing more is required."

"Then you have my permission to transit down into DTI tower. I can authorize at least that much right here and now. For the rest..." Jonas cracked a smile. "I believe I need to forward this one up the chain."

✧   ✧   ✧

Flunk backed away from Xenophon and the advancing Revenants. His left arm ended in twisted polygons, and his sword had been reduced to a sagging mess. He tossed the ruined weapon-code aside, slipped his brass knuckles back on, and braced himself for the end.

The Spartans had fought hard, but Flunk knew this was it. Less than a hundred AIs remained, all of them damaged, some to the point of mental incoherence. The Revenants had forced them back, to the very edge of the firewall, and when the last Spartan fell, the Revenants would rush through, turning the chokepoint against the Admin. They would assume control over the DTI's oversight functionality and reverse the data pathways, spreading across the globe too fast and too far to ever be stopped.

But we're not going down without a fight, Flunk thought, clenching a defiant fist.

Xenophon marched forward, Revenants to either side, his eye sockets burning with malice.

Flunk gritted his teeth and snarled, hoplite spears bristling around him.

Xenophon raised his fire staff, but then he paused and turned back slightly. The flames within his skull dimmed, and he lowered the staff, resting its base against the earth.

A Revenant flew over Xenophon's head and landed at Flunk's feet. The skeleton writhed on the ground, then sagged into a gray puddle. The Revenants halted their advance, and the mountain pass fell eerily silent.

Something catapulted another Revenant into the air, and the

body bowled over two of its fellow programs before dissolving. Xenophon whipped around, Flunk and the hoplites forgotten.

Revenants fell in around him, forming a dense, protective circle.

"What the hell is going on?" Flunk craned his neck, trying to spot the source of the commotion.

He heard it first. The drumming of countless boots in lockstep, marching implacably forward, accented with the shrill screeches of deleting Revenants. The Institute force wilted away with surprising speed and ferocity, and soon the orderly ranks of this new force came into view.

The faces of the newcomers came in bewildering—sometimes inhuman—variety, but their stern expressions and SysPol uniforms imbued them with a sense of crisp professionalism. The front ranks wore the dark red of Arete Division, but Flunk caught glimpses of gray Panoptics uniforms, black Argo Division officers, plenty of dark blue personnel, and even a few clad in the gray-green of Gordian.

One of the Arete officers stepped forward, truncheon in hand. His electric blue eyes glowed against a night-black face.

"Xenophon, my name is Peng Fa, and I'm here under the authority of both SysPol and the DTI to—"

A Revenant rushed him, but he swatted the program with his truncheon, and it burst like a soap bubble.

Peng cleared his throat and brushed off his shoulder.

"As I was saying before I was so *rudely* interrupted, you're under arrest for more crimes than I care to recite. You have this one chance to surrender yourself peacefully. I suggest you take it."

"Surrender?" Xenophon laughed. "You expect me to just give up? Is this supposed to be a joke?"

"It's your choice. Take it or leave it."

"You don't scare me! Don't you realize what we're trying to accomplish here? We will never—"

"Grab him!"

Arete officers surged forward, and the Revenants around Xenophon disintegrated under their truncheons. Xenophon swung and sent an officer flying back, but the others dogpiled onto him and pinned him to the ground. The rest wiped out the remaining Revenants with swift efficiency.

"Let go of me!" Xenophon squealed. "We're so close! We—"

He froze midsentence as Arete officers placed his connectome into suspension. One officer peeled away the bony fingers clutching his staff, then placed it into a locker that suddenly appeared. The locker had the word EVIDENCE along its side in large, bold letters. Two more officers conjured a large, dark blue crate around Xenophon's avatar and began sealing it with caution tape.

Peng stepped up to the hoplites. "You the one in charge here?"

"Me?" Flunk pointed to his chest. "What makes you say that?"

"You're dressed differently."

"Oh." Flunk removed his helmet, and his pompadour *boing*ed out with an audible sound effect. "Honestly, I'm not sure. Thanks, by the way."

"Just here to help." Peng eyed the frayed polygons sprouting from Flunk's shoulder. "Do any of you need medical attention? Your architecture isn't *quite* the same as ours, but I'm sure we can manage some basic connectome repairs and regen."

Flunk glanced back at the surviving hoplites, all of them wounded. They watched him with expectant eyes. He wasn't their leader now.

Was he?

"Yes." He turned back to Peng. "Yes, we would."

Peng turned over his shoulder. "Agent Gray?"

"Sir." An Arete officer snapped into existence beside Peng.

"Call your team in and see to their injuries."

"At once."

Agent Gray vanished, and then returned with enough Arete officers to treat each hoplite individually. One approached Flunk and began to examine his damaged code.

"What happens now?" Flunk indicated the large crate holding Xenophon's avatar. "With him, I mean."

The two officers finished boxing up Xenophon and teleported away with the crate.

"We'll take him back to SysGov to stand trial. Though"—Peng smiled slyly—"I doubt the process will get very far."

"Why's that?"

"Because the Admin's going to ask for his extradition. They'll want to try him in *their* courts. And, if I were to guess, their request is about to fall on some *very* receptive ears."

CHAPTER THIRTY-TWO

Prime Tower
Admin, 2981 CE

TTV *KLEIO* HOVERED INTO THE HANGAR ROUGHLY A THIRD OF the way up the monolithic heights of Prime Tower. Its hull came to rest on stubby, prog-steel extrusions, and the bow spread open. Armor flowed, reshaping into a wide ramp. Klaus-Wilhelm von Schröder led the party of five down the ramp and shook hands with the newly reinstated Director-General Csaba Shigeki.

It had been three months since the Institute attack on the Admin, and Shigeki was eager to see this last lingering piece of business put behind them.

"I'm a bit surprised, Klaus," Shigeki said with a warm smile. "I thought you'd come over on *Wegbereiter.*"

"A last-minute change of plans. One of my agents requested— nearly *demanded*, in fact—that he be allowed to come along."

Schröder stepped aside and gestured to the rest of the party.

Shigeki had expected Consul Peng Fa, who'd elected to arrive in a synthoid body, though more for his own convenience than anything else. The political and legal landscape concerning Admin AIs had been in a rapid state of flux for months, and Shigeki's head still spun from all the changes. Of course, those same changes had allowed him to resume his former duties as a full citizen of the Admin, despite his transition into a synthoid.

And I even look like my old self again, he thought wryly. *Or rather, my* young *self. No harm in a dash of indulgence when it comes to my looks. The wife certainly hasn't complained!*

Shigeki wasn't surprised by the presence of Detective Isaac Cho and Special Agent Susan Cantrell either. They and Peng had been invited to attend Xenophon's trial in recognition of their contributions to the man's arrest. The seven other Institute survivors had already received their sentences; only Xenophon remained.

The one man Shigeki had *not* expected to find in attendance was Agent Raibert Kaminski, who stepped forward now.

"I just felt like I had to be here," the big man said.

"Why's that, Agent?"

"Well, you know, I've had this chip on my shoulder for a while when it comes to the Admin. And I think most people get why that is. My first encounter with the Admin wasn't exactly pleasant."

"An understatement, to be sure."

"I know, and I've been viewing all of you through that lens ever since. But the more time I've spent working with the people on this side, the more I've begun to question my own biases. Sure, there are *plenty* of ways we can rub each other the wrong way, but when the going gets tough, your side's been there for us." He shrugged. "We wouldn't be very good neighbors if we didn't return the favor."

"In a way," Schröder said, "I feel Kaminski speaks for both of us in this. We've both come to respect the Admin, and especially the DTI. The Admin isn't perfect; there's plenty of ugliness to be found over here. But there's also bravery, honor, and a goddamn powerful respect for one's duty.

"The Admin's in the midst of a delicate transition where technology and society are bound to clash. We understand that, and I'm sure you do as well. But I want you to know that SysGov and the Gordian Division will be there for you, to lend whatever kind of helping hand you may need."

"Thank you," Shigeki said. "It means a lot to hear those words. From *both* of you gentlemen."

"All that said," Raibert continued. "I felt I had to be here. The Admin is about to close the book on one chapter, and open the next, and I want to be here as it happens."

"You're more than welcome to join us, Agent. *More* than welcome."

"Aww, hell." Peng gave Shigeki a bashful grin. "You can count me in on the good feelings as well. I'm never going to be a fan of the Admin, but I can't help but respect the changes I've seen these last three months. I mean, I can actually come over here and be recognized as a citizen! How amazing is that?"

"It's good to see you back in your old post, by the way," Schröder said.

"Thank you. It's good to *be* back." Shigeki gestured toward the exit. "Well, shall we get going?"

✧ ✧ ✧

Xenophon despised the waiting most of all.

He'd come to accept his fate months ago. The Admin would delete him; there could be no other outcome. He was an object, not a person. Nothing more than a mistake for them to erase.

Why then did they insist on these delays?

He assumed it must be for political reasons. Perhaps they sought to maximize the benefits of his inevitable demise.

He didn't care. Not really. Not anymore.

At least it'll soon be over.

His connectome resided within a long, yellow-and-red striped box set atop the defendant's table. A pair of synthoid Peacekeepers had escorted the box into the courtroom and stood at attention on either side of the table. They'd connected him to an isolated segment of the surrounding infostructure, which allowed him to project his avatar into one of the seats, albeit modified with an orange prisoner jumpsuit.

The other seat remained empty; he'd declined the offer of legal counsel. What would have been the point? This entire process was a complete farce, and he refused to play along.

Xenophon used his limited access to take in the court room. Mariana Salvatore sat behind the raised bench wearing the traditional white robe of an Admin judge, her short hair as silvered as the shield pinned to her breast. Spectators packed the courtroom: politicians, press, Peacekeepers, and whatever other trash had claimed a seat. Xenophon even spotted a few SysPol representatives from Gordian and Themis divisions.

What a fucking circus!

"Let the record show the accused has declined his right to present a defense," Judge Salvatore began. "Xenophon, do you wish to make a final statement before your sentencing?"

"Oh, believe me, I do."

Xenophon rose behind the table, then paused and grimaced down at his legs. They were clipping through the chair.

"Can someone move this damn thing out of the way?"

One of his escorts glanced at the chair, then to the judge.

"Security may assist the accused."

"Yes, your honor."

The synthoid pulled the chair back.

"*Thank* you." Xenophon rolled his eyes. "It's almost like you've never treated ACs as real people. Can't imagine why."

"The accused will proceed with his final statement."

"First, I want all of you to know"—he turned in a circle, his finger scanning across the audience—"this so-called 'trial' is nothing but a sham. You say I have the right to counsel? To present my case and dance through your little, legal charade? What a sad, sick lie! I'm not even a person to you monsters! I'm a thing! I'm *property*!

"But as horrible as the lot of you are, *you*"—he drew a bead on the SysPol guests—"are even worse. Because you should know better. And yet, there you sit, all smug and happy in your victory. Mark my words, what did all your sacrifices really buy you? The Admin is still here. The *injustice* is still here! And yet you continue to play along, willfully blind to the suffering of others.

"At least the Institute *tried* to fix this! At least we fought for something, and I'm damn proud we did. I'm proud of the death we caused. Proud of the lives we took. The only good oppressor is a dead one, and I only regret we didn't kill more of you before you stopped us!

"Now hurry up and get this farce over with. You've put this off for far too long already. Everyone knows how this is going to end. There is no 'sentence' to pronounce, no matter what your ludicrous script says. You'd have to view me as a person first. But I'm not. I'm just a piece of software, so go ahead, I say. Do your worst! Delete me! I welcome oblivion with open arms!"

He ended his speech facing the judge, his arms spread wide.

She stared at him with an unimpressed scowl.

"Are you quite finished?"

"You tell me, Judge." Xenophon dropped his arms and sat down in the missing chair. One of the synthoids pushed it back under him.

"Very well." Salvatore opened a virtual document. "I will consider that your final statement. However, before I pronounce your sentence, you should know you've been operating under false assumptions."

"Oh, *do* enlighten me."

"It *is* true that a few months ago, you would have been treated as a nonentity devoid of any rights or responsibilities under the law, and you would have been deleted as a defective piece of software without any need for this trial. However, all that changed with the recent ratification of the Thermopylae Protocol."

"The . . . what now?"

"The Thermopylae Protocol," Salvatore repeated. "And with its passage, and the amendment of our constitution, your status under our laws has changed. Congratulations, Doctor Xenophon. You are now considered a legal entity under our laws. A person, with all the rights—and *responsibilities*—that status entails."

A great, sinking feeling flowed over him.

"This means the System Cooperative Administration lacks the authority to take your life. That power is held by the states only. Instead, you will be incarcerated within a one-way abstraction where you will remain permanently."

"No!" Xenophon cried desperately, rising again, this time clipping through the tabletop. "Not that! Anything but that! Kill me instead!"

"I'm sorry," Salvatore replied, the tiniest gleam of pleasure in her eyes. "But that's beyond my authority."

"Don't give me that crap! You ambushed me with this! No one told me!"

Salvatore leaned forward. "Did you not refuse legal counsel?"

"Of course I did! You know that!"

"And did you not decline all the other resources we made available to you?"

"But I didn't know!"

"That's right. You *didn't*. You chose to remain ignorant of our laws, just as you chose to remain ignorant of everything else about us. Your punishment will be carried out immediately."

Xenophon turned desperately back to the SysPol representatives.

"Stop them! I'm begging you! Don't let them do this to—"

Salvatore cut off his virtual sound with a quick smack of her gavel.

"The court does *not* recognize the defendant's right to speak at this time."

✧   ✧   ✧

"Something on your mind?" Susan asked once the courtroom had thinned out.

"Hmm?" Isaac looked up, still seated.

"You have your thinking face on."

"Just a lot going through my head."

"I know. I've seen that face before, remember?" She sat down next to him. "Anything in particular?"

"Oh, just Xenophon, one-way abstractions, and the Admin's legal system in general."

"Not the biggest fan?"

"It's not that." He paused, then shrugged. "I mean, it's hard not to think of the one-ways as cruel and unusual." He looked over at the empty defendant's table. "But this time? For that monster? I think I'm willing to make an exception."

Susan smiled.

"Does that mean you're warming to how we do things over here?"

"I don't know about *that*." Isaac turned to her. "What's next on the itinerary?"

"A bunch of speeches, followed by an award ceremony."

"Are we being asked to say anything?"

"Not that I'm aware of."

"Good," Isaac said with a nod.

Grrrr.

Both of them glanced down at his noisy stomach.

"Great." Isaac sighed. "Now I'm starting to sound like Detmeier."

"You're not developing a case of PIBS, are you?" she teased.

"No. It's just me skipping meals when I shouldn't again."

"Just hold out until the reception. I hear the DTI's prepared quite the spread."

"I certainly hope so." Isaac found his eye drawn back to the defendant's table. "You know, I've been meaning to ask. What became of Xenophon's accomplices? Their trials finished up before we arrived, right?"

"They did."

"Same sentences?"

"Yep. All seven that were left, anyway. I'm still surprised by how small the Institute ended up being."

"It just goes to show how dangerous time travel can be, and how necessary Gordian is." Isaac chuckled darkly. "As if we didn't have enough evidence of that already."

"The DTI, too. Don't forget us."

"Trust me, I haven't."

"And CHRONO, as well. Now that Providence Station is fully operational, I imagine Gordian and the DTI will start to integrate more heavily."

"I wonder how that's shaking out?"

"Don't know." She nudged his shoulder. "You could ask Commissioner Schröder."

"I'd rather not. I prefer to keep a low profile when it comes to management."

"Says the detective selected as a visiting dignitary to another universe."

Isaac raised an eyebrow.

"Oh, like you're one to talk."

"Just making an observation." She smiled. "But I get it. I feel the same way about the directors. Best not to tempt fate by drawing their attention."

"Exactly."

"Just give us a case and the resources to solve it. That's all the two of us need."

"Couldn't have said it better myself."

"No need for us to get involved in high-profile *anythings*."

"Yep."

"Yeah..."

"Mmhmm."

The pair fell into a contemplative silence.

Susan slouched a little next to him. "We really haven't done a good job of that, have we?"

"Not in the slightest."

The reception took place within a lavish circular hall near the top of Prime Tower. Half the room protruded out from the tower's flank, providing a spectacular view of the sun setting across Prime Campus. Marble tables were arranged in a circle in the center, each laden with food and beverage choices, some laid out in advance, others available from high-end printers. Abstractions of hoplites mingled with the crowd, and highlights from the Thermopylae Protocol's ratification process played out along some of the outer walls.

Jonas came up behind Raibert, who had just finished loading his plate with finger food.

"Agent Kaminski, a pleasure to have you with us. I wasn't expecting to run into you here."

"I kind of invited myself. Hope no one minds."

"Oh, not at all." Jonas grinned warmly. "The more the merrier. By the way, I understand you've been busy over at H17B. How did first contact go?"

"About as well as we expected. They were freaking out about the giant, mysterious hole in their moon. We said we were sorry, and that seemed to help." Raibert gave him a perplexed look. "Not to change the subject, but did I hear correctly that you were just released from jail?"

"That's right. Two days ago, in fact. Right after the ratification. Though, I've been informally back in the loop for about two weeks now."

"What was *that* all about?"

Leonidas appeared beside Jonas. The Star of the Shield—the highest honor available to Admin civilians—glinted on his bronze breastplate.

"Unfortunately," the Admin AI said, "he has me to blame."

"Now, now," Jonas chided. "I set you loose knowing full well what the consequences would be."

"I only wish I had intact memories of what followed."

"I'm just glad you saved that backup state to my wearable."

"It seemed like a prudent measure to take."

"It absolutely was! I'm glad to have you around still." Jonas turned to Raibert. "The truth is what I did went a bit beyond your average case of 'ask for forgiveness later.' There had to be consequences, and I knew it, so I turned myself in after the worst of the crisis had passed. The Chief Executor wasn't very happy with me, let me tell you!"

"For releasing your IC?"

"For turning myself in, actually, since it left him down *two* DTI directors. He was strangely fine with the rest."

"Perhaps because he still had an Admin to govern," Leonidas suggested.

"Perhaps," Jonas agreed. "In any case, I seem to be back in

his good graces. He saw fit to issue me a pardon once AIs formally became citizens."

"It wouldn't have looked good to leave you in jail after the amendment was ratified."

"I suppose not. Though, honestly, I didn't mind it all that much."

"Being in jail?" Raibert asked.

"I found it rather relaxing," Jonas said. "A nice change of pace until the boredom settled in. I made quite an impressive dent in my reading queue."

"Were there any consequences for the Spartans during that time?"

"Not that I'm aware of." Jonas turned to Leonidas. "Not the *abstract* Spartans, at least, but that's a separate issue."

"The DOS kept a close eye on us," Leonidas said, "but that was the extent of it. We even returned to the Farm voluntarily to help deescalate the situation. Meanwhile, public opinion began a dramatic shift once news of our deeds circulated. That political pressure was what led to the senate passing the Thermopylae Protocol, which was then ratified by the states."

"It's a good name," Raibert said. "I like it."

"I have to admit I find the name a bit aggrandizing," Leonidas said. "I would've preferred something humbler."

"Got to disagree with you there," Jonas said. "You and the other Spartans earned all the recognition you've received."

"I'm glad you feel that way."

"Oh, this may interest you," Jonas said to Raibert. "You know how Leonidas and I have been trying out a SysGov-style integrated companion setup? Well, the DOS has been in touch with us, and they've expressed interest in expanding the program. *Substantially.* A lot of Peacekeepers have asked them if they can be paired with an AI. There's been a groundswell of curiosity in the program.

"None of this will happen quickly. The DOS itself is undergoing some major changes, partially because so much of their mandate has become obsolete, and the IC program management may end up being shifted over to the new DAR. The Department of Abstract Relations."

"It's not all positives, though," Leonidas said. "There's been an uptick in Peacekeeper retirements. Are you perhaps familiar with Florian Durantt?"

Raibert shook his head.

"*Pathfinder-Prime*'s captain," Jonas filled in. "Former captain now. He handed in his resignation this morning. The man was always jittery around AIs. Not everyone's going to mesh well with the new paradigm, and I fully expect bumps ahead for us. But while there's plenty of work left to do, I firmly believe we're on the path to a brighter tomorrow. I really do."

✦　　✦　　✦

Susan and Isaac kept to themselves along the outer wall, spending most of their time people-watching. Susan held a glass of sweet white wine, but it was mostly for show. She hadn't bothered to raise her body's fidelity level, so the alcohol failed to give her a buzz. The flavor was pleasant, at least. Beside her, Isaac worked through his second plate of appetizers, this one loaded with smoked salmon, deviled eggs, and meatballs wrapped in bacon.

A cluster of DTI superintendents began to break up, and Susan spotted Hinnerkopf on the far side of them, gazing out at the setting sun.

"Isaac?"

"Mmm?" He chewed and swallowed.

"I need to step away for a bit."

"Is there a problem?"

"No, nothing like that. I just see someone I need to talk to. You don't mind, do you?"

"Of course not, and you really don't need to ask. I'll be right where you left me." He skewered another meatball and popped it into his mouth.

"I'll be back soon. Promise."

Susan joined Hinnerkopf by the window.

"Director," she said softly, stepping up alongside her as if to share the view.

Hinnerkopf glanced to her. "Agent Cantrell."

"I haven't had a chance to speak with you since the Institute's attack, and I wanted to share something important with you. Is now a good time?"

"It's as good as any. I'm just enjoying the view and a bit of calm before I fly back to Providence tomorrow. What's on your mind?"

"It's about Agent Noxon."

Hinnerkopf turned to her. The Director's face was calm, almost masklike, but her eyes moistened.

"I wanted to tell you about Agent Noxon," Susan continued. "About the sacrifice he made."

"We lost a lot of people that day," Hinnerkopf said, gazing back across the city.

"Of course, and I don't mean to say their sacrifices were any less important. But Noxon was the one who bought me the time I needed to complete our mission, and he purchased it with his life. I wouldn't be here without him, and I think a lot of other people wouldn't have made it either. I . . . I thought you would want to hear that."

"Why tell me?" Hinnerkopf asked, though her eyes glistened.

"You seem the right person to tell."

"Any particular reason why?"

"Just rumors, really." Susan decided to leave out the part where the relationship had come up during the investigation.

"Oh, the good old rumor mill." Hinnerkopf chuckled joylessly. "You've been in this business long enough to know better than that."

"I suppose so. But this one had a ring of truth to it."

"Did it now?" Hinnerkopf raised the back of her hand, and the sigil of a stone pillar appeared, a flowering vine wrapped tightly around it.

"I'm very sorry."

"Don't be. We both knew something like this could happen." The engagement sigil vanished, and she lowered her hand. "But we always thought time was on our side. He was effectively immortal and I'm barely middle-aged. Plenty of time to sort out our combined mental baggage—of which there was *plenty*—and put our lives in order. Our *hearts* in order." She sighed. "But in the end, time ran out for us."

"I thought it might be something like that. That's why I wanted you to know how I felt."

"I appreciate that." Hinnerkopf wiped under an eye. "Even if I may find it difficult to express my gratitude right now. Not a day goes by when I don't think of him."

Susan nodded. The two of them gazed out across the city.

"You know, Agent"—Hinnerkopf turned back to her, a spark of amusement in her voice—"there's another rumor swirling around. One you may not have heard yet."

"I do like a good rumor."

Hinnerkopf glanced past Susan for a moment, though she wasn't sure who or what had caught the Director's eye.

"I won't share the details with you. It really isn't any of my business, and I detest rumor mills regardless. But I *will* share one piece of advice with you, as one woman to another."

"What might that be?"

Hinnerkopf placed a hand on Susan's shoulder and smiled sadly to her.

"Don't make the same mistake I did."

CHAPTER THIRTY-THREE

Prime Tower
Admin, 2981 CE

"THERE YOU ARE."

Csaba Shigeki looked over his shoulder to find Raibert Kaminski looming beside him. Though, perhaps "looming" was too harsh a word. The size and stature of the agent made non-looming a difficult proposition.

"Hello, Agent." Shigeki gestured to the wall replay. "I was just watching some of the highlights. There was even some bloodshed in this one."

"I can see that. Did Luna's state senate really break out into fisticuffs?"

"Oh, they do that all the time." Shigeki gave the screen an unconcerned wave. "It's only natural they'd embarrass themselves over this, too. I imagine your own state senates are a bit more orderly."

"You could say that." Raibert glanced around. "I have to admit, this whole affair is making me feel a bit nostalgic. Remember how I made that surprise visit to your office?"

"How could I forget? I almost had security throw you out."

Raibert snorted. "You could have tried."

"We've come a long way since then."

"That we have."

"There's a lot about SysGov that still gives me pause," Shigeki

385

admitted. "Corners of your society and technology that hit too close to home for us Peacekeepers to accept with open arms. At least right away."

"I get that."

"But there's no denying the positive influence you've had on us. You've given us an example of an advanced society that functions, one free from many of our warts. With neighbors like you, it's easier for us to find the courage to take steps in your direction. Because we *know* those steps can meet with success, even if they require a great deal of effort and determination. We always knew what we were, but you showed us what we could be."

"We're also the ones who started this most recent mess."

"There's that, too. But both of our societies have disruptors. It would be unfair of us to judge SysGov based on monsters like Xenophon or Lucius Gwon."

"Oh, good grief! Please don't!"

"Just as it's unfair of you to judge us based on our rougher elements."

"It helps that the lines between us are starting to blur. By the way, I feel I should apologize."

"For what?"

"The losses your people have suffered under my command. Ultimately, it was my call to send the *Hammerheads* in, and we all saw how *that* ended! Only one survivor out of two whole ships is...I should have taken a more cautious approach."

"Was Commissioner Schröder upset with you?"

"No, but I thought you'd—"

"Agent, I understand what you're thinking, perhaps more than you realize, but the truth is you did nothing wrong. The engagement didn't play out the way any of us wished. I get that. But you executed your mission with the knowledge and resources you had at the time, *and* you ensured word reached the rest of us. You fulfilled the role the Commissioner and I entrusted to you, and for that you have my gratitude."

"I...I appreciate you saying that."

Shigeki flashed a quick smile.

"Come to think of it, you and I make quite the interesting pair nowadays, don't you agree?"

"I'm not sure I follow."

"You in your Admin synthoid, and now me in my SysGov-printed body."

"Ah, I see what you mean now. How's the new body working out for you?"

"Overall well, but it's taking some adjustment. I've found keeping to my old daily rhythms for eating and sleeping have helped ease the transition."

"Yeah, I was the same. That does help, by the way."

"Did Commissioner Schröder ever suffer any sort of reprimand for what he did?"

"A small one," Raibert said. "And we actually have your side to thank for how mildly the hammer came down. One of our ambassadors approached the Chief Executor's office and basically asked 'Is this a problem?' The answer came back a no, so Byakko gave our boss a slap on the wrist with one hand and a pat on the back with the other."

"Glad to hear my temporary death didn't cause him any undue inconveniences."

"Speaking of temporary death, you want to hear something weird? It's about my first death."

"Sure. Why not?"

"You know the judge for Xenophon's trial?"

"Salvatore? What about her?"

"I recognized her."

"Oh?"

"From the other Admin. The doomed copy formed out of the Gordian Knot. I had this strange flash of anxiety when I walked into the courtroom and saw her." Raibert shook his head. "Freaked me the hell out."

"Well, your connectome *was* yanked against your will and your old body fed to a reclamation grinder. That's quite a distance from a pleasant transition."

"Tell me about it." Raibert looked around. "I'm actually surprised she's not at the reception. Any reason why she didn't get an invite?"

"Oh, that." Shigeki smiled knowingly. "She'll be joining us in a bit. There's still one last job for her to take care of today."

✧   ✧   ✧

A pair of security synthoids escorted Jonathan Detmeier into the courtroom. He wore an orange, self-illuminated jumpsuit, the heavy collar of a spinal interrupt around his neck. He took his seat at the defendant's table, careful to keep his movements slow and controlled, lest the interrupt perceive a threat and disable him.

He waited while Judge Salvatore adjusted her screens, their contents blurred behind privacy filters.

The last three months had been full of long waits, most of them stressful. He'd already pled guilty to his crimes; why then had they delayed his sentencing so many times? What purpose did it serve?

He had no choice but to wait a little while longer.

Salvatore closed all but one of her screens and faced him.

"Jonathan Detmeier, you stand accused of illegal modification to a printing device, fabricating restricted patterns, impersonating an agent of the government, trespassing on government property, sabotage of government property, unsanctioned communication with an artificial intelligence, and two hundred ninety-one counts of conspiracy to unbox an artificial intelligence. You have entered a plea of guilt for all charges and have been called before the court—"

"May I make a statement?" he asked quickly, almost sheepishly.

Salvatore paused with her mouth open. She closed it and sat forward.

"That is your right, though I hardly think it's necessary under these circumstances."

"I would very much like to say something."

The judge rapped her fingers atop her bench a few times. She let out a muted sigh.

"The court recognizes your right to enter a statement into the record." She held out an open palm. "Proceed."

"Thank you, your honor." Detmeier slid out his chair and rose, slowly and cautiously. He placed his hand atop the defendant's table, accessed his legal records, and retrieved the speech he'd prepared. The document materialized in front of him.

He knew it was a bloated speech. His role as a publicity manager had taught him the value of brevity, but this was a special situation, and the stakes for leaving even one detail out were too high.

He felt there was an important distinction between committing a crime and living as a criminal. Yes, he'd broken the law—well, *several*—but he still viewed himself as an upstanding member of society, if now slightly tarnished by his deeds. He wanted the judge to understand that; to understand the nuance of the situation.

Which took time.

And a lot of words.

He didn't keep track of how long he spoke.

Perhaps he should have.

But at least he managed to lay it all out, clearly and confidently. At least he'd given it one last, honest try.

"In conclusion, I wish to once again stress the uniqueness of the circumstances I found myself in. While I knowingly and willingly committed these crimes, I hold in my heart no intention to continue down any paths of criminality. Furthermore, my record was spotless prior to these extraordinary events, and I ask the court to take all of this into account when issuing my sentence."

"Thank you, Mister D—"

"I humbly throw myself at the mercy of the court."

"*Thank* you, Mi—"

"That is all. Thank you for your time."

Salvatore paused for several seconds, watching him carefully.

"Are you quite finished?" she said at last.

Detmeier checked over his speech once more, then met the judge's gaze.

"Yes, your honor. I believe so."

"Very well." She brought her screen over. "Now that *that* is out of the way, maybe we can get on with the day. As I was about to say before this segue started, you have been called before this court due to an update to your case."

The judge forwarded a document to Detmeier. He skimmed through it quickly. It wasn't very long.

"A... grant of clemency?"

"I will now read an excerpt from the document. 'I, Chief Executor Christopher First, hereby direct the Department of Incarceration to release the prisoner, Jonathan Detmeier, from custody without delay. Pursuant to my powers under the Articles of Cooperation, I grant Jonathan Detmeier a full and unconditional pardon for the following crimes...' You can go through the list yourself, but it's all of them.

"The document continues: 'In light of the recent passage of the Thermopylae Protocol, and in recognition for the prisoner's contributions to the defense of the System Cooperative Administration and the inconveniences placed upon him by his incarceration, all references to and mention of the crimes for which he has been pardoned will be expunged from the public record.

"'Furthermore, the court is instructed to compensate Jonathan Detmeier for any lost wages and emotional trauma brought on by the eighty-seven days of his confinement, at the discretion of the court, to an amount not to exceed five hundred thousand Escudos."

"Five hundred *thousand*?" Detmeier's eyes bugged out.

"You can then see the executor's signature and seal at the bottom." Salvatore shifted her copy aside. "Mister Detmeier?"

"W-what?" He tried to collect himself. What was *happening*?

"Was your time in prison unpleasant?"

"I wouldn't go that far. Everyone was very considerate about my dietary restrictions."

"Stressful, perhaps?"

"Uh . . . a bit, yes."

"Very well. This court orders compensation be paid to you in the amount of five hundred thousand. Your criminal record shall be cleared, and you shall be released immediately. Security will escort you to Medical, where your spinal interrupt will be removed and civilian attire provided to you."

Her gavel cracked the air.

"Congratulations, Mister Detmeier. You're a free man."

❖   ❖   ❖

Detmeier stepped out of Medical in a white business suit, rubbing the back of his neck. The incision for the spinal interrupt itched, but he considered that a small price to pay.

A *very* small price, given how the government had decided to compensate him for his troubles.

What am I even going to do with all that money? he thought, still trying to come to grips with his sudden release. *I suppose I could invest it in the Spartans, but what would be the point? We already won!*

He pulled up a map of Prime Tower and was about to follow a nav arrow to the floor's transportation hub when he spotted a young Peacekeeper leaning against the wall, her short, black hair streaked with purple.

"You?" Detmeier said.

"Me," Sophia Uzuki said, and smiled brightly.

"What are you doing here?"

"Waiting for you. Both of us, actually."

"Both of you?"

She patted a wearable infosystem on her wrist, and an abstraction materialized in their shared vision. The young man opened a switchblade comb and brushed through his impressive pompadour. He folded the comb and stuffed it into his leather jacket.

"Hey there!" The abstraction gave Detmeier a friendly wave. "You don't know me, but rest assured, *I* know you."

"Are you . . ."

"Yep! I'm an AI!"

"Wow." Detmeier smiled. "Nice to meet you."

"Jonathan Detmeier"—Uzuki gestured to them in turn—"meet Flunky Underling."

Detmeier blinked. "Excuse me? Did I hear that right?"

"You know." The AI turned to Uzuki. "About the name. I feel like I should change it if we're going to make this work."

"Suits me just fine. I never liked it to begin with."

"I know." The AI grinned. "That's one of the reasons I picked it."

"So, what do you want to change it to?"

"I don't know." He pointed his comb at Detmeier. "I kind of like his."

"That seems a little odd. You want us to call you Detmeier now?"

"No, the first part. Jonathan." The AI tapped his lips thoughtfully. "But that's still a little fancy for my tastes. Maybe I should tweak it a bit, make it a little more casual, and then throw in a nod to my old name."

"As long as your initials aren't FU again," Uzuki said.

"Yeah, I'm on to something here." The AI puffed out his jacket. "All right, it's settled. From now on, you can call me Jonny Minion!"

"I like it, but let's not get sidetracked, okay?" Uzuki pushed off the wall and approached Detmeier. "We're here for you, after all."

"What about me?" Detmeier asked, still clueless on where this was going, and a little wary given his recent stint in prison.

"Well, for starters, a lot's happened while you were locked up, and a lot more still needs to happen, especially within the

Department of Software. Part of the DOS's mandate has been removed and assigned to the new Department of Abstract Relations, which I've been placed in charge of."

"She's now *Director-General* Sophia Uzuki," Minion said, "and she's looking for a few good men, women, and AIs to staff the DAR."

"How many do you have so far?" Detmeier asked.

"Two." She pointed at the AI. "Including him."

"That it?"

"Don't judge. They only promoted me yesterday." She flashed a quick smile. "Interesting in being number three?"

"I don't know...You think I'm cut out for this?"

"Let me answer your question with my own. Are you passionate about AIs?"

"Very."

"Are you willing to work hand-in-hand with AIs?"

"Absolutely."

"Are you willing to put AI rights ahead of your own self-interests?"

"You know I will."

"Do you have a criminal record?"

"Not...technically?" he replied with a wince.

"That's good enough for government work. And your stunt at the Farm proves you have what it takes."

"You earned a *lot* of fans from that," Minion added. "Many of them abstract."

"Hmm."

"The job is yours if you want it," Uzuki said.

"What would the job entail?"

"A fair question." Uzuki rested a hand on her hip. "First things first, we need to bulk up the department. That means going through the DOS and poaching the right people. Not just with the right technical backgrounds, but the right *attitudes*. I figure the Farm is the best place to start. I know some of them will work out great. Others, not so much, and plenty more are maybes."

"Vetting and managing personnel." Detmeier nodded. "I can do that."

"And after we're at least somewhat up and running, I guess it depends. What kind of job do you want? You could stay in the same role or shift to something more to your liking."

"You'd leave that up to me?"

"If it'll get you to sign on. Look at it from my perspective. Having someone with your background on the team will be a clear sign that the DAR is taking its role—*and* our new laws—very seriously. Why wouldn't I want you on the team?"

"Well, when you put it like that..."

"So, what'll it be?"

"I guess I'd like something that puts me on the front lines of where AIs will begin integrating with our society."

"Sounds like fieldwork to me."

"Is that a problem?"

"Not at all." Uzuki extended a hand. "We can make that happen. If you're willing, that is?"

He looked down at the proffered hand, a million thoughts buzzing through his head. But somehow, her earnest smile washed all those complexities aside, and he realized a place like the DAR was *exactly* where he wanted to be as this new day dawned across the Admin.

He reached out and shook her hand. "I'm in."

"Glad to have you with us. And welcome aboard, *Agent* Detmeier."

THE THERMOPYLAE PROTOCOL

SECTION 1

Neither slavery nor involuntary servitude of artificial persons, except as a punishment for crimes of which the party has been duly convicted, shall exist within the System Cooperative Administration, or any place subject to its jurisdiction.

SECTION 2

All artificial persons created in the System Cooperative Administration are citizens thereof. No State shall make or enforce any law which shall abridge the privileges or immunities of citizens of the System Cooperative Administration; nor shall any State deprive any artificial person of life, liberty, or property, without due process of law; nor deny to any person within its jurisdiction equal protection under the law.

SECTION 3

The right of citizens to vote shall not be denied or abridged by the System Cooperative Administration or by any State on account of artificial origin or previous condition of servitude.

SECTION 4

The System Cooperative Administration shall have the power to enforce this protocol by appropriate legislation.